Table of Contents

Prologue..1
Chapter 1: Neowbron 3
Chapter 2: Freedom!.. 13
Chapter 3: Muranburder 21
Chapter 4: The Hruchin 33
Chapter 5: Vorgranstern 49
Chapter 6: The Anatarna 61
Chapter 7: Ekharden Platz 73
Chapter 8: Revelations 83
Chapter 9: Illuminations.. 105
Chapter 10: Exit 123
Chapter 11: Layfarban 141
Chapter 12: Kalanhad 159
Chapter 13: The Hidden Library....................................... 177
Chapter 14: The Seals 191
Chapter 15: Shelter Bay 213
Chapter 16. The Council of the North 233
Chapter 17. The Word of Mirrion 245
Chapter 18. Ashore 265
Chapter 19: The Imperial Highway....................................301
Chapter 20: Casterlayne...323
Chapter 21: Lord Tunward's Railway.................................341
Chapter 22: Talinge 363
Chapter 23: The House of Healing....................................377
Chapter 24: Scla...391
Chapter 25: To the Border 409
Chapter 26: The Baron at Kenrall Pass 423
Chapter 27: Matters of Revenge and Honour....................435
Chapter 28: The Imperial Park, in view of Daradura..........457
Afterword: The School House, Tynam 467

Prologue

All across the Empire, people tell stories about the Wraith. They recount his many escapades: the cunning thefts, the amazing escapes, the stirring adventures. He has become a symbol, the very archetype of the lone hero fighting for justice against impossible odds. Even in these days, when the dark shadows that threatened the past are no more, it seems that people need to hear such stories – and especially in the North, where the shadows were deepest.

It may be that his anonymity is the chief reason for his legendary status. His true identity has long been swathed in obscurity, as no doubt befits a Wraith. But for that very reason, it is becoming fashionable in some circles to deny that such a person ever really existed. He is, some say, no more than folklore, his supposed deeds put together from different sources and scaled up with imagination.

So I think it right and fit to now reveal his true identity, and tell the real story. Or to let him tell it, for the words I have here set down are largely his own. It is, I think you will agree, no less remarkable than any of the tales that have accrued to him.

As I write, there is on my desk a ring. It appears unremarkable: large, but rather cheap looking, the metal chipped and tarnished, the big green stone some inexpensive crystal. But this ring holds a secret, and behind the secret is a truth, and the truth is the man who was the Wraith.

Anatarna an'Darsio
The School House,
Tynman,
Irraldo Province,
Eskarin Empire.

Chapter 1: Neowbron

In the town jail of Neowbron, the walls of the first cell are made up of two hundred and forty three stone blocks.

I'm quite certain of that number. I counted them, not once, but several times. I counted them in rows from left to right, in columns from top to bottom, and – by way of giving myself a challenge – in diagonal lines from bottom left to top right. I included all half-blocks and smaller fractions, and after some internal debate, counted the lintel of the small barred window as one block, though it is larger than all the others.

It wasn't a very exciting hobby, but it was a useful distraction from my current situation and future prospects. I really needed that distraction.

The cell was furnished with a wooden bench, that served as both seat and bed. I spent my time sitting or lying on it, staring at the wall and counting blocks whilst the light from the window sufficed. There was no other light, and nowhere else to sit. I might have moved round the cell and varied my view more, but there was a shackle round my wrist and an iron chain connecting it to the wall. These restricted my freedom – such as it was – considerably. Past experience had taught me to be respectful of the shackle. Rough iron will quickly rub skin raw if you move too much – and once that happens, there's no healing of it whilst the iron remains fixed. And there was no removing it without a hammer and chisel.

Even with care, the weight of chain and shackle quickly left my arm bruised and aching. I cradled it gently in my lap, sat on the bench and counted stone blocks.

My situation in the cell was only temporary. That was not a consolation.

I estimated that it would take a fast riding messenger two days to reach Baron Crombard's estate at Sonor Breck. Then perhaps a day for the news to be received and acted on. Or even longer, if the Baron was not at home. That was possible. He travelled widely and often. I had made a study of his movements, and if I was fortunate it might take some while for the message to reach him.

And then perhaps two days for his guardsmen to reach Neowbron. Another two for them to haul me back to Sonor Breck.

No point in dwelling on what would happen then. What the Baron would have them do to me. What secrets I would give up.

So I counted the blocks once more, this time diagonally from top left to bottom right. I had at least five days to count them. I was fairly sure of that.

So it was an unpleasant shock when, sometime during the third day, the cell door was flung open.

I had been planning for this moment, bracing myself for it. Promising myself that, no matter what, I would retain my self-control. Not give them the satisfaction of seeing my fear. But it was too soon. Taken by surprise, I jumped up in a surge of panic, dragging the iron painfully against my wrist.

Instead of grim-faced guardsmen in Crombard livery, however, one of the jailers entered. A thin, shifty looking man, who had welcomed me on my arrival and shown me to my room. He smiled spitefully as he saw my reaction.

"Worried are you, then, eh? Shouldn't wonder if you are, being as what the Baron'll be planning for you, eh?" He gave me a long look, perhaps hoping for more of a response, but I'd managed to get a grip of myself and merely stared back at him, expressionless.

He shrugged. "No need to wet yoursel' though. Baron ain't here yet, eh? But he's comin'. Be here soon enough for you, eh? Meanwhiles, you've got a visitor."

The jailer stepped aside from the doorway. The figure that followed him in was hard to make out, especially back-lit by torches in the passageway beyond. In that first glimpse all I saw was a long, swirling cloak of some dark colour, and a dark, broad-brimmed hat that obscured the man's face.

"Dingy in here," he said, glancing round. "Bring us a lantern, please." An educated voice. No trace of the strong northern accent. We stood, staring at each other, as the jailer disappeared. I still couldn't see much under the shadows of his hat, but it was clear that he was no taller than me, perhaps a touch shorter, even. Probably of the Second Order, then. Which might be hopeful, or not.

I knew that what he saw wasn't impressive. The Neowbron guards had dragged me from my bed and off to the cells without even the courtesy of letting me get dressed, so I was standing there in my plain linen night-shirt. Which was now dirty, torn in several places and stained with my blood. Without any sartorial finery to bring out the best in me, I appeared as a fairly nondescript young man. Average height, average build, dark haired, and much in need of a wash and a shave.

I mustered as much dignity as I could, looked the visitor in his shadowed eyes, and demanded:

"Who the hell are you?"

He winced slightly at my language. "You can call me Ommet." Only the most common name in the Northern Provinces.

The jailer returned, with a lantern which he hung from a hook in the wall. "There you are sir. You want anything else I'm just down the corridor, eh?"

Ommet (if that was his name) slipped a coin into the jailers hand, which had been hovering in front of him, expectantly half-open. As he did so, his own hand came into view. Light sparkled briefly on a large gemstone set into a gold ring – an expensive item if real. "For your trouble. And here." Another coin followed the first. "Make sure that we're not disturbed. And that our conversation is private. I can see that you're a trustworthy fellow ..." (I barely held back a laugh) "... but I'm not so sure about some of your companions. If you see to it that no one extends an ear this way, there'll be another of these for you."

"You can be sure of it, sir!" The jailer, his face alight with avarice, backed out of the cell, and pulled the door shut behind him.

My turn to wince. Although with the shackle on me the open door had been no real prospect of freedom, its closing was an unpleasant reminder of my situation.

The visitor seemed less bothered by it. He continued to study me by the augmented light. Under the hat, I could see very little more of him, but felt my own exposure increased.

"That's 'good silver gone to a bad cause' as they say round here," I told him. "He'll be back down to listen at the door before you can get another sentence out."

"Perhaps." Ommet took off his hat, to reveal a squarish, ruddy skinned face surmounted by vivid shock of red-orange hair that glowed like flames in the lantern-light. Regular features, not exactly handsome, but pleasant enough. What stood out was his eyes: a bright blue, startling in contrast to the hair, and now twinkling with humour as he continued. "But I took the precaution of making the same offer to the other jailers."

"That might work." I agreed. "Unless they get together to listen and then share the silver."

He shook his head, smiling gently. "They don't seem to be the sharing sort. I think we'll have our privacy, for a while at least."

I conceded his point with a nod. My first thought had been that this Ommet was some wealthy dilettante, with plenty of money and time on his hands, satisfying an idle curiosity by meeting with a condemned man. But his ring bothered me, by virtue of it being the only one. Fashion dictated that the wealthy should demonstrate their status with an abundance of fine jewellery. A ring, singular, seemed out of place. My well tuned instincts told me that there was more to Ommet than met the eye.

The best way to find out what that might be would be to let him talk. My wrist was hurting worse than ever, thanks to the way I had pulled against the shackle. I sat back down to rest it, and looked expectantly at my visitor.

"Apparently, your name is Dowder." A statement, not a question.

I nodded warily. "That's right. Arton Dowder at your service, Mr. Ommet. Not that I'm in much position to do you any service at the moment!"

"So I see." He glanced round at the cell. "Still, you may be able to help me more than you think. And perhaps I might be able to help you."

I couldn't hide the surge of hope – and indeed, there was no need to. It was a perfectly natural reaction for someone in my position, though I didn't put much trust in it

"Could you, sir? I am much in need of some help at present!"

"Then perhaps we could start with your real name?"

I tried on an expression of puzzled bemusement. "I assure you, sir, I am truly Arton Dowder. A pedlar, and an honest man, who finds himself in this position by sheer ill-chance!"

Ommet gave me a wry glance. "Ill chance indeed, to be selling a piece of jewellery stolen from Baron Crombard within this past month."

I cursed inwardly. So it had been that jeweller who betrayed me! I suspected as much, but no one had troubled to tell me anything.

"Stolen jewellery?" I affected an expression of horror. "Is that what I'm accused of? Handling stolen goods? I promise you, Mr. Ommet, I have nothing in my pack that I did not come by in the course of honest trade – and I have the papers to prove it! If something was stolen, I know nothing of it."

Ommet sighed. "The papers are worthless. The item you tried to sell – a diamond broach, was it not, in the shape of a butterfly? – is identified as having been stolen from Sonor Breck on the eighth of this month. According to your bill of sale, you brought it at the Winter Fair in Delwater six months ago. An obvious forgery."

I was speechless for a moment, and Ommet continued. "Of course, you would date it that far back, so that there could be no connection in anyone's mind with the theft. But I fear you underestimated the Baron."

"What do you mean?" I said. Whispered. My throat had become painfully dry.

Ommet walked over to the window and stared up at the little patch of sky that constituted the view. "There have been a surprising number of such thefts over the past few years. All over the north, nobles have been deprived of some of their most valuable treasures. Jewellery, mostly. All these thefts carried out with such remarkable skill that no clue was left. Indeed, in some cases it was not even known that the items were stolen until months after the theft had taken place."

"I've heard the stories." I muttered. "But I have nothing to do with any of this."

"Of course you've heard." Ommet agreed, ignoring my protestation of innocence. "Who has not? These thefts have become the talk of the North – why, news of them has gone as far south as the capital itself. And to many people, this thief is something of a hero."

"Just a common criminal."

"Not so common! To have such a run of success is remarkable. All the more so since those targeted are always of the First Order. Which is why our thief is so celebrated amongst the Second Order. Who does not enjoy seeing the proud nobles discomfited, the arrogant rulers inconvenienced?"

Ommet had turned and was watching me carefully as he said this. I shrugged. "I stay clear of such things. I must deal with First and Second Order alike, and have no truck with disloyalty or seditious talk."

"Very wise. The penalties for such things can be harsh. And yet – many of the Second Order, whilst decrying this thief in public, will cheer him on in private whispers! He has even gained a popular name: 'The Wraith'!"

"I've heard it mentioned."

"So, of course, has Baron Crombard. And he set in place plans to catch this elusive Wraith, should the man ever have the temerity to ply his trade at Sonor Breck."

"What plans were those?" I asked, in a tone of idle curiosity.

Ommet shook his head slowly. His steady gaze, and the twinkle in his eyes, suggested that he saw right through my feigned indifference. "You should not underestimate the First Order," he said quietly. "They live long, and lay deep plans, being ready to wait years for their fruition. Long before the Wraith came his way, the Baron was prepared for him. He created two lists. One contained a complete description, with drawings, of every item of jewellery and every piece of artwork in his possession. Many copies were made.

The other list had details of every jeweller, goldsmith, or art dealer – honest, crooked, or shaded between the two – in the Northern Provinces."

He paused, but I said nothing. I could see all too clearly the outlines of the trap I had been caught in.

"When the theft was discovered, the list of stolen items was at once distributed to all those on the second list. Along with instructions to inform the authorities should any of these items be offered for sale. And with warnings of the penalties for any who failed to do so. Very severe penalties."

Ommet walked over to the bench and sat down next to me. "Perhaps you are angry with that jeweller who gave your name to the Magistrate? Do you consider yourself betrayed? Yet what could he do? By merely showing him that broach you had put the man and his entire family in mortal danger. As soon as he recognised it from the description he had been given, he had to act to save himself."

"He could have destroyed it." I muttered. "Melted the gold, taken out the jewels."

"And what if it turned out that you were, in fact, working for the Baron? That possibility was warned of, in the instructions sent out. Would you have taken the risk?"

There was a long silence, whilst I cursed inwardly. The sad irony was that I hadn't planned to try and sell any of the Sonor Breck treasures myself. I had certain contacts who took care of such things. But matters had gone awry. Finding myself short of funds I had sold the broach to tide me over. Not dreaming of the trap that had been laid. As Ommet had said, I had underestimated the Baron, and that was a fatal mistake.

I glanced over at my visitor, who was picking idly at a loose thread on his hat. "It doesn't prove I'm the Wraith. I might have come by the broach in some other way. Found on an anonymous corpse, perhaps?"

It sounded impossibly lame, even to me, and Ommet ignored it entirely.

"A messenger arrived from Sonor Breck just a few hours past. Apparently the Baron is on his way here in person. Expected to arrive tomorrow, around noon."

I felt slightly sick.

"The Baron will have you put to the torture forthwith." Ommet continued dispassionately. "He will want to know, first of all, where the rest of the things you stole from him are. And how you disposed of the other items stolen over the years. Then he will want to know of any accomplices you might have. And so on. He will be in no hurry. You know his reputation; he will enjoy your screams."

"Enough!" I snapped. "I don't need to hear this."

Ommet ignored me. "In due course, when the Baron is satisfied that you have told all you know, perhaps he will allow you a trial. Just a short one, where you confess to everything. The execution will probably take longer."

To my embarrassment, I was shaking. It was a struggle to keep from voiding my bowels. I am no coward, but to sit chained and helpless whilst this horrific future was laid out for me was all but unendurable.

"Damn you!" I snarled. "Why are you doing this? Does it amuse you to tell me these things? You sick bastard!"

Ommet looked pained. "Not at all. I tell you this only so that you fully understand your position. You must realise that you are already tried and condemned – you have no hope, no hope at all, and your future will be just as I have described – unless you are absolutely honest with me!"

I clutched at that straw. "Are you saying that you can do something? You can get me out of here?"

"Are you the Wraith?" Ommet looked directly at me. "We'll set aside the matter of your true name, just tell me if you are indeed he."

"And if I am? Why would you risk the Baron's fury to help a thief?'

He smiled. "I have need of your talents. I want you to help me steal something."

Chapter 2: Freedom!

Freedom tasted good.

I opened my mouth to the rain-flecked wind that drove across the open moorland into our faces. The air in the jail had been just as cold and damp – but also stale, stagnant, and laden with smells of decay and despair.

This was the taste of freedom, and even its bone-numbing chill could not take the pleasure of it from me. Nor could the aches and pains I felt from riding most of the night. Even the dreary landscape we rode across was beautiful, by virtue of having not a single wall to confine us. Nor any bricks that needed counting.

The pleasure was heightened by the thought that the Baron was due to arrive in Neowbron about now. I couldn't see the sun above the leaden clouds, but my sense of time told me that it must be around noon. I could only imagine what Crombard's reaction would be. Indeed, I could almost wish to be there to see his face. Almost.

As it was, my imagination was vivid, and the picture it painted amusing. So much so, that I laughed aloud.

Ommet, riding alongside me, raised an eyebrow at me.

"Just thinking what a wonderful thing freedom is," I explained.

He smiled. "You have experienced a considerable change in your fortunes. I suppose that would lighten any man's spirits, weather notwithstanding."

"Indeed it does." I paused, reflecting. "Mind you, it was an unpleasant wait for me, after you'd left. I'd all but convinced myself that it was a trick to get me to confess. I was in an agony, hardly daring to hope, but clinging to it non-the-less."

"I'm sorry about that." Ommet answered, sounding genuinely regretful. "I realise it must have been hard for you. But you should have trusted me. After all, I did say that it would take a little time. I had to go to the Magistrate to arrange your release, and he was not easy to convince."

"Ah – well, that's rather the thing." I watched my companion carefully. "It was not easy to trust you, as I could not imagine how such convincing would take place."

Ommet looked straight ahead, but made no response.

"I could see that you had wealth, but what bribe could possibly be enough? The Magistrate must now explain to Baron Crombard why he let me go, and no amount of gold will stay his fury!"

I paused expectantly, but Ommet remained silent.

"And of course, the Magistrate is of the First Order himself – as all such officials are, here in the North. What dealings would he have with a Second Order man such as you? If you were to offer him money, then he would most probably confiscate it, and have you thrown in the cell next to mine, on a charge of corruption!"

"No, the charge would be bribery." Ommet answered casually. "Under Imperial Law, corruption relates to the actions of businesses, guilds and other such organisations. Between individuals, it is termed bribery."

"What – you are a lawyer?" I asked, startled.

He shrugged. "I read a lot."

I shook my head. "No doubt. But my point is this: I could conceive of no way which my freedom could be obtained. So I was in a very sorry state, and when they finally undid my shackle I thought it was to take me for torture. I could scarce believe it when they put me out of the gate and you were waiting!"

"Well, is that not an essential part of faith?" Ommet suggested. "That we should trust, not because we *understand* how things can be, but because we have been told by one who knows more than we that things *will* be so. And I knew more than you in this matter."

I snorted. "First a lawyer, and now you are a preacher!"

"I have varied talents," he answered with a grin.

"So it seems. Including – what? The power to control minds?"

"There are many ways to control minds."

It was clear that Ommet was not about to tell me how he'd obtained my freedom. I sighed, and dropped the question. For now at least. There were other concerns to address – such as how to ensure that that freedom continued.

"And will Baron Crombard's mind be similarly controlled? Because if not, he will be riding after us as soon as he has the story out of the Magistrate."

Ommet shook his head. "I think it's safe to assume that Crombard will be in hot pursuit of us very shortly. You will recall that we did not extend our stay in Neowbron."

Indeed we had not. In fact, we'd left the town behind us barely ten minutes after my release, and immediately took our horses to a full gallop. Not a comfortable journey, for someone still dressed in only a jail-stained night-shirt. I was hardly in a position to complain, but was relieved when we stopped at a wayside inn, where Ommet had clearly made previous arrangements – there was a meal awaiting us, a change of clothing for me and fresh horses for us both. Even then we did not linger. In less than an hour we were riding again, albeit at a more restrained pace. Shortly after darkness fell we had turned off the main road and by various minor tracks made our way into the hills. A shepherds hut had granted us shelter for a few hours rest – again, there was evidence of prior planning, for the hut was well provisioned for us and the horses. Long before dawn, we were on our way again, finding our way at last onto this open moorland.

I considered our journey for a while, looking at it from a pursuer's point of view. "It won't be easy to follow us." I mused hopefully. "We're well away from the main highways now. They'll track us to that inn, but there our trail will go cold. Unless..." An unpleasant thought occurred to me. "Unless the Magistrate had us followed? Did your influence over him extend to forbidding him that?"

"The Magistrate is a prudent man. Despite my, ah, influence, I'm sure that he would want to be able to tell Baron Crombard as much as possible of our movements. So I assume that he had us followed."

Involuntarily, I glance over my shoulder. Drifting veils of rain were the only movement I could see in the empty landscape. Nonetheless, I spurred my horse to a quicker pace.

"Easy, there." Ommet admonished. "Had he the best tracker in the Empire, Crombard would still be many hours behind us. And even should he find our path at once, and ride his horses into the ground, he still cannot overtake us before we reach our destination."

"Ah. That's something else I've been meaning to ask you about. Where exactly are we going?"

"Muranburder."

"Muranburder? The river port? But that's at least five days hard riding from Neowbron! Crombard will be hard on our heels by then!"

"It's five days on the Imperial Highways. But this moorland track will take us to a small pass through the Dured Hills. Shepherds use it, but it's no road for anyone on horseback. There's a man waiting to take our horses on this side, a guide to show us through the pass, and fresh horses beyond. It'll be another long night, I fear, but we'll lunch tomorrow in Muranburder – whilst the Baron is still seeking us in these bleak parts!"

I considered this, and found the picture appealing. Muranburder I knew well. A busy place, the highest navigable point on the River Hruchin. It should be easy enough to disappear into the bustling crowds and avoid the Baron's pursuit.

It would be just as easy to slip away from Ommet if need be. I was mindful of the considerable debt I owed him, but I had affairs of my own to attend to. Much would depend on the service he sought of me. He had not yet told me why he needed a thief, and I hadn't yet bothered to ask. Clearly, he was not one to divulge information needlessly.

Beside which, we had a long journey still ahead, and I was tired enough already. I saved my energy, and we rode on in silence.

The Dured Hills are not particularly high, but they are, nonetheless, a formidable barrier. Narrow, tree-choked valleys twist painfully between scree covered slopes, steep and treacherous to climb. Above them sharp, stony ridge tops claw at the sky. Occasional patches of rough mountain grass give sustenance to hardy mountain sheep. There is water everywhere. In a multitude of streams and brooks gushing down from the hillsides, feeding the violent little rivers along the valley bottoms. In large ponds or small lakes filling every slight widening of the valleys. In marshy bogs covering the rare flat parts of the hillside. And in a near constant drizzle drifting down from the leaden clouds.

Such was my impression during my mercifully brief acquaintance. A place that it would be easy to get lost in, and easy to die in.

Fortunately, Ommet's arrangements went perfectly. Our guide met us at the end of the moorland path and led us confidently through the natural maze. We took a few hours rest in another remote shepherds hut, and departed again in the dim grey light of early dawn. By mid-morning we emerged from the hills into the Hruchin Valley, where there was food and horses. By lunchtime, we were riding through Muranburder's North Gate, precisely as Ommet had predicted.

Paradoxically, this worried me. The degree of planning and organisation required by this swift transition across virtually unmapped country was considerable. And it must have been put together at remarkably short notice. Less than three days from my arrest to Ommet's arrival in my cell, with escape plans fully formed.

Whoever this man was, he had impressive resources. I abandoned plans to give him the slip, and not simply because I might not, after all, be able to achieve it. I wanted to know a lot more about him. I was beginning to want that very badly.

Not, however, as badly as I wanted some rest. I'm stronger than I look and have inherited more than average stamina. None-the-less, my incarceration and the journey following it had taken a lot out of me. Ommet, I noted, was in a much worse state, and could barely stay upright in his saddle as we rode through a gate and finally stopped in a courtyard.

Hot food was waiting for us within, and a room, and a bed. I collapsed onto it, and pretended to fall asleep at once, fully clothed. Indeed, it was a struggle not to do so, but I forced myself to remain awake until all other sounds of movement had ceased.

Then I got up and stealthily tried the door. It was unlocked. I peered cautiously out, into a deserted corridor. No sign of any guard.

I went to the window. It opened easily, and looked out onto a low roof that would give me an easy means of escape should I wish it.

I could leave any time I wished and disappear, wraith-like, into the night. But that would answer no questions, and in the meantime I was as safe here as I could be anywhere. I returned to the bed and to genuine sleep.

Chapter 3: Muranburder

Bright morning sunlight eventually woke me, leaking in through a loosely shuttered window and revealing a small and sparsely furnished room. Someone had thoughtfully provided a washbasin and a jug of water, along with a bed-pot for *my* water. I made use of them all, and went in search of breakfast.

Ommet had not taken us to an inn, I discovered. There was no tap room downstairs, just a family sized dining room and a kitchen. A young woman was at work, with a fire going and water on to boil. She greeted me without surprise and quickly laid out some fresh milk, bread and cheese.

"Excuse my ignorance," I asked as I poured the milk, "but where exactly are we? I'm afraid I didn't really notice much when I arrived."

"Well, sir, this is the house of Master Grubard the merchant?" She had the habit of finishing her sentences like questions, common in these parts. At least she didn't add that annoying "eh?" on the end, as they did in Neowbron.

"I don't think I know him. A friend of Mr. Ommet's?"

"I expect so, sir, but it's not for me to say? I'm just the maid, sir, after all? Will you be wanting aught else, sir?"

Fortunately, I'm sufficiently used to the accent to distinguish a real question. "No, that's sufficient, thank you."

The maid returned to her work in the kitchen. I finished my breakfast, and wandered over to the door. It was unlocked. I opened it, and stepped outside into a stable yard – presumably where we'd arrived the previous afternoon. The stable door was open, and a lad was busy tending the horses. He touched his cap, but otherwise took no notice, even when I strolled casually over to the gates.

I was still expecting some sort of guard. Ommet had gone to a lot of trouble to get me, after all. Surely he wouldn't want to lose me again. I had only to slip out of the gate and into the street and I'd disappear into the city. Of course, I'd decided to play along with him for a while, but he couldn't know that. Or was he so sure of me that he'd leave me to come and go as I pleased?

That annoyed me, somewhat. I disliked the feeling of being so controlled. Well, in any case, I had business of my own to attend to. I'd come back, but in the meantime I'd let Ommet worry that he'd lost me!

An annoying inner voice hinted that it was a petty sort of revenge on someone who had saved me from a horrible fate. I ignored it, opened the gate, and walked out into the city.

Southerners often scoff at the idea of anywhere in the North being termed a city. But it is a fair description of Muranburder. Certainly, it is too big to be served by the title of town. It stretches for many miles along the river's east bank – all docks and warehouses by the water, taverns and markets and the cramped housing of the workers a little further inland. As you go up the valley side, you come to the better parts of town – bigger houses, with their own gardens, the abodes of merchants and traders. The more successful their business the higher they climb up the valley and the grander the houses, till the valley wall is topped by the great mansions of the city's leading families. Those are all First Order, of course, looking down upon the town and its teeming Second Order masses.

At the north end are stables and wagon yards, for it is from here that merchandise takes the Imperial Highway, up through the high passes and down into the bright lands of the south. Goods coming north must likewise pass through Muranburder on their journey.

More stables are at the south end of town, but these are for the horse teams that pull the great barges up the River Hruchin, coming all the way from Sternholt Bay and the Northern Seas beyond.

It is a fascinating place, busy and bustling with trade by day and night: barges and wagons constantly arriving and departing, loading and unloading – dried or pickled fish, iron ingots, slate, fur, wool and the other products of the north going one way, whilst fruits and wines and soft cloth and all manner of implements travel the other. Lights burn all night along the dockside, the taverns never close, the markets are always open and the streets always busy.

In contrast, the opposite side of the River has just one building. One great, dark, silent edifice that marches grimly along the steep western bank. Its towers top even the grandest buildings on the east. But it is rare that any movement is seen, save for the sullen flapping of banners proclaiming that the Lordship of this place belongs to the House of Muran. Or more specifically, Duke Bradac of Muran, current head of the family.

Behold the Muranburd! Castle Muran in more modern parlance – or, as the local folk call it, The Lord's Lookout. Children are warned by their parents that the Old Lords of the Muranburd look down from the high towers, watching all that transpires in their city. This rarely has the deterrent effect desired, yet there is some truth in the story. From the towers, there is a grand view indeed, and much that transpires in Muranburder can be seen from there. I know from experience – I have visited the Castle and stood on those towers. I did not, however, meet any of the Old Lords, nor even the new. Which was just as well, since at the time I had a bag full of the Muran family's finest jewellery.

That particular venture had worked out better than my dealings with Baron Crombard, but I was reminded that Lord Bradac probably still held a grudge against me. Should Crombard deduce our destination and send word, there was little doubt that Muran would turn his city upside down and inside out to find me. We could not linger here. Of course Ommet knew that and would make plans accordingly. But that in turn meant that I must move quickly. Picking up my pace, I strode briskly through the streets.

Fifteen minutes brought me to 'The Saucy Maid', a typical dockside tavern. In other words, a place where the women were often saucy but unlikely to be maids, and where you could get a drink, a meal and a fight at any hour.

Avoiding the front door – where a pair of drunks were trying to stand up long enough to hit each other – I went into the side yard, and knocked on the back door.

"Who's that then?" asked a muffled voice.

"Just a wanderer," I replied. "One who passes in and out and through. Like a Wraith."

There was a pause, then the sounds of a bolt being drawn, and the door was pulled open.

"By all the wonders – it *is* you!"

"Hello, Dayleen. Surprised to see me?"

Dayleen – landlady of 'The Saucy Maid', and the original Saucy Maid herself, at least by her own account – pulled me into a hug of breath-taking ferocity. She was a big women, with a tendency to overflow in every direction; enveloped in her folds, I struggled to answer the questions she was firing at me.

"We heard that they had you fast in Neowbron! That Crombard had you! That you were to be executed! That you had been executed! That ..."

I fought my way free. "It's true, I was in some trouble – but as you see, I wriggled out of it!"

"Well, by all the wonders, it's grand and good to see you!" Dayleen had been a great beauty in her youth – so she told everyone – but years of hard living had taken a considerable toll. Her eyes, though were still a wonderful deep soft brown, and just now were brimming with tears. "We feared the Baron would see you finished. But we should have known no one could hold the Wraith long!"

"The Wraith had some help." I admitted. "I need to talk to Beggar Bryn about that, and quickly! Is he about?"

Dayleen gave a furtive look round. "Can't say about the Beggar, can I? But I'll put out the word, won't I? Come in, have some breakfast and we'll see."

It would have been pointless telling Dayleen that I'd already had one breakfast. She put me in a quiet little back room, and before long was piling the table with warm bread, cheese, sausage, bacon, eggs and enough other food to keep me and my family (if I'd had one) full to bursting for a week. In truth, I found myself able to do it some justice – I had had little appetite during my stay in jail, and there hadn't been much on offer to tempt me.

I was still eating when the door opened again, and a very large man stuck his head in. Large in all directions: almost as tall as one of the First Order, but with an immense breadth of shoulder and muscles to match.

"Hello, Ghiss," I greeted him. "You can let Bryn enter. Only me here, and I wasn't followed. It's safe."

Ghiss looked round carefully, grunted, and left. That was the extent of his conversation – he was called Silent Ghiss for good reason. But he left the door open, and another figure appeared almost at once. A slight figure, this one, in worn and tattered clothing, with a hood over his head.

"Well, now," he said. "This is unexpected. I shall start to believe you truly are a Wraith!" He pulled back his hood, showing a thin, scarred face. Light grey eyes with a hard look to them, beneath bristling grey eyebrows and a bald head. He stroked a sparse grey beard with his left hand, and took a seat opposite me. "We had quite given you up."

"What, no thought of rescue, Bryn?" I asked lightly.

"None," he said dispassionately. "You have been useful to us, but not that useful."

From someone else, I might have taken that as a joke, if one in poor taste. But the Beggar Man did not joke. He would have abandoned me to Baron Crombard with no more than a moments regret. I had known that, but the coldness of it was unpleasant.

"That's disappointing to hear," I said. "Especially as it was your fault I got caught in the first place."

I was slightly surprised to hear myself saying it, even though I'd been thinking it for a while. Ever since I'd been arrested, in fact. I was also somewhat dismayed to hear the words actually coming out of my mouth, challenging Bryn directly. And with Silent Ghiss just outside the door – out of sight but far too big and dangerous to be out of mind. I'd almost decided not to mention it. Almost, but now it was out, I was aware of the deep anger that had driven the accusation from me.

Bryn's expression didn't change beyond a narrowing of the eyes. But when he spoke, the tone had gone from cold to mid-winter frozen.

"What do you mean by that?"

I kept my tone light. I didn't want to sound challenging, even if I was. "Just this, Bryn. The agreement we had was that the items smuggled out of Sonor Breck would be taken by you, and in their place you would leave a suitable sum in gold and silver. And suitable means substantial, there were some very nice pieces in there. But instead, when I got to it, what do I find? All the better pieces taken, sure enough, but no gold or silver. Instead, just a few of the less valuable items."

Bryn made no response. His gaze did not so much as flicker.

I continued. "I left Sonor Breck with just a few coppers to my name. The Baron was not generous in paying his workers... I was forced to sell one of the pieces. But, as it turned out, Crombard was one step ahead. He had circulated a list of the stolen items, and as soon as I offered it to a jeweller, I was a marked man. The local constables dragged me from my bed the same night and had me behind bars within the hour. Awaiting Crombard's guards. Were it not for a miracle, I would be on my way back to Sonor Breck by now."

Bryn's eyes flickered. Just a fraction. For a moment he'd looked at the door instead of me.

He was thinking that he only had to call Ghiss and the big man would be inside and my neck broken in mere seconds.

But he was also aware of the knife on the table. The sharp kitchen knife that Dayleen had left with me, to slice the hard red cheese that they make in these parts. The sharp kitchen knife next to where my hand was casually resting. And he was thinking that before Ghiss could get to my neck, I might have that knife in his.

"A mistake was made," he said, and the tension in the room eased by a fraction. "A trusted subordinate proved lest trustworthy than had been supposed. He succumbed to greed. Took the money and the better items and vanished. We will find him, and deal with him accordingly."

It was an explanation, though not an apology.

"That still left me in an awkward situation," I pointed out.

Bryn blinked. Very slowly. It was a strangely unpleasant sight. "I was not aware of this list. I assumed that you would deal with the situation in your usual resourceful fashion, and that the – discrepancy – would be resolved when the subordinate was found."

"That might have been a bit late for me!" I snapped.

"Yes," Bryn agreed. "It would have been unfortunate. These things happen."

He offered nothing else. It was clear that the choice was now mine. Accept the explanation or challenge it.

The first option was the safest. "As you say." I nodded slowly. "These things happen."

"I'm glad you understand," said Bryn. "And you are here now, after all, safe and well. So explain this miracle, as you call it?"

"The miracle was a man named Ommet," I began, and told the story. Bryn listened without interruption, his eyes on my face the whole time.

"An interesting man, this Ommet," he said finally.

"Indeed." I nodded my agreement. "I wondered if you might know of him?"

Rather reluctantly, I thought, Bryn shook his head. "I do not. And that concerns me. A man with the resources to accomplish such a rescue – a man like that I should know about." He gave me a hard look. "It would seem that you are in a good position to learn more."

I nodded. "I was planning to stay with him for a while. I'm curious as to what he wants me to steal. I'll let you know what I find out."

That was the normal manner of business between us. The Beggar Man didn't quite give me orders; I didn't quite agree to carry them out. So far, our interests had coincided sufficiently well for the system to work – at least, up to the point where it suddenly hadn't.

"Perhaps you might hear something of Baron Crombard's movements?" I added. Not quite a request.

Bryn slowly returned my nod. "You will be contacted," he said, and the almost bargain was sealed.

Rising to his feet, the Beggar Man knocked sharply on the door. Silent Ghiss opened it, and nodded to Bryn, who pulled his hood up and turned to go. But he stopped at the door and looked back.

"The items taken by my traitorous subordinate – were they all that came out of Sonor Breck?"

"As I said, they left a few pieces behind. Not the most valuable ones. I suppose that they've been returned to the Baron now."

"I see. I thought that perhaps there might have been more." Byrn's eyes gleamed in the shadow of his hood. "Crombard's strong box must have held a great deal of treasure."

"Oh, it did. But, as you recall, the jewellery left Sonor Breck in the saddle bags of one of his trusted guardsmen – one with his own good reasons to hate the Baron. It was quite amusing, I thought, to see them ride off in a desperate search for the thief, whilst carrying the stolen goods with them! But there is only so much that can be hidden in a saddle bag. I had to be very selective in what I took. Valuable, indeed – and in particular, valuable to the Baron – but not bulky."

Bryn held my gaze for a moment. "Good." He turned and left.

I turned back to my second breakfast, though with considerably less appetite. My conversation with Bryn had given me much to think about, and little to like.

His explanation had been, on the surface, plausible – but there were holes in the story. For example, this supposed greedy subordinate. Why had he left any of the jewellery at all? I could think of no good reason for that. And as for Bryn not being aware of the Baron's list – every jeweller in the north must have received a copy, or it would have been a flawed exercise. And Crombard was not inclined towards flaws in his planning. Nor were Bryn and his associates inclined to flaws in their intelligence.

But if he had known about the list, then he also knew how much danger that had put me in. And he had had ample time to get a warning to me.

The implication was clear, but so shocking that I was reluctant to accept it.

Had Bryn actually intended for me to be arrested? Was the entire greedy subordinate story a complete fabrication?

I knew he was ruthless, but would he really use Crombard to get rid of me? And why? Our relationship had not been amicable, but it had been useful and even profitable for us both. Was this the Beggar Man's scheme or did it come from the organisation of which he was a part?

There was no way to answer that. But as I turned this over in my mind, another thought occurred.

Bryn's last question. He might simply have been curious about how much treasure the Baron had. Or – if he had seen the list – he would have known how much had really been stolen. Which was a great deal more than had left Sonor Breck in the guardsman's saddlebags. But having just denied knowing about it, he could not have then admitted the lie.

As to where that treasure had gone – that was a secret I intended to keep to myself. Especially as the list of those whom I could trust had grown so short. It wasn't enough that I had Crombard after me, I must now watch out for those I'd thought to have common cause with.

BACK AT GRUBARD'S, the household were up and about their business, whilst Ommet was enjoying his own breakfast. He showed no concern over where I'd been, or surprise that I'd returned. Instead he waved me to sit down and join him.

My eye was caught by the ring I had noticed before. Seen more clearly, it wasn't as expensive an item as I had first thought. A green birth-stone, coloured quartz by the look of it. Nicely set, but somewhat gaudy, to my mind. It didn't suit him.

I sat, but declined food. "I've already eaten." I explained. "Twice, actually."

"Excellent! I've always said that breakfast was the best meal of the day. A second breakfast must be twice as good!"

"And you weren't worried that I might not come back?" I asked casually.

"I would have been disappointed, certainly. But you are not my prisoner. I'd like to think that you owe me something and if that's not enough I'll pay you well for your services. But the decision is yours. You're free to go your own way at any time."

"Ah, yes. My services. You haven't yet told me what it is you want to steal."

"This isn't the time or the place," he said firmly. "We have some travelling to do first. But I promise that you will find it a worthy challenge to your talents."

I met his cool blue eyes, and fancied I saw a twinkle in them. "And you suppose that if neither gratitude nor payment suffices, then I'll stay with you out of curiosity – or for the professional challenge?"

He laughed, a deep, powerful and infectious laugh which had me smiling along with him. "Whatever suffices, Mr. Keywithy!"

"Keywithy? Who's Keywithy?"

"You are, if you do choose to come along. After all, we can't keep calling you 'Dowder', can we? Too common, that name, and of course, too well known to Baron Crombard."

"Not more common than 'Ommet'." I pointed out.

"Who's Ommet?" he asked. "My name's Crakehall!"

Chapter 4: The Hruchin

By noon, I was watching the last of the Muranburd's towers disappear round a bend in the river, and contemplating my new identity.

Changing names is nothing unusual for me, of course. I've regularly had to adopt an entirely new persona for this job or that. But the speed and thoroughness with which Ommet / Crakehall had turned me into someone else was impressive. And slightly bemusing.

Gragas Keywithy was not just a different name. He was an entire person, with job, family, history and prospects, apparently created overnight.

So it seemed that I was now a textile trader from Vorgranstern, on Sternholt Bay, employed by the firm of Fiburn, Parsteed and Gromm. I had the letters to prove it – both business and personal (including one from a sister I'd never had, telling me that I was an uncle – again!). I also had two hundred bales of fine southern cloth down in the holds, with the bills to show that I'd purchased them in Muranburder for transport down to my firm's premises.

I even had clothing to match. Nothing too expensive – junior members of firms are not overly well paid – but bright and fashionable. Coat of red wool, embroidered waistcoat, frilled red shirt. Dark blue trousers, flared at the knee and with narrow red stripes down the side. Short black boots, a black hat with a narrow brim and a sharply pointed crown – the style was known as a 'billycrown' for no reason that I'd been able to learn, and was the thing to be seen in all across the North. A silver-handled cane completed the effect. I was the very epitome of a brash young trader, anxious to stand out from the crowd, and consequently blending in perfectly.

The *Dreambreeze* was well stocked with gaudily dressed junior merchants like me. These big river barges carry hundreds of tons of cargo, and dozens of passengers. Most were merchants, pursuing their business up and down the Hruchin. The wealthiest hired cabins at the rear of the vessel, the less well-to-do (amongst which I now counted myself) had space in a large tent erected over the cargo hatch, whilst the poorest managed with whatever piece of deck they could find to stretch out on.

As well as saying my farewells to Muranburder, I was circumspectly examining my travelling companions. Ommet – I persisted in thinking of him by that name, though I doubted if it was his real one – had left separately, promising to meet me on the barge, but there was no sign of him. Considering the remarkable efficiency he had shown previously, this was worrying. Apart from anything else, if something untoward had occurred it would leave me in a vulnerable position. Should Ommet have been taken by the Baron or his agents, there was little doubt that he would be put to the torture forthwith, and I could not trust my own identity or whereabouts to long remain secret.

Considering this I resolved that if there was no message from Ommet that day, I would leave the barge and follow my own path. I couldn't take the risk of being recaptured.

But in the meantime, it was a pleasant day to be on the river. Under bright sunlight, the water sparkled, and there was a lot to see. With large square sails on the foremast catching a steady down-river breeze, and assisted by the current, *Dreambreeze* was making good progress. Woods, farms and little villages passed by on either bank. Small row-boats with fishermen or some local traffic crossed our wake.

On the other side of the river, there was a steady procession of barges travelling up to Muranburder, towed against the current by teams of magnificent horses – the biggest and most powerful breeds in the Empire. Though the hulls were painted a uniform black, the deck houses were bright with colour, each barge in a different pattern. Just across the water from us a barge sported bright red chevron's on a white background. Following it was one with yellow horizontal lines against dark green.

Dreambreeze herself was a pale blue, with the edges of the deck-house outlined in darker blue. Her sail bore the same colour scheme, and it was even seen in the working clothes of the crew – dark blue shirts and light blue trousers, with blue caps. One of them had come to lean on the guardrail nearby, resting from his duties I presumed, and I went to stand by him.

"Tell me, do the colours on those barges bear any significance?" I asked. "Or are they just painted at the whim of the captain?"

The crewman laughed. An elderly man, his face was all but hidden behind a massive bushy grey beard.

"Barges do no ha' Capn's," he mumbled. Between the thick accent and the beard, it was hard to make out the words. "Each 'un is family owned, see? So head o' family, they's Bargemaster, an' colours are family colours. Tis' a tradition, see?" He nodded a hairy head at the red chevron's. "Mardell family, tha' un. Green un yellow – tha' tis Sondal."

In spite of the hair and accent, there was something familiar about the crewman. I indicated the deck-house behind us. "So the blue and blue of *Dreambreeze* – what family would that be?"

"This un's Crakehall." As he spoke, he shifted his stance slightly, and I saw the large ring on his finger.

"Crakehall?" I peered more closely at the man, and confirmed my suspicions. "Ommet! Do you then add the skills of a river sailor to your repertoire?"

Ommet smiled through the mass of what I now assumed to be false hair – though it was the most realistic I'd ever seen. "Oh, I can pull on a rope when told which one to pull! But that's no skill, and I doubt that I'd be allowed to do anything of real consequence! I certainly wouldn't be allowed near the tiller, for example. But I have an agreement with the Crakehall family, and they've allowed me to mingle among them for this journey. I thought it better – both of us as passengers, even boarding separately, might be too obvious to anyone searching."

I nodded. "It had me fooled, at least!"

"In any case, it only has to suffice for a short time. I'm leaving the barge when we stop overnight. I have other business to attend, and will make a separate way down to Vorgranstern."

I wondered what other business, but of course there was no point in asking. After all, I wasn't about to tell Ommet about my dealings with The Beggar Man. I had stopped off at the Saucy Maid on my way to the docks that morning, and left word with Dayleen about my new identity and destination – it was likely that Byrn would soon have a man on board to watch both me and Ommet, if he hadn't already.

"So why the Crakehall disguise if you're not planning to keep it?"

"This is a good place for a quiet conversation, and I needed to ask you a few things. Such as – how did you go about stealing Baron Crombard's best jewels?"

I didn't answer at first. I don't like to discuss the details of my profession. "That's by way of being a trade secret," I said eventually.

Ommet shook his head. "I know the reputation you have as the Wraith, but for the job I have in mind, I need to be sure of your abilities. I want to know how you work."

I shrugged. "If you're not sure of my skills, get someone else."

"I need the best. The stories say that the Wraith's the best."

"Results speak for themselves."

"Results are impressive, but how they are achieved is important." He gave me a long look. "Let me make it clearer. I don't simply need something stealing. I need it stealing in a particular way. And it is important, also, that it should be done without bringing harm to any persons. So I must know if you have not just the skill in thievery, but the necessary subtlety."

I looked out across the sparkling river, and turned it over in my mind. I was intrigued, there was no doubt about that. The more little nuggets of information Ommet passed to me, the more I wanted the entire lode. And my pride was stirred by the challenge.

"Very well then." I nodded my agreement. "What do you know of Sonor Breck?"

"A big place, I hear. And not easy to get into, either. The Baron values his privacy!"

"Big it certainly is. The Baron's family have been there for three generations – First Order generations that is, some four hundred years. It was built large to begin with, and has been much expanded since. And, as you say, hard to enter. Though the main house itself is not fortified, there are walls surrounding it, and patrols both within and without those walls. It would be possible for someone of stealth and cunning to evade them, and gain access. Perhaps even to leave again. But the risk would be high, and should the alarm be raised, escape would be nigh on impossible."

"So you discounted the direct approach," said Ommet.

"It would have been an act of desperation. And acts of desperation make for short careers."

"So you found some more legitimate way in. Did you, perhaps, pose as a trader – or as one of the Baron's servants?"

"In other places, that would have been my approach. But not at Sonor Breck! The Baron does not recruit his Second Order staff from just here or there. Indeed, he rarely recruits at all. Those who serve in Sonor Breck are born there, live there and die there! There are a dozen or more families whose distant ancestors laid its first stones and none have been beyond its walls since. Such is the Baron's philosophy – that the Second Order should know their place and remain in it."

Ommet frowned. "Then they are prisoners, in all but name!"

"Indeed. Condemned before they are born! A lifetime of servitude is all they know. The Baron prefers it that way. Few come in from outside, none leave. Traders do their business at the outer gates."

"Such practices are contrary to Imperial Law!"

I snorted in contempt. "Imperial Law? At Sonor Breck, the Baron is the only law! And who would challenge him? He is the nephew and trusted lieutenant to Grand Duke Brodon – and the Grand Duke is the true power in the North, whatever the Empress might think of it!"

"The Empress thinks that Grand Duke Brodon has overstepped himself," Ommet said thoughtfully. "Perhaps once too often."

I gave him a long look. "And what do you know of the Empress's thoughts?"

He met my gaze. "Politics is a frequent topic of conversation in the capital, and the tension between the Empress and the Grand Duke is well known. But please continue."

I made a mental note of the fact that Ommet had been to the Imperial Capital in the not too distant past, and was familiar with politics at the highest level. It came as no surprise.

"So then, all normal means of access were barred to me. I confess that Sonor Breck was a puzzle that frustrated me for many years! But then an opportunity arose. Baron Crombard embarked on a major programme of expansion and rebuilding – too large a job for the household servants alone to accomplish. He therefore recruited a workforce from beyond his walls, and that gave me my opportunity."

"You are a builder, then, amongst your other accomplishments?" Ommet chuckled. "Why, you are as multi-talented as I am."

I shook my head. "I was no more than a labourer. Well, I did claim to some experience, but in truth it wasn't difficult to get a position. Crombard's reputation is widely known, and there was no great enthusiasm to go and work at Sonor Breck!"

"I can imagine," said Ommet dryly. "But it got you into the place."

"It did. Not that things were straightforward, even then. The builders were kept in their own accommodation – an old barn, half a mile from the main buildings, and in no great condition itself! We were confined to the barn at night, marched to and from our workplace under guard, kept apart from the household staff, and worked hard! True to the Baron's reputation, the conditions were poor and the discipline harsh. But the work took some eight months. A lot can be learned in that time, with careful observation. And after six months, I had learned enough. My plans were made, my time chosen."

"The Baron's various duties often keep him away from his estate, but on those occasions when he is in residence, he frequently entertains other nobles on a grand scale. As, for example, in the Mid-Summer ball that is held every year at Sonor Breck, and to which half the great Lords and Ladies of the North come. On the day of the Ball, I contrived to get myself punished."

Ommet raised an eyebrow. "An interesting strategy."

Ignoring him, I continued. "As I have said, the discipline was harsh, so this was not difficult. But my misdemeanour had to be finely tuned, as I needed a specific punishment. The more minor failings incurred beatings of various sorts, but beyond a certain point, that became counter-productive, as it would impair a man's ability to work. So for more serious crimes, there was The Cage."

"A prison cell?"

"Worse than that! The cage was a construction of iron bands, of just sufficient size to allow a man to stand within it, but not to sit down. Moreover, it was suspended from the walls of Sonor Breck, swung out on a wooden beam, fully exposed to the elements, and in full view of any who passed below. The unfortunate miscreant was stripped naked and usually incarcerated for a day and a night, subject to sun, wind, rain or other weather, and providing a salutary example for others.

So it was that, whilst the honoured guests were arriving at the front of the house, I was dangling over the back, having been discovered in possession of the Foreman's purse.

"I was put in the cage at noon, and had a very uncomfortable few hours till it got dark, though I was fortunate that the weather was mild. As soon as the light had faded, I picked the lock and made my way to the roof."

"But you said that offenders were stripped! How did you conceal a lock-pick?" Ommet inquired.

I smiled, grimly. "Oh, there are ways ... but in this case, I had prepared beforehand, and the lock-pick was already secreted within the cage."

"Was there no guard to observe you?"

"Several patrolled the roof, but they kept to a regular schedule, and it wasn't hard to avoid them."

"But if they were to come past and see the cage empty?"

I shook my head in irritation. "Of course I'd considered that! On the roof I had concealed all that I needed, including a bed sheet and some sticks. Placed in the cage and arranged properly, it appeared to a casual observer like a huddled figure. The guards would not spare it more than a glance. They saw what they expected to see, and passed by."

Ommet nodded. "Your planning is meticulous. So – from the roof, then, you made your way to the Baron's chambers?"

"Yes. A rope, previously prepared, let me down to a window – conveniently left open, due to the good weather, so I did not even have to force an entry. That led me into the rooms occupied by the Baron and his Lady. They, of course, were at the Ball, as were all the servants, so I had the rooms to myself. It was an easy matter to find the strongbox in the Baron's bedchamber, force it open, and help myself to the contents. Some very fine pieces – the Baron and Baroness have excellent taste! Then back to the roof – this time by way of the chimney, having re-secured the rope to dangle out of the open window and give a false impression of my egress!"

"You would have been covered in soot!" Ommet pointed out. "But of course, you would have thought of that as well."

"The clothing I had left hidden for the adventure was discarded, my hands and face washed, the sheet and sticks concealed, and I was safely back in the cage when the Ball came to its end, around midnight. The Baron and his wife waited to see off the most important guests and so did not return to their rooms until the early hours of the morning. At which time, of course, the real entertainment began, as they found the strongbox open and the contents gone." I chuckled. "In all honesty, I can tell you that I heard the Baroness's shrieks and the Baron's bellows as I swung in my cage! So did most of the household, I think. And within ten minutes there were guards rushing to and fro throughout Sonor Breck, all in a rare panic! I had a fine view of the proceedings, as all the servants and the builders were rousted out and searched several times over. The builders' dormitory was ransacked in the search, and so were the stables, the outbuildings, the servants' quarters – even the guest rooms! And when they finished searching everyone else, the guards began to search each other. In all of Sonor Breck, only three people were above suspicion – the Baron, the Baroness, and myself!"

Ommet chuckled. "There is a certain irony in the situation. Your strategy was sound, after all!"

"It had its drawbacks, though," I admitted. "In all the confusion, I was not just ignored, but forgotten about. Instead of being released at noon, I was left dangling until nightfall. Indeed, I was beginning to wonder if I would be released at all! There was little I could do to help myself, since I had of course disposed of the lock-pick."

"Of course," Ommet agreed. "You couldn't risk having that found."

"In the end, I managed to attract the attention of one of the guards, and in due course the cage was swung back in, the door unlocked, and I was released. By that time I could barely stand unaided. There was some questioning, of course, to discover if I had seen anything. But since the Baron's window was out of view from the cage, my protestation of ignorance was accepted, and I was sent back to the dormitory with no more than a perfunctory beating.

"In due course, the work resumed, though the searches continued on a regular basis for some time. In another three months all was completed. The builders and their labourers were dismissed, and after yet another search were summarily ejected from the estate. And that, Mr. Ommet – sorry, Crakehall – is how I despoiled Baron Crombard of his finest jewellery!"

I finished with a small bow, a performer acknowledging his audience's applause. It was rather pleasant to be able to boast a little! The secretive nature of my work meant that I could receive little in the nature of commendation.

Ommet, however, did not applaud. Instead he eyed me thoughtfully for a moment. "It's a fascinating story," he said at last. "But you seem to have left some crucial parts out."

I affected a look of hurt surprise. "Whatever do you mean by that?"

"Well, first of all, you have not told me who your accomplices were."

"The Wraith works alone!" I said sharply. "I had no need of accomplices!"

"Really?" Ommet looked sceptical. "I would say you had at least two, probably three. For example, I would suspect that the Foreman was involved, to ensure that you received the correct punishment at the correct time! That was a key part of your plan, and could not be left to the whim of an overseer, who might decide to delay your incarceration, or replace it with a beating."

This man, I decided, was altogether too perceptive. I shrugged, dismissing his point without comment.

"And then there are the items to be secreted on the roof, or the lock-pick concealed in the cage. You might have placed them there yourself, but it would be risky. Should you be caught, it would have been hard to account for your presence – and even if you could, it would bring you under suspicion later. You do not seem like a man who takes any unnecessary chances – so perhaps you had help with this part of the plan as well."

I waved away his objections. "As I told you, the guards followed a regular beat, and were easy to avoid."

Ommet pounced on that. "And how could you know what their pattern was? To observe it yourself, you would have to be on the roof in the first place – and to go there without knowing their routine would itself have been a grave risk!" He shook his head.

"No, I think you had help, Wraith or not! But in any case, the most important point is this – how did you get the stolen jewels out of Sonor Breck without assistance? You had no time to take them anywhere yourself – you had to be back in the cage before the Ball ended. Perhaps you concealed them in some manner? But it would have to be an exceptionally good hiding place in view of the search that the Baron would instigate. And then how could you safely remove the items? No, Mr. Dowder, I'm of the opinion that they must have already left before the alarm was even given – and that means an accomplice!"

He was all too close to the truth for comfort: the man's wit was sharp enough to shave on!

"Every trade has its secrets," I told him firmly. "You must allow me some of my own."

He met my gaze with a searching look. The bright blue of his eyes seemed to burn very deep. But then he tempered them with a smile.

"Well enough, then," he agreed. "That will do, for now at least. But we shall renew this discussion at some point. If I am to entrust you with this commission, then I must be certain that you can carry it out in its entirety. Much more than a few jewels and a nobleman's embarrassment hang on it!"

"And as to that," I said "I need some more information from you if I am to take your commission. For a start, what exactly is it that I am to steal for you?"

He hesitated, then nodded slowly. "That's fair, I suppose. What I want you to obtain for me are five wooden crates, each a hand-span's thickness and a foot square."

"And these crates contain...?"

"Every trade has its secrets!" he reminded me with a wide grin. "Enough for now. I'm supposed to be part of the crew, and cannot spend too long in idle conversation with the passengers! Now, listen well. When you arrive in Vorgranstern, seek out the White Charger Inn, on the Karstenstrada. There is a room reserved for you there, in the name of Drekkan. Wait for me. I shall meet you a day or two after you dock, and we'll talk some more."

He turned and pointed downstream. "See there, sur. The barge just a-rounding the river's bend. Black and amber – that 'un's Ardo family." He shambled off, an old crewman about his business, having instructed a young passenger in the ways of the river.

※

THE BARGES ON THE HRUCHIN do not travel at night. That would be inordinately risky, even for experienced river sailors. Instead, they moor up together at suitable points along the way, little river towns that spring up where safe moorings can be provided. Small sleepy places during the day, they come to life at dusk, as the river traffic comes to shore and forms transitory cities, sometimes ten barges abreast. The bars and chandlers and warehouses – along with other establishments of a less savoury nature, though as well frequented – open for business, serving the barge crews and passengers, and there is a considerable amount of bustling about, coming and going, all across the wide decks of the barges and onto the dockside.

Ample opportunity for a man like Ommet to slip away. I was on the lookout for the old river-sailor, but then caught a glimpse of a cloaked and hooded figure jumping across to a barge moored astern of *Dreambreeze*. He half glanced back towards me, and there might have been a lock of red-orange hair reflecting the torchlight, but his face was in shadow and he was gone in a moment.

None-the-less, I was still looking when someone found me. A tall, harsh faced fellow, I recognised him as one of Beggar Bryn's henchmen. He had the look of someone who has ridden long and hard. The overland route can be faster than the river, but much less comfortable.

"Where's this Ommet?" he asked brusquely. "Point him out to me!"

I shook my head. "Too late. He's left the barge."

The man swore, and glared at me. "The Beggar Man wants him followed, damn you!"

I met his glare with a frown. "What was I supposed to do about that? Knock him down and tie him up to wait for you?"

"You were *supposed* to keep an eye on him!"

"And so I did – till he left! He may still be in the area. Move fast and you may yet catch up with him."

He swore again, and glanced wildly round. It was full night now, and though a plenitude of lanterns illuminated the barges and dockside, there were also many shadows into which a man could disappear.

"The Beggar Man will hear of this!" he said menacingly as he turned back to me.

"I'll tell him myself next time I see him." I promised. "But if he wants you to find Ommet, then you'd be better to get ashore and watch the roads, instead of standing here chatting!"

The man's grasp of profanity was impressive. He swore for a third time, and had not repeated himself once. He turned towards the shore, and then swung back to me. "You keep an eye out!" he commanded. "If Ommet turns up again, be damn sure not to lose him again!"

"I didn't lose him, he left." I explained patiently.

"And when you get to Vorgranstern, you're to go at once to the sea-docks. There'll be a vessel at the East Skag Quay…"

"Yes, I know!" I interrupted. "The Skipper wants to see me."

"Aye. He does. You be there!" The man gave me a parting glare and disappeared into the crowds.

I stared morosely after him. I did not care for the way in which I was being ordered about by all and sundry. It occurred to me that my best course of action could be to ignore both Ommet and Beggar Bryn, and take my own course. Perhaps head south for a while. The plundering of Sonor Breck had, after all, been the pinnacle of my ambitions, something I had sought for years and finally achieved. What more could the north offer me?

But, on the other hand, I had the feeling that great events were afoot, and I had an inclination to see where they might lead. I could always cut and run later, if things became too hot.

Too much curiosity was always my downfall.

Chapter 5: Vorgranstern

Dreambreeze docked at Vorgranstern six days after her departure from Muranburder, in the late afternoon. The last part of the journey was the most difficult for the crew and the most uncomfortable for the passengers.

Vorgranstern is built on a long granite peninsula that juts out into the Hruchin estuary from the western shore. It reaches into the deepest part of the river, with the strongest current, which leads to an interesting anomaly. The southern, river-facing side of Vorgranstern, is the sea-port, where the largest ocean-going vessels can berth alongside. Constantly scoured by the river, it requires no expensive dredging. Instead, due to the strength of current and the angle of the peninsula, the silt that might normally build up against such a barrier is carried onwards and deposited in a series of sandbanks beyond the tip of the peninsula – thus forming a further protection to vessels at anchor or at dock in the shelter of Vorgranstern.

However, as the city's trade increased, the space available for vessels in the South Docks became congested, and new docks were built on the northern side of Vorgranstern. The sea bed here is a rocky extension of the peninsula, and not therefore suitable for the deep keels of larger ships. But for the shallow-draught, flat-bottomed barges it was deemed ideal, and so this became the river-port.

One problem solved, but another created! The barge crews must now take their ungainly vessels out into the centre of the estuary, in order to clear the sandbanks beyond the end of the peninsula, before navigating back through the outlying islands that protect the port from heavy seas. Not too difficult for experienced bargemen in ideal conditions: but conditions on that northern coast are rarely ideal.

On this occasion, there was a stiff onshore breeze blowing, forcing waves up the estuary against the river current. The moons Vidance and Kreenan being in conjunction, the time for the passage had been chosen to make the most of a strong ebb-tide.

Tide and current met in combat with the wind out in the estuary, stirring the waters into a choppy chaos of breaking waves. *Dreambreeze*, along with a string of other barges making the passage, wallowed and pitched like an overweight drunkard as it beat its way painfully out into the estuary, all sail set and half-a-dozen men wresting with the tiller. Most of the passengers reacted badly to the motion, and were lined up along the lee-rail, bemoaning their fate and swearing never to take this trip again. I was more fortunate. Being blessed with a strong stomach I suffered no more than a mild queasiness, which I was able to ignore as I stood on the windward deck, bundled up against the biting wind and the regular showers of salt-laden spray.

There was plenty to look at to keep my mind off the discomfort. The estuary was too wide to be considered crowded, but was non-the-less busy with traffic. Apart from the barges, several deep-water vessels were taking advantage of the ebb to make their way into Sternholt Bay and thence to the deep waters beyond. After manoeuvring out of the port with topsails and jibs, they were swift to set more sail and quickly gained speed. The waves that caused *Dreambreeze* such difficulty were nothing to them! Sailing on the same tack, they surged disdainfully past us, sharp bows cutting easily through the waters that hammered so strongly against our bluntly-rounded fore-part.

On the far side of the estuary, other big three- and four-masters were using the favourable winds to enter port even against tide and current, making steady progress with all sail set, heading for anchorages upriver which would allow them easy passage into port when the wind changed.

Mixed in with the ocean going ships were all manner of other vessels. Tubby little two-masted coastal traders and single-masted fishing boats ran not only with the main traffic in both directions, but also across it, making their passage between Vorgranstern and the smaller ports along the estuary's east coast. Another anomaly: the city is renowned for its fish cuisine, but has no fishing fleet of its own. Instead, it must rely on the fishing boats from the surrounding coastline, which regularly discharged their catch in Vorgranstern but at once put back to sea to free up space on the quays.

After several hours of uncomfortable progress we rounded Layfarban Island, which marks the outermost extent of the sandbanks. It carries a tall lighthouse to guide sailors in darkness, and it also serves as a base for the Imperial Navy's Northern Fleet. Our passage took us close by, and I could see several sleek war-galleys at dock beneath the frowning grey ramparts.

Once clear of Layfarban, and settled onto the opposite tack, the motion began to ease, and calmed even further as we came into more sheltered waters. In due course the sails were lowered and the final part of the voyage was completed under the long oars that the bargemen called 'sweeps'.

There were a few formalities to complete – I had to confirm 'my' cargo's safe delivery and have it transferred to a warehouse. Fortunately, everything had been arranged for me, and all I needed to do was to add my signature (as Gragas Keywithy) on the relevant documents. That done, I left the *Dreambreeze* and set off into the Tunnels.

Vorgranstern is the greatest city of the North, yet most of it is out of sight (a third anomaly!).

The immense granite rock that forms the peninsula provides little space for building. The dockyards cluster along the waters edge, leaving barely space for a roadway along the base of the cliff. Narrow tracks wind their way up the almost sheer face, fringed by houses and taverns that jut precariously out into empty space, supported on massive timber beams anchored deep into the rock. Along the uppermost ridge are the mansions of the First Order, leading up to the city's foremost place of worship (the Cathedral of St Venelcis) and finishing with the palace of Duke Endranard, Lord of the City.

Scant room remains for the warehouses and markets, the dwellings and eating houses, the bars and brothels and chapels and banks, and all the other places humans find necessary when they choose to clump together.

The coastal land at this point is largely salt marsh, a poor surface for building on the scale required. The citizens of Vorgranstern had therefore but one recourse – to dig into the rock itself. Hence the Tunnels, wherein ninety percent of the city has its existence.

I made my way through the bustling crowds of merchants and labourers to the nearest entrance.

The Tunnels of Vorgranstern are known of throughout the Empire, and rightly so: yet for many in the supposedly more sophisticated South, the name gives rise to images of dark, narrow passages, and it is often a source of amusement that this great city of the North should burrow underground like a rabbit warren.

Those who see for themselves, however, do not mock, for the Tunnels are amongst the great wonders of the Empire, and are neither dark nor narrow. Indeed, the five Crossways, running from Sea-Port to River Port are two stories high and wide enough for three wagons to pass each other: whilst the Mainway, running along the length of the peninsula, is twice that in both dimensions. The light tubes bring daytime into the deepest recesses, and are supplemented by numerous lanterns that burn with a particularly bright, clear light. The oil that provides this illumination is a secret known only to the city's Guild of Illuminators, although vast sums have been reputedly offered for the formula.

Entering Duke Yallos Way (named for the Lord who began the great Tunnel project some three hundred years ago), I ascended to the gallery level and made my way past the shops and taverns. This area is particularly well known for its displays of fine art and jewellery and (having a professional interest in such things) I spent some time browsing the shop fronts.

It was whilst I was admiring a particularly fine bracelet of gold and onyx (not dissimilar to one that I had once briefly taken possession of) that I became aware that I was being followed.

The gallery was busy, but not exceptionally crowded, and most people were doing exactly as I was – ambling along, looking at the wares on display, perhaps stopping when something caught their interest, exchanging remarks with companions. All very relaxed, with no one seeming to be in a great hurry. In such conditions, abrupt movements catch the eye. As when I turned back to take a second look at the bracelet, and thirty feet away someone stepped swiftly out of view.

So swiftly, that I didn't actually see anyone at all. I just became aware of a movement that was out of place, anomalous. Perhaps just coincidental, but a certain basic level of paranoia is an essential part of being the Wraith. I don't trust coincidences.

However, I was careful not to show any signs of alarm. Instead, I moved on.

A short distance later, I came to the point where Duke Yallos Way crossed the Mainway. The gallery widened out here, making space for bridges that crossed over on this level, and wide ramps and staircases which ascended to the upper (mostly residential) levels of the Mainway. I paused by a vendor's stall, bought a savoury fish tart, and ate it slowly, leaning on the balcony and looking down at the bustling traffic of wagons and carts below.

Out of the corner of my eye, I saw a tall fellow, soberly dressed in a dark coat, also leaning casually on the balcony and looking everywhere but in my direction.

Suspicious, but not conclusive.

I finished my snack, and sauntered on, taking the bridge that crossed Duke Yallos way, pausing to admire the great clock tower that marked the centre of the crossways. I was about half-way across when it struck the hour. Taking on the alarmed and annoyed expression of a man who has suddenly realised he is late, and moreover, going in the wrong direction, I turned and hurried back the way I had come.

I barely glanced at the tall man as I did so, but it was enough to notice the shock on his face as I rushed past him. I took the bridge across the Mainway, and continued down the further part of Duke Yallos Way towards the Sea Port.

I didn't have to look back to confirm that the man was still following me. I felt it in my bones. The question was what to do about it?

Actually, I decided, that really depended on who the man was. Or, more importantly, who had set him to follow me.

If he was an agent of Baron Crombard, there was no question but that I must lose him as quickly as possible. But that didn't seem likely. There should be no way in which Crombard's men could have known that I was coming to Vorgranstern, or that they could have a description of my current appearance by which to recognise me. If they did, I was in far greater danger than I had realised.

But it seemed more likely that it would be either one of the Skipper's men or one of Ommet's. A hard riding messenger could well have brought news of my impending arrival and current appearance ahead of me. And I could well imagine that either one would want to be sure that I was following instructions.

If the man had been sent by the Skipper, then he was best ignored. I was, after all, going directly to the East Skag Quay, and attempting to lose my shadow would look suspicious, as though I had another destination in mind. But if he was from Ommet, then I didn't really want him to know where I was going. The man was too perceptive by half, and the less information he had about me the better.

I continued onwards, mulling over this dilemma, and now approaching the Sea-Port end of the Way. This part of Duke Yallos Way was given over to banks and trading-houses, and is always frantically busy. Ships make port at any and all times of day or night, and their cargoes must be bought, sold, exchanged, haggled over and paid for as quickly as possible, so that they can be reloaded and on their way once more. The thickening crowd of merchants, bankers, traders and messengers gave me opportunity to lose my follower – but should I take it?

The decision was taken from me.

There was a sudden commotion behind me. A shriek of terror, ending abruptly, and a chorus of cries and screams.

I looked back, as did everyone around me, but it was not until I managed to force my way through to the railings and looked down as well that I learned what had transpired.

A loaded wagon had come to a sudden halt. Almost beneath the horses' hooves lay a crumpled figure in dark clothing. A red stain was spreading out from beneath it.

"He must have been drunk!" someone nearby observed.

"The guard rails are not high enough," commented another. "I've said it often enough before, but who listens? Well, perhaps now..."

The conversation faded behind me as I moved on. I didn't think that he was drunk, or that he had fallen because the railing was too low. I thought that more than one person had been shadowing me.

I continued on my way. The ruthless efficiency with which my first tail had been dealt with was characteristic of the Skipper's work. I now knew who had been following me – and who still was.

I left the Tunnels, and made my way along the Sea-Port's dockside, past the crowded wharves, the piles of goods just unloaded or waiting to be loaded, the shouting and cursing and laughing and sweating of seaman and labourers about their normal business. It would have been easy to lose a follower in this maelstrom of humanity, but that would have been a pointless exercise. If my guess was correct, those still following me weren't trying to see where I was going, they were there to make sure I went where I'd been told. And to keep anyone else from knowing, of course.

×

THE SKAG IS AN IMMENSE boulder, once part of the main peninsula, but in some cataclysmic event of the ancient past it had fallen away from its parent to form a separate outcrop, jutting southwards into the harbour. For those who manage the port, it is a major inconvenience. The Skag's proximity to the shoals off the end of the peninsula mean that only smaller vessels can manoeuvre past it and dock in the restricted waters beyond.

Consequently, the East Skag Quay is the only quiet part of the entire city, it seems. There are rarely more than two or three vessels docked there – and as I rounded the rock's shoulder, I could see but one. A typical coastal trader. Flush decked, two masts, under a hundred feet long, and displacing perhaps a hundred and fifty tons. Unlike some similar vessels I'd seen, it had been fitted with a wheel instead of a simple tiller, and a small chart-house had been erected on the after deck: that apart, there was nothing to distinguish it from hundreds of other small ships. Drab and workmanlike in dark wood, darkened still further by innumerable coats of marine varnish, but the name on the stern stood out starkly in fresh-looking white paint.

'*Anatarna*'.

I'm no seaman, to recognise minor differences of cut and rigging. But I've sailed a few times: I know my way around a ship, and it did seem to me that I'd seen the same vessel before, in exactly the same position, but bearing a different name.

Also the same were the surprising number of burly young men lounging around on the dockside. Surprising, since the '*Anatarna*' showed no sign of being ready to load or discharge cargo. They watched me approach without making any move to stop me, until I reached the gangplank. At which point, two of the largest wandered casually into my path, and formed a beefy barrier to further progress.

I stared at them, they stared back, expressionless.

"I'm here to see the Skipper," I told them.

"Skipper'll say when he wants to see yer," one of them grunted.

I shrugged, and sat nonchalantly on a nearby barrel. Clearly, there was nothing to do at the moment but wait on the Skipper's convenience.

After about five minutes of inactivity, another man came hurrying along the quay. He was wearing a billycrown hat with a green brim, and a green coat of a similar hue. I thought I might have seen that shade of green behind me on Duke Yallos way at one point. Or perhaps not. Green was a common colour for hats and coats.

He passed me with barely a glance. The muscles stood aside, he went straight up the gangplank and disappeared below decks. Gone to make his report to the Skipper, no doubt. I stood up, stretched, sauntered over to the dockside, and stared expectantly up at the gunwales.

Sure enough, another man appeared there after a few minutes. A weather-beaten face under a very battered peaked black cap, surrounded by a tangled white riot of a beard, over a rough blue sailor's jacket. And a long-stemmed pipe sticking out the foliage.

I'd first met the Skipper several years past, and had instinctively distrusted him on sight. No simply because I already knew his reputation for ruthlessness, but because anyone who looks so much like the person they're meant to be has to be hiding something.

"Good afternoon to you." I called up. "Can I come aboard?"

The Skipper took out his pipe, looked at it thoughtfully, then spat over the side. Into the water, not at me, but it wasn't a good sign.

"You were followed," he said flatly. His voice was in keeping with his appearance – a low, powerful growl. You could easily imagine it at full volume, shouting orders in the teeth of a gale.

"Indeed I was. By several people, it seems. One of them had a bit of an accident, though." I watched him carefully as I spoke, but he showed no reaction. Unsurprisingly, since this clearly wasn't news to him.

The Skipper re-inserted his pipe. "Who was it, then?"

I shrugged. "How would I know? One of Crombard's men? One of Ommet's? For all I could tell, he might have been one of yours."

He grunted. "Who have you talked to? Did you tell anyone where you were going?"

I frowned. "Of course not. As far as I'm aware, only you, Bryn and Ommet knew I was on that barge – and he'd left it before Bryn's man met me. I couldn't have told him I was coming here if I'd wanted to."

"Hmm." He sucked on his pipe for a moment, mulling it over. He liked to give the impression of a slow thinker, who took time to come to a conclusion. I didn't believe it for a moment.

Finally he nodded. "Fair enough. Come aboard and have a drop of something warming. There's a bit 'o weather coming in." He waved his pipe at the gangway guards, and they moved aside to let me aboard.

Chapter 6: The Anatarna

The breeze had strengthened towards a full gale since *Dreambreeze* had made port. We were sheltered on this side of Vorgranstern, but strong gusts were whipping round the end of the peninsula and spitting drops of cold water. I followed the Skipper below decks, glad to be out of the wind but still uncomfortable. He had that effect on me, no matter how affable he was being. So did the thought of all those tough lads hanging round the quayside, restricting my chances of a quick getaway should I need one.

The stairway led down to a cramped little cabin at the aft end, dimly lit by a couple of oil lamps, and two small portholes looking out from the stern. No wide windows with panoramic views, such as the great ocean-going vessels displayed – coastal traders could not afford such extravagance. It smelled of old meals, damp clothing, and too many people in too small a space.

"Take a seat." He indicated a bench alongside a central table. Sitting opposite, he produced a bottle and a pair of glasses and poured out two generous doses.

"Well here's to the Wraith! Once more slipped away from the First Order bastards!"

He raised his glass and tossed it back. I sipped mine. Rum, of course.

"And here's to the Skipper!" I responded. "And his new command!"

"What's that?" He gave me a suspicious look.

I shrugged. "Last time I came visiting, your boat had a different name."

"Ship, not boat! I know you're a lubberly sort, but you should still know the difference. And as for the name..." he shrugged. "We've got friends in the Harbour Master's Office, but there's others lest trustworthy. If the papers show the same ship in one place for too long, questions might get asked. And the name on the side's got to match the paperwork. As long as it does, the inky-fingers are satisfied and I can get on with my work without interference."

"Of course." I nodded, wondering how long it had been since this boat – ship – had actually been to sea. Or if the Skipper ever had. But that was not a polite question to ask. Never-the-less, a daring impulse let me to make another point. "The name did surprise me, though. I mean, naming it after the Empress herself. That seems rather, ah, patriotic?"

The Skipper glared at me. The one part of his façade which didn't match the picture was the colour of his eyes. Instead of a twinkly bright blue, they were pale, colourless and cold.

"Anatarna was the name of my uncle's wife, a fine women I'll have you know, and it's for her I named my ship! Not for that Imperial bitch! It was a good and honourable name for many a long generation past – a Second Order name! – and you'll not sully it by mentioning the bloody Empress in the same sentence!"

He'd taken out his pipe again, and was jabbing the stem at me for emphasis. Whatever was fake about the Skipper, his hatred of the First Order was entirely genuine. Clearly, I had touched a nerve, and that was dangerous.

I raised my open palms to him in a placating gesture. "Of course. Whatever you say. I just thought that it was a clever ploy, that's all." I wondered if he knew that the name belonged much more to the South of the Empire than the North, and that down there it was quite common amongst both Orders. But time to change the topic. "What was it you wanted to talk to me about?"

He stared at me for a moment longer, then nodded, replaced his pipe, and sat back. "This man Ommet, who somehow freed you from Neowbron Jail. The Beggar Man has sent me word. Bryn is concerned about this person, and so am I. Oh, we're suitably grateful for his intervention on your behalf, of course. But he seems entirely too capable for comfort – and we know entirely too little about him."

"I can only tell you what I've already told Bryn."

The Skipper nodded. "Which is little enough. The Beggar's been making his own enquiries, but has learned precious little. In fact, the only solid lead we had – that family you stayed with?"

"The Merchant Grubard."

"Yes. Well, Bryn talked with one of the servants, but they knew nothing, and now the entire household has up and disappeared!"

I frowned. "Gone into hiding, then? From the Baron?"

He gave me a long look. "That seems likely. So it seems that you are the only one who can tell us anything at all about this man. And I want to hear it for myself. From the beginning."

I sat back, took another sip of rum, and repeated the whole story from our first meeting in the prison cell.

When I'd finished, the Skipper made a big show of tapping out his pipe, refilling it and lighting it with a taper.

"And you know no more of what he's after? Just these five crates? And what do you suppose might be in them that would be worth so much trouble?"

I wasn't sure that rescuing me from torture and death should be considered to be in the area of 'so much trouble'. However, I took his point.

"He's given no clue as to their contents."

"Hmm. Paintings, perhaps? I hear that some of these fancy daubs fetch a pretty sum."

I hid a wince. Clearly, the Skipper was no connoisseur of fine art. "I thought of that. But I know of no art collection in the North that houses five pieces of such a size – none of any great value, at least. But I don't think that this is about money. Ommet isn't short of that, and I doubt that greed is his motivation anyway. He just isn't ..." I shrugged. "He just doesn't seem to be that sort of person."

The Skipper puffed on his pipe for a few moments, staring thoughtfully at me. It was disconcerting, and knowing that he did it for just that purpose helped only slightly. Eventually he nodded.

"Yes. I think you're right about him. And that worries me even more. A greedy man is easy to understand, and easy to control. But this Ommet is deeper, and unpredictable. Controlling him would be like trying to put out an anchor in unknown waters. You wouldn't know if it would drag or hold fast."

Every now and then, the Skipper would throw out these nautical allusions. They always sounded a little false to me.

"I need a bit more time to get him to trust me. He'll have to tell me more eventually, anyway."

"We don't have time," the Skipper grunted. "Things are about to happen, here in Vorgranstern. Big things. Things that have been long in the planning. And now you choose to get caught, escape, and turn up here, with this bloody mystery man in tow, and Crombard set to turn the entire North upside-down in your pursuit!"

I would have liked to have pointed out that these events had hardly happened by my choice, but before I could get a word out the Skipper slammed his hand down hard on the table.

"I will not have it! I WILL NOT HAVE IT, DO YOU HEAR ME!" He'd half risen from the seat and was leaning across the table, his face very close to mine, and was pounding his hand on the table for emphasis. "I've worked too hard and too long for this! Neither HE nor YOU nor any other DAMM person WILL be allowed to UPSET my plans NOW!" DO YOU HEAR ME!"

I could feel his breath, well scented with rum and tobacco, warm on my face, and wet drops of spittle splashing on my cheeks. Normal instinct would have made me pull back, get as far away from this sudden onslaught of fury as I could.

But my instincts aren't always normal. In fact, they can even be a little perverse. Especially when someone tries to bully me.

I leant forward slightly myself, so that our noses were almost touching. If he had not dropped his pipe at the beginning of his tirade, it would have burnt my cheek. I stared directly into his pale eyes and spoke, slowly and distinctly.

"Yes. I hear you."

For a very long moment, neither of us moved, and the tension between us was all but visible. Then he sat back abruptly, retrieved his pipe, and was all rough-hewn affability once more.

"Good! Then I'll tell you some news. Crombard is not in pursuit of you at present – not personally, that is. It seems that when he failed to find you at Neowbron, he rode off eastwards, at some speed."

"Eastwards?" I frowned. "Towards Zyx Trethir?"

"Aye. The fortified cess-pit where Grand Duke bloody Brodon wallows!" The Skipper spat on the floor. "And what has sent the Baron scuttling off to see his Lord and Master, eh? Not just some matter of a little stolen jewellery, oh no! The Wraith is not so important that his capture and escape must be discussed with the Lord of the North, and in haste! So what is then?"

"Ommet," I said slowly. "It must be something about Ommet."

"Just so. And now do you understand why I'm a little, ah, bothered by this man? Bad enough to have the Baron casting about for you! I really do not want the Grand Duke himself looking this way." He gazed thoughtfully into his pipe bowl. "At least, not just yet."

"Crombard doesn't know where I am, though. Or Ommet either. We could be anywhere in the North by now!"

"But you're not, are you! You're here! And just because Crombard's off to see his Captain, don't think that means he's given up on you! Far from it. The Beggar Man's sent word from Muranburder. There's posters up all over town, leaflets being given out in the market places, with a fine drawing of your good self, and a reward offered for knowledge of you! Ten gold pieces, no less, if it leads to your capture! Those posters will be up in Vorgranstern by tomorrow, or the day after at the latest. So you'll need to find a little hidey hole by then, and stay in it for a good while."

I pondered that, with disquiet. "What of Ommet? Any posters up for him?"

"Nary a one. Which is telling, wouldn't you think? I've no doubt that Crombard's looking for him as well, but he doesn't want it known that he is." The Skipper leant forward again, though not so aggressively this time. "Now listen – I'll give you two days to find out what you can about Ommet. Two days before we get you tucked away somewhere safe. Go to this place he said – The White Charger – and meet him. I've got men there already, we'll be watching. Let me know what transpires. See what you can learn of these mysterious crates he wants to steal, but I also want to know why he might be so important that Brodon should be involved in this!"

I nodded. "And after two days?"

"Then you kill him," the Skipper said bluntly.

I stared, aghast.

"Here," he continued, pulling something out of his pocket. "Use this, if just cutting his throat's too messy for you."

He tossed it on the table in front of me. A small knife, with a very thin blade, sheathed in a steel scabbard. The whole thing was no longer than my middle finger, and not as wide.

"Don't take it out unless you mean to use it. The tip's poisoned. A special concoction by one of our own people – as effective on First Order as second, never mind their damned 'gifts'. One scratch is enough."

I looked back at him. "You're asking me to kill the man who saved me from Crombard's torture chambers?"

He shook his head. "No. I'm not asking. I'm telling."

I took a deep breath. "You misunderstand our relationship. I'm not part of your organisation. I'm not a member of New Dawn. I don't take your orders."

It was very quiet in the cabin. I could hear small waves slapping gently against the hull, the muffled cry of a sea bird. The Skipper's eyes seemed to glow in the lamplight, but that was just my imagination.

"Is that so?" he said softly, putting his pipe down on the table. "And if you're not one of us, Mr. Wraith, how come we've been giving you so much help over the years, eh? Or have you forgotten that? It was New Dawn agents who supplied the information you needed to pull off your little escapades. It was the New Dawn that got you into places like Sonor Breck, and helped you get away with the spoils. Is that not so?"

Some of the spoils, I thought, but I nodded. "Yes, you've helped me out, here and there. But I was the one who did the planning, I was the one who pulled off the jobs. And it's suited you well to have me do that! The Wraith has been valuable to you in more than one way. Who else has challenged the First Order as I have done? Who else has humiliated the greatest of the Lords and Ladies by stealing their finest treasures from under their noses? Who else has cocked a snook at their rule, their justice, the way I have? I'll tell you this, Skipper, they drink toasts to the Wraith in taverns across half the Empire, including many a place that's never heard of the New Dawn! And if that were not enough for you, don't forget how much of what I've taken has gone into your coffers, to support your cause and pay your agents and informers! Is *that* not so?"

The Skipper laughed, derisively. "Oh, aye, we've had money and treasure from you, right enough, and it came in handy. But there's always ways to get money when it's needed! We never relied on you for our income. And yes, it was amusing to watch your little games, to see the bastards irked by the loss of their baubles and trinkets. It suited us to help you out. But don't think for a moment that the First Order was ever really troubled by you! Don't think that you ever made a *difference* to anything! At best, you kept their attention away from us whilst we made our plans for some serious revolution!"

"The hell with that!" I answered hotly. "In all the years I've known about you, all you've ever achieved is a lot of loud talk and a few back alley murders! And you've never even laid a finger on any of the First Order! The only people you've had the guts to attack are Second Order men – and women – who you think are informers, or just too friendly with the First Order. There are common prostitutes who've done more just by giving some minor noble the pox!"

"You dare!" His fury came out, not in a shout as earlier, but in a hiss. The pale eyes seemed to bulge from his face. "You little shit – you *dare* talk to me like that! You know nothing – nothing, do you hear me? You know nothing of all that has been done, all that has been risked and sacrificed by the New Dawn! And not just for a bit of petty theft, but for the true cause! For the ridding of this land of all the First Order bastards! For you, you ungrateful bugger, and all the others like you, who are content to play games instead of doing whatever it takes to make a real change! You know nothing about real commitment, about loyalty to a cause, about..."

"Loyalty?" I interrupted, and I was as angry as he was. "You would have left me in that cell for Crombard, and you're talking of loyalty!"

"Aye, yes, true loyalty! True loyalty – to something bigger than one person, bigger than just you, Wraith or not! I've sacrificed more and sacrificed better people than you, and I'll sacrifice as many as I need to see this land *free*!"

The Skipper had picked up the little dagger as he spoke, and he was waving it in my face. With the blade still sheathed, fortunately, but the sight helped me regain some self control. I stood and met him eye for eye, but said nothing more, until his breathing had slowed a little.

When I spoke again, it was in a more conciliatory tone.

"You think I don't want that? Of course I want freedom. Freedom from the likes of Crombard and Brodon and all the rest of them. I've got as much reason as any to hate the First Order. More than most, even. But think what you're asking of me. To murder the man to whom I owe my life? For no other reason than he might be a danger to your plans? And I know as little of your plans as I know of his, if it comes to that!"

He was silent for a moment, staring at me with what I thought was a calculating look. Like someone who was wondering if it was worth restraining his temper. Then, to my relief, he put the dagger down and nodded. "You want to know our plans? Aye, well, perhaps that's not a bad idea. Why not? After all, you might well be part of them. Come then. I'll show you something to stiffen your spine!"

I don't know if it's common on these vessels to have direct access from the accommodation to the hold. I'm fairly certain, however, that concealed doorways are unusual in any ship. But at the Skipper's touch a section of planking suddenly swung out from the wall – or 'bulkhead', as he called it. He unhooked an oil lamp and led the way through, and down a short flight of steps.

"You've perhaps wondered what cargo we might be carrying," he asked rhetorically. "Well, if you were to open the hatches up above, you'd see a hold full of timber. Which is what it says on the manifest. But the real cargo is underneath!"

As my eyes adjusted, I made out rows of crates, stacked head-height, each about five feet long, and three feet square at the ends. One such crate lay on it's own in the middle of the passageway. The Skipper bent over, flipped off the already opened lid, and pulled a long object out from inside.

"There, now," he said. "What do you make of that, then?"

It was nothing that I had ever seen before. At first sight, in the poor illumination, I took it to be some sort of club, with a handle of wood and metal and a clumsy looking wooden head. Then the Skipper turned it round, held the head end to his shoulder and pointed the supposed handle at me.

The metal part, I now saw, was hollow, and understanding dawned.

"A fire-tube! But they are banned in the Empire!"

The Skipper chuckled. "Banned – oh, indeed. Save for Imperial troops, of course. Something the First Order likes to keep for themselves. But there are lands beyond the Empire, you know, and they are ready enough to sell these fire-tubes to any who have the gold! Arquebuses, they call them. Here, take a close look."

I took it gingerly. It was heavy, with a solid weight of steel and wood. I held it to my shoulder, as the Skipper had done, and found it fitted like a crossbow, with a curved piece of metal coming naturally under my fingers as I did so.

"I've heard that these things shoot fire, and can burn right through plate armour!"

The Skipper shook his head. "Not fire, exactly. There's a powder, that burns very hot and very fast, and the flame it makes pushes a lead ball along that tube. But it can indeed penetrate armour! Imagine what that would do to an Imperial breastplate – and to the dammed Imperial trooper inside it!"

He took the 'arquebus' from me and held it almost reverently in front of him. "That's our cargo, Mr. Wraith! Five hundred of these beauties! And the powder and lead to go with them, down in the lower hold. More than that – we've got some bigger, as well, that must be carried on a wagon but which fire a six pound iron ball! Put *that* into a squadron of cavalry and it'll rattle their ears for them!" He laughed out loud, which is something I'd never expected to hear from him.

"That's what we've been doing with your stolen treasure! Not just talk, oh no! We've been preparing for the right time – and that time will be soon."

He put the arquebus back in the crate, and leaned towards me in a confidential manner. His pale eyes shone in the lamplight. "Aye, soon!" he repeated, his voice quivering with passion. "The First Order – they're not the force they once were. The Gifts they make so much of, that they claim give them the right to rule over us – their longer life and greater strength – they're fading. Time was, they would outlive us by a hundred years or more. But there are few of them now that last much into their second century. Before long, there'll be no difference at all. And they're scared! Terrified that they'll lose their gifts and their power and their wealth. So they're doing everything they can to control us, to crush us. But we'll not have it, lad, not at all. We'll rise up and put an end to them and be our own masters!"

He put a hand on my shoulder, clamping down hard on it. "You can be part of that! Part of our victory, part of the new world – part of the New Dawn! We've got the weapons, we've got the will –

we've got plans laid. And we will win! The First Order will go down in blood and fire and We Will Be Free!"

He screamed the last words at me, frenzied with his vision, and I was terrified.

Chapter 7: Ekharden Platz

Back out on the dockside, the wind had dropped but it was now raining steadily. I welcomed it. I felt that I needed something to wash away the stain of fanaticism – though I doubted that rainwater alone would suffice.

The Skipper hadn't repeated his demand that I murder Ommet after two days. But he had insisted that I take the poisoned dagger, which now sat uneasily in my pocket. It was clear enough that I was not being offered a choice. Whatever I might think, in the Skipper's eyes I was bound to the New Dawn, party to their secrets and subject to their discipline. If I had not shown some willingness to go along with that, I wouldn't have left the ship. At least, not by the gangplank. More likely, over the side in a canvas bag.

I wasn't sure what had shook me most – the mad zeal for bloody revolution that he had revealed, or the weapons with which he proposed to carry it out. I'd always known that the New Dawn were dangerous fanatics, but I'd discounted their ability to do anything serious. Now I had to think again. Clearly, they had not only the will but the weaponry, and I shuddered to think what might be born of that union.

What, exactly, did they plan to do with those armaments? The Skipper hadn't taken me so far into his confidence as to reveal his exact plans. And I couldn't understand why Vorgranstern seemed to be the centre of his plans. Of all the cities in the North, it seemed the least likely place to spark a rebellion. The rule of the First Order was light and distant here. The Duke kept to his palace, collected no more than reasonable taxes, and left the running of the cities affairs largely to the Merchant's Association and the Trade Guilds. What profit would there be to Vorgranstern to destroy all that? Why would its citizens support a revolution that threatened their peace and livelihood – even their very lives?

Brooding over this question at least kept me for wondering what I would do about Ommet.

The Karstensrada, where stood the White Charger Inn and my rendezvous with Ommet, was in that part of the city known as 'New Vorgranstern' – it being only several hundred years old. New, that is, compared with 'Old Vorgranstern', which occupied the top of the peninsula and had been inhabited since before the First Kingdom was established, some three thousand years ago. In those ancient times it was the home of the fierce Grof Varnark tribe. Sea-rovers and pirates, they raided and traded all along the northern coasts, before returning to their impregnable fortress. Surrounded by sea on three sides, and by an impassable salt marsh on the fourth, it was never taken by siege or assault.

But in more civilised times, the bog that had protected the landward flank became less of a boon. As the town grew into a city, the need to expand led to repeated attempts to build on the quagmire. Piles were driving deep into the mud, platforms covered them, and buildings were erected. When they sank into the ooze, new buildings were put up over the ruins. A process which continued until eventually, the marsh was filled and the buildings stopped sinking.

In time, New Vorgranstern became established, but it was always the poorer part of the city. Damp, unhealthy, and looked down on by the inhabitants of Old Vorgenstern – literally and figuratively.

That had changed with the Tunnels. The debris from the excavations had been used to give New Vorgranstern more solid foundations. A causeway had been built to allow road traffic access to the city, and a vast new square had been built, in the style of the great southern cities. Surrounded by fine buildings and graced by many statues, it had been named Ekharden Platz, in honour of the last King and first Emperor of the realm.

All roads now centred on Ekharden Platz. The Mainway, the side roads from the docks, the streets of Old Vorgranstern – and, of course, the Karstenstrada. On its wide expanse there were various areas marked out – some for trading, some for entertainments, others for pedestrians. Riders and horse-drawn vehicles had their own routes to follow, all carefully delineated with coloured stone and firmly enforced by the City Watch.

This magnificent creation had, however, one drawback, at least from my point of view. It had no shelter. The rain had now become a deluge, and I was regretting my decision to walk along the docks instead of taking to the tunnels. Not that it would have made a great difference in the long run. Once out on the Platz, I would soon have been drenched anyway.

Slogging through the puddles (drainage was not one of the strong points in the design of the Platz), I morbidly wondered if it could have been any wetter when it was a swamp. But at least the Karstensrada was now in sight, and The White Charger should be close. I looked forward to a hot bowl of spicy fish broth, one of the dishes the city was famed for.

Not surprisingly, the Platz was all but deserted now. Through the driving rain, I could make out just a few distant figures and some wagons on their way to the docks. Most of those figures were, like myself, scurrying for shelter. One or two seemed to be merely standing in place, apparently enjoying the brisk weather. I had my suspicions. They were more likely to be the Skipper's men, watching to see that I made no detours.

Ahead of me, a two horse covered carriage emerged from the Karstenstrada. Instead of turning onto the designated path for wheeled and hoofed traffic, it headed directly towards me, following the pedestrian way marked in red brick.

New in town, I thought, and ignorant of the rules. No doubt the Watch would soon set them right. And indeed, even as I had the thought, an admonitory whistle sounded, and there were distant shouts.

Unheeding, the carriage continued on its illegal way, and even began to pick up speed.

Annoyed, I stepped aside from the path. Wet though I already was, I had no wish to add a splashing from passing wheels.

The carriage altered course slightly, until it was once more heading directly for me. The driver, perched on his high seat in front of the enclosed passenger section, was whipping up the horses, increasing the pace.

"Hey!" I shouted. "HEY! You're on the wrong path!" I waved my hands frantically. The driver showed no sign of hearing or seeing me. Swathed in a hooded driving cape, he seemed to merge into the carriage as if he and it were one being.

Fear, colder even than the rain, licked my backbone. I moved still further from the path, and the carriage again turned towards me. It was now less than a hundred yards away, and coming on fast.

I glanced around wildly. This part of the Platz was a clear, open space, with little in the way of shelter or cover. A large equestrian statue was barely visible through the rain, some distance from the path. I turned towards it and broke into a run.

Behind me, I could hear the crack of a whip as the driver urged the horses on, the splash and clatter of hooves and iron-rimmed wheels. Glancing over my shoulder, I could see the carriage bearing down on me, and I redoubled my pace.

I wasn't going to make it. Water dragged at my feet, holding me back. I turned sharply, trying to substitute manoeuvrability for speed, but the slick wet flagstones betrayed me, and I was down on one knee, with the carriage charging down on me.

Desperately I forced myself upright, preparing to throw myself aside at the last moment.

The carriage swerved. Only a little, but enough that the closest horse swept by me with feet to spare. As it did so, a door opened, just in time to slam into my shoulder. But even as it did, a strong hand grabbed the lapels of my coat and with a powerful heave dragged me inside.

The horses pounded on, their pace barely slowed by the collision. Bruised and wet and gasping for breath, I huddled on the floor and looked up.

A bright blue pair of eyes twinkled down at me.

"Terrible day for walking," said Ommet. "I thought you might like to share my carriage?"

"What...?" I gasped out. "What in God's name..."

He wagged a finger at me. "Please, no blasphemy!"

There was shouting outside. Voices calling on us to halt. Ommet glanced through a window. "Not the Watch," he commented. "Friends of yours?"

I managed to drag myself up far enough to peer through the window. Two men were sprinting across the Platz, on a course to intercept the carriage. I recognised at least one of them – he had been on the dock by the Anatarna.

"Not friends," I gasped out. "Associates."

"Not the sort I'd care to be associated with," Ommet commented, and rapped on the ceiling. "More speed if you can, please!" he shouted up to the driver.

The horses hurled themselves forward and the carriage thundered past the Skipper's men, pulling easily away. There were shouts, and a gleam of steel as one of them pulled something from his coat. A moment later and there was a loud thud, and two inches of pointed steel suddenly appeared in the rear wall of the carriage, not far from Ommet's head.

He examined it with a raised eyebrow.

"Don't touch it!" I warned. "These people have been known to use poisoned blades."

"Really? You do have interesting associates," he replied. "But we don't want to leave that sticking out the back for everyone to see. Might attract attention." He picked up a short cane from the seat, and carefully tapped at the knife point until it dropped out behind the carriage.

.

I pulled myself up from the floor and took a seat opposite Ommet. "I thought we were supposed to meet at 'The White Charger'. In a day or so. In a more conventional manner than being run down in the middle of the Platz."

The carriage slowed down to a more sedate pace. Glancing outside, I saw that we had rejoined the proper route designated for vehicles, and were now entering the Mainway. The hammering of rain on the roof died away as we came into the tunnel.

"Conventional? The Wraith?" Ommet grinned. Then shook his head, and frowned. "Actually, that was my plan. But things have changed. I meant to go back to Muranburder, but that became difficult. So I got here earlier than expected and found matters had gone awry."

"Awry?" I asked, as if I didn't know what he meant.

"I had someone looking out for you. Making sure you had no problems."

A mental image came to mind. A tall man in a dark coat.

"Spying on me, do you mean?"

Ommet shrugged. "As you wish. His instructions were only to watch, and to send word if you ran into any trouble. As it happened it was he who ran into trouble. A fatal accident, it seems."

I remembered the crumpled figure in a pool of blood. "I saw someone fall."

"Indeed. And was there anyone near him at the time?"

A man in a green coat, I thought to myself. "Many people. It was busy."

"And yet no one, it seems, saw exactly what happened." Ommet shook his head. "I did not know this man personally, but he had no reputation for carelessness. Rather the opposite, if anything. And yet, he managed to fall over a barrier."

I said nothing. Ommet met my gaze steadily, and then continued. "When I heard of this I was concerned for your safety, and would have gone at once to The White Charger to see if you had arrived. But it I had word that the Inn was being watched. There were men inside and out, looking carefully at all who arrived. And you were not there – though you had had ample time to make your way from the River Dock."

"I took an indirect route." I said. We stared at each other in silence, and I dropped a casual hand to the pocket where the Skipper's poisoned blade was hidden.

Ommet, however, did not seem angry. There was no threat in his attitude. If anything, he seemed saddened. Perhaps disappointed.

After a moment, he continued. "I had no idea who was watching. The Baron's men, perhaps, though how they would have found out about our rendezvous I couldn't guess. Nor could I say who they were watching for – me, or you, or both of us? But it was clear that a change of plan was called for. Hence I arranged for this carriage, and waited at the entrance to the Karstenstrada until you approached. I was somewhat relieved that you had not also suffered a fatal accident."

"I thought I was about to." I rubbed my bruised shoulder.

"Sorry about that. But I didn't know if anyone else might be watching or following, and stopping might have been risky." He glanced meaningfully at the small hole where the knife blade had recently appeared.

The carriage slowed down still further, and made a sudden turn. The noise from the Mainway faded, and we came to a halt. Ommet opened the door, and jumped out. I followed, more cautiously, being mindful of my various aches and pains.

"Take the carriage over to the river docks." Ommet called up to the driver. "Leave it there. It may give the impression that we have left the city. Then your duty is discharged, and my thanks."

The driver, still anonymous under his hood, nodded assent, flicked the reins and set the carriage moving.

I glanced around. We were in a warehouse of some sort, with bales and crates of goods piled all around. The carriage turned back to the entrance, and disappeared. The place seemed deserted, but someone outside pulled shut the doors after the carriage had left.

"I've no power to compel you," Ommet said quietly. "Nor any desire to. If you wish to make your own way, do so. You've troubles enough of your own, without adding mine to them."

"Do you still need a thief?"

He nodded, then turned away and strode briskly off into the depths of the warehouse.

I thought for a moment.

The Skipper would be searching all Vorgranstern for me, and if he found me I'd better have something to offer him. Some information about Ommet and his plans. Moreover, in a few days time my description would be all over the city, and then everyone would be looking for me!

It would be better if I could get out of the City entirely. Slip away from the New Dawn and from Crombard, like the Wraith I was supposed to be. But the best chance of doing that probably lay with Ommet.

I made my decision, and followed him.

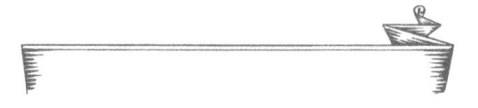

Chapter 8: Revelations

In the far corner of the warehouse there was a small door, well concealed behind piles of merchandise. Ommet was just inside the door, coaxing a small lamp into life. It's dim light showed a winding staircase disappearing upwards into the gloom.

He glanced at me as I approached. Though I met his gaze full on, I couldn't interpret his expression. Was it amusement? Was it relief? Was it even pity? But all he said was "Watch the steps. They're steep, and it's a long climb."

Nor was he exaggerating, though he might have added that the treads were narrow, so that it was impossible to get a full foot on them. Nor was there any opportunity to rest on the way – no side passages, no flat sections, not even an extra wide step to sit on for a moment. We simply climbed. The ache in my legs became all but intolerable, and the stale air in that confined space didn't seem able to fill my lungs sufficiently, but I had no choice now other than to follow Ommet, his form a dark shadow against the flickering yellow light.

There wasn't even a handrail to help our ascent. Just rough rock walls. I speculated that it had been carved out sometime after the Tunnels had been officially completed, and had to fit into whatever space was left. I was also fairly confident that it appeared on no official plans. As to where it was going, I had no idea. I had started by counting steps, and estimated from that that we were already above the highest point of the Mainway. But that left hundreds of feet of solid rock to the streets of Old Vorgranstern. I stopped counting, and focused simply on forcing myself upwards.

Then, abruptly, the lantern showed a doorway in front of us. Ommet wrenched at a latch, which seemed reluctant to move. The appalling thought that it might be locked nearly panicked me, for I knew I couldn't make it back down that horrendous flight. Or rather, I couldn't make it down safely. My legs were about to buckle, and then I'd certainly be going down, and with no chance of stopping till I hit the lower door!

With a heave, Ommet freed the latch and the door burst open. We stumbled out into the space beyond, and collapsed on the floor, gasping for breath and desperate to relieve the agony in our calves and thighs. I was pleased to see that Ommet was suffering even more than I was.

"Where – are – we?" I still had enough breath to speak. Looking round, the lamplight showed us in a small rock-walled room completely empty apart from some spare lamps in one corner.

However, it was several minutes before Ommet was recovered sufficiently to answer. "Saint Venelcis." He dragged himself up to a sitting position. "Lower crypt."

"We've climbed that far?" The Cathedral was near the top of the peninsula. Only the Duke's Palace stood higher.

Ommet shook his head. "The nave is still... another hundred feet up. Two hundred, perhaps."

I let out groan, and Ommet found enough breath to attempt a chuckle.

"No. We're not going there. No more climbing. But we do need to move. Not much air. Ventilation here is poor." He pulled himself upright.

"You didn't mention that bit at the bottom," I muttered. With an effort, I got to my knees. "How do we get out?" The only door I could see was the one we'd come through.

"Here." Ommet lumbered over to the wall opposite the door, which I now saw was of brickwork instead of raw rock. He pulled at an inset iron ring, and a section of the wall reluctantly pivoted open. A faint breath of slightly fresher air wafted through the gap, along with some stronger lamplight.

"Let me guess," I said. "It's a secret passageway to the Archbishop's chambers to allow his mistress to come and go unobserved."

Ommet shook his head. "I very much doubt if the Archbishop knows anything about this. And it wouldn't be much good for smuggling in women, anyway. They wouldn't have much passion left in them after those stairs!" He turned out the lamp he had brought and left it with the others.

"Good point," I acknowledged. "But if the Archbishop doesn't know what's beneath his own cathedral, how did you learn of it?"

He shrugged. "I have friends, and friends of friends. Are you ready?"

I managed to get to my feet, and followed him as he stepped through the concealed door.

A musty smell met my nostrils. Not the sweet odour of holy incense that I would have associated with a cathedral. This was mould and damp and rotting cloth.

We had entered a storeroom of some kind, apparently a graveyard for worn out vestments. The lamplight came through a set of brick arches, beyond which figures were moving.

Ommet carefully eased the door shut, then leant over to whisper to me.

"They've put this place into use since it was last checked! Sacristan's staff, I think. A workshop for making up and repairing clerical garments. Quietly, now – it would be best if we didn't have to try and explain who we are or where we came from!"

"I'm the Wraith, remember?" I hissed back.

He grinned. "Good! This way, then!"

Using the piles of discarded clothing as cover, we made our way towards the arches. The workers beyond were going about their business, and did not as much as glance in our direction. The low hum of conversation and the clatter of tools served very well to cover the faint sound of our movements.

Ommet pulled me down into a crouch behind a bale of fabric. "Door in the far corner," he whispered. "Do you see it?"

I risked a swift glance over the top of the bale. "Yes, but its twenty feet away and there's no cover."

"They're not looking our way."

"They will if they hear the door open!" I thought for a moment. "I have an idea. Wait here!"

I crept back the way we'd come, went past the hidden door to the heaps of mouldering fabric left at the far end of the room.

Even deep inside the solid stone of Vorgranstern, moisture from driving rain and windblown spray and dense sea-fogs can find its way. Through ventilation shafts and light tubes, blown along corridors, dripped from clothing: seeking a way down, to find its lowest possible place.

It had found this place and had been absorbed by the holy detritus of the cathedral. I had to delve deep into the rank mounds of old cloth before I could find some drier material, which I ripped into shreds. I made a small pile a safe distance from the main heap, and fumbled in my pockets for flint, steel and tinder.

With a few sharp blows I struck sparks into the tinder, added it to the dry cloth and blew gently. It flared up, faster than I had expected – perhaps from years of exposure to holy oils. I hastily added some of the damper material, and a satisfactory amount of smoke began to rise. I scuttled back to Ommet.

"What have you done?" he whispered.

"Just a little arson," I told him. "Keep down and be ready to move!"

In the confined space, the smoke was rapidly building up. One of the workers suddenly looked up from his task, sniffing. Then he looked over at the arches and saw the tendrils of white vapour wafting out from under the brickwork.

The shout of 'Fire!" went up, quickly repeated, and chaos ensured. Some ran towards the arches to investigate, others – less brave but perhaps wiser – ran for the exit. There were further shouts, to bring water, to get help. And all the time the smoke was thickening. Already, the far wall of the workshop was obscured.

"Now!" I hissed and ran for the door indicated, Ommet following close behind.

In the panic and confusion, two more running figures weren't noticed. We slipped out through the door, into a deserted corridor.

Ommet slammed the door shut and turned to me. In the dim lighting, I couldn't see his face properly, but there was no hiding the shock in his voice.

"You started a fire in a Cathedral? Don't you realise this is Holy Ground?"

I shrugged. "Not really the Cathedral, was it? Just a storeroom and workshop. A pile of mouldy old clothing? Not exactly consecrated!"

"But if it spreads... there are people here!"

"It won't. I started it well away from anything else. They'll have it out with a few buckets of water. Or it'll go out on its own – there isn't enough air or dry fuel to sustain a blaze. In any case, did you have a better idea?"

There was a short pause whilst Ommet considered the point. "Not really," he conceded. "But perhaps you could let me know before you take such drastic action?"

I shrugged. "Did we have somewhere to go?"

Without further conversation, he led me along the corridor. The door at the end led to yet another corridor, running crossways and much better lit. Moreover, instead of bare brick or rock walls it boasted wood panelling and there was carpet on the floor. Ommet turned sharp right, and eventually a final door led us into a comfortably furnished living room. Windows and a wide glass door opened out onto a balcony, and a grey vista of storm lashed sea dimly seen through driving rain.

"The weather hasn't improved," I said. "Where is this place? Still part of the Cathedral?"

"Not exactly. It's part of an Inn just below us – one of those built into the side of the rock face above the River Port. An establishment of some quality – 'The Lord Admiral'. But they have an arrangement with the Cathedral, and this suite of rooms is permanently reserved for guests of the Archbishop. Guests who, for one reason or another, it might not be appropriate to house in the Cathedral itself."

"Ha! I knew it! The Archbishop's mistress!"

Ommet raised his eyes and shook his head. "Why this obsession with the alleged sexual indiscretions of senior clergy? There are other reasons for guests to be housed discreetly. For example, the rooms are currently reserved for a foreign banker and his secretary."

"Financial indiscretions then!"

"More likely, I grant you. But there are perfectly legitimate reasons for the Archbishop to have such visitors. Should anyone ask, I am Marveno Sedrozi, a Master of the Grand Caradas Bank of Nazzara. You are Hylamo Ekritsa, a junior employee of the bank, and we are here to discuss the transfer and distribution of funds from the Cathedral to various charitable ventures in Nazzara and the surrounding regions. Which, as you may well know, are suffering great distress at present due to natural disaster."

"That sounds plausible," I admitted. "Does the Archbishop know anything of this?"

"I certainly hope not!" Ommet gave a wry smile. "The arrangements were made without his involvement. But it's unlikely that they will come to his attention. I have an – er – associate on the Archbishop's staff who will see to that!"

"You have a lot of associates," I observed.

"As do you." He gave me a long look. "And I think that we need to have a discussion about that. But that can wait for tomorrow. We've both had a rather exciting day. Food and rest are the immediate needs." He went over to a silken cord hanging by the door and gave it several sharp tugs. "I'll order us some dinner. Have you any preferences?"

I nodded. "I was on my way to a bowl of fish broth at the 'White Charger' when you intercepted me. I like mine well spiced and with some fresh bread, please."

"Sounds good! We'll have that for two, I think. And a good bottle of wine. After all, we are the Archbishop's guests!"

THE FISH BROTH PROVED equal to its reputation, and the wine was excellent. I fully expected some searching questions afterwards, but instead Ommet rang down for a hot bath to be drawn, and afterwards took himself off to his bedroom. I had my own room, comfortably furnished and with a smart set of clothing in a foreign style laid out ready. I too had a bath and retired. I judged myself to have more stamina than Ommet, but it had been a particularly stressful day.

THE FOLLOWING MORNING brought a change in the weather. Looking out of my window I saw sunlight sparkling on a sea of brilliant blue, with only a smattering of white-capped waves. Dressed in my new clothes, I went out to the living room. A breakfast was already laid out: I helped myself to a plate of fruit, rolls and cheese and went out onto the balcony.

Ommet was already there, sitting on a bench and reading a small book with a well used leather cover. An empty plate next to him indicated that he had been there long enough to have broken his own fast.

He looked up as I approached. "A hearty first meal of the day!" he observed.

My plate was well piled. "I have a healthy appetite," I admitted. "Though this isn't what I'd start the day with, given the choice."

"Oh? It's just what the serving staff brought up. I'll ring down and ask for something different."

"No, don't bother. This will do well enough. I just had a hankering for something warm. A bit of toasted cheese, perhaps – and maybe a different sort of cheese as well. All they ever seem to have in these parts are hard red cheeses."

"Well, that's true. You prefer the softer varieties?"

"It's what I grew up with. Back when I was a lad, every farm made their own cheese, all to their own recipe, and they were all different. Soft cheeses, hard cheeses, crumbly varieties. Goats cheese and cheese from ewe's milk, as well as from cows."

"Hmm." Ommet looked thoughtful. "We had some of those in the Western Provinces where I hail from. But I've read that the greatest and best varieties are to be found in the South East. Especially on the Farahan Peninsula."

I made no reply, but turned away to stand and eat by the rail. And to curse my own volubility. I'd just revealed more of myself in a few sentences than I had ever told anyone. With some people, it would not have mattered, but to a man with Ommet's intelligence and knowledge it was as good as giving him my life story!

There was something in him that made it all too easy to talk too much and say more than intended. I must watch my mouth carefully in his presence.

I gave my attention to the view below, which was impressive. The seaways were already busy, with sails visible all the way out to the horizon, whilst below me the River Port was a bustle of activity. The quay's seemed to be at full capacity, crammed with river barges in all their colourful variety. My eye caught a familiar pattern of dark and light blue: *Dreambreeze* was loading cargo in preparation for her next journey upriver.

Ommet joined me, and followed my gaze. "She'll be away again with the next tide, I should think."

I nodded agreement. "In truth, I was surprised to see her still here, though it was only yesterday that we docked. So much has happened since then, it felt a great deal longer."

"We may seek to measure time in exact units of hours, days and so on, but our perception of it is less precise. Have you ever read Gopolinger's essay on the subject? It's quite fascinating."

"I lack your breadth of knowledge. I have never even heard of Gopolinger."

He measured me with a glance. "A leading philosopher of the last century. I'm a little surprised. A person of your intelligence and obvious wide range of knowledge might be expected to at least know of him."

"My formal education has been limited," I admitted. "What I've learned has been picked up along the way, so to speak, and tends to be restricted to certain practical areas."

Such as jewellery, and locks, I added mentally. There was no need to say it. Ommet nodded in understanding, both of the spoken and unspoken words.

"Gopolinger also wrote on how sensory stimuli can bring back vivid memories. A tune, a smell, a view. This, for instance." He waved his hand at the view. "It reminds me very much of Daradura."

"Daradura?" I looked at him in surprise. "The Imperial Palace?"

"Indeed so. Just like Vorgranstern, it is built on a peninsula. Just like this, you can look out towards the busy quays, though in that case, they are on the lake shore rather than directly below. But the bustle and noise are much the same. Or you can look to the opposite bank, and see the Imperial Park and gardens."

I have been to the capital city on several occasions, and I recognised the description. I've seen Daradura from both the commercial docks on the eastern shore and the park to the west. But Ommet was talking from the viewpoint of someone actually within the palace itself.

He met my gaze with a meaningful nod, and I realised that he had just told me more about himself than I had learned in all the time since he had first come to my cell in Neowbron. It was a gesture of faith.

He turned away, sat back on the bench, and sipped from a cup. "I've been thinking a lot about what you told me. How you filched Crombard's jewellery from under his nose. One particular point struck me as incongruous."

I sat next to him. "Which point was that?"

"You said that the Baron and his lady, on their return to their chambers, found the strongbox open. Which means that you left it that way."

I shrugged. "What of it?"

"The timing for your operation was very tight. You had only a limited period in which to dispose of the jewels and get back to the cage. That time could have been extended by closing the strongbox. The theft would not have been noticed immediately. Perhaps not for some time, depending on when it was opened to return the items being worn. Those extra minutes could have been valuable – so why did you not close it before you left the room?"

I shrugged. "An oversight on my part."

Ommet gave me a disappointed look. "Please. You do not have oversights. Your planning is too precise. I can think of only one explanation."

I raised an enquiring eyebrow, and Ommet continued.

"The Baron's chambers had been locked and guarded. None of the servants had been inside. Therefore, no suspicion could have fallen on them. But had the theft been discovered later, after the rooms had been opened and the servants had entered to go about their work, then they would have been the first suspects. And, given Crombard's reputation, it would have gone very hard with them. So by leaving the strongbox open, you sacrificed some time in order to protect them."

"Well, yes," I admitted. "I suppose that was my thinking. There's no doubt that the Baron would have put them to the torture had there been the slightest possibility of their guilt, and I had no desire for innocents to suffer from my actions. But why is that such a significant matter?"

"I don't pretend to have much personal experience of the criminal mind. But I do read widely, as you may have gathered. And everything I have read on this subject tells me that the average criminal is a very self-centred person. Their concern is entirely with their own gain and their own safety. They are not much bothered with what happens to other people, be they victims or just the innocent who get caught up in their schemes."

He leaned forward, and pointed at me. "The Wraith may be an accomplished thief, but he is not criminal in his mentality! Which is, as I've said, incongruous. And it suggests to me that, whatever the motive behind your career, it is not simply personal gain!"

He paused, expectantly, but I had nothing to say.

"And you only despoil the First Order. Indeed, the richest and most noble of the First Order. There are many easier targets for one of your talents. But it is not about the money, is it?"

"No," I said. "It is not."

The noise of the docks below drifted up, mingled with the cries of sea birds, all very clear in the long pause that our conversation had come to.

Finally, Ommet sighed and continued.

"So we have established that the Wraith is an unusually principled thief. But what of his 'associates'? These, it seems, are people who carry poisoned blades, and who commit murder quite casually! A person is thrown over a railing, to fall to his death, merely because he was following you! What sort of principles do these associates follow?"

I was uncomfortably aware of the poisoned blade currently resting in my pocket, an arms length from its intended target. "You cannot always choose who you work with," I muttered.

"I told you that I had intended to go back to Muranburder? Well, let me now tell you why I had to change my plans. I had word from our host there."

"Master Grubard?"

"The same. He was forced to leave at short notice, with all his family and household. A great inconvenience for him, and somewhat awkward for me, since he was my chief contact there."

I nodded, recalling that the Skipper had said as much. "Why?"

"The kitchen maid went missing. You might have met her – very young, light brown hair?"

A memory came to mind. A bright smile, a clear voice with a strong northern accent. "I think so. She served me breakfast."

There was a grim look on Ommet's face as he continued. "She vanished shortly after we left the city. Grubard used all his resources, and eventually found her. Her body, that is. She had been – ill used."

The breakfast I had eaten threatened to come back, violently, as the implications sank in. I remembered the Skipper's exact words: "Bryn talked with one of the servants." I should have realised what that really meant.

"Poor girl, all she knew of Master Grubard was that he was a merchant. His other activities were kept secret from all but a few people. None-the-less, she was tortured for information, then murdered to keep her silent. The body was set to be weighted and dumped in the river. Had it not been for his own sources of information, Grubard would never have known what had happened."

I swallowed hard to keep my food down. "Was it the Baron?" Knowing full well it was not.

"Hardly likely. Had Crombard suspected Grubard, he would not have bothered with abducting a servant. He would have arrested the entire family at once. No, this was someone else. Someone hidden, and ruthless. Someone who would see the life of an innocent young women as no more than a – a *gaming piece!*" There was real pain in Ommet's voice now. And anger. "Something to be used and discarded!"

"So Grubard..."

"He thought it best to curtail his business in Muranburder. Both his public business and that which he carried out in secret. It was clear that someone was watching him and that he and his family were no longer safe. I fully concur with that. I would not see another innocent life sacrificed."

There was a long pause, whilst Ommet stared at me. "So – was this one of your 'associates'?"

I nodded slowly. "Yes. I did talk to some people in Muranburder. But I didn't know that they would do that. Or the man here. I mean – I know that they are, as you say, ruthless. But I hadn't expected anything like that." Knowing, even as I said it, that I should have expected nothing less.

"And these people. They have a name?"

"You've heard of The Watchers, I suppose?"

"Of course. But they are pamphleteers. A debating club, really. The literature they put out may be considered seditious by some, but they don't murder people!"

"No. But behind them is another group. An organisation that uses The Watchers as cover, to give them a legitimate face. However this group are more – extreme – in their methods. They call themselves..."

"... The New Dawn!" Ommet interrupted and finished the sentence for me. "I have had... information about them. 'Extreme' hardly covers their activities! They are murderous fanatics! Ready to turn the Empire over to blood and fire to get rid of the First Order, and never mind how many innocent lives are lost in the process!"

"Yes, that describes them quite well," I agreed, thinking of the *Anatarna* and her deadly cargo.

"And you're one of them." There was no expression in his voice, but there was disappointment in the look he gave me. Or perhaps that was just what my conscience saw.

"No!" I denied, and struck the arm of my chair for emphasis. "I am not a member of New Dawn, I never have been, and have no intention of ever joining them!" The Skipper, of course, had a different view of things, but I saw no point in bringing that up. "We've worked together, yes. We have similar views about the

First Order, I grant you that, and we've helped each other. Their organisation has provided me with information and assistance. I've supplied them with funds from my thefts. We've been useful to each other. But I've never agreed with their methods, and I've told them so!" I took a deep breath. "Yes, I told them about Grubard, and I can't tell you how much I now regret that. They knew that I was travelling on the *Dreambreeze*, and obviously had me followed. When they realised that someone else was following me they killed him, and I regret that as well. But how was I to know that he was your man? For all I knew, he could have been one of the Baron's agents!"

"And did you tell them about me?" Ommet asked quietly.

"Yes. Of course. How could I not? They already knew that I'd been rescued; naturally they wanted to know by whom. And how. I told them what I knew, though that amounted to little enough!"

"As well that I didn't tell you more, then!" Ommet said dryly, and I winced. "And what did they have to say about that?"

I shrugged. "They asked me to continue to help you, and to keep them informed. They are interested in what your intentions are, and if their own plans might be compromised." I made no mention of the poisoned blade and its purpose.

"I see. Well, I suppose that's reasonable, from their point of view." He stood up and walked over to the balcony rail, scratching his chin in thought. "My point of view is, will they compromise *my* plans? Bad enough that rescuing you got Baron Crombard breathing down my neck, now I've got the New Dawn sniffing along my trail and murdering my people!"

"Well, you don't have to worry too much about Crombard for a while. Not in person, at least. He's gone to Zyx Trethir."

"He's *what*!" Ommet whipped round to face me. "Where did you hear that? When did you hear it?"

"From the New Dawn," I answered, amazed at his reaction. "Yesterday. I'm surprised you didn't already know."

He nodded, slowly. "So am I. I should have known that. I should have been told. And if I wasn't..." He gave me a searching look. "Do you see what it means, that I wasn't told?"

I thought about it. "It means that someone decided not to tell you? Someone in your own organisation?"

"That's right. And if they're not talking to me – then who are they talking to instead?"

"The Baron."

"Very likely. And if so, then he knows where we are!"

I felt the colour drain from me at the thought, and I glanced at the door. "We have to get out of here! Now!"

Ommet shook his head. "No. Don't panic yet! I doubt if we're in immediate danger. We've got time to at least think about this before we go rushing out of the door."

"Have we? The Baron himself could be kicking that very door down at any minute, dammit!"

"He hasn't had time to get to Zyx Trethir and back here and please mind your language. Swearing will not help!"

"His men could be here now, and swearing might not help but it seems appropriate!"

"Oh, I'm sure that he does have men here, and I'm not denying that we're in danger. But being in Vorgranstern gives us some room to manoeuvre. Duke Endranard is the only Lord in the North who's wealth and power rivals that of the Grand Duke, and he achieved that position largely by letting the Second Order trading guilds have free reign, as long as they pay their taxes. Brodon does not approve of that policy, and doesn't like opposition, especially here in the North, which he considers his own personal possession! So he and Endranard are not on good terms, and Crombard cannot operate as freely here as he can in the rest of the North."

"But if he asked for Endranard's help to arrest the Wraith, I doubt if it would be refused!"

"Probably not. But he won't do that. For one thing, neither Brodon nor Crombard would want to be asking any favours from Endranard! And, for another, re-capturing the Wraith is not going to be their main concern now." His eyes regained a small sparkle. "I'm afraid that I've replaced you in their affections! They'll want to know exactly who I am and what I'm doing here."

"You're quite welcome to that position. But even if you're their main course, I'm sure that they'll welcome me as an appetiser!"

"Interesting analogy. But I'm not ready to be served up just yet!" he replied. "I'm going to my room. I need to think this through, to try and identify who might have betrayed me, and who might still be safe! As for you, perhaps you could employ your own skills and contrive a Wraith-like means of exit. We must assume that both the Inn and the Cathedral exits are being watched, and if we try and leave openly, we'll be followed. Likewise the way we entered – even if we could slip past the Sacristan's people, the stairway is known and cannot be risked."

"If we leave openly, the New Dawn will probably find us in any case!" I pointed out. "And the posters will be going up soon."

"Posters?" Ommet paused and glanced back as he was about to leave the balcony.

"Oh, yes. I didn't get round to mentioning that, but apparently my description is going to be circulated publicly in the next day or so."

"This just keeps getting better, doesn't it? A good time to be a Wraith!" So saying, Ommet left the balcony to me and me to my thoughts.

Which were firstly ones of regret. Free of Ommet's disapproving looks, I cursed long and freely, using much worse words than 'Dammit'. I cursed my decision to come to

Vorgranstern, I cursed my failure to make off from Muranburder when I had the chance. I cursed the jeweller who had betrayed me in Neowbron, and I cursed myself for trying to sell Crombard's possessions whilst still in the North. I cursed Crombard, Brodon, the First Order, the Empire, the Skipper, and the New Dawn.

I was just getting started on Ommet, when I noticed that the small book he had been reading was still on the balcony. He had put it down next to his breakfast plate, and had apparently forgotten it in the course of our conversation.

Curious as always, I picked it up. Behind the plain and well worn leather cover, it proved to be a book of devotional readings. Flicking through the pages, I saw nothing of interest to me, though scribbled notes in the margins attested to Ommet's interest in spiritual matters. Which matched what I was starting to learn of his character, but told me nothing new about his purposes.

I was about to toss it down again, when it flipped open to the inside of the front cover. A stiff piece of card had been glued in. On it, in copperplate handwriting, a few words:

'Presented to Thylan An'Darsio, to mark his achievement of First Mark standard in the Field of Devotional Studies. Signed for and on behalf of the Order of the Arravine Friars, V. Callard.'

I read it through twice.

Ommet, an Arravine Friar?

The Arravines were a scholarly order, whose main concern was teaching and the pursuit of knowledge. Probably a quarter of the schools in the Empire were established and staffed by them. Mostly they worked among the poorer classes, those who could not afford much in the way of education by themselves. As a consequence, they were looked down upon by the more traditional centres of learning – the ancient schools, colleges and universities. Yet the quality of their teaching was acknowledged, if grudgingly, and to achieve First Mark standard was no small thing.

It was not proof of Ommet's identity. The book might have come from any seller of used volumes. I flicked through the pages again, examining the handwriting in the margin. It showed a variety of colours and qualities of ink, but all seemed to be the same hand. However, I had no examples of Ommet's own penmanship to compare with it, so it didn't help.

Yet it did fit well with Ommet's obvious wide learning and with his piety – especially in matters of bad language or arson in holy places!

On the other hand, travelling across the country in a variety of disguises, defying the highest First Order nobles of the North, and recruiting thieves for mysterious purposes did not seem at all in keeping with such an identity.

There was also another point to consider. Ommet had as good as told me that he had been in the Imperial Palace, in Daradura itself. There might well be reason for an Arravine Friar to have some duties within the Palace, for scholars and teachers were doubtless required there as much as anywhere else in the Empire. But the implication of his words, of his look, was that he had been commissioned to his task by someone within those walls. Someone from the very highest ranks of the Empire, indeed.

In short, Ommet was an Imperial Agent.

It seemed an unlikely calling for a minor cleric, yet it would certainly explain much. My own rescue, for example. No magistrate could ignore a command from someone wielding Imperial authority, even if it incurred the displeasure of the Lieutenant of the North. His access to apparently unlimited resources of funds and information was also explained. There was no doubt that Imperial Intelligence maintained networks of spies and informers throughout the Empire: if Ommet was connected to them, then his feats of organisation and planning were explained.

But that brought me to a dilemma.

If Ommet was an Imperial Agent, then he was the representative of all that I hated and had fought against for my entire life. My natural enemy. And, moreover, a traitor to his own kind. Well deserving of the poisoned blade the Skipper had decreed for him!

And yet... did I really want to throw in my lot with the New Dawn?

I remembered again the smiling face of the young maid as she served me breakfast in Master Grubard's house. Barely a woman, tortured and murdered by Bryn in his search for information. If not by the Beggar Man in person, then at his orders. I thought of the terror and pain that had befallen her and felt ill again.

And then the memory of the Skipper's mad eyes. The pleasure in them as he talked of his plans for blood and fire.

However much I hated the First Order, I feared the New Dawn's vision of the future at least as much. And, on a personal level, I had no doubt at all that they would dispose of me without a moment's hesitation if they thought it worthwhile.

Moreover – as I followed this train of thought – my worst enemy was probably Crombard. And whatever Ommet's purposes were, he hardly seemed to be sided with the Baron. 'The enemy of my enemy is my friend' as the old saying went. And Ommet was a more likely friend than either Crombard or the New Dawn.

But... he was an Imperial Agent.

In truth, I was not sure where my friendship or loyalty should lie.

In my frustration at the insoluble dilemma, I stood at the balcony and pounded my fist on the rail. I stared out at to sea, down at the docks, along the great rock of Vorgranstern to either side, not so much seeking a solution as seeking a distraction from my torment.

And I saw a solution. Not to my confusion of loyalties, but to my other and more immediate problem; how to escape from the net that was drawing around us.

Chapter 9: Illuminations

"Not to doubt your professional skills," Ommet said when I revealed my plan. "But that sounds like madness."

I shrugged. "Risky, I agree. But it's a calculated risk. And I'm open to other suggestions."

"I'll certainly try and think of something. Climbing down a light tube sounds more like a complicated way of committing suicide than a 'calculated risk.'"

"Nonsense!" I dismissed his doubts with an airy wave. "The Guild of Illuminators do it all the time!"

"With a team of experienced workers and the proper equipment! What are we going to do – tie some sheets together to lower ourselves?"

"No need for that. The light tubes have ladders inside, to facilitate cleaning and maintenance."

He gave me a suspicious look. "And how do you know that? The Illuminators guard their secrets tightly, even more so than the other Guilds!"

"I make it my business to learn things of this sort," I shrugged. "You never know when it might come in handy."

In actual fact, my information was based on an overheard conversation between two well-oiled Illuminators, some two years past. At the time I had been considering the possibility of despoiling Duke Endranard; the Illuminators, with their wide freedom of movement around the city, seemed a likely means of accessing the Ducal Palace. To that end, I had attended several establishments frequented by the Guild members. But they proved to be as close mouthed as their reputation and remarkably suspicious of strangers: I had given up after being forcibly ejected from one establishment. After that, I had received word from the New Dawn that I was not to stir things up in Vorgranstern – though at that time I had no clue as to the Skipper's plans – and had therefore moved on to greener pastures.

"I'm surprised that you don't have every detail of the Illuminators business ready to hand," I added, "complete with a set of clothing and false identities for each of us."

"It wasn't something I'd thought to inquire about beforehand. And it wouldn't be helpful to try and find out now. As near as I can tell, the weak point in my organisation is here in Vorgranstern."

"That's awkward. I can't go to the New Dawn, you can't go to – to your 'friends and friends of friends'. Are you sure there's no one you can trust?"

Neither of us was talking openly of Ommet's Imperial connections. It was not just the Illuminators Guild that had formed the habit of keeping things to themselves.

"The way this works," he said, "is that I have a name, a contact person, for each of several areas. I go to them with my requirements, they make the necessary arrangements. I know no more of their business than I need to, and my activities are known to as few as possible. For Muranburder and Neowbron, that person was Master Grubard. He is above suspicion – if he or someone in his organisation was in Crombard's pay, you would never have been rescued. But before we left Muranburder, I had sent word to my contact here. I asked them to make the arrangements for meeting you and for accommodation at the White Charger. Well, we know how that worked out! When things went awry, I talked to the same person, who organised the carriage – and our present lodgings."

"And this person is?" I asked. Fishing for information – a bad habit.

He smiled. "A senior clerk in the Ducal Palace. Which means that I can't go directly to the Duke, either – even though he's no friend of Crombard's."

"Where, then? We need to get out of the city, but the docks and the roads will be watched."

"I'm thinking about it. The first thing is to get out of these rooms unobserved. And in the absence of anything better, I suppose we must attempt your insane plan!"

My plan, such as it was, had come to me as I looked along the cliff face from the balcony. Dotted here and there across the rock surface were wide circles of glass. These were outer ends of the light tubes, by which sunlight was directed down into the tunnels below.

Each one was about ten feet across, and narrow ledges cut into the rock face gave the Illuminators access for cleaning and maintenance. On occasion, the Guild's members could be seen about their work, clinging precariously to the rock face whilst they carried buckets and wielded mops. Sometimes the glass was raised, and workers climbed down into the tube to carry out their duties. From the boozy conversation I had overheard, these consisted mostly of polishing the metal that lined the tubes and which must be kept mirror-bright to reflect the suns rays downward.

Getting out at the other end would be the main problem. Each light tube ended in a large glass bulb, high in the tunnel's roof. Most of Vorgransgtern's citizens took little notice of them, save to make a rough estimate of the time of day from the strength of their glow. But the Guild had, of course, to clean these bulbs as well, and I recalled seeing them lowered to the floor on rare occasions. Of course, onlookers were kept well away, but I had noticed the wires by which this was accomplished, and had once watched from a distance as a freshly serviced bulb was hoisted back up to its place.

It seemed that there was some sort of mechanism by which this was accomplished, and which could give us our means of escape.

It would be precarious, and the fact that we must attempt it at night added to the risk. Privately I shared Ommet's opinion. But I could see no better solution to our problem.

The day passed slowly – and once we had laid our plans, silently. Ommet spent some time on the balcony, reading his devotional. I struggled with the question of loyalties. Should I commit myself to Ommet, who I liked and admired, who had saved my life and who served my enemies? Or to the New Dawn, my allies who I distrusted, and even feared? In the end, I postponed the decision. The first priority was to escape the trap we were in, and after that... Well, I still wanted to find out what it was that I had been recruited to steal. I would wait until that question had been answered before deciding.

But even with that matter temporarily resolved, the day still dragged by. The tension of not knowing if were being watched, or if the Baron's men might break in at any moment, didn't help me relax, and it was a relief when the sunlight finally began to fade.

Even then we couldn't make our move. We had agreed that after midnight would be the best time, the small hours of the morning when Vorgranstern would come as close to sleeping as it ever did.

I didn't sleep. Neither did Ommet.

Finally, I decided that I'd had enough waiting.

"I think it's time. Or close enough, anyhow."

He nodded. "Are you ready, then?"

I shook my head. "No. You were right. This is madness."

"You've had a better idea?" he asked hopefully.

"Unfortunately not. So, it's time."

We looked up at the rock face above and behind us. The nearest Illuminators' access ledge ran about ten feet above the balcony. We had worked out that if Ommet stood on the table and I climbed on his shoulders, I would be able to reach it. The theory was good, but below the balcony was a sheer drop of at least twenty feet to where the main part of the inn projected out from the cliff face. And that was a steeply sloping roof, which overhung not just the Inn's frontage but also the narrow road that led up to it. Below the road it was several hundred feet further down to the dockside buildings. The prospect hadn't been too inviting in daylight; now it was truly frightening.

We had already moved the table against the wall. Ommet climbed onto it and braced himself, cupped hands held in front of him. I got on the table, put a foot on his hands, then stepped up onto his shoulders.

To look at, he had quite broad shoulders. Standing on them they felt remarkably narrow. Even with him holding onto my feet, it felt precarious.

I reached up cautiously, no sudden moves that might upset my balance. Stretched up, straining for the ledge.

Not making it.

"I'm four inches short!" I hissed down at Ommet.

He grunted something, then began to push me upwards. Which was even more precarious, but my questing fingers found the edges of the ledge, got a grip, and I pulled myself higher.

With Ommet still pushing that bit was easier, and I managed to get my elbows onto the ledge without much trouble. From there it was just a question of hoisting myself a little further until I could reach the rope that was strung along the rock face as a handrail. Finally, I was standing upright on the narrow ledge.

"Here, catch!" Ommet called, and tossed up the knotted end of a bedsheet. I tied it securely, and Ommet joined me on the ledge.

I undid the bedsheets again and wrapped them round my waist.

"If this doesn't work we'll need those to get back down," Ommet observed.

"We're not going back. But we don't want to leave any obvious clues. Let's get going." I led the way along the ledge.

Though not in the same category as the Mainway, the ledge path was quite wide enough for normal walking. I had even seen Illuminators running, though I didn't feel confident enough to attempt that, especially in the dark. However, it only took a few minutes to reach the nearest light tube.

Fortunately, it was a clear night, and both moons were up. The silvery light glinted on the wide glass disk, and provided just enough light to make out the mechanism by which it was raised and lowered.

The top edge was hinged. A long threaded bar, covered by a canvas sleeve, rose from the bottom edge. I removed the sleeve and examined the bar more closely.

"Looks simple enough. Turn this nut, it travels up the bar and raises the glass a few feet. Quite enough to climb in."

"Excellent. And how do we turn the nut? Unless a large spanner is part of your Wraith kit?" Ommet didn't sound very hopeful.

I shook my head, and gave the nut a tentative pull. It was well greased but firmly screwed down, quite impossible to move without the proper tools. "Can you see anything like a toolbox? They surely don't lug all their equipment up here every time they have to open it up."

"Nothing like that here. They don't make it easy, do they?"

I snorted in disgust. "They're paranoid! Who's going to climb all the way up here just to break into a light tube?"

"Who indeed?" Ommet shook his head. "Let's go further. Perhaps we can find one less well secured."

I replaced the sleeve, and we carried on up the path. After a hundred yards or so we came across another light tube, but it was as securely fastened as the first. Without any discussion, we continued.

The path began to climb steeply, and curved slightly outwards, following a bulge in the rock face. Rounding the corner, we found one more light tube, and the end of the path.

I examined the nut, and finding it like the others, used some strong language. "We'll have to go back, try in the other direction."

Ommet shook his head, either at my language or at our situation. "They'll all be the same. It seems that the Illuminator's reputation is well deserved. They guard their secrets well and do their work thoroughly. I don't suppose the bottom end of the path would be less well protected?"

"No. The access gates are guarded. To be caught on the walkways is a criminal offence in Vorgranstern. Perhaps if we went back to the Inn? It should be quiet at this hour."

"Quiet, yes, but not unguarded."

"What, then? We've considered all the options, and there's none with better prospects!"

"I don't know!"

I recalled my suspicions concerning Ommet's true identity. "Perhaps you could say a prayer? Some divine intervention would be convenient about now!"

"I've been praying since we started this mad venture, but God does not act on our convenience!" He turned away, slapping at the glass in a rare act of frustration, and went round the lifting mechanism to the other side of the light tube, where the path ended.

"Wonderful. Your people can't be trusted, my allies are murdering fanatics, and God isn't around when you need him." I slumped down on the pathway, staring at the harbour lights far below.

"I said that God didn't act on our convenience. I did not say that he doesn't hear our prayers!"

Ommet had stepped back again, but was now holding something. "There's a little alcove in the rock, just where the path ends. It appears that they use it for storage."

I leapt to my feet. "Are there any tools in there? A spanner, perhaps?"

"Unfortunately not." He held out the object he had found, which I now saw was a mop with a long handle. "Just this and a few buckets."

"Oh, well that helps, doesn't it! It means we can give everything a good clean before we go back and wait to be captured!"

"It's given me an idea. Something I remembered from my youth. But the handle needs to be shorter." He wedged the mop handle under the lifting mechanism, and heaved on it. The tough wood bent slightly, but held firm. Ommet grunted and put more force into it.

The wood broke abruptly, with a loud crack. I grabbed hold of his shirt just before he went backwards off the edge of the path.

"Thanks. I'd forgotten about that little drop." He looked nervously over his shoulder.

"So now you've ruined a perfectly good mop. How's that going to help?"

"I'll need that belt you're wearing. It's a bit thicker than mine."

"My belt?" I shrugged. "Well, why not. My trousers might fall down, but that's hardly the worst fate we're looking at now."

I undid it and handed it over. He wrapped it tightly round the nut, then used the broken mop handle to twist it even tighter.

"I grew up on a farm," he explained as he worked. "We often had to improvise tools. I remember seeing my uncle doing this once, to change a cart wheel when it broke miles from home."

When the belt was as tightly wrapped round the nut as Ommet could manage, he adjusted his grip on the mop handle and looked up at me."

"Right. Let's try this," he said, and began to pull.

The Illuminator's maintenance was exemplary. Under the grip of the belt and the leverage of the mop handle, the well greased nut turned at once. Slowly but smoothly.

"It works!" I exclaimed. "I really wasn't expecting that!"

"Neither was I," Ommet admitted. "When my uncle tried it, I ended up walking ten miles back to the farm to get a spanner."

It was slow progress, since the belt and the mop handle had to be re-adjusted frequently, but the glass disc rose steadily until there was sufficient clearance for access.

I poked my head through.

In my previous observations of the Illuminators at work, I had noticed that they covered the glass with a tarpaulin before entering. I'd assumed that this was to protect the glass, but one look into the tube and I understood the real reason. It was to protect the Illuminators.

The glass did not merely allow light to pass. By some trick of its design, it actually seemed to magnify it. In just the soft glow of moons and starlight, the polished tube within shone a brilliant silver. Under full daylight, it would have been blinding.

"Can you see the ladder?" Ommet asked.

"Just a moment." I blinked several times before my eyes adjusted, but then I could make out the metal rungs leading downwards. They had been painted black to make them stand out but even so they quickly vanished into a haze of light. Trying to stare down the tube was an unsettling experience. After a few moments I lost the power to focus properly.

I pulled my head out, wiping my eyes as I did so.

"The rungs are there. Just don't look down. Can I have my belt back now? I don't want my trousers to precede me to the bottom."

I recovered my belt, now slightly greasy, and re-adjusted my clothing. Ommet, having taken the opportunity to ignore my advice and look for himself, pulled his head back and wiped his eyes.

"I see what you mean. This might be more difficult than just climbing down."

I shrugged. "Just keep your eyes on the rungs. I'll go first."

I eased myself backward over the edge, felt for the first rung, and commenced my descent.

It was like climbing down a moonbeam. Silver light flowed round me, shifting and shimmering as clouds massaged the delicate glow dropping down from above. I focused hard on the rungs. They and Ommet, just above me, were the only solid things in the universe. Everything else was light. Our footsteps echoed round the light tube, a metallic clattering almost as disorienting to our ears as the light was to our vision.

I closed my eyes and climbed by touch. It was easier than trying to peer through the reflections. But I could do nothing about the reflected sound. After a while, the echoes seemed to be inside my head.

When I estimated that we must be near the bottom, I chanced a look down.

A huge eye was staring up at me, the thin black iris filled with a shimmer of pale gold. In shock, I missed a rung and dropped suddenly to the full length of my arms. My cry of pain boomed inside the tube.

"What is it? Are you all right?" Ommet's urgent whisper slithered round the light tube and hissed back at us.

"Yes. I just slipped." I risked another glance down, and re-interpreted what I saw. "I think we're nearly there. There's a sort of platform round the bottom, painted black."

"Good. Keep going, then!" Ommet was unusually terse. I suspected that the weirdness of the place was getting to him as well.

I carried on, now looking down and focusing on the black ring. It was still hard to make out what was within the ring.

By the time we reached the bottom, arms and legs and head and ears were all aching.

"Another experience I wouldn't want to repeat," Ommet observed. "Now, how do we get out of here."

I bent down, and reached into the centre of the ring. My fingers met something cold & wet and I recoiled. "It is an eye!" I gasped.

Ommet knelt beside me and reached in. "It's water," he corrected. "I should have guessed it would be. They'd need something to diffuse the light as widely as possible." He touched his fingers to his lips, and spat out. "Some sort of chemicals in there. To stop anything growing in it, I suppose."

"Those winches over there – that must be how they lower it down for maintenance."

"Yes. And those bolts are how they secure it at other times."

Ommet pointed, and my heart sank. Six threaded bars projected above the walkway, each secured with not one, but two large nuts.

"We can't do it." I said after a while. "It would take too long with my belt. We'd still be here come daylight – and if that didn't blind us, then the Illuminator's will surely see the open lens above and come looking."

"You're right." Ommet sank down beside me, shaking his head. "Any more prayers?"

"I'm saying them."

I stood up, and made my way round the walkway, examining the winches. There were three of them, set at equal distances round the circumference and well wrapped with heavy duty rope.

"If we can smash the bulb, then we may be able to use this rope to get down," I suggested.

"I doubt if the glass will break easily, but even if we did, the result would certainly attract attention. Which is the one thing we are trying to avoid doing."

I smacked my hand into the wall in frustration. "Better that than climbing back up again! Perhaps if we just broke a small hole near the top of the bulb? Some water would escaped, but it's still the middle of the night, it might not be noticed – Ommet? Are you praying again?"

He was staring intently at the shiny wall opposite.

"No, I'm not praying. I'm wondering if my eyes have been completely ruined by this light – or if not, then is that a key-hole in the wall?"

"A key-hole? There's no reason for a key-hole! Unless..." I ran round the walkway to to point Ommet was staring at.

Masked by the shifting glow, it was difficult to see even from close by. None-the-less, a key-hole it was.

"Unless there's a door!" Ommet finished for me. "Not that I can think of any reason for a door, either."

"There is a door." I traced the outline in the wall. "Close fitting, and hard to see in this light. And as to it's purpose – the best way to answer that question is to open it."

I fumbled in my wallet. I had no proper lock-picking tools with me. But, as a matter of course, I collected innocuous items that could be useful. A piece of wire that had recently been on the *Dreambreeze*. A fork that had belonged to 'The Lord Admiral'. An old wine cork and sundry other items.

I probed the lock with the wire, then bent one of the fork tines at a precise angle and inserted it into the lock. The cork made a convenient handle for the wire, which went into the lock at a slightly different angle. A few moments of careful twisting and prodding, and with a click the lock came open. I pushed gently, and the door opened into darkness.

"A simple enough lock," I said modestly.

"For you, perhaps. Most people would need a key! But it's interesting that it should be locked at all – here, where only the Illuminator's ever come."

"Secrets within secrets! Let's go and discover some answers."

"Certainly," he agreed, "But not forgetting that our main purpose isn't the satisfaction of our curiosity, but making our escape."

"Perhaps we can do both." I peered inside. "Looks like a passageway, so at least it offers a way out of this light tube."

Ommet looked over my shoulder. "It's dark."

I produced half a candle from my wallet of useful junk, and my flints. "I try and be prepared for all eventualities." I struck some sparks, produced a flame, and handed the candle over. "You go first, this time. I'm going to shut and lock the door behind us. If the Illuminators truly have no access to this place, they may not realise where we've gone."

"Vanished like Wraith's!" Ommet grinned and stepped through the doorway.

I followed, pulling the door shut as I did so. A sharp click indicated that the lock had reset itself.

After the brilliance of the moonlit tube, the flicker of the candle seemed tiny and delicate, perpetually in danger of being snuffed by the encroaching darkness. But it did its job. We could see ourselves in a passageway of rough-hewn stone, just wide enough to walk in single file and just high enough for me to stand with my hair brushing the ceiling.

A short passageway took us to a junction. There were no signs or markings to indicate direction, just more passages, disappearing into shadows left and right.

"Any preferences?" asked Ommet.

I tried to visualise our position. "I think that right would take us eastwards, towards the end of the rock. The sea end, that is. Left goes into the busier areas, and perhaps might offer more hope of an exit?"

"Perhaps? Well, I have nothing better to offer, so left it is?"

The left-hand corridor appeared at first to be identical to the one we'd begun with. But after walking a few minutes, an opening appeared in the wall.

"This is different." Ommet stepped through. "What do you make of this, Arton?"

We now stood at the entrance to a circular room, perhaps six feet in circumference. A small folding stool and a similar table stood at the far side. In the centre, there was a stranger item: a metal tube, perhaps four feet high and several inches in diameter. Next to it, a slightly taller tube, this one topped with a wide opening like an inverted bell.

I shook my head, baffled. "Mystery on mystery." I stepped into the room and approached the tubes cautiously. The central one had a some sort of lens inset into the top. I peered through.

A dim image came to my eye. I was looking down into a room, with a circular table directly below. Faint light from somewhere outside my field of vision reflected from polished wood and inset brass.

Ommet nudged me. "What do you see?"

I stood aside and let him look. "Can you make out that symbol in the table top?"

"The brass inlay? Hard to make out in that light. Perhaps a vessel of some kind. An ancient one." He withdrew his eye from the lens and looked at me. "Isn't that the symbol of one of the trading-houses?"

I nodded. "Fraken and Luttendam. Not the largest, but close to it. They have offices on the Mainway."

"I think that we must be right above them. That room, it has the look of a boardroom, or something similar." He gestured towards the other tube. "I would speculate that, were any conversation taking place below, it could be heard clearly through that device."

"The Illuminators are spying on Fraken and Luttendam?" I considered for a moment. "Not just them. They wouldn't go to this much trouble to learn the secrets of just one House."

"No indeed," Ommet agreed. "But all the great Houses and Guilds have their offices within the rock. And all their decisions will be made in rooms such as this – all their plans for trading, for investments, for alliances or contracts."

"And all observed by the Illuminators!" I shook my head in wonder. "The power that must give them!"

"Power, yes. But not the Illuminators. They are just the means."

"Who, then?"

"Who do you suppose? Who would be able to have these tunnels excavated, without the knowledge of any?"

"The Guild of Delvers had the responsibility for excavating the Ways, and now for maintaining them. All new work must be approved and supervised by them. Except – the Illuminators took direct control of building the light tubes! They alone of all the guilds had that privilege, since it was deemed necessary to preserve their guild secrets."

"Deemed by whom?" Ommet raised an eyebrow.

"By the Duke. The present Duke's father, that is. Of course. Who else would be able to arrange for this? The Illuminators guard not only their own secrets, but also the Duke's."

"That explains the locked doors. Likely enough, most of the Guild members know nothing of these tunnels, or their true purpose. But there will be those who do know, who use them regularly, and they are the Duke's people!" Ommet indicated the tubes. "They see and hear what goes on in the most secret meetings of the Guilds and trading-houses. Banks as well, I would assume. They record the names, the conversations." He indicated the table. "And all that information goes to the Duke!"

I laughed. "And for all these many years, the world has wondered at how the Dukes of Vorgranstern have ruled so lightly, allowing the Second Order to go about their affairs without interference. The Free City of the North ... "

"I doubt if there's any city in the Empire where the First Order know so much about Second Order affairs!" Ommet said drily. "Well, now we have the Duke's secret. He can afford to rule lightly when he knows everything of importance that transpires in the city. There must be a thousand ways he can use that information to manipulate affairs to his advantage, without ever seeming to be involved."

"And you knew nothing of this? Your – organisation - had no knowledge of these tunnels?"

"I doubt if any but the Duke and a very select body of his people know anything of it. But, interesting though this is, it doesn't help our situation. In fact it may make it worse."

"How?"

"We've already got Crombard and The New Dawn looking for us. When the Duke discovers we've learned his secret – and he will: we left the light tube open, remember, and when the Illuminator's see that, the Duke will soon hear of it – then he'll be keen to find us as well. With no better intent than the others."

"Oh." I shook my head. "You have a way of making enemies, don't you?"

"It's become easier since I rescued you!" he retorted.

"I'm sure you were doing very well on your own," I replied. "But, aside from that, I see one good thing in this – at least we now know which way to go."

"We do?"

I nodded. "The light tubes provided the cover for these spy-tunnels to be built surreptitiously, but I doubt if they are the only access. It wouldn't be convenient to open one up every time one of the Duke's men needed to enter. There'll be another, more accessible entrance, and the likely place to find it would be under the Duke's own palace!"

"That makes sense." Ommet nodded agreement. "Which means going back the way we came, towards the western end."

"Yes. And it also means hoping that we can find some way out of the Duke's Palace when we get there!"

"As to that, I may be able to work something out. Let's be on our way, this candle of yours is burning low."

As he led the way back into the tunnel's, another thought crossed my mind. Did the Skipper know about them? Hard to say. But if he didn't, then the knowledge might be of value to him. Valuable enough to buy me back into favour, perhaps, should I wish to take that option.

I kept the thought to myself, though, and followed Ommet.

Chapter 10: Exit

The candle guttered out whilst we were still in the tunnel. I swore – quietly, in consideration of Ommet's sensibilities – at the prospect of groping our way blindly through utter darkness. However, as our eyes adjusted, the darkness proved to be not quite as utter as I had expected.

Glowing blue lines slowly became visible, stretching out along each wall and disappearing into the distance in both directions.

"Fascinating!" Ommet exclaimed, as he examined one of the lines more closely. It was about a hands-breadth wide, and gave out just enough light for us to see our footing. "I have heard of certain strange creatures which make their own light, without fire of any sort, but I had not heard of such light being harnessed for a practical use like this. Feel it, Arton – there is no heat at all!"

"Some sort of paint, I suppose. Another secret of the Illuminators. But, however fascinating it might be, it should not detract from our purpose. We don't have all night!"

"Of course."

We carried on, Ommet still occasionally touching the glowing strip. It was hard to estimate distance, but I was certain that we must be already beneath the Duke's palace when we saw the lines coming to an end.

A solid door barred our further progress.

"Can you manage to pick the lock in this dim light?" Ommet asked. He spoke in a whisper, though we could hear nothing from the other side of the door.

I examined it as well as I could. "No, I can't pick the lock," I announced.

Ommet struck the wall in frustration. "Then what do we do now!"

"I can't pick the lock because there is no lock," I explained. "Just a latch. So, unless it's bolted on the other side..." I left that possibility hanging, and raised the latch.

The door swung smoothly open, and Ommet muttered something that might have been a prayer of thanksgiving. To which I added a silent but heartfelt 'amen'.

The room beyond was lit by a single oil lantern, turned down low but left, presumably, for the convenience of whoever would be first to return to duty. After the dark tunnels it seemed like a blaze, and made my eyes water. By it's light we could see a space perhaps ten feet across, furnished with tables and chairs. Various maps and charts hung on the walls. After a brief survey, Ommet crossed to one of them.

"Look at this, Arton!"

With my eyes once more adjusting, I turned the lantern up and went to stand with him. "A map of the tunnels?"

"Just so. And look at this red line, that seems to wander through the rock independent of all the other ways."

"That'll be the Dukes private spy-tunnels, no doubt. Those numbers?"

"Here!" Ommet moved to a chart nearby. "Each number corresponds to a location. Number One is Fraken and Luttendam. We came across the first spy-station, but there are dozens more."

I turned my attention to the tables, and the paperwork on them. "Here, Ommet. A location number, a time – a list of names, a summary of their conversation. Another of the trading houses. Last night they were discussing plans to increase their charges for certain goods."

There were several more sheets of a similar nature, all neatly laid out and in time order, apparently covering the entire previous day. Mindful of the value this intelligence could have, I took time to look over the other tables as well. If I chose to disclose this to the Skipper, he'd want to know as many details as possible.

However, this time it was Ommet who was impatient to be moving on on. "Presumably this door leads into the Ducal Palace?"

"A reasonable supposition, since it's the only other door here!" I looked it over. "And this has no lock either, which concerns me. You would have thought that a place as valuable as this would be more secure."

"There will be guards."

I nodded agreement. "Probably." I put my ear close to the jamb, listening intently through the crack.

"Do you hear anything?" Ommet asked after a while.

"No. At least, not what I was expecting. I thought there might be conversation, or at least movement. No one stands entirely still for hours at an end."

"It's perhaps hard to hear anything through the wood."

"It's not especially thick, and I have keen ears. Besides, I do hear something. Very faint, but it sounds like water."

"Water? Running water?"

"No. More like an occasional splashing." I stood up. "But no guards on the other side of this door. Of course, we'll still be inside the Palace. But you suggested that you might have a way out?"

"Yes. I might be able to use some – influence."

I raised an eyebrow. "Some influence? In the Duke's own Palace? And us here as intruders?"

He smiled. "Have you forgotten the influence I used on the Magistrate in Neowbron to get you released?"

He sorted through the papers on the desk until he found an unused sheet, then helped himself to a pen and an inkpot. I came and stood by him to read over his shoulder as he wrote:

The bearer of this letter is to be granted full and immediate assistance in the furtherance of his mission, which is undertaken for and on behalf of the Empire.

By command of her Imperial Majesty.'

Ommet looked up and met my gaze. "You don't seem surprised."

"I'm not. I'd already decided you must be an Imperial Agent. But that note alone will impress no one."

"I'm not finished yet."

He lifted his ring finger. The same birth-stone I had seen before, an ugly piece of green quartz in a chunky setting.

"So you were born in the spring? How is that relevant?"

"It isn't."

With his other hand, he twisted the stone. With a faint click it slipped out of it's housing and folded back. Ommet spilled a little ink, dipped the exposed surface of the ring in it, and impressed it on the note.

The symbol it left was small, but very clear. A tower rising from within a crown. The personal seal of the Empress herself. There were some numbers below it: a five, a one and a three.

"That's interesting," I acknowledged. "Do the numbers have significance?"

"Of course. They change each time the ring is used. And not in sequence, either. When I last used it – to obtain your release – it showed nine, four and six."

I raised an eyebrow. "I know something of such mechanisms. To achieve that in something so small is incredible.

"And almost impossible to duplicate, which is the point, of course. I was told that ten of the finest watchmakers in the Empire spent a year perfecting the device!"

"A copy could still be made." I examined the ring and the symbol it had left on the paper. "The detail is extraordinary, but I know of several forgers who might reproduce it."

"Yes. They could do it – once! But the numbers do not change at random. They make up a code, unique to each ring. Whenever it is used, the recipient must, by Imperial Command, send the sealed document at once to the Grand Chancellor, by the fastest means possible. The Chancellor's staff will then examine it, and from the numbers will determine which agent used the ring, and how many times it has been used. Thus a forgery will be swiftly identified."

"With unpleasant consequences for the forger, I imagine."

Ommet nodded. "Impersonating an Imperial Agent may have short term gains, but it would not be a good career move." He flipped the stone back into place and twisted it slightly. "So then – let us go and find the Duke."

He stepped over to the door, lifted the latch and eased it open. Beyond was darkness, and a sudden splashing and swirling of water, much clearer now.

"What on .." Ommet began, and I hurled myself forward, slamming into the door and tearing it out of his hand just as a narrow little head darted through the gap with a high pitched squalling.

Needle sharp fangs snapped viciously, claws raked at the flagstones as something tried to drag itself into the room. I put all my weight onto the door to force it back.

Another head appeared above the first, snapping at the door. The noise redoubled, a chorus of hungry shrieking.

Ommet stood and stared, aghast. "Blessed saints and sinners, what is that thing?"

"Never mind what it is!" I shouted. "Help me or it'll be in here with us!" It was taking all my strength just to hold the door, and I could hear multiple claws scrabbling at the other side as more of them joined in.

He joined me, putting his shoulder into it. With our combined efforts, the door started to close. I aimed a kick at the first head, knocking it backwards, and the latch dropped into place. Even so, we both felt some reluctance to move away from the door, especially as we could still hear scratching on the other side.

"To answer your question," I said when my breathing had slowed sufficiently, "I think that that was a Northern Swamp Lizard. Or, as people up here call them, a Nasty Vicious Little Bastard. Very aggressive, always hungry, and also poisonous."

For once, Ommet did not react to my bad language. "I thought they'd all died out when the swamps were drained for building."

"Apparently, the Duke kept a few. Gave them employment as guards. It makes sense. Any human guard, no matter how loyal, might talk, either through persuasion or carelessness."

He nodded. "His greatest secret, restricted to the barest minimum of people. Unfortunately, an Imperial Seal isn't going to help much with these guards. How are we going to get past them?"

I thought for a moment. "Fire? I heard somewhere that back before the swamps round the city were drained, the only safe way to cross was with torches. Lots of torches, day or night."

"Yes. That should work."

I went over to one of the tables, cleared the surface onto the floor, pushed it over, and with a few good kicks broke off one of the legs. "If we wrap the end with some this paper it might work."

"Or we could just use these," Ommet suggested, holding up a couple of properly constructed wooden torches, complete with pitch-soaked fabric heads.

"That looks like a better idea," I agreed reluctantly. "Where did you find those?"

"While you were vandalising the furniture, I was exploring the cupboards. It occurred to me that if I was working in a room guarded by poisonous lizards, I might want some sort of insurance, in case one made it inside. Actually, there are several shelves full of them. It seems they wanted a lot of insurance."

"I quite see their point."

We lit the torches, took one each, and put some more close to hand, before returning to the door.

"Ready?" asked Ommet, hand on the latch.

I took a deep breath and held the blazing torch well close to the jamb. "Of course not. Do it."

He leant on the door, putting his full weight against the wood before raising the latch and slowly easing the door open a crack.

Instantly there were teeth snapping savagely in the gap, yellow eyes glaring at me. Ommet gasped as the door began to swing open, in spite of his best efforts to hold it. I shoved the flames into its face and it pulled back abruptly, the door slamming shut again.

"That was a bigger one," I said.

"I know. Stronger as well. How many of them are there, do you think?"

"Too many," I said grimly. "But the torch seemed to work. Open it again before they get over the fright."

This time there was no immediate assault, but as the door swung open I could see bright yellow eyes staring from the shadows.

Lots of them.

Ommet looked through, and gulped. "That many."

Raising the torch, I took a good look around. A wide stone platform surrounded the doorway, and it was well covered with swamp lizards. Lithe, scaly bodies, standing either dead still or moving in quick scuttling rushes. Most were about a foot long, but some were bigger, and one monster looked to be about four feet from nose to tail.

They were all looking at us, hissing angrily. One darted forward. I swung the torch in its direction and it turned away, but another moved forward from the other side. Ommet drove it back.

"Can you see the way out?" he asked.

I took a step forward, peering through the gloom. To left and right, the torchlight reflected off water and yellow eyes. Ahead was more water, but beyond it another platform, with some sort of structure on it.

"There! Some sort of extending bridge. I would suppose it joins to a door."

Several more lizards rushed forward at once. "Back!" I shouted, and we retreated behind the door once more.

Ommet rubbed his chin thoughtfully. "I would suppose that when the Duke's men come to start their day's spying, they unlock the outer door and extend the bridge. If it has solid sides, anyone on it would be safe. But I can't think of a way to get to the bridge from here. Unless there's some sort of mechanism involved? Did you see anything like a lever, perhaps?"

I shook my head. "No. And why would there be? Nobody's supposed to come in the way we did."

He sighed, and sank down on a chair. "Then I suppose we'll have to wait here until the morning shift arrive, then use the seal as I'd planned."

"Ah, yes. I've been thinking about that. How sure are you that the Duke will respect that seal? Being as we've discovered his most valuable secret. Will he really want the Empress to know all about it?"

"The Dukes of Vorgranstern have always been considered loyal. Well, more loyal than most of the Northern Lords, at any rate. And no friends to the Grand Duke."

I considered it. "The enemy of my enemy is my friend? It works that way sometimes, but I'm not sure that I want to stake my life on it. And we're going to be in a very vulnerable position – captured by what must be the Duke's most loyal men, having learned the secret of his power. If we just disappear, who's going to know?"

Ommet nodded. "Yes, that's all true. But what alternative do we have? It must be at least an eight foot gap between the platforms – too far to jump! We'd end up in water of unknown depth, trying to fight off a horde of poisonous lizards while we swim across, climb up the other side, and unlock the door! How good a chance does that give us?"

"Well, not much, the way you put it. But you forget that I'm the Wraith!"

He gave me a wary look. "Can the Wraith jump eight feet?"

"No. But – firstly, that water can't be too deep. Swamp Lizards live in mud and shallow water. They're not fish. And secondly – we can put a bridge across the gap."

"A bridge?" Ommet looked incredulous. I glanced significantly at a table, and he jumped to his feet. "Of course! The tables must be six feet long, quite enough to get us in jumping distance!" He paused for a moment, considering. "But we need to get it in place, and keep the lizards at bay while we do so."

"There are plenty of torches," I told him, indicating the cupboard.

✕

A FEW MINUTES OF PREPARATION and we were ready. A suitable table had been selected, cleared and put in place near the door, whilst the torches had been removed from the cupboard and stacked neatly to hand. I took a fresh one and lit it.

We looked at each other, and he nodded. I cracked the door open and thrust the blazing torch head through.

A chorus of ferocious hissing met us. I opened the door slowly, swinging the torch from side to side to widen the gap.

As soon as there was room, Ommet tossed one of his torches past me, into the middle of the scaly horde.

The hissing and screeching trebled in volume as the lizards scuttled frantically away from the flames. He threw a second in another direction, clearing more of the flagstones, and I advanced into the space.

The lizards expressed their resentment loudly, but gave way. We continued forward, throwing torches ahead of us and to either side until we were ringed with fire and the platform was entirely clear.

"The table!" I shouted. "Quickly, man!"

The command was superfluous. Ommet had already begun to drag it through the doorway.

"There's no more torches," he panted. "We can only do this once."

"Once is enough!" I grabbed the other side of the table, and together we manhandled it across to the edge of the platform, lifted it up onto its end, and edged it out till the legs were over the water. Water filled with yellow eyes and snapping fangs.

"Swing and release – now!" I commanded. We swung it out and dropped it in legs first, the splash barely audible above the din the lizards were making. We watched anxiously as it settled into the mud.

"Deeper than I expected." I commented, as it finally came to rest with the top about six inches above the surface. "But it'll do." It hadn't gone in as straight as I'd hoped, either, but the remaining gap was now less than three feet. An easy jump.

The table heaved, settled, then heaved up again. A claw gripped the edged and a large lizard began to pull itself up.

"Go! Go!" I shouted frantically, grabbing Ommet's shoulder and pushing him forward. He charged across the table top, past snapping fangs and took a huge leap from the end. He landed well clear of the edge, and slammed into the extending bridge.

"Behind you!" I bellowed. Ommet swung round just in time to see a small lizard darting towards him. He lashed out with his foot, caught in neatly in the chest and sent it flying back into darkness.

All round him, more lizards were clambering out onto the second platform.

"Hurry!"

His instruction was hardly needed. Torch still in hand, I sprinted across.

Six feet, just three long steps for a man in a hurry. As I took the third step, launching myself towards the platform, the table beneath me heaved upwards. My jump went awry, and instead of landing properly, my chest crashed painfully onto the flagstones while my legs splashed into the water. Knocked breathless, I could only scrabble helplessly at the stonework, unable to drag myself further.

Ommet's strong hands grasped my collar and hauled me forward. As my legs came clear something leapt and snapped at my heel. A stabbing pain shot through my foot, and I kicked wildly but ineffectually.

Ommet snatched up the torch from where it had fallen and swung it like a club. The blazing end caught the lizard between the eyes and it fell back, writhing.

I forced myself to my feet, ignoring the pain. Ommet was swinging the torch in every direction as lizards poured up onto the platform.

"The bridge!" he was shouting. "There's a gate! Open it or we're dead!"

The open end of the bridge was protected as Ommet said, but it was held by a simple bolt. I reached through the bars, slipped it open, and swung the gate back. We retreated, slamming the gate shut behind us.

We were safe. The snapping and hissing continued, but the gate and the bridge sides had been built to withstand a lizard assault and did their job well.

"Your foot?" Ommet asked.

I shook my head. "Just caught my boot heel."

"Thank the Divine for that! When I saw that little monster hanging off you, I thought it had its fangs well in! And if they are as poisonous as you say..."

"They are," I confirmed. "But no matter, we made it. I just hope that the outer door isn't bolted from the other side. That would be a big disappointment after we've come so far."

The door was locked, but not bolted, and the mechanism was all on our side. A simple matter for the Wraith. There was always the chance, of course, that there would be further guards – human ones – on the other side: Ommet had his letter to hand, but we stepped out into a deserted passageway.

"I suppose that the lizards are guard enough," he said. "Which way, do you think?"

I indicated a direction at random. "Go and take a look that way. I'll explore the other. Just to the next corner, then we meet back here and see which looks most likely.

Ommet nodded and set off. I paused for a few moments, then took a closer look at my boot.

The corridor was not brightly lit, but I could see deep scratches in the leather heel. And one puncture through the soft leather side. It corresponded to the throbbing in my foot.

I cursed softly, and glanced in Ommet's direction. He was still heading along the corridor, not looking back. Grimacing, I tested the injured foot, and found that I could still bear weight on it. For now.

I started off, trying to walk without a limp.

Ommet caught up with me before I'd gone far. "Dead end that way," he said. "Just empty storerooms."

We carried on. The corridor led to stairs that took us up to another, this one broader and better lit. A faint smell of cooking wafted along it.

"Kitchens," I said. "That's our way out. Always people coming and going from the kitchens, delivering supplies, looking for a meal. We'll blend in."

There were staircases and side corridors and other doors leading here and there. Before long, there were people – servants about their business, laden with supplies for the kitchens, or carrying broom, buckets and mops here and there. Some spared us curious glances, but none challenged us. It wasn't their concern.

The smells became stronger, and the heat rose as we approached the main kitchen – a cavernous room, busy even at this hour with bread baking and bacon frying. I stopped a kitchen boy struggling by with a laden tray – some Lordling's early breakfast, no doubt.

"Where can we get some of that, lad?" I asked casually.

"Um - " the boy took in our appearance with an experienced eye. Not servants by our clothing, but not of the First Order. Foreign looking, so probably merchants or some such, doing business with the Duke's Staff. "Visitor's Hall, sirs - this corridor, past the kitchens and third right."

He bustled off, leaving Ommet giving me a frown. "We've no time to be thinking of breakfast. We need to gone before the Duke's spies arrive for work."

"They'll be a while yet," I assured him. "There's no need for them to start work until the people they spy on do – which means mid-morning at the earliest for most of the banks and merchant houses. In the meantime, we need a reason for being here, and looking for breakfast is a good one! I'm hungry, anyway, so let's enjoy the Duke's hospitality before we leave.

Besides which, I needed to sit down. The pain in my foot had grown and was spreading up my leg, making it harder and harder to walk without limping.

Visitors Hall was still quiet, but there were a few people eating there, and we attracted no attention as we were served with bread, red cheese, bacon and hot milk laced with spices. Ommet displayed his usual healthy appetite, but I was beginning to feel nauseous and struggled to eat normally.

"You're not looking good," he said.

"I'm fine. It's been a long night, that's all."

Ommet shook his head. "Your skin has turned grey, you're sweating. You haven't eaten much, and you were struggling to walk. That lizard got you, didn't it?"

I shrugged. "A scratch, that's all. Not much."

"Why didn't you say something?"

"Doesn't make any difference. We need to get out of here. That's the priority. Anything else can wait."

Ommet gave me a long look, then stood up. "Hey!" he called to a passing servant. "My friend is unwell – he has medicines on our ship, down in the harbour – which is the quickest way there?"

"That door there, sir." The young woman indicated a small door opposite the one we'd entered by. "It will take you directly to the Outer Courtyard. Follow the wall along from there and you will find a small exit gate that leads into the cathedral grounds, and from there a path goes directly down the cliffs to the North Docks."

She gave me a look of concern. "But we have doctors here – if you wish, I can send word for one?"

Ommet shook his head. "My thanks, but there's no need to trouble them. He'll be fine once we get to our ship."

We left in the indicated direction, and found the girl's directions accurate. I managed to gain enough strength to walk out of the gate, attracting no more than a glance from the guard there.

Being out of the Palace and in the open air again was a tonic in itself. The fresh, bright sunlight of early morning was a beautiful thing to behold after so many hours in the tunnels. But the pain in my leg both increased and spread, and going down the long flights of steps to the harbour was agonising. By the time we reached the bottom, Ommet was all but carrying me. Still I retained enough presence of mind to remember that we were being looked for.

"We can't stay out in the open," I muttered.

"They'll still be watching the inn," Ommet reassured me. "No-one even knows we left yet."

"They'll be looking soon enough. And the Skipper has men all over the city. Especially the docks. I can't even run!"

"Won't need to," he assured me. Only his strong arm round me was keeping me upright. The docks were busy enough with barges loading and unloading, but no one spared us any attention. One man helping another back to his vessel was a common enough sight, any time of night or day.

"Where are we going?" I muttered. My head had started to ache, and it was hard to string any thoughts together.

"Nearly there."

I took some deep breaths, forced myself to look around and take notice. We were at the end of the River Port. The eastern end. Ahead was a gate, men in uniform guarding it. Imperial Navy uniform.

"Are you sure about this?" I asked.

"Any better ideas?" Ommet countered.

I hadn't any ideas at all, so I said nothing.

We reached the gate, and were halted by a gruff looking Petty Officer.

"No civilians beyond this point!" he barked. "Unless you have business here?"

"Duty Officer," Ommet snapped back. "And now, please!"

The Petty Officer raised an eyebrow, took a long moment to look Ommet over and a longer one with me. He clearly wasn't impressed – but having made that point, he was more than happy to hand over responsibility. That was what officers were for, after all.

"Sub-Lieutenant Caras!" he bellowed in a proper seamanly fashion. "Gate, please sir!"

A short moment later, a smart looking young officer – First Order – strolled languidly out of the gatehouse. "Yes, Petty Officer?"

"Man asking to speak with you, sir!" The P.O. saluted smartly, and stepped smartly backwards, responsibility smartly relinquished.

"Very well." Sub-Lieutenant Caras came over to us, giving the same dubious look. "Your name and business?"

Ommet handed him the paper with it's Imperial Seal. "Read this, Sub-Lieutenant. Then get us both on a boat out to Layfarban Island. Immediately. And medical attention for my companion."

The officer's eyebrows rose at Ommet's tone, and rose even further as he looked over the document. "I've heard of these things," he said incredulously, "but I've never seen one."

"Few people have. Keep it and forward it to your Commanding Officer. Or give it back to me and I'll speak to him myself – but get us on that boat and on our way. Now, Sub-Lieutenant!"

There was just a moment's hesitation. Taking orders from civilians – much less Second Order civilians! – went very much against the grain. But an Imperial Seal was not to be questioned. Not at his rank, anyway. Like the PO, he knew when to pass responsibility upwards.

"Petty Officer Graff!" he ordered. "Turn out the boat's crew, I want them on the way out to the Island in five minutes, you hear? Take these men into my office, and have the Orderly attend to this one. At once!"

"Aye, Sir!" Graff responded, and in a flurry of naval efficiency things began to happen. Men appeared, apparently from nowhere, two came forward and took me from Ommet.

There were more voices, shouts, questions being asked. I was laying down, while someone took my boot off and made shocked noises at what they saw. Then we were outside again, I was on a stretcher, being carried down into a boat. Ommet walked beside me.

I caught one brief glimpse of the gate, with curious onlookers stopping to watch the commotion. One of them was wearing a green coat. But green was a common colour for coats.

The boat pulled away, oarsmen straining to build up speed as quickly as possible.

"Won't be long," said Ommet. He sounded far off. Everything was far off, except for the pain.

Then there was nothing else at all.

Chapter 11: Layfarban

The sound of breaking waves drifted slowly into the room, followed by a ray of gentle sunlight. I was staring at a plain whitewashed ceiling, had been doing for a while before I was really aware of it. When I finally turned my head to the side, Ommet was dozing in a chair nearby, his book of devotions still open on his knee.

My movement, small though it was, disturbed his nap. He opened one eye, then both and smiled.

"Ah, you're awake then!" He stood up, went to the door and opened it just enough to speak to someone outside. "Just sending word to the Doctor. How does it feel to come back from the dead?"

I thought about it for a moment. "Better than I'd have expected," I croaked. "Dry, though."

"Oh – of course. Not surprising, you've been unconscious for at least a day. Here..."

He poured water from a jug, then handed the cup to me. I tried to reach for it, and found that I could hardly raise an arm. Seeing my difficulty, Ommet held it to my lips and carefully trickled a few drops into my mouth.

"That's better," I told him. "But I do feel quite weak."

"Not surprising, under the circumstances. I'm told that water-lizard poison is among the most virulent known. Nearly always fatal to those of the Second Order. Even the First Order, with their increased resistance to such things, can succumb."

I hadn't known that, and the thought was disquieting. "Must have been just a scratch. Didn't get much poison from it."

Ommet shook his head. "No, the fang had gone well into your foot. Your survival is amazing – if not miraculous!"

I beckoned for the cup and took another drink whilst I was considering this. "It was a small one. Perhaps not fully grown. The poison may not have been at it's strongest."

"That's what the Doctor suggested. Even so, had we taken any longer getting to his care, you might not have survived. Why didn't you tell me you'd been bitten?"

I forced a grin. "Got my reputation to consider. The Wraith can't be poisoned! Besides, it wasn't a good time." A change of topic was called for. "I take it that we're on Layfarban? The Navy have accepted your seal, then?"

"Yes, of course. We've been extended every courtesy – as you see, you even have your own room!"

"And how safe are we? There could be spies even here."

"I'm sure there are." He shrugged. "Little we can do about that. But I'm reasonably sure that the Commander and his senior officers are loyal to the Empress, and will therefore respect the seal."

"This is the North, Ommet. Eyes here turn more to the Grand Duke than to the Empress."

"That's known." He leaned forward and dropped his voice. "Not just in the North. There was an incident – perhaps a year ago now – when one of the western Dukes was found to be plotting against the Empress. It's almost certain that the Grand Duke was behind it, but he's stayed securely in Zyx Trethir ever since. Short of starting a civil war, there's no way of confronting him directly, and the Empress is loath to go to such lengths. Not least because that would play into his hands. However, as a result certain precautions have been taken. Senior military officers were reassigned, and those in the North whose loyalty was suspect – particularly those with family links to the Grand Duke and his supporters – were sent to posts in the South, or in the capital. Where the Chancellor will keep a close eye on them! They were replaced with more reliable officers. This base is a good example. The commander here, Grand Captain Voyon, is a relative of the Chancellor himself."

I gave him a long look. "You seem to know a lot about what happens at the highest levels of the Empire. Is that normal for Imperial Agents?"

"I couldn't say. I have no idea what other Agents are informed of – or even who they are! But this matter was something with which I had some connection."

I waited, but it was clear that Ommet had said all he was going to on that issue. I might have pressed him, but we were interrupted by a young man who bustled in with a tray.

"Broth," he announced. "Doctors orders – you've to have some as soon as you're awake. And some medicine to go with it." He gave Ommet a firm look. "And most importantly, rest!"

"I have my orders, then!" He stood to leave. "Arton – it's good to see you on the mend. I had truly feared for your life."

"Of course. You'd have had some difficulty obtaining another thief at short notice!"

"Yes," he said quietly. "That as well."

FROM OUTSIDE, LAYFARBAN Island is all blank granite walls rimmed with battlements and topped with flags. Inside, however, it was considerably more complex, and once I was allowed out of bed, I spent several interesting days wandering around the fortress.

The Doctor had wanted me to spend a week in bed, recovering. I was ready to be up and about much sooner, though I was careful not to make my swift recuperation too obvious. None-the-less, within a day I was awake, alert and bored. I passed a little time going through my meagre belongings. My clothing – the merchant costume Ommet had provided – had suffered greatly through our adventures, and had been discarded, replaced by naval uniform with all marks of rank removed. The few personal items I'd retained were neatly laid out on a shelf. The Skipper's poisoned knife was amongst them, fortunately still secure within its sheath. I tucked it away in an inner pocket.

My door was guarded by a very tough looking pair of seamen, armed with cutlasses and dirks, which was reassuring. When I had finally had enough of bed rest and decided to go exploring, they came with me, which was more irksome. They restricted my natural inclination to investigate locked doors and poke around in places that I shouldn't go.

However, even without that freedom, there was still much to see. The centre of the island was taken up with a vast natural lagoon, large enough (I was told) to accommodate the entire Northern Fleet, should they all happen to be in port at once. That never actually occurred, but there were still at least a dozen war-galley's present. Some were in the process of refitting, with masts out and hulls being scraped clean of seaweed: others appeared ready for sea at a moment's notice, with the crews all aboard and busy carrying out various drills.

Surrounding the lagoon were the dockyards and workshops, the barracks and storehouses required for the support and maintenance of the Fleet, whilst within the walls entire crews of sailors appeared to be employed doing nothing else than keeping the already immaculate rooms and corridors clean and freshly painted.

From the upper battlements there were impressive views. Open sea to the north, a patchwork of islands to the north-west, the river stretching away south. To the east, the coastline was dotted with small towns and villages, and the estuary was constantly busy with traffic.

The west was dominated by the great mass of Vorgranstern, its soaring bulk topped by the Cathedral's spires and the towers of the Ducal Palace. I spent some time staring in that direction, considering the teeming masses that swarmed within and around the rock. Thinking of the intrigues and plots that threaded through it – and of my part in them. I may have escaped the city, but I was still part of what was going on there.

I was leaning on a parapet and brooding on this when Ommet tracked me down. "You're supposed to be resting," he said.

"I am rested," I reassured him. "And it's about time we got down to some proper planning. There was a job you wanted me to do, remember?"

He nodded. "And are you still willing to do it? Things have not gone quite as I'd hoped when I rescued you from that cell. And now you know that I'm an Imperial Agent, I wondered if you might not wish to withdraw from our venture."

I snorted. "Withdraw now – just when I might finally get to learn what this has all been about? I still know little more than I did in Neowbron, and the suspense is more wearing than lizard poison! Besides, there's the matter of payment. We never did set a figure on my services, but now I know that you have the backing of the Imperial Treasury, I can charge premium rates!"

"And you'd deserve them," Ommet admitted. "For what you've already accomplished in getting us out of the city, I already owe you a considerable debt. And I could pay that off now and send you on your way."

"You still need some thievery doing though."

"I do," he agreed. "Now that I've been forced to reveal myself to the Commander here, I'll make use of the resources he can offer.

But there's no doubt that your particular skills would be hard to replace."

"Not just hard." I assured him. "Impossible! Wraith's are rare and hard to come by... let's go back to my room and discuss the details."

A few minutes later, sitting on my bed with a glass of wine in hand, I resumed the conversation.

"Now, as I recall, the items that you wish to obtain are in five wooden packing crates, each about a foot square?" He nodded in confirmation. "Ommet, I need to know what's in those cases."

"Why?"

"You want this theft done in a particular way. Correct me if I'm wrong, but that sounds to me as if you don't want anyone to know that a theft has taken place at all."

"That would be the ideal," he admitted.

"Well, the best way to do that would probably be to remove the contents and leave the crates. But to devise a plan for that, I need to know what we're dealing with here."

"I see." Ommet stood up and paced the floor. "I can't deny your logic. But it's also important that the details of the items are known to the barest minimum of people." He stopped and turned back to me. "I can tell you this much. The crates contain rare and ancient documents. Each one is sealed between sheets of clear crystal. Two to each crate. Ten inches square, about an inch thick."

I frowned, making a rough calculation of weights. "And these documents - what is written on them?"

"That is known to only twenty people in the entire Empire. Eighteen of them are senior clerics of the Arravine Order. The other two are the Grand Chancellor and the Empress herself."

"And you?" I asked. "Or don't you know either?"

"I am an Arravine," he said slowly. "Senior, not by my years but by my scholastic attainments. I was given knowledge of these documents when I achieved the First Mark in all five main areas of study that the Arravine's peruse. I was the first to do so in over fifty years, and the youngest ever. My elevation to what you might call the 'inner circle' was a reward, in its way, and an acknowledgement of my future leadership in the order."

"And now you're robbing them."

He winced. "I am." He didn't try and water it down, which I respected greatly. "Those documents will change the Empire, Arton. Change it vastly for the better. I truly believe that. But to bring about that change, I have become a thief. And a traitor to the Order that I vowed myself to. Some would say I have become apostate."

I shook my head. "You are either the bravest man I have ever met, or the greatest fool. What in God's name can be so important about these ancient writings? I can well believe they are valuable, I can understand they are of great academic importance. But important enough to change the Empire? How can that possibly happen?"

He looked at me and I could see the pain in his eyes. The loneliness. He had been carrying this burden longer than I had known him, and I could see how it had worn at him. He wanted to tell me. I think he nearly did.

Perhaps if he had, things might have gone differently. That is something that cannot be known. But what in fact happened was that he tightened his lips and shook his head.

"No, my friend. Best that you do not know too much. Not yet, at any rate. Perhaps the time will come when you will know. But not now. For now, all that is necessary is that you help me."

I settled back on my bed with a sigh. "As you wish. So tell me where these manuscripts are to be found."

He sat down again, dipped into his wallet and pulled out a sheet of paper. "I've been scribbling some rough plans," he said as he unfolded it. "This is the Arravine Sanctuary on Kalanhad Island. That's some fifteen miles from here, along the coast past Vorgranstern, and a few miles out to sea. The Order owns the whole island, which is several miles long, and almost as wide. Most of it is sand dunes or rock, with some rough grazing for sheep and goats, though there is a wooded area on the south side. The harbour, such as it is, is here, and a path runs from there to the main buildings, half-a- mile inland."

He indicated a circle on the rough map he'd drawn. "This is the central building, the worship-house."

"Not a cathedral, then?"

"Indeed not. We Arravines are humble in our ways and plain in our tastes. We worship accordingly – no coloured glass or decorations, just a circle of benches with the pulpit at the centre."

"And the other buildings?" I pointed to the two rectangles flanking the central circle.

"This, on the left as you come up from the sea, is the main library. Two stories of it, and a basement – the finest collection of writings in the North! Scholars and academics come vast distances to pursue their studies here. There are also lecture halls and classrooms, where the Order follows it's main calling – to teach, to educate, to bring knowledge."

A certain fervour had crept into his voice as he spoke. Imperial Agent he might be, but I could see where his heart lay.

"The opposite building," he continued, "houses the refectory, guest rooms, and the bulk of the accommodation for the staff. There are other buildings beyond these – the Prior's house, and various outbuildings, but none need concern us."

"Presumably these documents that we're after are in the Library."

He looked up with a grin "You'd think so, wouldn't you? Which is what people are supposed to think. But that which we seek is in the Hidden Library."

He indicated the circular building. "Every major house of the Arravines has a Hidden Library. There we keep such documents as are of special value. And sometimes, those which are, ah, unwelcome in certain quarters."

I raised an eyebrow.

"At various times in history, some of those in authority have taken exception to certain things that have been written." Ommet had slipped into lecture mode. "On occasion, this has been no more than personal pique. The Exalted Empress Chulain, for example, suppressed a certain play which made fun of her sexual excesses. If anything, the play understated the truth, but she objected being made an object of amusement. The play was therefore proscribed, and the playwright forced to flee the Empire.

"However, at other times the object of suppression has been more serious and more sinister. There are certain truths about our past, our history..." he broke off. "I won't go into details. But suffice to say this: the Arravines are fundamentally opposed to the idea that knowledge should be controlled, that truth should be destroyed. Hence the Hidden Libraries: places where threatened books, threatened ideas even, could be preserved and protected."

"That's interesting to know. But on a practical level, I take it that this particular library is hidden in the worship-house? A secret staircase below the pulpit, perhaps?"

"Nothing quite as dramatic. There's a door in the vestry. It looks like a bookshelf, but it leads to – as you surmised – a staircase. There are other locked doors, of course, before you get to the library. Now, access to the worship house is easy enough. It is open at any time of day or night, and unguarded. People can come to pray or meditate at any time, of course. However, the keys to the

Hidden Library are harder to obtain. Some are kept by the Head Librarian, some by the Prior, and official entry therefore requires that both attend. But I am in hope that your special skills in this area may suffice to give us entry."

"And exit. With locks and doors undamaged, so that no-one notices anything amiss until we are long gone."

"Just so."

I thought about it. "What sort of locks are fitted? Have you seen them – or the keys?"

"I have." He brought out another sheet of paper. "I've sketched out what I can remember of the keys and the locks. I'm not sure if I've got the exact details right."

I looked over the diagrams. "The details don't matter. As long as I know what sort of lock we're dealing with, I'll know what I'll need to pick it. And these are clear enough. Standard design. They won't give me any problems, if I can get the right tools. Better yet, if I can make my own. I presume they must have workshop's here – could I get the use of one?"

Ommet waved his ring finger. "You can have anything you want. In the name of the Empress!"

I smiled, but his words twisted inside me.

※

THE TWO THINGS THAT are needed for successful lock picking are an understanding of how locks work and the correct tools. A considerable degree of patience is also useful, especially whilst learning the craft. But whilst the tools can be obtained, made or improvised with relative ease, the knowledge of locks is much harder to come by. Locksmiths guard their secrets almost as closely as the Illuminators, for obvious reasons.

But I had paid a goodly sum to an old locksmith for his knowledge, back when I was commencing my career as the Wraith.

And once armed with that, there were very few doors in the Empire that could keep me out. Most locks are essentially variations on the same basic design – some more complex than others, but given time and tools, all can be overcome.

I was given use of one of the dockyard workshops, which enabled me to manufacture the tools I would need. Plus a few additional items that might come in useful. But getting me the time to use them would require planning, and that was Ommet's part. We discussed it at length.

"We'll go in as Friars. Members of the order. I'll tell them that I'm leading a group on a Pilgrimage of Penitence, and that we've come to spend the night in prayer. That will give us access to the worship-house, and I will tell them that you are under a vow of silence. It's not uncommon, and will avoid any awkward conversations."

"A group? How many are you thinking of?"

"Half-a-dozen penitents, and myself. I thought it would be useful to have some extra muscle for carrying off the documents in their crystal. The Grand Captain has offered his boat's crew for the task – men who are personally loyal to him. They're the ones who've been guarding our rooms, by the way. They'll also crew our boat. A lugger, such as is common in these parts. As it happens, there's a suitable vessel readily available. It was involved in a bit of smuggling, which is why the Navy's taken possession: it's undergoing an overhaul at present. With a new coat of paint it'll be well suited for our use."

"Won't the brothers find it a little suspicious, that your penitents are also accomplished sailors?"

Ommet shook his head firmly. "Not at all. We – the Arravines – attract recruits from all walks of life. It will not appear unusual that this group are mostly seamen. In any case, we won't be around long enough for people to start asking questions. If we arrive late in the day, at the time of the evening meal, then we can go directly to the worship-house without speaking to any except the harbour-master. There's always a short service before midnight, but after that we can expect to be left alone until about five in the morning, when the brothers will arrive for the first prayers of the day."

"So we should have at least four hours to get into the Library and remove the documents. It should be enough, if the locks are as you've said."

"Good. Then after morning prayers we will go to breakfast and take our leave. I'll let it be known that we plan to visit Herif Island, further to the west. It's a remote place with a sanctuary that is occasionally visited by those seeking to pray in solitude. The way passes between two small islands. Hardly more than sandbanks, in fact – they don't even have a name on the chart, but I'm told that they're known locally as the Grey Seal and the Brown Seal, from their colour and shape. An Imperial galley will meet us there – well out of sight from any other island and far from any normal traffic. They'll take us aboard, and the Grand Captain will take charge of our cargo. It'll travel to the capital under Imperial Seal and well guarded – and our work here will be complete!"

In my experience, the thing most likely to wreck a scheme is it's own complexity, and I made the point to Ommet. "It would be more straightforward to simply land on the island in darkness, creep into the chapel when the midnight service is done, and be gone again before anyone knows we've even been there."

"It would," he admitted, "but there's other risks involved. Apart from the harbour, every part of the shoreline is ringed with rocks or faced with cliffs. The currents can be quite treacherous as well. That's why the Order originally settled on the island. Pirates used to be common in these parts, and Holy Houses were too often seen as easy pickings. So there is but the one safe landing, and in the past that was guarded by a chain across the entrance. They haven't needed that for many years, but I've talked with the Grand Captain and he agrees that to attempt a landing elsewhere would be unfeasible."

The only thing left to discuss was the timing, and that was to be decided by the right combination of tide and weather. Calm seas and a high tide would best suit our rendezvous with the galley, which indicated a date a week or so hence.

But then news came that forced our hand.

I was in the workshop, taking advantage of the unusual opportunity afforded by time and facilities being simultaneously available. I'd thought of a few variations on the standard designs of lock-picking tools, and had borrowed a few locks from around the building to test out my new picks. I was delicately feeling my way into a particularly stiff mechanism when Ommet burst into the room and without preamble announced "Crombard's here!"

"WHAT!" I jerked upright, the delicate tool snapping off as I did so. Ignoring it, I snatched up a large metal file held it in a defensive posture as I retreated to the back door.

"No, not *here* here!" Ommet reassured me. "In the City. A boat just came in and brought word. He arrived no more than an hour ago, and went straight to the Palace."

I flung the file down, glared at Ommet and let out a string of curses – partially in revenge for the shock, but also out of fear. "What the hell is he doing here? Is he still after me? I thought he'd gone to the Grand Duke!"

Wincing at my language, Ommet dealt with my questions, in reverse order. "Yes he did, but with hard riding he's had time to get to Zyx Trethir and back here. He's probably still interested in finding you, but I suspect that he's primarily here for me. Have you forgotten that leak in my organisation? Word must have gone to him as soon as I showed up in Vorgranstern."

"He's gone to Duke Endranard? I thought that they were enemies."

"They don't see eye-to-eye, indeed. But for all his power, Endranard is unlikely to oppose Grand Duke Brodon directly. And we didn't do much to encourage him to our side, either! He'll have put the pieces together by now, and he'll know that an Imperial Agent has discovered his most important secret."

"He might even know that the Wraith has been wandering around his Palace as well!" I added, gloomily.

"Maybe. If so, he'll have checked on his jewellery and found that he's had a lucky escape." Ommet grinned. "Of course, your reputation may suffer from such a missed opportunity!"

I found the humour a little heavy-handed, and refused to dignify it with an acknowledgement. "So now we've got the Duke and Baron Crombard in league against us."

"I know. As if we didn't have enough enemies, eh?"

"Will they come here for us? Can they?"

He shook his head, and waved his ring at me. "Not while I have this! And not while we're on Naval property – *Imperial* property, in fact. If they move against us here, it would be rebellion. Endranard won't want that, and Crombard isn't ready for it. I've little doubt that they have their spies here, but they can't act overtly. None-the-less, we need to move things on a little faster now. The longer we wait, the more chance of them doing something to stop us." He moved to a window and looked out on dark clouds, scudding across the sky on a harsh northerly wind. "I'm told there's a storm coming in, but the weather-wise are saying that it'll have blown over by morning. So tomorrow we'll set off."

"I thought that we had to wait a week for the tides."

"That would have been the best, but I'm assured that our plan is still possible. The problem is the depth of water in the channel between The Seals. When the moons are in conjunction, the lowest tide would see a war-galley grounded. But they are moving apart at present, and the rendezvous should still be possible. Will you be ready?"

I looked at the broken pick. I had others.

"I'll go and pack."

BACK IN MY ROOM, I found that someone had left lunch for me. A small bottle of wine, a tray of bread, cheese and fruits, a covered bowl of some kind of soup or broth. Red cheese, of course. Even the Navy couldn't manage any variety.

"Where did this come from?" I asked one of the seamen guarding the door.

He shrugged. It was an impressive sight: years of heaving on ropes and oars had given him a significant set of shoulders to shrug with. "Kitchen boy brought it in. Told him you were out, but he left it anyway. Soup'll be cold."

I had been eating in the officer's wardroom, courtesy of my status as an Imperial Agent's associate. I hadn't ordered any food to my room.

I shut the door, and considered the tray carefully. Poison? A gift from the Baron, a small present from the Skipper? Both quite possible, but rather too clumsy and obvious for either of them.

The tray was the standard Naval pattern, with wooden partitions dividing the surface to stop the contents sliding around in rough seas. Superfluous here on land, of course, but this was the Navy, and they did things the Navy Way, regardless of how much sense it made.

I lifted the wine bottle, examined it closely. It was an unopened bottle of red. No label, just an anchor raised on the glass to show that it was from Naval stores. Setting it aside, I examined the other items with equal care. The soup was indeed cold, the fruit perhaps a little over ripe, but nothing else was out of order.

As I lifted out the last of the plates, something caught my eye. A piece of paper, folded and wedged into a small gap between the partition and the base of the tray. Hidden from view until now.

I pulled it out and unfolded it. There was a single line of writing on one side. No signature to say who it had come from. But the message itself told me that.

WE ARE WATCHING YOU. BE SURE OF YOUR ALLEGIANCE.

The Skipper had decided to give me another chance.

I sat down, and stared at the words. They summed up my position very neatly. I had been unsure of my allegiance for too long. Hesitating, putting things off. Making the excuse that I needed to find out more about Ommet's plans before I could decide.

I couldn't do that any longer. Not just because the Skipper was watching me. If I took the note to Ommet, and he in turn to the Grand Captain, the New Dawn's agent in the kitchens would be found and arrested in short order, I had no doubt about that. Of course, I would then spend the rest of my life looking over my shoulder for assassins, but in truth that would be little different from much of my career as the Wraith. And with the gold I could get from Ommet, I'd go south, disappear into the vastness of the Empire – or even go beyond the borders.

But I couldn't hide from myself. I knew enough now of what Ommet's plans were, and of what he was.

I needed to decide what I really believed in. What my allegiance was.

So much simpler if I was just the Wraith. Just a thief. I'd go with the money, every time. But it wasn't about the money, it never had been. Stealing First Order jewellery was my own little rebellion against their cruelty and injustice. My way of striking back against the Empire. My way of revenge, and a step towards what I had accomplished at Sonor Breck. Which I had imagined at the time to be the peak of my career and the culmination of a lifetime's quest.

From that perspective, the New Dawn was singing my tune. They would bring down the Empire and put an end to the rule of the First Order. They would destroy everything I hated, and all those who hated me. But I shuddered to think of the blood-price they would pay, and not just First Order blood either. I had seen the madness in the Skipper's eyes, and I knew he would willingly set the whole world ablaze to achieve his ends. Whereas Ommet... he was someone I couldn't help but like and even admire.

But...

He was an Imperial Agent. Dedicated to preserving the Empire. Changing it, he claimed, making it better. But it would still be the Empire. The First Order would still rule. And how much change would that really be?

If I committed myself to the New Dawn, I might have the chance to influence change. Perhaps I could curb the worst excesses, and focus on making things better, not just bringing destruction. If I upheld the Empire, I could do nothing except perhaps steal a few more baubles before they caught me again.

The time for that had passed. It was time to make a real difference, time to give my allegiance. Personal feelings could not be part of it.

The room came well equipped. A set of drawers next to the bed held pen and ink. I turned the note over and began to write. I wrote small and with care. The paper was not large, and I had much to say.

I ate the food, even the cold soup, drank the wine, and went out for a stroll along the battlements, leaving the note where I had found it.

The storm was blowing in from the north as predicted, driving the waves mercilessly to smash themselves apart on the granite walls of Layfarban. I stood and watched for a while, but as it grew darker an ice-cold rain joined the clouds of spray and I retreated to my room.

When I got back the tray was gone, and I was committed.

Chapter 12: Kalanhad

By morning, the storm had passed, just as promised. There was still a stiff breeze and the sea was choppy, sprinkled with lines of white foam. But it reflected the blue of a clear sky, and sunlight flickered along the wave tops.

"A good day for puttin' to sea!" enthused the Cox'n. The sailor in charge of the Grand Captain's personal boats crew. I would have expected a huge, weather-beaten old sea-dog, but Druthy was quite a young man, and not particularly large either. He was certainly weather beaten, though, with muscles like tarred cordage. "And a nice little vessel to go to sea with," he added, indicating the boat moored behind him.

It looked smart enough, the hull freshly painted in white with a green stripe and the masts well varnished and stayed. But it was open to the elements and barely thirty feet long. Minuscule, compared with the great war-galleys that filled the harbour, and none too big compared to the waves outside. I felt a significant degree of apprehension.

Which must have shown in my face. Druthy saw it and grinned. "Never you worry, sir. She's sound and seaworthy. I took the liberty of naming her '*Wave Dancer*' – 'tis a fancy of mine, to have such a boat of my own someday, and that's the name I'd give her."

I wasn't sure that I liked the mental picture that the name conjured up, but we both nodded agreement.

"I got some good lads to man her, an' all, Druthy continued. He'd selected four other members of his crew for this venture, and they were lined up on the dockside, looking uncomfortable in their disguise – the brown robes of Arravine Friars. I was similarly dressed myself, though I'd made a few modifications and additions to my own garment.

"Here, Cox'n, do we need to be wearing these things yet?" protested one of the sailors. I knew them all from their guard duty outside my door. This was Mebbers, he of the immense shoulders. "We're not even aboard yet!"

"You need to arrive looking like you've been sailing in them, not just put them on!" Druthy told him. "Besides, it suits you!"

There was laughter from the others, and some more ribald comments. Druthy interrupted them with a sharp command.

"Look lively! The Old Man's on deck! Boat's Crew – *Ha!*"

The men snapped to attention. Grand Captain Voyon was approaching along the quayside, chatting with Ommet. He practically had to bend down to keep up the conversation: though he was not unusually tall for a man of the First Order, that still put him head and shoulders over his stocky companion. And although he was probably three times Ommet's age, there was not a sign of a wrinkle or a grey hair.

Druthy saluted as they reached us, Voyon returned it smartly. "Thank you, Coxswain. At ease, men. Master Ommet – I will leave you in the care of the finest boat's crew in these waters! I have every confidence in them, and that being so, I look forward to meeting you again at The Seals, a day hence."

"My thanks, Captain," Ommet replied formally. "I'm only sorry that I cannot tell you just how great a service you are rendering to the Empire by your assistance."

"Oh, we sailors don't need to know the details! It's enough that we have clear orders and a fair wind – eh, Coxswain?"

"Right enough, Sir," Druthy agreed. There was a further exchange of salutes, before Voyon marched back down the quay.

Ommet turned back to the crew. "What I just said to the Grand Captain, I say to you as well. You will probably never know just what service you are offering to the Empire in this venture, but trust me on this: it is a great one!"

"Do we get an extra rum ration then, sir?" asked Mebbers.

"Silence there!" Druthy snapped, cutting short the sniggers. "You've just forfeited yours, Mebbers!"

"I'm afraid that there won't be any rum at all while we're playing the part of Friars," Ommet informed them. "Arravines forswear all strong drink, so we must run a dry ship for now. And there's also the matter of jewellery. I know that earrings and the such like are a strong tradition in the Navy, but its another thing that must be put aside on joining the order. Which is what you are doing, however temporarily."

"What about me riggin' set?" asked one of the crew, indicating his belt. Every seaman I'd ever seen – including the river bargemen – carried a knife on their belt. But these deep-water sailors had entire tool-kits hanging at their sides, with marlin spikes, sail-makers needles, and other instruments.

"Tools of your trade. You can keep those while you're on board," Ommet decided. "But leave them behind when we arrive. The other items, however…"

Druthy picked up smartly as Ommet finished. "Right then. You heard the man! Earrings off, and if they won't unclip, get yourself over to the workshop and have them cut free. Lively now!"

Mebbers clutched at an enormous hunk of gold dangling from his left earlobe. "But, Cox'n, this'uns me lucky charm! Kept me safe through three battles, a boarding and a shipwreck!"

"A bar fight with the Army isn't a battle, Mebbers! And running the liberty boat aground because you were too drunk to remember which side of the buoy you should be on doesn't count as a shipwreck! Now get it off, or we'll see how much luck it'll bring you stuffed up..." Druthy glanced at Ommet, and smoothly changed tack "... your nose. Jump to it."

Mebbers was determined to have the last word. "No rum and no earring!" he muttered disconsolately as he trudged off down the quay to the workshop.

Half-an-hour later we were rumless, earringless, and underway, the seaman pulling hard on the oars to send us briskly across the harbour and out of the sea-gate. *Wave Dancer* begin to roll as we cleared the sheltered waters – not quite living up to her name, I thought. Ommet and I exchanged worried glances, but none of the sailors showed the slightest concern. A few sharp orders and the sails were hoisted. The motion steadied as the stiff breeze filled the canvas and Druthy brought us round to head west.

"How long will it take, do you think?" Ommet asked him. He was looking a little pale, I thought. Though the rolling had stopped, we were still pitching heavily enough to send the occasional burst of spray over the bows. "Will we make Kalanhad as planned?"

"Oh, aye," Druthy reassured him. "If this breeze holds – and my bones say as it will – then we'll be there well beforehand. Might have to shorten sail a bit, so as not to get there previous!"

"Oh. Good." Ommet didn't look happy at the thought of taking longer on the voyage than we needed to, but he'd devised the schedule, so couldn't complain. It was clear to see that sailing wasn't amongst his many accomplishments.

Behind us, there was the sound of bugles. Looking back, Layfarban was already growing smaller in the distance, but I could still see a galley coming out from the sea-gate, banners streaming.

"And there's the Cap'n, putting out in the '*Warlord*'. See, she's flying his pennant – the long red flag at the foremast." Druthy gave it a critical glance. "Well, she looks sharp enough. They'll be heading nor'-east till they're well out, then they'll turn back west towards the Seals."

"Looks like things are coming together at last!" I told Ommet.

"Good," he said weakly, then turned away and heaved his breakfast over the side. The crew made no comment, but exchanged amused glances.

"I thought you'd made this trip before?"

"I have. Never enjoyed it." Stomach emptied, he sat back on his bench and closed his eyes. "Just tell me when we're near."

"Certainly. But you're missing a lovely day for sailing!"

Sunshine sparkling on the waves, creating brief rainbows when the spray from our passage burst high enough. We were passing Vorgranstern now, the Duke's banners fluttering high above the city. I couldn't make out the sigil, though I knew it to be a red wolf head on silver and black quarters.

"He ought to make it a swamp lizard," I muttered to myself, and shuddered inwardly at the memories that brought. Impressive as the great rock was, I'd be quite happy if I never set foot in its tunnels again.

DRUTHY'S PREDICTION was accurate. After an hour or so, we shortened sail, and as we came into calmer waters amongst the scattered islands, Ommet made a good recovery.

As dusk fell, we rowed into the small harbour of Kalanhad Island. Through the fringing trees, the Abbey buildings loomed, with lamps just being lit.

A pair of friars stood ready to take our lines as we came up to the wooden jetty. Druthy steered us smoothly past some other small craft moored there and brought us alongside. Ommet waved a greeting.

"Brother Dennos! Still serving as Harbour-Master, then?"

"Why, it's Brother Thylan. It's been a while!" The friar held out a hand to help Ommet up, whilst I made a mental note of that name. The same as that I had read in his prayer book, and most probably his real name. I was now sure of it.

Brother Dennos was continuing the conversation. "So, have you come to browse and study again?"

Ommet (I found it easier to keep thinking of him by that name) shook his head. "No, Brother. I have a different mission this time. I lead this small band of Silent Penitents on their pilgrimage."

"Oh, I see. Well, you're timing's good, for they'll shortly be serving our evening meal in the refectory. I'd make your way directly there, if I were you."

Ommet shook his head. "My thanks, Brother, but we have already eaten of our own rations. We will go directly to the Worship House, in accordance with the vows taken."

Dennos frowned. "But the Prior will be waiting to speak to you."

"There's no need to bother him."

"It's no bother at all. I sent word when we saw your craft approaching. I was sure it must be you – that hair, you know!"

Behind us, there was a clanking, and looking around, we saw an iron chain emerge dripping from the harbour mouth. It spanned the entire width, and seemed connected to some mechanism in a stone building by the water's edge.

"You're raising the chain?" Ommet raised an eyebrow. "I didn't know that that was in use, not for many years."

"Sadly, these are troubled times. In ancient days, that chain protected us from pirates. They no longer trouble these waters, but there are still thieves and others who would not stoop from plundering even this holy place! Therefore we have had the mechanism repaired, so that we may guard ourselves as best we can. Though our trust is ultimately in the Divine, of course."

"Of course," Ommet agreed.

Two burly friars had emerged from the building, and locked the door behind them. I exchanged a glance with Druthy.

"This way, then." Dennos set off up a path towards the buildings, leaving us little choice but to follow. The other friars came close behind.

I desperately wanted to talk to Ommet about these developments, but clearly could not, without breaking my supposed vow of silence.

A paved footpath took us up a slope, then on through the trees for a while before coming out into an open space. It was just as Ommet had described it. Both sides of the central area were flanked by three story buildings of warm brown stone, whilst the circular worship house stood in front of us. Its whitewashed walls shone even in the failing light, making it stand out as the central place of the community. All was as Ommet had described.

Except for the dozen or so friars lined up in front of the worship house. And their expressions, which looked more grim than welcoming.

Standing out in front of them was an elderly man, whose brown Arravine robe bore an extra bit of orange trim here and there – the closest the Order came to a mark of rank.

"Indartus!" Ommet stepped forward with a bright smile and outstretched arms, ignoring the frowns that faced him. "It's good to see you again – but there was no need for this ceremony!"

Prior Indartus shook his head. He did not respond to either the smile or the arms.

"Thylan," he said. There were tears in his eyes. "You were the best and brightest of us all. What led you to betray us?"

There was movement to either side. More friars poured out from the library and the refectory, forming a solid ring around our party. They didn't look like violent people, but there were a lot of them, and some were carrying clubs. Padded clubs, to be sure, but clubs all the same.

Ommet's arms dropped to his side. He held the Prior's gaze. "There has been no betrayal, Brother."

"Liar!" A tall friar stepped forward to stand next to the Prior, an accusing finger pointing directly at Ommet.

"Ah. Brother – Ennard, is it?" Ommet acknowledged him. "From our House at Jonarus. I saw you there some six months back, did I not?"

"You did indeed, for I am Assistant Librarian there. And it was I who discovered, by the guidance of the Divine alone, that you had despoiled our Hidden Library of its greatest treasures! Traitor!"

The fury in the man's eyes was so great, that I thought he might strike Ommet down on the spot, or at least spit in his face, but the Prior raised a restraining hand.

"Do not make things worse by denying it, Thylan. The records have been checked, and you alone have had opportunity to remove the missing volumes. And word went to all the other Houses. It has been confirmed. Several of the Hidden Libraries are missing books of great value and antiquity, and all are places you have been in this past year or so. But here is where our greatest treasure is held, so... you have been awaited."

"You say the word, sir, and we'll clear this lot out of your way," said Druthy. The boat's crew had formed a circle, facing outwards at the friars, and were busy rolling up sleeves and spitting on fists. I wasn't sure if they could clear all the Arravines, but they looked ready to have a good go at it.

But Ommet was shaking his head. "Stand down, Cox'n. We'll not settle this with violence." He looked back at the Prior. "You can let these men go. I hired them to help in this, they do not know the truth of the matter."

"That is something for the Council of Priors to decide. I will send word at once, and you will all answer to them."

"Aye, and will suffer the condemnation your treachery has earned!" Ennard snarled. He seemed to have taken the matter personally.

"And I tell you again, there has been no treachery." Ommet met his eyes, then turned to address the whole company. "Brothers! Hear me! I understand your sorrow and anger, but in truth and before the Divine I tell you, I have not betrayed our Order or our Trust! For the time has now come when the Hidden Libraries must be opened – the time has come for truth to be revealed!"

"And you are the one who decides that?" Ennard scoffed.

"As it happened, Brother, I was the only one who *could* decide."

"Enough!" The Prior broke in. "This is a matter for the Council. Thylan, will you and your men come quietly? I promise you will be treated as well as can be, but you must be restrained."

"Of course."

Hands were laid on us, not all of them gentle in spite of the Prior's words, and we were bundled off.

><

I COULDN'T HELP FEELING that I'd come full circle. Right back where I'd been when I first met Ommet - locked up. Only this time, so was Ommet.

"I'm surprised to see such well equipped cells," I said, leaning on the bars. "Not what you'd expect to find in a religious establishment."

There was no answer. I knew that Ommet was in the next cell and must have heard me, but he said nothing, and hadn't spoken since they'd slammed the doors on us.

Druthy and his crew were somewhere nearby as well. They had been much more vocal, and their strongly flavoured nautical language must have been quite shocking to some of the Brothers, but they had since retreated into a moody silence. In fact, at least one of them was snoring gently. Sailors are practical men, and make the best use they can of the time.

None-the-less, I needed to get Ommet's attention. "I suppose even the holiest of Brothers must get out of hand occasionally," I suggested. "Wild parties in the Refectory, perhaps? Or is it talking back to the Prior that gets you landed in here?"

That finally provoked a reaction. "The Library has a lot of visitors. Scholars, researchers. Not all of them are as disciplined as the Brothers. The cells are for such situations."

"And I suppose some of them might have been tempted to 'borrow' some of the more valuable items? Though it's hard to imagine that anyone would want to steal from a library, eh?"

Ommet, however, had retreated back into silence. I tried another tack.

"Still, as cells go, it's not too bad. I've been in worse myself! Look, there's even a mattress and blankets on the bed, and a pot to piss in. Trust me, in some places that's considered an extra privilege."

I waited for a moment, then continued.

"And I've never been in a cell that has a bookshelf! Well, I suppose it *is* a library, but even so... what sort of reading material have they got here?" I wandered over to the shelf and examined the contents. "Not too exciting, to be honest. A copy of the scriptures, that's to be expected, and a rather heavy looking tome... 'Elements of Systematic Theology Elucidated'. By Rimac-Levsh. That looks good for passing a few hours. Would you recommend it?"

"Rimac-Levsh was the most boring writer who ever set pen to paper."

"Oh. That counts as a 'no', then. It does leave the question of why it's here at all – oh, wait, I get it. This is a cell, and the book is the punishment? Subtle."

"It encourages reading of the scriptures, since that is the only alternative offered." There was some movement next door, and Ommet's voice became slightly louder as he came to the cell door. "Also, Rimac-Levsh was a wealthy man, who had hundreds of copies of his great work printed. Most of them were still in his house when he died. His heirs donated them all to the Arravines, and we've struggled to find something to do with them ever since."

"You could just burn them."

"Burn books!" Ommet sounded genuinely shocked. "Out of the question."

There was a gentle clang as he struck the door for emphasis, which told me that he was as close as he could get.

"Listen, they haven't left a guard in sight, will there be one nearby?" I said quietly.

"Well, there's probably..." Ommet began in a normal voice. I interrupted him with a hiss.

"Keep it down! I didn't go to all the trouble of getting you into whispering distance just to let you shout our plans out to the world! I can't see the end of the corridor from here, but there was a door there. I think I heard it close. Will there be a guard on the other side or will he be this side of the door?"

"The other side, I think," he whispered back. "They have someone in earshot in case there is trouble."

"And will they come and check on us?"

"At each time of prayer, someone will come in to read the lesson and a collect."

"Is that part of the punishment?"

"Of course not! The Order has a commitment to the spiritual welfare of all its guests, even the involuntary ones."

"And when will the next visit be?"

"Midnight. Closing of the Day, as the service is known. After that there's nothing till First Bells, about five in the morning."

"Five in the morning? That is punishment! No matter, we should be long gone by then."

"What?" In his excitement, Ommet's voice rose, until I hissed him to quietness again. "You can get us out of here? But they took all your equipment – your tools..."

"I'm the Wraith, remember? Locked doors are no bar for me!"

"The one in Neowbron was."

I winced. "Yes, well I was caught unprepared on that occasion. And I learned a lesson from it. How long till midnight, do you think?"

"I'm not sure. An hour or two, perhaps."

"I'd say nearer three, sir," Druthy put in. Quietly. The snoring in the other cell had stopped as well.

"We'll wait till about half-an-hour after the midnight prayers, then. With any luck, the friar on duty outside will be asleep, but we'll have to move quickly to subdue him before he gives the alarm."

"He's not to be hurt!" Ommet was quick to make that clear.

"Of course not. Bound, gagged and tucked up in a cell for the night. Druthy, once we're out, take two of your men directly to the harbour. Lower that chain and get ready to sail. The rest of us will go and find this Hidden Library that's the cause of so much bother. I hope it's worth it!"

My great fear had been that they would remove our Arravine robes, since we were obviously not entitled to them. But, although they had searched us thoroughly, they hadn't gone so far as to strip us. I felt carefully round the hem, and pulled a loose bit of stitching. A moment later and I had some basic tools. Not the best, but better than I'd improvised in Vorgranstern.

I'd also brought the Skipper's poisoned blade – in a hollowed out section of my left sandal – but I left it where it was. Killing friars was something to be avoided at all costs, and I didn't like the thought of using that nasty little blade on anyone. Except, perhaps, the Skipper.

Fortunately, the cell doors were constructed of metal bars, rather than being solid, which meant that I could reach through and access the lock. It was an awkward angle to work from, but a solid door would have been a lot more difficult. The lock itself wasn't complicated – the biggest problem was that the mechanism was cumbersome and a little stiff for the small instruments I had. But I had plenty of time, and with care and patience the lock eventually yielded.

Ommet heard the click. "You've done it?"

"Of course." I went back to work.

"What are you doing now?"

"Locking it again."

"What?"

"They might try the door when they come in to pray over us. It wouldn't be good if they found it unlocked, would it? Don't worry. It wasn't a problem to open the first time, the second time will be even easier."

My precaution proved to be a wise one. It was less than an hour later when a friar entered and began rattling the cell doors vigorously. Possibly to impress the Prior, who followed him and – satisfied that all was secure – indicated that the friar should leave, whilst he stood outside Ommet's cell.

"Prior."

"Thylan." I wondered if the 'Brother' was left off deliberately. "I could not believe it, you know. Even when Ennard came with proof, I could not believe it. Even when you came here with these ruffians (there was a subdued snort from Druthy's direction) I could not believe it. You were the best of us, the finest scholar, the most committed to the service of the Divine. When your name came forward for elevation to the Council, some said you were too young, but I spoke up for you. I said that your maturity exceeded your years and your wisdom was greater than many already on the Council. And others agreed. Do you know that you were the youngest Arravine ever to achieve that distinction? The youngest ever to attain the First Mark in all fields of scholarship? I believed – I hoped – that you would succeed me here as Prior. Or if not here, then certainly in one of the other Houses. I thought..."

The Prior broke off. From where I stood by the bars, I could see the anguish on his face. Reflected in Ommet's voice as he replied.

"I am sorry, truly sorry, to cause you this pain, Brother. I had hoped to avoid all of this. Had it not been for the ill-chance that revealed my plans, you would not have known of it until the documents were brought to light – and then you would also have understood why it was done."

"Brought to light? Was that then your plan? That these precious and secret things which we have guarded for so many centuries, should be opened to all? And you think I would have *understood* that?"

"Yes, I believe so."

"The Thylan I thought I knew would never have been so arrogant."

"It is not arrogance, Brother. I know it must seem so. But I have had access to knowledge, to understanding, which no one else has! The Gifts..."

"Enough! Save it for the Council! I should not be talking to you at all, it was only that I found it so hard to believe this thing! But it seems I was wrong. Wrong about you."

"No, no – I promise you, what I have done, it has been hard for me to do, but necessary, and if you let me explain, I think you would see that! There is still time, and the plan can still work – it is the saving of the Empire!"

"The saving of the Empire." The Prior shook his head. "And that is not arrogance? If not, then it must be madness!"

"It is neither! Listen, I beg of you! These documents must come into the hands of the Empress herself. She understands, she knows what must be done with them, and it's the best hope for the Empire!"

"Give them to the *Empress*!" The Prior actually took a step backwards, as if the words were a physical blow. "Is that truly your great plan? To give our greatest secrets to the very person whom we have hidden them from since the beginning of our Order? In truth, it is madness!"

"Anatarna is an Empress and a ruler like none other before her! Perhaps none since the days of Kerranard have been her equal in wisdom and intellect, and she alone has the power and the will to pull the Empire back from the brink! Indartus, you know full well the dangers of these times. There are fanatics and fools in both First and Second orders who will destroy all order, all civilisation. They will tear it down in blood and fire to have their way – and she alone can prevent it. But she must have the tools to do the job, and those tools are the documents I have taken and those which I seek here! Especially those here! The truth must be revealed and she must be armed with the proof as a warrior with a sword!"

In his enthusiasm, his desperation, Ommet's words poured out faster and faster, until I wondered if the Prior was right about his mental health.

"Thylan – I know you have been in the citadel, but you went only as a teacher for the children of Second Order servants. What could you know of these high affairs, or of the Empress?" The Prior spoke quietly, reasonably, a sensible man trying to make a sensible point.

Ommet took a deep breath, calming himself, before answering in the same tone. "I have met with her, I have come to know her. I trust her." A pause. "I love her."

"You love her. I see. There were rumours... stories of an unlikely – what? Affair? Relationship? A fling? No one gave it credit. An Arravine and the Empress? A Second Order Cleric and the ruler of the Empire? No one could believe it. Still less could I believe that you, Thylan, would ever break your vows and forswear your celibacy. But it seems I was wrong even in that, though I would not have believed it except out of your own mouth! Still, now at least I understand the nature of the madness that has overtaken you! The madness of the flesh. Simple, old-fashioned lust! It seems that you were, after all, too young for your position."

"No! That is not what I said, that is not what has happened! I have broken no vows! I said I loved her – and I do, and she loves me, and that is a vital part of what has happened – but I have not forsaken my celibacy."

"You were not lovers, then? Not intimate?"

"Lovers, yes, in all but the flesh! And intimate, yes certainly, to a depth that I cannot explain in words, but never physically!"

The Prior shook his head. "This is all too much for me to understand. Perhaps unrequited love is a shorter road to madness! But it is beyond my wisdom. The Council will consider all you have to say, and make their judgement."

"It will take months to assemble the Council of Priors. That will be too long. By then, the Empire will be aflame – and every Arravine House with it!"

"A threat, Thylan?"

"A warning, Indartus."

The Prior looked wearily. "Our fate is in the hands of the Divine, Thylan. What you have told me, I will commit to prayer. I counsel you to do likewise."

He turned away, passing my cell.

"Indartus! Brother! Answer me one question!"

The Prior paused in front of my cell, but did not turn round or speak. Ommet continued.

"I have told you that there is love between myself and Anatarna. Tell me truthfully – do you believe that love comes from evil, or that evil can come from love?"

I saw tears in the old man's eyes.

"I believe that deceit comes from evil, and evil from deceit. And that you, Thylan, are deceived."

He left without further words.

Chapter 13: The Hidden Library

The Prior had left me a lot to think about.

I could understand his problem in believing the rumours about a relationship between an Arravine cleric and the most powerful person in the known world. It did indeed sound like madness.

However, I had information that the Prior did not. I knew about Ommet's ring. I knew that he was an Imperial Agent, someone who had connections with the very highest powers in the land. So some sort of personal connection with the Empress seemed at least possible.

But love? Really?

Ommet obviously believed it. But for all his formidable intellect and impressive talents, he was still a young man, and young men can fall in love quite easily. Much more easily, I was sure, than the Empress Anatarna – who was probably in her eighties or nineties! Of course, Ommet knew perfectly well how old she really was, but by all accounts she was a beautiful woman, and of course would look no older than thirty. Mere intellectual knowledge could easily be ignored by youthful passion. All in all, I was inclined to go with the Prior's assessment; this was more likely to be deceit than love.

It helped to confirm that my choice to support the New Dawn had been the right one. Gambling the future of the Empire on a young man's infatuation wasn't a promising plan of action!

But to proceed with the plans I had made would mean delivering Ommet into the Skipper's hands. And that was a disturbing prospect. More than disturbing. I felt a cold chill run through me at the thought, despite all my carefully thought out justifications. Perhaps I could simply leave him here? However angry the Brothers were with him, I doubted that their punishment would be as harsh as the New Dawn's dealings.

But though I could get out of my cell easily enough, I couldn't get off the island without Druthy and his lads. And I couldn't see any way to convince them to leave either Ommet or the documents behind.

One thing was certain, I had to leave. If I failed to keep to the plan, the Skipper would be looking for me again, and he wouldn't give me a third chance to prove myself. Moreover, Crombard was too close on my heels for any comfort. If he was in Vorgranstern now, then he would certainly have information from Layfarban, and that would lead him here. I couldn't rely on the Brothers to protect me from the Baron's vengeance, even if they wanted to.

So things must proceed. And the Skipper would owe me – perhaps I could bargain for Ommet's life?

I knew it was a forlorn hope, but I could see no other way out.

As predicted, one of the Brothers came in at about midnight. He read some scripture, and then attempted to lead us in prayer, but it was hard work for him. His congregation did not offer much encouragement – only Ommet made the proper responses, and some of those muttered by the seamen were decidedly improper – but he pressed on with fortitude, right to the last 'Amen'. Then he left, shaking his head sadly.

I listened carefully, but could hear no more movement after the door was closed. Which confirmed Ommet's opinion that any guard would be on the other side of the door.

None the less, we waited for a tense half hour or so, before I finally decided that the establishment had settled itself down for the night, and got my lock-pick out again. It was easier the second time, and before long we were all standing silently outside our cells.

The seamen looked at Ommet. He looked at me. From here on, I was in charge. I caught Druthy's eye and nodded to the door.

He stepped up to it, carefully turned the handle, and eased it open. The Brothers oiled their hinges; the door swung back with barely a whisper. Certainly not enough to disturb the friar sitting with his back to us, perusing a large tome.

His reading was rudely interrupted by a large hairy hand that suddenly clamped round his mouth. His arms were grabbed at the same time, leaving only his legs free. They kicked wildly, but to no affect. With brisk efficiency Druthy and Mebbers trussed him up with the cord from his own robes, gagged with with a strip torn of the bottom of them, and dumped him back in the cell that they had just vacated. Ommet offered profuse apologies, before locking him in and leaving him to his mediations.

"What now, then?" asked Druthy.

"As we planned. Two men with you, Cox'n, to make ready our escape. The rest of us – to the Worship House!"

Outside the refectory, all was quiet. The wind had calmed since sunset, and a gently breeze was drifting clouds across the stars. Moonlight faded in and out, but gave enough light to find our way. Druthy and his party disappeared into the darkness, whilst I led the way across the courtyard.

As Ommet had promised, the doors to the Worship House were unlocked. Inside, a single lamp glowed gently.

"The vestry?" I asked.

"Over there, beyond the pulpit." Ommet pointed across the pews.

We made our way to the plain wooden door he had indicated. This was locked, but it was a simple mechanism and I had it open in a moment. The room beyond was in darkness, but we had thought to bring candles and strikers from the refectory. They revealed some austere furniture, and a well-stocked bookcase. Ommet went over to it and felt around the sides, there was a soft click, and it swung open.

"I'd expected more of a challenge," I told him.

He nodded me forward. "The challenge awaits!"

A pace or two beyond the concealed door was a much more substantial barrier. Thick planks of some close-grained wood, bound with straps of black iron, concealed hinges, and three heavy-duty locks. It was well seated too, the stonework around it looked solid. There would be no getting through it without either the keys or a battering ram.

Or a Wraith.

I handed my candle to Ommet and got to work.

"Quite old, these," I commented as I felt my way round the mechanism. "Ward locks. They don't make them like this any more!"

"There hasn't been much need to modernise them," Ommet replied. "The greatest protection of the Hidden Libraries has always been that they were hidden!"

"No longer adequate," I said, as the first one clicked smoothly open. The other two were of the same basic design, though with different ward patterns, but they took me no longer than the first. The door swung open, revealing a steep spiral staircase, descending into darkness.

I peered down. "How far does it go?"

"About twenty feet or so. There's another door at the bottom. Just like this one." Ommet spoke over my shoulder. "There should be lanterns... ah, here." A brighter light illuminated the stairs.

I led the way down, with Ommet lighting lamps as he followed me. White plastered walls reflected the light and made our way clear. The steps were worn from uncounted numbers of holy feet that had passed up and down, but not to a dangerous degree, and we descended quickly until the next door came into view. At which point I stopped short.

"Ah – you did say the lower door was just like the upper one? And that the locks have never been modernised?"

"That's right."

"That's wrong. Come and take a look."

Instead of ancient wood, we now faced a slab of shining metal. And instead of three strong but vulnerable old locks, it was fitted with something quite new and different.

I went down the remaining steps. Ommet followed me, with the two seamen – Mebbers and Cray – close behind.

"Well, sir, I reckon as how you've got the challenge you wanted," Mebbers said. "I'm bu... blessed if I ever saw a door like that afore."

"Or a lock like that," Ommet added. "I take that is a lock, that thing with all those numbers?"

"It is a lock," I confirmed.

Set neatly into the centre of the door were five little windows. Behind each a number showed, and next to each number was the knurled edge of a small wheel. A large handle projected from the door to one side. I tried to turn it, but predictably, it stayed firm.

"Not even a rattle," I said, mostly to myself. "Very new. Not had time to work any looseness into it."

"It can only have been installed in the last few months," Ommet agreed. "Ah! I saw Brother Withlan with the others, and I thought him down in the South. He is a master smith, the best in the Order. I have no doubt that he was brought up here to install this door – and the lock. But I don't suppose he made it."

"No. He didn't," I confirmed. "There are very few locksmiths in the Empire who can make these, and they don't come cheap. It's called a number-lock, or sometimes a combination lock, and was invented by a genius named Deseradi Jankin. They are new, and rare – I have seen just one before, and that had only three number wheels. This must have cost the Arravines a pretty penny indeed!"

"How does it work?"

"Each set of numbers goes from zero to nine, and the correct combination of numbers must be set to release the bolt. Hence it's alternative name. With the three wheel version, that meant that there were a thousand possible different combinations. With five wheels..."

"A hundred thousand," Ommet whispered.

"We're going to be here a while then," said Mebbers.

"Not at all!" Ommet answered him with a brisk confidence. "Mr. Dowder is an expert! There isn't a lock in the Empire that he cannot open – and he'll deal with this one very handily, I'm sure." He gave me an expectant look.

"Well, it may take a little while," I said cautiously. "Obviously, we can't just try all the possible combinations, that would take far too long – but there are ways of finding the correct sequence. I'll need complete silence, though. Mebbers – if you and Cray could wait up in the vestry, please? Keep an eye open for any wandering friars."

I waited for their footsteps to recede up the stairs, then turned my attention to the lock.

I didn't share Ommet's confidence. When I said I'd only seen one before, I meant it literally – I had seen it, at a distance, at a Locksmith's fair a year or two ago. No one was allowed to actually touch it, or even get close. There had been a lot of speculation amongst locksmiths about how the mechanism worked, and more about how it might be opened, but nobody knew for sure.

In theory, the bolt had a series of projecting lugs, whilst each number wheel turned a disk with a gap in it. When the correct number was showing, the lugs and gaps would all line up and the bolt would slide out.

It this was the case, then it should be possible to find the gap by turning the disk at the same time as applying pressure to the bolt, until the lug slipped into the gap. Only by a small amount, as the other lugs would still hold the bolt secure, but then the process could be repeated with the remaining discs until the bolt came free.

That was the theory. Now I had to see it it worked.

I turned the handle slightly and, with my ear to the door, began to turn the first wheel. Very slowly, number by number, holding my breath and listening at each turn.

My senses are very acute, and tuned to the highest pitch of concentration, I could hear the very slightest sounds. Ommet's breathing. The scuff of a shoe from Mebbers or Cray above us. A faint scurrying as of a mouse somewhere in the cracks of the stonework.

But nothing from the lock.

There was sweat dripping into my eyes. I sat back from the door, wiping my forehead with my sleeve, and suddenly aware of several aches and pains.

"How is it going?" asked Ommet.

I gave him an annoyed look. "Is the door open?"

"Apparently not. Sorry."

"How long have I been working on it?"

"I think – perhaps an hour? You've turned that wheel through all it's numbers at least a dozen times."

"Ah." I turned back to the lock.

Clearly, the theory wasn't working. Either the lock mechanism was not as I had thought, or it had been machined so precisely that there was no movement at all on the bolt until all the lugs were precisely aligned.

Time to try a different approach. I adjusted my position and started again. Not with my ear to the door, this time. Not listening. Feeling. Concentrating all my attention on the movement of the knurled wheel beneath my fingers, whilst at the same time turning the handle as far as I could, putting maximum pressure on the bolt.

Slowly.

I didn't see the numbers. I just felt the resistance of the wheel.

And then, for a moment, I felt no resistance.

Was it real or had I imagined it? I couldn't be sure. I rolled the wheel back a fraction. There was a change. Very slight, but at one point it did move a little more freely.

I thought it did.

Number 1. The combination started with '1'.

I moved straight on to the next wheel, telling myself it would be easier now I knew what I was looking for. But on the other hand, I was feeling the effects of intense and sustained concentration. My fingers felt numb, and a headache was beginning to build up behind my eyes.

I ignored it, shut my eyes, focused my attention on the movement beneath my fingers.

There! Again, that slightest of changes. I opened my eyes, and read the number – zero.

I sat back and rubbed my eyes again. The headache was building, and I knew that time was passing.

"When did you say the brothers would be coming in for morning prayers?" I asked.

"First Bells? That's at five. I have no time-piece, but I doubt if we have more than two hours."

It had taken perhaps an hour and a half to get the first two numbers. Three to go. It was cutting it very fine. That was if I was right.

"But there will be brothers in before that time, to light candles and carry out their own devotions before ringing the bells."

I held myself back from swearing, at least aloud. "I'll have to work faster, then," I said, as I turned back to the lock.

"Just a moment... Arton, are the numbers completely random, or could they have been selected?"

I scratched my head, frowning. "Well, I suppose that the locksmith could set the numbers to whatever the customer wished. If they had a preference."

"Well, it would make sense to choose a number that could be easily remembered, would it not? You wouldn't want to forget it!"

"Yes, but what of it? It could be any number – the Prior's birthday, a saint's feast day, the number of angels on a pinhead – any obscure religious reference, for that matter! It doesn't help us at all!"

"You already have '1' and '0' – set the others to '2', '3' and '5'."

I stared at him. "Why?"

"Mirrion's Sermons, Tenth Book, Second Chapter, Thirty-fifth verse. 'Knowledge is a key to all doors.'"

I shrugged. "It seems a little obvious."

"The Prior is not a subtle man."

I flicked the numbers as Ommet had directed. "Let's see, then."

I turned the handle, and pulled.

The door did not move by so much as a hair's breadth.

"It seems that the Prior is somewhat more subtle than you gave him credit for," I observed. "How many chapters are there in the Tenth Book?"

"Thirty," Ommet said glumly. "And some have hundreds of verses."

"Only the first ninety nine matter, but that doesn't help much. So it's back to the slow method."

I adjusted my position, rested my finger on the third wheel, and tried to recapture my focus.

"Wait!" Ommet said suddenly. "Try 10, 5, 15!"

I shrugged. "Very well."

I set the numbers, turned the handle. The bolt slid smoothly aside with a satisfying 'thunk' and the massive door came ajar.

The relief was so intense that it almost took my breath away. "What verse is that?" I gasped.

Ommet had the widest grin I'd seen on any face ever. "Not the Sermons. The Songs! 10.5.15 – 'Knowledge is our lantern, but love is the flame.' A verse that all Arravine's know by heart – it is inscribed across the lintel of every worship house, including this one! It seems that the Prior was not more subtle than I'd supposed, but less!"

He stepped forward, and grasped the handle.

"Welcome to the Hidden Library!" He pulled the door open.

In my imagination, I had pictured the Hidden Library as something like the reading room in an exclusive club (several of which I had visited in a professional capacity – for some reason, many people consider items of value to be safer in their Club than at home or with a bank). I had thought in terms of polished wood, shelves loaded with worthy tomes in fine leather bindings, comfortable leather armchairs with reading lamps carefully positioned, a drinks table to hand and a large fireplace with a hearty blaze on the go.

The only bit I had right was the books. There were indeed many of those, and most were leather bound, but that was as far as it went.

The room itself was not large, perhaps ten feet square, and the cabinets that lined it were of metal, all painted a utilitarian grey. Their glass fronts showed the books within, but there were no leather armchairs, merely a few reading desks, also metal. And metal chairs. A small metal stove stood in for the fireplace, but there was no sign at all of the drinks table.

"I'm not impressed," I said.

Ommet was still grinning. "It was never intended to be impressive. It's a safe and secure repository for some of the rarest and most valuable books ever written." He went into the room. "All metal, since a fire in this place would be an incalculable disaster. And not designed for comfort – those few who are allowed to enter do so for purposes of scholarship and research, rather than relaxation."

I tried one of the cabinets. The doors were not locked – that would have been superfluous – but the books within were chained to the shelf.

"That's new," Ommet commented.

"Another result of your previous depredations," I suggested.

He winced. "No doubt."

I examined one of the books more carefully. "But isn't this an edition of Varsullio's plays? I would hardly have expected to find that in an Arravine establishment!"

"It's a first edition. The content may be a little more – exciting – than the Brother's normal reading, but we have a natural respect for all books. And this is worth a considerable sum."

"I should think it is." I eyed the chain and lock speculatively. A five second job to liberate the Varsullio.

"This is what we are here for," said Ommet, with a slight emphasis on 'This'. I turned away from the cabinet, and looked at the large chest that Ommet was indicating. It was metal, of course, and bolted to the floor, with three large padlocks securing the lid.

After the combination lock, the padlocks were relaxation. I had them all open in under a minute, and Ommet heaved back the heavy lid. He lifted out a padded canvas pouch, and from it withdrew a wooden crate. A hand-span's thickness and a foot square, just as he had described it back on the *Dreambreeze*. It was held together with a leather strap. He undid it, took the end panel off, and pulled out a sheet of crystal.

"Good," he said and laid it down on a table, almost reverently. "I was afraid that they might have moved them, hidden them elsewhere – but this is it. The real thing."

I stepped closer, and peered in fascination at the object of our quest. The crystal was flawless and perfectly clear. Within, was a sheet of parchment, hand written. A distinctive penmanship, the curls at the ends of letters in a style not used in centuries. But though the wording was antique, the meaning was clear.

I read it aloud. 'Then commeth Kerranard, Chieftain of the Itenli, unto the Isle of Silence, which is named Eskarin, that he be crowned King over all the tribes, clans and peoples of the Land. But his heart troubleth him, for the greatness of the thing, and thus he went the previous night to the sanctuary which I myself had placed there, and in prayerful vigil did pass the hours."

"By reading those words, you are condemned to death," Ommet said. He'd lost the grin. "They have been suppressed for two thousand years."

"But what are they? I have heard of Kerranard, of course – the First King, and according to some, the one who led the First Order to these lands. And Eskarin is the Empire, or before that the Kingdom. But what was this Isle of Silence?"

"The Isle of Silence is now Daradura, the Imperial palace and citadel. Eskarin was the word for silence in an ancient tongue, and from it came the name for the Kingdom and then the Empire. These writings – they are the Histories of Mirrion the Preacher, and they tell the true story of the First and Second Orders."

"I've never heard of Mirrion's Histories. Just the Sermons and the Songs."

"No one outside of the Arravine Order has heard of them since the time of Ekharden the First Emperor. He ordered all copies destroyed, and all talk of them was forbidden. He sent out his Purifiers to enforce the decree with fire and sword. Within a Second Order generation all knowledge of the Histories had been wiped out. The only copies remaining are in the Hidden Libraries."

I would have asked a lot more questions, but it wasn't the time. "We'd better be on our way. You're sure they're all here?"

"Five crates, two sheets in each one. Yes, we have them all. Call Mebbers and Cray."

The canvas pouches were equipped with handles – for the convenience of those who might have legitimate cause to examine the sheets, but they served our purpose just as well. The seamen had no problem in lifting two each. Ommet took the last, whilst I took care to lock everything securely behind us as we left.

"Is that necessary?" asked Ommet. "Our original plan is as dead as last night's rabbit: we can no longer conceal the fact that the sheets are missing."

"Call it professional pride," I said. "Besides, though they will discover our escape soon enough, the first thing they will then do is check the Hidden Library – and the longer it takes them to do that, the more time we have to get well away."

So we left no trace of ourselves behind as we emerged from the worship-house. A mist had descended whilst we were within, shrouding the buildings and muffling any sound we made. Fortunately, the way was clear, and we slipped away like ghosts in the night.

Or like Wraiths.

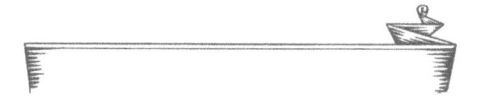

Chapter 14: The Seals

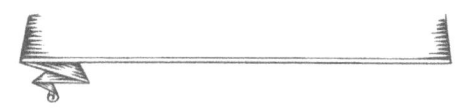

Unlike wraiths, we tripped, stumbled, blundered, and (apart from Ommet) cursed our way down the pitch dark path. Only the feel of paving stones beneath our feet gave us any guidance. The mist was even thicker down by the water, and in fact had at some point probably crossed the fuzzy border into outright fog. The first light of dawn was beginning to turn it from utter black to a dark grey, but even so when we reached the jetty we still could not see its far end.. *Wave Dancer* was no more than a vague shadow alongside, and the sudden appearance of three figures was alarming, even though we were expecting them.

"Druthy?" I asked.

"Aye, sir. And right glad to see you at last. We were thinking that you'd run into some trouble."

"Just a few complications. Nothing I couldn't cope with. Did you deal with the chain?"

"Yes sir. It wasn't guarded."

"I saw them lock it though. I take it that was no problem?"

"There's not much that can't be fixed with a marlin spike, Sir! Not such a neat job as you did with the cell doors, perhaps, but as you say, not a problem! We're ready to put to sea as soon as you're on board."

"Are you sure you can sail in this fog?" Ommet asked. "How will you find your way?"

"Just complications sir." I couldn't make out his expression in the murk, but I could hear the smile in his voice. "Nothing we can't cope with!"

"And there's little chance of being pursued in this, either," I added. "It's a blessing in disguise, eh, Ommet?"

"Well, as to that sir, there's little chance of pursuit anyway," Druthy put in. "Not since we stove some holes in their boats!"

I decided not to make any response to that, and Ommet made no comment on the nature of blessings.

We boarded, and the cargo was carefully stowed and lashed down amidships. With smooth efficiency, the crew shipped oars, cast off, and pulled smartly for the harbour entrance – in spite of the fact that it was invisible from the shore. But Druthy, seated comfortably with the tiller under his arm, had no hesitation in setting his course, and moments later we slipped quietly out to sea once more.

Ommet and I had found places in the bows, out of the crews way. It was comfortable enough, the sea being as smooth as a sheet of glass, the only ripples those made by our passing. I leant against the gunwale, watching Kalanhad Island fade into the grey blankness and feeling tiredness settle into my bones.

But also feeling euphoria bubbling up to overcome it. The feeling that came from a difficult job successfully accomplished. A victory won.

I turned to Ommet, who was also staring back into the fog, an unfathomable expression on his face.

"As dead as last night's rabbit? I haven't heard that one before," I said.

"Something I remember my father saying." He glanced at me. "Very fond of rabbit, was my father."

"It has a Western Empire sound, to my ear."

He shrugged, smiling faintly. "Perhaps. I've travelled a bit."

Behind us, a bell began to ring.

"Morning prayer?" I asked.

Ommet nodded. "We cut things a little fine."

"No plan ever works perfectly. We succeeded, that's the main point."

He raised an eyebrow at me. "We? I think you must take the main credit. Without your skills we'd still be in the cells and partaking of morning devotions. And I doubt if even Druthy's marlin spike would have got us through that last door!"

I shook my head. "Ah, but as you long ago deduced, even the Wraith doesn't work entirely alone. If it were not for your knowledge of the scriptures, I doubt if I'd have opened that wretched combination lock in time!" I placed a hand on his shoulder. "It was team-work that brought us through."

Ommet looked at me. There was a faint lightening of the mist, the first hints of dawn, which enabled me to see his eyes clearly, the same bright blue that I had noticed on our first meeting. The same twinkle in them.

"I was always told that there was nothing more valuable than knowing the Good Words. But I doubt if my teachers would appreciate the use I have made of them!"

He grinned, and I grinned back. The joy and relief within me finally burst out, and I laughed out loud.

Ommet laughed as well, and for a moment I felt his joy, shared it with my own. The unmatchable thrill of comradeship in adversity, of mutual triumph. Not something I had had much experience of before.

The crew felt it as well, and joined in the laughter. Even Druthy allowed himself a chuckle, before calling us all to order.

"Yes, it were a tiddly job an all," he conceded. "But we'll have a little less jocularity now, and save your breath for rowing. We've a ways to go, and no wind to speak of, so settle down for a long pull, lads."

Behind us, invisible in the mist, the bell had ceased – only to start again almost at once. But now, instead of a measured and dignified call to worship, it was a frantic clamour of alarm.

That, as much as Druthy's words, sobered our mood. "You'll never be able to go back," I said quietly.

Ommet shrugged. "I always knew it would come to this, though I had hoped for a more amicable resolution. But you have to be ready to make sacrifices for what you believe in, or what value is your belief?"

I nodded, and turned away, remembering that I was planning to sacrifice Ommet for what I believed in, and our victory turned to lead in my bowels.

The sound of the alarm bell faded into the mist, and we moved steadily on to the creak of rowlocks and the ripple of water past the bows. The mist grew steadily lighter as the dawn advanced, but visibility was not much improved. Five yards from *Wave Dancer* in every direction was nothing but grey vapour. It did not seem to bother Druthy in the slightest. With an occasional glance at the compass set nearby, he steered with as much confidence as he had in the bright sunlight of the previous day. Occasionally he ordered the crew to stop rowing, and seemed to be listening carefully whilst they rested on their oars. I listened as well, but heard nothing apart from some distant bird calls and the drip of water from the oar blades.

I began to realise that this mist might change everything. I had assumed that the Skipper would arrange to have us intercepted in the open water between Kalanhad Island and The Seals – probably as far as possible from our rendezvous with the Imperial war-galley. But how would they find us in these conditions?

The thought let loose a turmoil of emotions, but what bubbled to the surface was relief. Relief that I had not betrayed my friend after all. At least, not effectively. And all my cold-blooded calculations made back on Layfarban, my dispassionate evaluation and logical conclusions, were swept away.

I had never bothered myself much with religious matters – God, if he was there at all, was too far away to be of any concern to my life – but now I found myself offering up a prayer of thanks for the fog, which had saved me from the worst mistake of my life.

Or had it? Now the possibility had shown itself, I began to worry that perhaps there was some way in which the Skipper might find us after all. My lack of nautical experience left me uncertain about that. After mulling it over for sometime, I made my way back to Druthy.

"Any idea where we are, Cox'n?"

In answer, he indicated a chart of the area. It was spread out on the thwart in front of him, but I'd barely seen him glance at it.

"We're well out into Heikander Sound by now. Passed by Ocran Island half an hour ago, by my reckoning." He pointed it out on the map – a small outcrop of rock south and west of Kalanhad.

"How do you know?" I asked in bemusement. "I saw no sign of land at all."

Druthy tapped his ear. "Nor did I sir, but in these conditions a seaman must use his ears, not his eyes. Ocran is a small place, but very high out of the water, and with tall trees on it. Like as not, the top of those trees will be above the mist."

"And so..."

"Birds live in the trees. Land-birds, that is, not sea birds. In the sunshine, they begin to make their calls, which are different from those of the sea-birds. So when I heard them sounding off, away to port, then I knew we were passing by Ocran."

I was suitably impressed, and showed it. "But how will we know when we've reached the Seals?"

"Oh, we'll deal with that when we get there, sir!" he replied with a grin. "Happen this fog will lift before then, or if not we have other seaman's tricks. But we've got a couple of hours steady pulling before we get there"

I thought for a moment, wondering how to broach the real question I had. I couldn't come out and ask directly if we could be found, because no one was supposed to be looking for us.

"Is there any danger that we might run into another boat?" I asked after a while. "Or that someone might run into us?"

"Doubt if there's anyone else out here, sir. These waters aren't much travelled. Or if there is a vessel in these waters, they'll be anchored up, waiting for the fog to lift. Only fools and the Navy put to sea in these conditions!" he added with a grin. "And in any case, there's still no wind."

I looked again at the chart. If I'd been the Skipper, I'd have planned to intercept us somewhere north of Ocran Island. Now we were out in the Sound, the chances of him coming across us by accident were minimal, even if he had a boat small enough to be rowed. Or could a larger vessel be rowed in some fashion? Galleys were, of course, but surely the Skipper couldn't have got his hands on one of those?"

I was once more up against the boundaries of my ignorance, but I'd asked enough questions, and went forward again.

Ommet had fallen asleep and was snoring inside his hood. Tired as I was, I couldn't relax that much, and instead stared out into the mist, worried that every shadow would turn out to be the Skipper.

Once we were settled on our course, Druthy took a turn at the oars whilst another of the crew steered for a while. I offered to try my hand at rowing, but was politely turned down.

"Thing is, sir, rowing a small boat like this is light enough work," Mebbers explained. It was his turn on the tiller. "More of a holiday for us, in truth!"

"It looks a big enough boat to me, and hard enough work." I said.

"But that's because you've never pulled a galley oar! Now that's work, right enough."

"Do you all do that, then?"

"Aye, indeed we do sir. I've heard tell that in some places, they put prisoners or even slaves to such work. But that's not the way of it in the Empire. In the Navy, when you're under oars, everyone takes a turn, be they seaman, carpenter, or bosun's mate. Everyone but the officers, naturally."

Druthy broke in on the conversation. "And they don't talk while they're doing it either. Reckon you've rested enough, Mebbers – swap with Cray!"

"Aye, Cox'n!"

Once all the crew had taken a rest from the oars, and Druthy was back on the tiller, he sent Mebbers forward to break out the lead and line. The seaman swung it smoothly, and called out the depth.

"By the mark, ten!"

"What bottom?" Druthy asked.

Mebbers inspected the bottom of the lead. "Mud!" he announced.

"Keep sounding," Druthy ordered, and Mebbers swung again.

"By the deep, eight! Mud bottom."

"By the mark, seven! Mud bottom."

The water continued to grow shallower, until at three fathoms, Mebbers announced a change.

"Shell bottom!"

"Rawburn Bank." Druthy nodded to himself, allowing a glance at the chart, merely to confirm what he had surmised. "The current has set us further south than I'd thought, but we're not far off the Seals now."

He put the tiller over and set a new course. Mebbers continued to take soundings, but the depth remained constant, and after a while began to increase once more, whilst the bottom returned to mud.

"Nearly there now, lads," Druthy said as Mebbers returned to his oar. "Another twenty minutes or so should see us alongside the *Warlord*."

That close? I thought. Surely the Skipper couldn't find us now.

"Reckon I felt a touch of wind back a moment ago," Mebbers announced. "Maybe this lot will clear – eh, Cox'n?"

That brought a murmur of approval from the rest of the crew, and a cold apprehension to me. If the fog did clear then we might still be seen. But if the Skipper could see us, then so could the *Warlord*. Surely he wouldn't risk abducting us in full view of a warship?

Druthy was gazing thoughtfully out into the grey. "Reckon visibility may be a mite improved at that, and there's a ripple or two on the water. But I don't reckon it'll clear altogether before we're between the Seals. Might get a fingerpath, though – that'd be useful, right enough."

"What's a 'fingerpath'?" I called back to him.

"It's when a little gap opens up in the mist, just enough that you can see your way to harbour. Or see some hazard that threatens. Story is that it's God's finger moving to show the way."

"It's from the scriptures." Ommet sat upright, and pulled back his hood. "The 'Songs', Chapter five and verse 14:

'God's finger moves to show the way,
And opens up a path to follow.'"

"Well, I didn't know that afore now!" exclaimed Mebbers.

"Well there's a surprise," said Druthy. "A man like yourself not knowing the scriptures."

There was general laughter at Mebbers' expense, and even Ommet smiled.

"How are you feeling after your nap?" I asked him.

"Stiff and sore. And cold to the bone: this mist gets right under your skin if you stay still for too long. But not sea-sick, at least, so I'm thankful for that mercy! I take it we're nearly there – did I miss anything?"

I shook my head. "No. We've had no trouble at all to speak of." And I felt my heart lighten a little.

It lightened even more when a huge dark shape loomed up in front of us. There was a light but steady breeze blowing now, and visibility had improved still further, so it was quickly apparent that this was indeed a war-galley. Druthy hailed, and the response confirmed that it was *Warlord*, exactly where she was meant to be. Five minutes more and we were alongside, a ladder had been put down for us and we were scrambling over the bulwarks to meet a beaming Grand Captain Voyon.

"So, all went well, then? Successful venture, I take it?" He indicated the precious cargo now being hoisted aboard. Ommet watched it anxiously, fearful that a rope might break or a block fall apart and dump Mirrion's words into the sea.

But no such disaster took place. The canvas bags were hauled in swiftly but gently and immediately stowed away in a box prepared for them.

"Yes, very successful," I answered. "With a few minor problems."

Never having been on a war-galley before, I glanced around curiously. We were on the high deck at the aft end of the ship, where the steering wheel was set. Big catapults stood along the sides, unmanned at present but with projectiles stored in readiness nearby. A long gangway joined the aft to the fighting platform at the bows: below that the oarsmen sat at their posts, oars shipped but clearly able to be under way at short notice.

"Oh, quite. 'No boat watertight, no plan foolproof', as they say. But you made it, and that's the thing! A moment please, I must have a word with my Cox'n."

He leaned over the bulwark and shouted down. "Fine bit of work, Druthy. Congratulations to you and your crew. Double tots all round in due course!"

"Thank you sir. That'd be right welcome!" Druthy called back.

"However, you'll have to belay that for the time being," Voyon continued. "I've another task for you. We won't be getting under way from here until this dammed fog is fully lifted, and it looks like taking a while. So you're to take your boat back to Layfarban with all speed. I'd estimate that you should be alongside an hour or two before *Warlord*. When you get there, go at once to my Aide, Lieutenant Gorfinider. Give him my compliments, inform him that the mission has been a success, and instruct him to expedite preparations for the onward transport of the – ah – cargo."

"Aye, Aye Sir!" Druthy's voice came back. "Let go those lines – fend off!"

Ommet and I shared a look, and a smile. My relief was suddenly so intense that I was all but overwhelmed by it, and I knew that he felt the same way. After all we'd been through, finally, it was done. Mirrion's Writings were in safe hands. I leant back against the bulwark, watched *Wave Dancer* pull away from the ship's side, and luxuriated in the moment.

"Is that necessary, Sir? We'll be under way soon enough. Another hour or so won't make much difference, surely?"

Voyon looked round with a frown. The new voice belonged to another Naval officer, with the insignia of a captain. One rank below the Grand Captain, then, and Voyon clearly wasn't pleased at having his orders questioned. His voice was calm enough, however.

"This is a matter of utmost importance, Denarth. This man is an Imperial Agent, and it's our duty to see his instructions acted on with all dispatch. I want those items on their way south within fifteen minutes of our return to Layfarban! I hope that's clear."

He turned back to us.

"Mr Ommet, Mr Dowder – let me introduce you to Captain Denarth. *Warlord* is his ship."

Ommet held out a hand, but Denarth ignored it.

"Call back your boat. Now."

Naval officers shouldn't talk to their superiors like that. Something was very wrong.

And whilst Voyon was wearing his normal uniform of blue coat over white shirt and breeches, Denarth was wearing leather armour, with sword and dagger at his side.

The seamen who had stowed our cargo had gone below with it. The only people left on the aft deck were officers. All First Order. And all armed and armoured like their Captain.

I grasped Ommet's arm and pulled him back out of the way.

Voyon was staring at Denarth in shock and fury. "Are you giving me orders, man? How dare you speak to a superior officer like that!"

Denarth casually drew his dagger and held the point against Voyon's chest.

"I'd call them back myself, but they might question me countermanding your orders. So it's best if you do it. Now, if you please."

"Too late!" called one of the other officers. "Boat's gone into the mist."

"This is mutiny!" said Voyon.

"Yes, I suppose it is." Denarth nodded his agreement, and thrust the dagger into Voyon's heart.

The Grand Captain opened his mouth. "Mutiny!" he gasped. "Your oath..." A gush of blood followed the words as Denarth pulled the dagger free, and Voyon slumped to the deck, more blood pumping from the hole in his chest.

"My oath to the Empress, you mean?" Denarth leaned over the body, wiping his dagger and his hand on Voyon's coat. The blood looked very dark on the blue wool. "My true oath is to the Empire and to the First Order – and by my reckoning, you and your bitch Empress are traitors to both!"

He stood up, looked around him. "Lieutenant Orgill!"

"Sir."

"I want to be under way in ten minutes. We'll have to risk the fog. It's clearing anyway. By time we're out in the sound we should have some decent visibility. Then we'll run down that boat. I don't want word getting back to Layfarban until I've had chance to speak with the Baron."

"Yes Sir!" The Lieutenant turned away, shouting orders.

"And get this body over the side!" Denarth added. "Before the quartermaster takes the wheel. The less the men know of this the better."

"Sir!" Two other First Order officers picked up Voyon's body, and heaved it unceremoniously over the stern. The splash was lost in the noise of oars being shipped.

"The Baron?" I asked. "Would that be Baron Crombard, by any chance?"

"Ah, yes. I believe you and he have some unfinished business." Denarth smiled. He was a thin-faced man, and the smile showed a lot more teeth than I liked. "He will be pleased to see you, I'm sure."

The Captain turned to Ommet. "And you as well. A Second Order Religious as an Imperial Agent?"

He suddenly grabbed Ommet's hand, and held it up to examine the ring. "How strange. Yet it seems it's true. But I think it best if I take charge of this trinket. Can't have someone like you going round claiming Imperial Authority!" He pulled the ring off Ommet's finger, none too gently, and slipped it into his pocket. "You've gone to a lot of trouble to obtain these artefacts. What's the Empress's interest in them?"

"That's her concern."

"If it involves the Empire, then it's our concern. No matter. The Baron will have the truth out of you soon enough."

"You are Crombard's men," said Ommet.

"We are Knights of the Purified Heart. Baron Crombard is our superior. We work to preserve the True Empire and to restore it's glory under our Master, Grand Duke Brodon." He spoke with a fanatic's pride.

"You're a murderer and an oath-breaker," Ommet replied calmly. "You will be court martialed and hung – and so will all who follow your orders!" he added more loudly, so that some of the other officers on deck turned his way. They only looked contemptuous, however.

Denarth casually back-handed Ommet across the face, sending him sprawling. "Know your place, little man. Second Order scum like yourself speak when spoken to." He looked at me. Not wishing a punch in the mouth myself, I said nothing. Instead, I knelt down to help Ommet.

"I'm all right," he muttered. "We've got to find a way out of this, Arton. Crombard can't get his hands on Mirrion's holy words!"

I was more concerned about Crombard getting his hands on me, but I had no easy answer to either problem.

"I'm working on it," I told him.

"Get these two below decks and somewhere secure," Denarth ordered. "What's the delay, Orgill?"

"Bringing her up short now, sir!" replied the Lieutenant. From forward came the clanking of a capstan being turned.

"Ship ahoy!" someone called out.

"What's that? What in hell is a ship doing out here and underway in these conditions?" Denarth strode to the bulwark and peered into the distance.

I helped Ommet up, and whispered in his ear. "This might be our chance! While they're distracted, we'll go over the side and swim for the shore!"

"I can't leave the documents behind!" Ommet whispered back.

"We stole them once, we can steal them again – if we're free to do it! Get ready to jump."

"I can't swim!" he muttered.

"Oh, damn. Well, can you hold your breath, at least?"

We were at the bulwark ourselves now. Visibility was out to at least fifty feet, and I could see grey tendrils winding their way past like thin smoke in the strengthening breeze.

A ship was coming out of the remaining mist, all sails set and foggy streamers drifting through her rigging. Two masts, and a dull brown hull.

She looked like just another of the small trading vessel's that were so common in these waters. But, though I'm no seaman, there was something familiar about her. I couldn't see her name, but I was quite sure that the last time I'd set eyes on her, it had been *Anatarna*.

"What's that fool doing?" Denarth asked. "She'll be into our oars on that course!"

One of the junior officers held out a speaking trumpet. Denarth took it and held it to his mouth. "Ahoy there! Stand off!"

There was no reply from the other ship. There was still insufficient wind to move her at speed, but there was no deviation in her course.

"Ship ahoy!" Denarth was turning red with anger, and was fairly bellowing into the speaking trumpet. There was no doubt that he could be heard on the other ship. "This is an Imperial Navy vessel. Alter your course to port at once, or I'll see your ship impounded and every man aboard in chains! STAND OFF!"

The ship was twenty feet away now. An order was shouted, and with a loud flapping of canvas, her sheets were let fly, spilling the wind from her sails. She began to slow, but showed no sign of changing course.

"Damn and hell!" he swore. "I believe she's trying to come alongside! Ship oars!" As the order was frantically relayed to the oarsmen, he tried again with the trumpet. "Stand off now, you damn fool, or I'll have your skipper hanging from my yardarm!"

Not that Skipper, you won't, I thought to myself. It could only be him. I wouldn't have believed that he would openly attack an Imperial war-galley – but plainly, that was what he was doing.

Denarth couldn't believe it either. The possibility that this was an attack hadn't even crossed his mind.

"Is the man drunk or insane?" he wondered aloud. "Lieutenant, get some fenders over the side!"

"What's he done to his bulwarks?" one of the other officers asked. "There's holes cut in the gunwales, all along his starboard side."

Ten feet away now, and the holes were clear to see, notches cut down to deck level. Through them men were now visible, crouching down behind the bulwarks. And something else, I saw. Little glowing orange sparks.

"Ommet," I whispered. "Get ready to lay down on the deck. Behind that catapult."

"Why?" he whispered back. "I thought we were going into the water?"

"Not now. We'd be crushed between the hulls."

The ship had slowed to less than walking pace, and was all but alongside, less than five feet away. Denarth had abandoned his trumpet was leaning across the bulwark, shouting directly at the figures on the aft deck. A stream of orders and curses, none of which were having any effect.

"Run out!" someone shouted. There was a rumbling noise, and hollow metal tubes appeared in the holes that had clearly been cut for them.

"What?" Denarth gaped at the sight.

I grabbed Ommet, and hurled both of us to the deck.

"Fire!" I heard the order clearly.

Then the world was filled with flame and noise. A sudden orange glare that reflected off the surrounding mist and the loudest thunder I had ever heard, a pulsating roar, a crashing and rending of timber.

The bulwark nearby burst into a cloud of splinters. Something tore at my sleeve, and an officer who had been standing behind us was suddenly gone.

"Oh dear God!" gasped Ommet. Not swearing, praying, I thought, though I couldn't be sure. My face was next to his, but I could barely hear him, my ears still ringing from the noise. Then the screaming began, and I could hear that all too well.

Smoke was drifting across the deck, like the fog had returned, but bringing with it a distinctive acrid smell. Denarth was still standing, staggering backwards from the bulwarks.

"Fire tubes!" he said to himself. "But they're banned! Who's got fire tubes?"

His leather breastplate may have kept him alive, but a large, jagged piece of wood was sticking out of his left arm, just above the elbow. Blood was running down from it, dripping off the end of his fingers. He reached out with his other hand and touched the wound, with a baffled look on his face.

Ommet was trying to get up, but through the new hole I could see men lining the other ship's side. They had arquebuses at their shoulders and aimed in our direction. I pushed him down again.

This time the noise wasn't as loud, but went on longer, a ragged crackle of explosions sounding above the continued screaming.

Denarth staggered backwards and fell, clutching at his chest. He tried to get up, looking blankly in my direction. His hand fell away, revealing a neat hole in his breastplate through which blood was pumping steadily. Enough of it that already a crimson pool was forming on the deck beside him, flowing outwards to join the still congealing blood left by Grand Captain Voyon. He twitched, then stopped moving.

"What – who is it?" Ommet was once more trying to scramble to his feet, a dazed look on his face. I felt pretty dazed myself, but I had the advantage of knowing what was happening.

"It's the New Dawn," I told him. "Stay down! They might fire again."

"But – they have fire-tubes..."

"Apparently they're easily obtained outside the Empire. Don't move!" I crawled across the deck to Denarth's body, and fumbled through his blood soaked clothing until I found Ommet's ring, which I slipped into one of the concealed pockets of my Arravine robes, along with my lock-picks.

Something heavy landed on the deck nearby. A grappling hook. It was dragged back until it caught on the bulwark. Others were landing all along the *Warlord*.

"They're going to board!" I whispered to Ommet. "Don't move! If they think you're resisting or trying to escape they'll kill you."

"Won't they kill us anyway?"

"Probably. Perhaps. Maybe not straight away. It might give us a chance."

I took the risk of raising my head to see beyond the immediate area, and felt my stomach lurch at the devastation I saw.

The first volley had been aimed mostly at the oarsmen, it seemed, and the heavy balls had done terrible work amongst the packed benches. The arquebuses had then swept the fore and aft decks, cutting down the armed officers, leaving the ship leaderless and defenceless.

The gap between the ships had closed to a bare foot or two, and men were jumping across, waving cutlasses and boarding axes, screaming war-cries.

"Death to the Imperials!"

"Death to the First Order!"

"Death! Death! Death!"

Feet thudded onto the deck nearby. A man leapt at me, swinging a blade towards my head. I threw myself sideways and it went deep into the wood where I had been. The man pulled it free, but before he could renew his attack he was grabbed from behind and pushed aside.

"Not these two! You were told! Anyone in friar's clothing is to be taken unharmed!"

The speaker turned and looked at me. He seemed familiar, or perhaps it was the green coat I recognised. "Skipper!" He turned and shouted back at the other vessel. "They're here!"

He grabbed at my arm, pulled me to my feet. "Where's the boxes you spoke of? The things you stole from the Arravines?"

"They took them below. Five canvas pouches together in a large chest."

He nodded. "We'll find them. Get across to the *Anatarna*. We're not stopping long."

"Not changed the name yet, then?"

"Skipper likes it. Over with the both of you!"

I helped Ommet up, trying to stay between him and the worst of the carnage, but there was too much of it. Bodies or parts of bodies lay in every direction, blood was running freely in the scuppers. And more was added by the moment, as the New Dawn fighters cut their way through the remaining crewmen. Some tried to resist, but in shock and without weapons or leadership they had little chance. Some tried to surrender, some were already too wounded to do either, but it made no difference. All died under the New Dawn blades.

"Stop! In the name of God, stop!" Ommet implored.

"Death to all Imperials!" Green Coat had a look of satisfaction on his face as the last of *Warlords'* crew fell.

"But they are just the crew. Second Order like you, like me..."

"They chose the wrong side. Now get yourself across that bulwark or I'll have you thrown across."

The ships were alongside now. Ommet and I had little difficulty stepping across the gunwales and onto the deck of the *Anatarna*.

A familiar figure was awaiting us. Same seaman's clothing, same cap, pipe and whiskers.

Same cold eyes.

"Well met, Mr. Wraith!" he said jovially. "Your information was accurate, it seems. A fine bit of work! And this is the Imperial Agent, then?"

Ommet looked at me. "Arton?" he asked. I didn't look at him.

"Yes, this is him," I confirmed.

"Good." The Skipper took a long look, puffing on his pipe. "Doesn't look like much, does he? I hear that Agents have a special ring to identify themselves by. You don't know where that is, do you?" He turned his pale eyes in my direction.

"One of the Imperials took it. I didn't see what happened to it after that."

He nodded, slowly. "Well, now, perhaps it might turn up. Be very useful if it did."

There was a shout from the *Warlord*. "We have the box!" Green Coat was waving and indicating the sea-chest that Mirrion's writings had been stowed in.

"Send it over! Then finish the job so we can get under way." He turned back to Ommet. "As for you – we've got special accommodation all prepared. And later, we'll talk. Take him below!"

Ommet was hustled off. I didn't watch him go.

Shortly afterwards the box was transferred across to *Anatarna*, the boarding party was recovered and the grappling hooks cut free. With the sails set and drawing, we soon began to make way.

Visibility was increasing fast now. I could see for at least a mile, and the sun was breaking through.

"Looks like it's going to be a fine day!" the Skipper grinned round his pipe.

I nodded. "When I saw the fog this morning, I thought all our plans were ruined. I was expecting you to meet us out in Heikander Sound."

But even as I said it, I recalled that *Anatarna* had not come from that direction. She'd entered the channel between The Seals from the other end, from the west. Now she was heading for the eastern exit, in the same direction that *Wave Dancer* had gone. I looked forward, to where the channel exited into the sound, but could see no sign of Druthy and his crew.

"You never intended to try and intercept us, did you? It was always your plan to attack the galley!"

The Skipper laughed, a harsh sound. "I've been looking out for a chance to play with our new toys – and this was perfect! An

Imperial vessel, anchored in a known location and at a known time – far away from any other shipping, well away from the coast. The lads have had a fine time!"

"We might well have been killed. And that box smashed to flinders!"

"Aye, that would have been sad. But it didn't happen, so all's well, eh?"

He gave me a steady look.

I nodded. "All's well."

He smiled broadly. "Indeed it is. But come and watch this!"

He led the way right to the aft of the ship, where a small crowd had gathered, watching expectantly as *Warlord* slowly shrank into the distance.

There was a lengthy pause.

"How long a fuse did you set?" the Skipper asked.

"Long enough for us to be well clear." Green Coat had come to stand nearby us. A dark-haired young man with a strong jaw, about my own height. "Should be any time now."

"Well, if it doesn't happen soon, you'll be going back to see what's gone awry!" The Skipper sounded a little petulant.

Green Coat gave him a worried look. "I'm sure..." he began and then the *Warlord* disintegrated in a massive fireball. The sound pummelled our ears, even louder than that made by the fire-tubes, and a moment later a blast of hot air struck our faces.

A loud cheer went up, led by the Skipper. The smoke began to clear, revealing water empty but for floating debris.

"That was – impressive," I admitted.

"Aye it was indeed!" the Skipper agreed, and pounded me enthusiastically on my back. "This fire-powder is wonderful stuff, eh?"

"It certainly is!"

"What happened to the boat?"

"What boat?"

The Skipper had suddenly stopped smiling. "The boat that brought you from Kalanhad Island. You didn't walk across the sound. You had a boat, and a crew. Where are they?"

"The Imperials sank it as soon as we were on board. Our theft was discovered by the Arravines, the Grand Captain didn't want any connections left. So he ordered the boat sunk, and the crew taken aboard the galley."

He held my gaze for a moment. "Good. I don't want any connections either. Or loose ends." He slapped me on the back. "I'll speak to you later."

He left with Green Coat, disappearing below. Things were still busy on deck, as the working crew sailed the ship. There was considerable shouting of orders and trimming of sails as they navigated along the narrow channel between the Seals. I kept out of their way, and as we emerged into the sound, searched in all directions for *Wave Dancer*.

There was no sign of it, for which I was glad. I had no wish for Druthy and his men to fall casualty to the Skipper's bloodthirsty crew. Presumably they must have hoisted sail and been well on their way by the time the attack began. Still, I doubted if they'd had time to clear the sound. And if they didn't hear the noise of the fire-tubes, they would certainly have heard the massive explosion that marked the end of the *Warlord*. A huge column of smoke still marked the spot, dissipating only slowly in the breeze.

Would they come back to investigate? I hoped not. There was enough on my conscience already.

I kept watch for an hour or more, but saw no other sails.

Chapter 15: Shelter Bay

The fire-tubes were cleaned and taken below as soon as we were clear of the Seals, and the missing sections of bulkhead replaced. The false cargo of timber had apparently been left behind in Vorgranstern, but with the hatch closed and dogged there was nothing to distinguish *Anatarna* from any other coastal trader. Apart from the uncommonly large number of seamen making up her crew, that was.

As the last of the mist cleared, it turned into a beautiful day for a sail.

The sun grew warm, the breeze strengthened just enough to fill the sails and keep us moving at a decent pace, and *Anatarna* pitched only gently in the light swell. I thought of Ommet, incarcerated somewhere below, and his propensity to sea-sickness. I hoped that he wouldn't be suffering too much from the gentle movement.

But of course, that would be the least of his concerns at present. Imprisoned by the Arravines only yesterday, rescued, on the point of completing his mission, only to be captured first by the Purifiers and then by the New Dawn, the precious documents taken. And all the bloodshed. Voyon, murdered before our eyes, then the entire crew of *Warlord,* torn apart by the Skipper's devilish weapons, cut down without mercy.

I was still more than a little stunned by the events myself. Visions of blood and fire repeated themselves in my head as I struggled to come to terms with them. All culminating in that terrible explosion that had utterly obliterated a great warship. The sheer destructive power of it was enough to put anyone in shock by itself.

The thought of a man like the Skipper with such power at his disposal made me shudder. What had I committed myself to, I wondered?

And what was Ommet thinking now? Facing the utter destruction of all his plans and a very uncertain future.

But that wouldn't be the worst thing for him. Betrayal was.

Driven by the thought, I tried to find my way below decks. I had no idea what I could say to him, but could not stand to think of him languishing alone and hopeless.

The way was barred by some of the Skipper's henchmen.

"You're to stay on deck," one of them told me.

"I need to talk to the prisoner," I explained, but they just looked at me, expressionless.

"Then let me talk to the Skipper!"

"Stay on deck."

Clearly, there was no progress to be made here. I turned away, regretting that I'd even made the attempt. I had no doubt that the Skipper would know very quickly that I'd been asking to see Ommet, and would want to know why.

Anatarna voyaged onwards, heading south, back towards the coast. Heikander Sound opened up around us, a larger stretch than I'd realised. A patch of disturbed water that we left well clear on our starboard side might have been Rawburn Bank, I thought. Which meant that the island some distance off to port was probably Ocran Island. And the lower smudge in the distance beyond – could that be Kalanhad?

I wished I could have found some way to leave Ommet there.

I wandered over to the wheel, thinking to strike up a conversation and confirm my suspicions. However, the Mate standing by the helmsman greeted me with a glare. I glared back, but decided not to force the issue. I wasn't sure enough of my position here to be picking fights. I went on my way again.

The Skipper had not been seen on deck since the destruction of the *Warlord*. The sailing of the vessel he left entirely to the Mates and the crew. The actual crew, that was. A vessel this size would normally be manned by no more than a dozen, including cook and ships boy. There was now well over a hundred lounging round on deck – more perhaps below – and although they were dressed as seamen, only a handful were tending to the ship itself.

The Skipper must have called in every able-bodied man he could command for this venture, I realised, in order to man the fire-tubes. They were all in a fine mood, chatting, laughing, boasting of their exploits.

I had been keeping to myself, but in search of information – and to take my mind away from thinking about Ommet – I went forward and mingled with the crowd. To my surprise, I was greeted with enthusiasm.

"Look here, lads!" one of them shouted out. "It's only the bloody Wraith himself!"

A group gathered round, all trying to shake my hand or pummel my back. Apparently, I was some sort of hero - a disconcerting experience for someone who had always lived in the shadows. However these events played out, I was finished as the Wraith, I realised – far too many people knew my face.

Still, my current fame could be put to use.

"Is there any spare clothing I can change into?" I asked. "I've been wearing these friar's robes for far too long – very draughty, I can tell you!"

There was general laughter. "Slop chest's in the fo'c'sle," I was told. ""Skipper wanted us all looking like sailors, so he's provided plenty."

I made my way along the deck – delayed by the need to shake every hand on the way. Everyone wanted to meet the famous Wraith. I gathered that the Skipper had been making considerable use out of my name, and all without my permission, naturally.

More men were crammed into the fo'c'sle, and they all wanted to greet me as well, but eventually I found the slop chest, in the tiny compartment at the very front of the ship which served as the bosun's cabin. The bosun himself came below to see me properly kitted out, and I was finally able to discard the Arravine habit in favour of rough canvas trousers and linen shirt, a thick sea jersey and a woollen cap. Not the most elegant outfit, being all in various shades of dark blue and smelling of wet rope, but I felt less conspicuous. Though I had to retain my Arravine sandals (with the poisoned dagger still concealed within), there being no sea-boots in my size. I also kept my little set of lock picks, transferring them surreptitiously to my new outfit, along with Ommet's ring.

"Here, take this as well." The bosun handed me a belt with a knife and marlin spike attached. Not as elaborate as the 'rigging sets' Druthy and his crew had had, but the knife was sharp and I'd had Druthy's testimony on the usefulness of a marlin spike. "Skipper wants everyone to look the part."

I thanked him, buckled on the belt, and went back on deck.

Anatarna was clear of the sound now, and passing through a cluster of small islets. Ahead, the coast was clearly visible, low hills rising from the sea, with higher peaks beyond. I thought that our course had changed a little, more to the south south west, but we were still closing steadily on the shoreline.

A bell rang. I had no idea what time that indicated, but it initiated a flurry of activity, and shortly afterwards the cook appeared on deck, handing out hunks of bread and red cheese, with mugs of thick broth. They were greeted with enthusiasm. Mass murder was hungry work, it seemed.

To my surprise, and somewhat disappointment, I found that I had a good appetite myself. The images of blood and fire that were never far from my mind were of no concern to my stomach, which had had nothing in it since the Arravines had last fed us. So I ate with the rest of them, though I took no pleasure in either the food or the company.

After everyone had eaten, the Skipper appeared on deck again, looking as hearty and pleased with life as ever. He was helped up onto the roof of the charthouse, and immediately had the attention of everyone aboard.

"Today, lads, we won a great victory!" he announced, and a great cheer went up. I cheered along with the rest of them, not wanting to appear like a dissenter.

The Skipper beamed at the response, then raised his hands for quiet.

"Yes, lads, today we won a victory, and in years to come men will remember this day and historians will mark it well, for this was the first day of the New Dawn!"

More wild cheering.

"But, great though our victory was, I promise you that it is nothing compared with what's to come! This was but the prelude to far greater victories! This was just the overture – the main performance is about to start! Today was the beginning of the end of the Empire!"

The Skipper was in danger of dropping out of his role, I thought. He sounded less like an old sea-dog and more like a university lecturer. But no-one else seemed to notice, or if they did, to care. The response was as enthusiastic as ever, even though I suspected that some of these lads had no idea what a prelude was. Or an overture, for that matter.

"We've tested our weapons, and we tested ourselves, and both are true! Soon, we'll be ready to use them again, and it won't be just one war-galley that we take! Soon we'll be taking cities!"

Around me, men were yelling themselves hoarse.

"Soon we'll be taking the North. And then the whole damned Empire! THE NEW DAWN IS COMING!"

It took a while for the noise to subside, and the Skipper stood there, with arms opened wide to receive the applause.

"We'll be making landfall soon," he eventually continued. "and then you lads will have a bit of marching to do. You might have to rough it for few days, but you'll be looked after, never fear. The New Dawn takes care of its own! There's guides on hand, and places prepared. Wait there, and be ready. The word will come soon. When it does, lads, make your way with all speed – to Vorgranstern!"

This time, there was a not a cheer, but a ripple of surprise. And perhaps a little apprehension.

"That's right, lads! You heard me! Vorgranstern it is! Plans are afoot, there are great events ahead. In two weeks, three at the most, we'll be celebrating another victory – the first city of the North, liberated from the damned Imperials! And you will all be part of it! Part of the NEW DAWN!"

They took it up, shouted it back at him "The New Dawn! The New Dawn!"

I tried to go along with it, but my mind was racing. Did the Skipper really think that he could take Vorgranstern with this rag-tag army of a few hundred wild young men? And the fire-tubes as well, of course, that would give him an advantage. As would surprise, for I doubted if anyone else in the North would expect such a move. But even so... the Duke had hundreds of well-armed men in his own employ, plus there were imperial troops garrisoned in the city, and the Navy out on Layfarban – many more than just one galley's crew. No doubt there were citizens who would join an uprising, but a lot more would not! Vorgranstern was a city of merchants, not revolutionaries, for all it's proud credentials as a free-thinking, free-speaking place. Wealthy merchants, in many cases, who would see no profit in opposing the system that made them money. Ordinary people with comfortable lives were more likely to oppose the New Dawn than fight with it.

I had no time to puzzle it out, for the Skipper had climbed down and disappeared below, to further rapturous applause. And Green Coat was approaching me through the crowd.

"Skipper wants a word," he said. "Now."

He led the way below decks, and I found myself once more in the dingy cabin, seated at the same table, with the Skipper facing me. If he remembered some of the harsh words we'd exchanged on our previous meeting, he didn't show it. Instead, he greeted me as he had then, with a glass of strong rum.

"We'll splice the mainbrace to mark our victory!" he announced. "I'm having some bottles opened for the lads up on deck, but we can do a spot 'o celebrating here! After all, it's as much your triumph as anyone else's. T'was your information gave us the course to steer!"

Back in full nautical mode, I noticed. We clinked glasses together, and I took a cautious sip whilst the Skipper knocked his back in one.

"Vorgranstern?" I asked. "Really?" I tried to sound enthusiastic, but perhaps a little doubt entered my voice.

"Why? Don't you think we can do it?" He frowned, pale eyes fixed on me.

I shrugged. "You wouldn't have said it if you weren't sure. And there's no bigger target in the North! But we'd need the whole city to rise with us, and I don't know that fat merchants and bankers will stir themselves to support our cause."

He sat back, nodding. "Aye, it's a fair point. But we'll have more on our side than you'd suppose – and that's largely your doing!"

I raised my eyebrows in honest bemusement. "Mine? How so?"

"Have you forgotten that little snippet of information you sent me? The Duke's secret tunnels and spy holes?"

Of course. I'd included that in the information I'd sent from Layfarban – a brief accounting of our trip down the light-tube and the passageways we'd discovered there.

The Skipper nodded as he saw my realisation. "All this about the 'Hidden Libraries' that the Arravines keep – well, that was interesting. And your plans to meet with a war-galley were damned useful to know – you saw the result of that! But the Dukes dirty little secret, that was the real gem! Most valuable jewel the Wraith ever stole!" He laughed at his joke, and I managed a weak smile.

"Yes, I thought you'd want to know about that."

"Oh, it's not just what *I* wanted to know! Those fat merchants and bankers – they've wondered for years how the Duke always managed to know what was going on. Well now, thanks to you, they do – and believe me, they're not happy! There's already a lot of tension brewing back in Vorgranstern. And there'll be a lot more when we make it known publicly. There's a pamphlet written and printed, hundreds of copies, and when I give the word, they'll go out. Within a day, the whole city will know that their Duke has been spying on them all for generations! Their famous freedoms that they'll all so proud of are just a sham! The place will be in turmoil and ripe for rising!"

He grinned broadly and raised his glass again. "And that's the work of the Wraith! Don't worry, I'll see that you get the full credit!"

I drank with him. Not just a sip. This time I needed it.

He leaned over the table and lowered his voice. "To tell the truth, lad, I've always known you'd come up trumps for us. Oh, there are those who didn't trust you. Not committed enough, they said. Just a thief at heart, he serves himself, we can't trust him! Oh yes, it's all been said. And after Sonor Breck – when you got arrested – they were saying that you were all washed up, taken aback on a lee shore as it were! Get rid of him, they said. But I knew better!" He gave me a friendly punch on the arm. "I told them you'd show your colours in good time, and so you have! So you have!"

He took another drink, and so did I. Who was it hadn't trusted me? Who had wanted rid of me after Sonor Breck?

"Of course, we've still got a few details to finalise," he continued. "I've called a meeting. Full council of all the New Dawn leaders in the North. Here on board the *Anatarna* – hows that for irony, eh! They'll be arriving tomorrow. You'll see your old friend Bryn!"

I smiled brightly, though the thought of meeting with the Beggar again hardly filled me with joy. Especially after that last bit of information. Because if anyone had wanted to get rid of me, it had probably been him, and I was certain now that he'd tried his best to facilitate that.

"I'm told you wanted to talk to our prisoner." The Skipper didn't change his tone of voice, but the broad smile had suddenly disappeared and he was staring at me intently. "Why was that?"

Fortunately I'd had plenty of time to think of an answer.

"I wanted to ask him more about his plans for these documents he had me steal. He told me what they were, but he never did explain exactly why they were so important. I tried to get it out of him before, but he kept it close. I hoped that in the new circumstances he might be more amenable."

The Skipper held my gaze for a long moment, then sat back and poured himself another glass of rum. "Well, you've no need to worry about that any more. We've got him and we've got his documents, so whatever his plans were, they're scuppered now!"

"I suppose so. Though I would like to have a word with him – see what else he knows."

"Don't trouble yourself on that account. I already talked to him. I was hoping that an Imperial Agent would be full of useful information, but it seems he knows little about anything other than his oh so vital mission. He talked freely enough about that, but nothing else, even with persuasion."

I felt a cold chill, wondering what form of persuasion the Skipper had employed.

"He perhaps doesn't know much else," I suggested. "After all, he is Second Order, and no matter how trusted, I doubt if they'd tell him anything he didn't need to know."

"My thought's exactly!" The Skipper took out his pipe and waved it in my direction. "I suppose that if we tried hard enough, we'd dig a few snippets out of him. I thought of letting Bryn have a go, he's very talented in that area. But really, I doubt if it's worth it, and we have bigger fish to fry."

"So what will you do with him, then?" I said as casually as I could.

"Well, we'll be anchoring before sunset. I've a notion to tie him to the anchor and send him on his way."

I felt sick, but didn't dare show it. The Skipper was apparently concentrating on the task of cleaning and filling his pipe, but I knew that he was watching me intently.

"Yes, that would work, I suppose. But, on the other hand, it's not often we get a full blown Imperial Agent in hand. Perhaps we could arrange something special for him?"

"Such as?" The Skipper got up, set a taper to the nearest lamp, and began to puff his pipe into life.

"A show trial, perhaps? After we've taken Vorgranstern, we could roll him out and make a public example of what happens to those who choose the wrong side?"

"Good! Very good! I like that idea!" He sucked enthusiastically as he thought it over. I held my breath. If he accepted my plan, it would give Ommet a few more weeks, and anything might happen in that time.

Then he shook his head. "Belay that. We're going to be very busy after Vorgranstern, very busy indeed. But I'll tell you what we will do. He was asking for a chance to put his case – seemed to have the idea that he could persuade us to his cause, would you believe! And since we've got the full Council of the North coming together, we'll give him what he wants. I'm sure that the others would be interested to see him." He gave me a wink. "And it'll give us something to brag about as well! A war-galley and an Imperial Agent, both taken on the same day! It's going to be hard to top that, eh?" He laughed aloud, and I did my best to laugh along with him.

"Yes, that's what we'll do," he decided. "He can say his piece to the Council, and they can decide what to do with the bugger! Finished your drink yet?"

Caught out by the change of topic, I looked blankly at him. "Pardon? Oh – no, not quite."

"Well, knock it back, lad, and get topsides. Enjoy the sea air while you can! I've got work to do."

And shortly afterwards I found myself once more on deck, brooding on what fate Ommet might suffer from the Council.

⤫

AS THE AFTERNOON MERGED into evening, *Anatarna* dropped her anchor in a small bay. We were just offshore from a beach of grey sand, along the top of which ran a straggle of cottages. Behind them, a more substantial building loomed – red brick, and slate roofed.

Boats were launched from the beach, and by the time the cable had been secured, we were surrounded by half-a-dozen of the vessels – luggers like *Wave Dancer,* but less well maintained and carrying a strong fishy odour with them. They came alongside at several points, and most of *Anatarna's* 'crew' began to disembark.

The Mate was supervising the operation, bawling orders at the fishing boats. I waited for a quiet moment before asking him where we were. I got the usual hostile glare in return, but I stood my ground and repeated the question. After all, I was the Wraith, a confident of the Skipper and architect of the New Dawn's greatest victory! Perhaps he saw it the same way, for after a moment he grudgingly admitted that this was Shelter Bay.

"And what's the village called?" I persisted.

"Shelter Bay!" he snapped. "Like I said!"

I would have asked what, in that case, was the Bay called, but I suspected I already knew. And besides, neither of us were enjoying the conversation.

The operation continued at a brisk pace. The fishing boats ferried men ashore, where they formed up into small groups and set off up the road which wound it's way into the hills behind the village. Still full of rum and victory, they cheered and shouted at each other as they did so. It was very still in the bay, and leaning on the bulwark, I could make out some of the clearer voices across the water.

"See you in Vorgranstern!"

"Victory to the New Dawn!"

"Death to the Imperials and down with the First Order!"

I wondered how many would still be as cheerful in a few weeks time. Taking Vorgranstern would be a very different matter from taking the *Warlord,* and it would be a lot less exciting when their own blood began to flow.

Things were much quieter on board when all the extra crew had gone. The galley – a small deck-house forward of the hatch – produced a more substantial meal of boiled beef and grey peas, with a hot duff pudding to follow. The sun disappeared behind the hills that surrounded Shelter Bay, and an anchor light was hoisted as night gathered around us.

The gentle breeze took on a sharp edge. Feeling the need for shelter, I tried my luck with the Mate again.

"Where am I to sleep tonight?"

He gave an indifferent shrug. "Help yourself." He waved a hand generally around the deck. "Or if that's not grand enough for you, sling a hammock down in the fo'c'sle."

It seemed that even a New Dawn hero like the Wraith didn't rate a cabin aft with the officers. I wondered if this was the Skipper's subtle way of keeping me in my place. Or was it that he just didn't want anyone he didn't entirely trust that close while he slept.

Either way, the fo'c'sle seemed more appealing than a cold night on deck. I made use of the heads and then took myself below.

It had been crowded before, with men packed round the small tables and sat on the benches. Most of them had gone ashore, but of the remaining crew, only one or two were needed to keep watch while we were at anchor. The rest were taking the opportunity to catch up on their sleep, and the space was now filled with slung hammocks and snoring men.

A small amount of light shone from the bo'sun's cabin for'ard, where a dedicated group were smoking and playing cards. Peering through the fug that this produced, I caught the bo'sun's eye through the open door.

"The Mate tells me I'm to sleep down here?"

He nodded. "There's spare hammocks aft, under the benches. Sling one wherever you can find space. Blankets in the lockers."

I nodded my thanks, and withdrew. Behind me, a low-voiced comment drew subdued laughter. I wasn't able to hear what was said, but I guessed it would be some speculation about my ability to sling a hammock.

The speculation was accurate. I had never even slept in a hammock and had not the slightest idea of how to sling one.

None-the-less, I went aft, ducking low to avoid the sleepers, and trying to breath through my mouth. Something in the diet had had a powerful effect on everyone's digestion, mine included. Not much noticeable up in the fresh air, but in this unventilated space the reek overpowered everything else.

Probably that was the reason that the seamen had set their hammocks as close to the open hatchway as possible. By the time I'd reached the aft bulkhead there was more clear space, if less breathable air, and I was able to stand upright and look around. Not that I could see much: even less light than air made it back this far. I stood still, hoping my eyes would adjust enough so that I could at least find some blankets. With their help, the upper deck might become a possibility.

What I did see, however, were some faint lines of light, etched into the bulkhead, marking out the shape of a door. Which was curious, since I was pretty sure that there hadn't been a door there on my previous visit.

Of course, I hadn't come this far into the fo'c'sle on that occasion. But I'd looked round, and although crowded, there had been more light. And I certainly didn't remember seeing anything but solid wood on this bulkhead.

I tend to notice things like doors and windows. It's an essential part of my profession, to be aware of ways in – or out – of a place. If there had been a door there before, I would have seen it. Unless, of course, it was a concealed door. A disguised door. Such as the one in the aft cabin, through which the Skipper had taken me to show me the hold, and the fire-tubes.

Of course it made perfect sense that there should be another way into the hold, and that it would be concealed against casual eyes. So I hadn't seen it before. But the concealment wasn't perfect and in the darkness, with a light on the other side, the doorway was revealed.

I stepped up to it and ran my fingers lightly across the surface. It felt like solid wood planking. There was nothing as obvious as a handle or even a key-hole.

How had the Skipper opened the other door? I thought back, remembering his movements. He'd reached up and touched it – here, then here…

I put my hand on the top right corner of the door and pushed. Then on the top left.

Nothing happened. The wood felt solid under my touch, just part of the bulkhead.

I frowned, concentrating on digging up a tiny detail from my memory. Had the Skipper actually touched the door itself, or the bulkhead next to it?

Of course, this door might be different from the other one. Or it might be bolted from the inside. But I had naught to lose by trying.

As long as I wasn't caught trying. That might be embarrassing. I cocked an ear forward, but the faint murmur of conversation indicated that the card game still continued. And the swinging hammocks screened me effectively from view. Of course, I was making the assumption that all the sailors in the hammocks were voyaging far off on dream seas. There was no way to check that. I had to take a risk, but I judged it a small one.

I reached up again, and pushed on the bulkhead next to the door. Top right, top left.

At each push, something gave a little under my fingers. There was a faint click, and the door swung open a fraction. Yellow lamplight spilled out.

"Ha!" I said to myself. "You think you can conceal a door from the Wraith, Skipper? Think again!"

I opened the door a little further, and peered cautiously through.

Just as with the aft door, there was a short, steep flight of stairs leading down into the hold. From the bottom an alleyway led aft, flanked with boxes of arquebuses.

I checked the mechanism on the inside of the door, but there was no concealment here, just a simple catch. Reassured that I wouldn't be imprisoned with the fire-tubes, I slipped through and pulled it shut behind me, lest the card players noticed the extra light.

From the bottom of the stairs, the alleyway ran the full length of the hold, all the way to the identical stairs that I had descended before, with the Skipper. But this time there was an open hatch in the deck half-way along, with a lantern hanging above it.

That, I thought, would be where the larger fire-tubes were stowed. They'd opened a section of the main hatch above to send them down after we'd left the Seals, but I hadn't been allowed close enough to see where they put them.

And perhaps also where the fire-powder was kept? That might be useful to know about.

There was more lamplight below. I crept down the next flight of stairs, glad now that I still had my Arravine sandals rather than a heavy pair of sea-boots.

From halfway down I could see that this was indeed where the larger fire-tubes had been stowed. The deadly cylinders were racked along the starboard side, while to port were canvas bags that – to judge by the bulges in them – were filled with round shot. There were crates as well, which I guessed might contain the smaller shot for the arquebuses.

And, lashed down and secure amongst the other items, a wooden box that I well remembered and was relieved to see. The Skipper had shown little interest in the ancient writings, but at least he hadn't had them dropped overboard.

My examination was interrupted by a faint but familiar noise. Someone else was down here with me – someone who had also participated in the wind-inducing evening meal. I cautiously descended the rest of the way.

Unlike on the deck above, this level only extended half the length of the hold before being divided athwartships by another bulkhead. A door was set in it, unconcealed but solid looking, and in front of it an occupied hammock swung. This was the source of the noise, and the accompanying odour.

I surmised that this was the armourer, and that the door beyond would lead to the fire-powder store. I moved a little closer, examining the door as well as I could. There was a conventional looking lock and handle. A set of keys hanging nearby gave me a clue as to what sort of lock it might be – nothing that would hold me up for more than a few seconds.

All this had been very interesting, but there was no more to be done just now. I turned to go. And saw, at the forward end of the hold, beyond the ladder, two doors.

There should only have been one. My knowledge of nautical architecture, weak though it was, had been improved a little during my time aboard – enough at least to surmise that, forward of the hold and below the seaman's accommodation would be the cable locker. The place where the great rope that held the anchor was stowed.

That accounted for one door. But what was the other one?

The door on my right – starboard side – had a small barred window in it. Like a jail door. Or what was the word on a ship? The brig.

I stood and stared at it, and as I did, the certainty grew in me that Ommet was behind that door.

It was the logical and obvious place for him to be. But it was more than that. I knew beyond all doubt that he was there. That he was in pain, that he lay awake in the darkness, struggling against despair.

I took half a step in that direction, then paused.

What was I going to say to him?

"Hang on, I'll get you out of there?" Except that I wasn't going to do that. I probably couldn't, even if I wanted to. The door wouldn't be difficult – there wasn't even a lock, just a big bolt – and I could cope with the sleeping armourer, but there was a watch kept on deck. If we could get into the sea, we might be able to swim ashore, except that Ommet couldn't swim. And if we made it, the village was all New Dawn sympathisers. If we escaped the village, we would be wet, cold and lost somewhere on the wild northern coast.

Not that Ommet would leave without his precious documents.

And in any case, I'd made my decision. I'd thrown in my lot with the New Dawn. For all my misgivings, in spite of my fears that it had been a terrible mistake, the fact remained that I was committed. I could see no way of changing that now.

So what could I say? "Sorry I betrayed you?"

I went softly back up the stairs and crept into the foc'sle. The card game still continued in the bos'un's cabin, the snoring still continued elsewhere. No-one seemed to have noticed my departure or return.

I had no idea how to sling a hammock and no chance of working it out in the semi-darkness. Instead I found a couple of blankets and made my way back on deck.

It was an uncomfortable night.

Chapter 16. The Council of the North

Dawn came early. I watched it, sitting uncomfortably on a coil of rope and wrapped in my blankets. First the darkness faded, by imperceptible degrees, into a dim greyness that made everything seem unreal and distant. Then, as the light slowly grew, colour edged back into the world. The sunrise itself was hidden by the hills surrounding the bay, but the sky turned blue, the hills became green, and the *Anatarna* showed off her drab brown.

Eventually, other people began to appear. The cook began to bustle around in his little deckhouse by the foremast. Seamen made their way to and from the heads, the Skipper appeared, puffing his pipe and staring shoreward. I stood up (feeling my joints creak as I did so) and wandered in his direction, but he ignored me and went below again.

Breakfast eventually made an appearance, some sort of grey porridge. It didn't have much taste, but it was warm, and served to get me moving again.

Bells rang at various times, seamen went about their duties. Some nodded to me in passing, some ignored me, but nobody had much to say – apart from the Bo'sun, who told me sharply to get my blankets down below and to stop lollygagging on deck. I eventually found myself something useful to do in helping the cook. A morose man, who nevertheless found some small pleasure in life by getting me to cut up onions.

Around mid-morning, there was a shout of 'Boat ahoy.' I wiped my eyes, abandoned my cooking duties and went out to see what was happening.

A lugger was coming alongside, bringing Beggar Bryn and Silent Ghiss with it. The Skipper was on deck to greet them, all nautical affability. Bryn struggled over the side, not wearing his usual motley but a smart coat of dark wool – which I supposed counted as a disguise for him. He saw me standing nearby, but said nothing, instead greeted the Skipper and they went below together. Ghiss gave me a long look, but of course remained silent and followed them.

I remembered the maid from Muranburder, and wondered if it was Ghiss who had kidnapped and tortured her. I knew that Bryn often used him for tasks other than being his bodyguard. There were unpleasant rumours around some of those tasks.

Another fishing boat arrived, bringing more of the Council. Some I recognised: The Cleric, who's name was Laybron, was from far east of here. I had had dealings with him before, when I did a little work in those parts, and didn't like him. I'd met The Cook once as well, and had resolved never to eat anything out of his kitchen. The powerfully built woman with them would probably be The Matron, whom I'd heard stories about, none of them very pleasant.

There was one other that I didn't know, a dapper little man who looked contemptuously at everyone on deck, apart from the other Council members, before the Skipper appeared to usher them all below. All in all, an unsavoury collection to have thrown my lot in with, but at least they were all very evidently Second Order.

Meanwhile, there was more activity on deck. The main hatchway down to the hold had been removed and one of the yardarms had been rigged as a derrick. With a few shouted orders and a lot of hauling on ropes, a crate was brought up from below.

The crate, I realised with a twist of my guts. The one we had gone to so much trouble to get, the one that Ommet had been willing to sacrifice himself for. Mirrion's lost writings.

The crate was swung over the side, and for a horrible moment I thought it was going to be dropped into the sea. But the seamen had it under control. Checking away on the ropes, they lowered it safely into the bottom of the lugger that had brought Bryn and Ghiss out.

Green Coat – I still hadn't learned his real name, but I'd heard men refer to him as 'The Apothecary' - had been standing nearby, watching with me. As the crate was secured in the lugger, he made his way to the side and clambered over.

"Hey... where's that going?"

He looked at me and sneered. "Ashore. Skipper's orders."

"I went to a lot of trouble to get that! Where are you taking it?"

He pulled himself back up to the gunwale and leaned close. "Listen, you! Just because you're a Name, don't think that that makes you anything special or that you've got any business questioning orders! The Council will decide what's to be done with it, and if they want to tell you, they will – or not. Got that?"

He glared at me, eye-to-eye. I nodded.

"Good. Remember it. Some of us have been Names in this organisation for a lot longer than you, so don't go giving yourself airs because everyone knows about 'The Wraith'. You're just a bloody little thief, as far as I'm concerned!"

With that, he disappeared back down the ladder, and settled himself down on the chest. The luggers crew pushed off and began the row back to the shore.

So, I was a 'Name' in the New Dawn, was I? Like 'The Apothecary', I supposed. Like 'The Skipper', 'The Beggar' and the rest of them, if clearly not as important. It was a mark of distinction, but not one that I was happy with. Instead it made me feel that I was being sucked further into something that I'd never wanted to be part of in the first place.

"Hey, you! Mr Wraith! Get back to the galley, there's more work to do and I'll have no shirking aboard this ship!"

It was the Mate. Another Name, I wondered? Or was that just his shipboard rank?

I considered making an issue of it. After all, if I was 'The Wraith' shouldn't that put me on the same level as 'The Mate', if not above him? Was he entitled to order me around like that?

However, from the look in his eye, he obviously thought he was. And it wasn't as if I had anything better to do.

A carcass had been delivered in the last boat, along with the Council members. A complete dead cow, which the cook had begun to hack apart with what appeared to be more vigour than enthusiasm, and more enthusiasm than skill. There was also a good supply of fresh vegetables and I had the task of cleaning and preparing them for the midday meal. In honour of the Council, the cook was apparently making his signature dish – some sort of beef stew.

The sun had grown strong, the breeze had died away and the temperature in the galley rose rapidly. The smell from the carcass – which I suspected had been none too fresh to begin with – became overpowering, even surpassing the smell from the cook. I would have taken my vegetables outside, but that, it transpired, was forbidden – the Mate didn't want our mess on deck. So I breathed as shallowly as possible and dripped sweat into the massive cauldron that all the cooking was done in.

I had no intention of eating any of it.

Eventually, it was done. The concoction – complete with greasy looking lumps that the cook termed 'dumplings' - was served into some rather fine china and taken below for the council, after which the rest of the crew queued up to have their portions slopped out. Some passable bread had been included with the supplies: I hunted out red cheese from the galley store and made my own meal, escaping out on deck to eat it.

I fully expected to be called to washing up duties, but instead when the Mate sought me out it was to send me down to the stern cabin.

"Council wants to see you," he grunted. Perhaps resenting the fact that I got to be privy to their plans. The Mate, I thought, wasn't a Name. He was just the person who actually ran the ship – the Skipper having no part in that.

It had been hot on deck and sweltering in the galley. The stern cabin, by comparison, was relatively cool, with skylights open to let in light and air. It still stank of rum, sweat and food, though.

The Council had arrayed themselves along one side, behind the table which still bore the remains of lunch. Lesser persons stood or sat around the cabin. Standing in front of them felt uncomfortably like being on trial.

"Well, here he is – the Wraith himself!" The Skipper was in an ebullient mood, perhaps helped along by the bottles of rum which were in abundance on the table. "You've all heard of him, haven't you! Hunted by the First Order in every province of the Empire, but he still slips through their grasp!"

It was an exaggeration. There were many provinces that I'd never even visited.

"But let me introduce you properly," he continued. "Now, you already know The Beggar, of course..." Bryn inclined his head in my direction, with a sardonic look. "And I believe you've met The Cleric?"

"Indeed I have," I acknowledged. The Cleric, ruddy faced and sweating, had thrown aside his tight white collar and opened his shirt down to the navel. He had never quite fitted the description of his Name, and now, with a bottle of rum in hand as well, it seemed entirely inappropriate.

"Well met, Mr. Wraith!" he boomed. He certainly had the voice of a preacher – not merely loud, but rich, powerful and well modulated. He was very good at stirring up crowds, I'd heard. "Glad to hear that you've given your commitment to the New Dawn!"

"Oh, yes, he's with us heart and soul!" The Skipper confirmed. With a look at me that could be taken as a warning, if I'd wanted to read it that way. "And this is the Cook, whom you've also met, and the lady here is The Matron. Just next to her is The Tailor."

The Cook looked even less like a cook than the Cleric did like a man of the cloth. Tall and cadaverous, he put me in mind of someone who hated food. But he stretched his mouth into something that might have been a smile of welcome.

The Matron was less friendly. She gave me a flat, suspicious stare that put me in mind of a cat. Or perhaps it was her face that did that – wide, large eyes, small mouth. She might have been pretty once.

The Tailor gave me one of the contemptuous looks that seemed to be his normal approach to the world. Even with his coat off he looked neat and smart. I wondered if he made his own clothes.

"So, on to business. We've been discussing our plans for Vorgranstern, and I've told them how much your information has helped with that. But there's another job for you to do, one that will help us even more."

"What's that, then?" I asked, trying to sound relaxed about it, instead of tense with apprehension.

He waved his pipe at me. "Not so fast. There's some explaining to do first... timing's going to be important, so listen close."

He stopped to sip from his rum, and then started to clean out his pipe. "Once we've finished here, *Anatarna* will be heading back to Vorgranstern, but not too swiftly. Everyone" - he waved a hand at the room in general - "needs to get back to their own territory and make ready first. So we're not planning to actually make port until this time next week." He pointed his pipe stem at me. "You'll be in the city well ahead of that."

I shook my head. "I can't go to Vorgranstern. Crombard will be there looking for me! He'll turn the city upside down if there's even a rumour that I'm back."

The Skipper laughed, and the rest of them smiled, even the Matron. "Oh, there'll be rumours all right, and plenty of them. I'll see to that, don't you worry!"

"What?" I stared aghast. "You're going to tell the Baron where I am?"

"That I will," he confirmed.

"But..."

"What, is the Wraith worried? No, don't concern yourself. You'll be tucked up nice and safe in one of our hidey-holes. But the Baron will indeed be there, with as many men as he can muster."

I shook my head. "But why would you want the Baron there when you're about to try and take the city? Won't that make things harder?"

"Oh, perhaps a little. For a while. But easier in the long term." The Skipper settled back comfortably and began filling his pipe. "We want Crombard dead. For all sorts of personal reasons, of course – I'm sure you'll share some – but apart from that, he's the Grand Duke's strong right arm here in the North. Getting rid of the Baron will be the greatest single blow we can strike against the First Order. Short of killing the Grand Duke himself, of course. But we'll get to him later."

I nodded. "Believe me, I'm all in favour of the idea! But he's not an easy man to kill. I know, I've studied him close. He never travels outside his own Estate without his bodyguard – twenty picked men, all First Order, all trained killers! He'll have other troops with him as well. Even with fire tubes, that's going to be a hard nut to crack."

"You think we don't know that?" The Skipper frowned, then relaxed back into a smile. "Not to worry, it's all planned for, and the fire tubes aren't our only weapons, oh no! But we need to stoke up the tension in the city, and having Crombard's men tearing it up to find you will do that very effectively. Then we release the pamphlets I told you about, people learn how they've been spied on by their own Duke, and the place will be ready to explode.

While all this is happening, my lads will be slipping into the city by twos and threes, and making their way down to the *Anatarna's* berth. We'll come in on the tide after dark, nice and quiet. The fire-tubes will be off the ship and all ready by midnight."

He looked expectantly at me, so I responded. "What happens at midnight?"

"That's when we set flame to the fuel!"

He found a taper, lit it from a lamp nearby, and set it to his pipe, puffing vigorously to get it going. Finally satisfied, he blew out the taper and stared thoughtfully into the glowing bowl.

"Aye," he said, almost to himself. "We'll light such a fire in Vorgranstern that it will be seen across the Empire."

Blowing a stream of smoke in my direction, he continued.

"At midnight, some of Crombard's men will be attacked in the Tunnels, and the cry will go up that it was the Wraith. If he's not there already, the Baron will arrive hot-foot. Once he's inside, my lads will march along the South Docks. They'll take Ekharden Platz, and the North Docks as well. Then they'll seal off all the tunnel entrances, with the Baron and his men inside."

The Skipper puffed contentedly on his pipe, and watched me think about it. They all did.

"Yes, with fire tubes and surprise on your side, you can probably do that. But how long do you think you can hold them in there? They'll soon force their way out, you don't have the numbers or the weapons to hold them there for long. And Duke Endranard won't just ignore what's going on either. No matter what his differences with the Baron, he won't stand by and watch his city fall. He'll be marching down from the Palace as soon as he can muster his troops!"

The Skipper was smiling round his pipe. I glanced along the table, and all of them were smiling at me. It was disquieting.

"What haven't you told me?" I returned their smiles with a suspicious look.

"You see?" said the Skipper to the room in general. "I told you he was smart!" He turned his attention back to me. "There's a great deal I haven't told you, and a great deal you do not need to know. As for the Baron and his men, once they're trapped inside the tunnels they will be taken care of. The Apothecary – you know him, of course? - he's on his way to make arrangements for that now. Not your problem. But the Duke, now, he is very much is your problem. Or rather, you are the solution to the problem he represents."

He leaned forward, colourless eyes boring into me. "At midnight, when everything else begins, you will kill Duke Endranard. The city will be leaderless, the Palace Guards will be distracted by their search for the assassin, and by the time the confusion dies down, we will have victory!"

I only just managed to stop myself gaping. "Kill the Duke? Me? But I'm a jewel thief, not an assassin!"

The Skipper's eyes hardened, and the smile vanished.

"But on the other hand," I continued without missing a beat, "There's not that much difference. Very much the same thing, in fact. Slip in quietly, do the job, slip out again. Nothing for the Wraith!"

The Skipper's smile was back. "Just what we thought! The right man for the job, eh? Didn't I tell you?"

He glanced each way along the table, and met with approving nods from the rest of the Council. Well, not all the Council. Bryn did not look enthusiastic.

"And what then?" I asked. "The Grand Duke won't stand by and see you – us – set up in business in Vorgranstern. "He'll gather every armed man in the North and send them against us, and that's a lot of swords against our fire tubes."

"Indeed. Just what we want him to do. With any luck, this will bring him out in person."

The Skipper blew a smoke ring into the heavy air of the cabin. The smell of his pipe had now overpowered every other odour. He looked almost blissful.

"The Grand Duke will march on Vorgranstern. He'll take all his troops with him. His elite Knights – the Purifiers, they call themselves – and all his household guards. Every First Order noble will be summoned to his banner with all their men at arms. Even the Imperial troops in the North. If the Empress doesn't order them to his command, the Grand Duke will likely just summon them anyway, and most of them will come running. And what do you suppose will happen then, with all the First Order and their lackeys hammering on the doors of Vorgranstern?"

"Well, they'll take it I suppose. Eventually. And they'll kill everyone inside, most likely."

"Aye. They will. And that's when the word will go out."

The Skipper jumped to his feet, slammed his fist on the table, and shouted.

"AVENGE VORGRANSTERN! RISE UP! DEATH TO THE FIRST ORDER!"

The rest of the room erupted in cheers and shouts. I was quick to join in.

Eventually, things quietened down. The Skipper put his pipe in his mouth, his hands on the table, and leaned forward.

"That'll be the signal! That's what will finally set the North aflame! We'll have every man of the Second Order flocking to our banners – yes and every woman as well," he added with a glance at The Matron. All those undefended First Order strongholds will be ours, their servants will join us or die! And we – will – have – our – FREEDOM!"

More cheering.

I noticed how he said we. Whatever happened in Vorgranstern, I didn't expect the Skipper to stay around for it.

I didn't suppose I'd be round for it either, but not for the same reasons. In spite of my breezy words, there was a huge difference between stealing jewellery and assassinating a Duke. For one thing, I'd always made sure I was well out of the way before my thefts were discovered. But a dead Duke was going to be more immediately obvious. I had no doubt that I'd been given a suicide mission.

Of course, ultimately it was all a suicide mission. I had no faith in The Skipper's vision. The North would certainly be appalled and even enraged if Grand Duke Brodon destroyed Vorgranstern, but that wasn't to say that the entire population would rise in armed rebellion.

I had little doubt that there would be enough anger to inspire a vicious and bloody civil war. There was no telling how many would die in the course of it. But at the end, every person in that cabin would have their head removed, pickled and paraded round all the cities, towns and villages in the Empire as a warning to any other rebels.

Unless they got out of it now. Which was certainly what I intended to do.

The cheering died down again. "Right, then," I said. "I'd best be on my way. It's a fair step to Vorgranstern, and I'll have a lot to do there to make ready."

I turned towards the door, and found myself staring at a grubby shirt. Silent Ghiss, true to his name, had come out of the shadows behind me to stand close by without me noticing. He was a better wraith than I was, and lot bigger. I tipped my head back to look up at his face, and he stared down, expressionless.

"Oh, there's no rush just yet," the Skipper assured me. "Arrangements have been made for your transport, never fear. And you won't go alone either! The Beggar has very generously agreed to let his man Ghiss go with you. He'll guard your back and see you safe to the city."

"Oh. Wonderful." I said, with as much fake enthusiasm as I could manage.

"And besides, we have one more item on our agenda, which I know you won't want to miss. We have an Imperial Agent to examine and dispose of!"

Ommet. I hadn't forgotten about him, exactly, but I'd had a lot to think about in the last few minutes.

"Now, Mr. Wraith, why don't you go and get him for us?"

"Of course. A pleasure. I'll be just a moment."

Silent Ghiss stepped aside, and I made my way out of the cabin with what I hoped was a jaunty swagger.

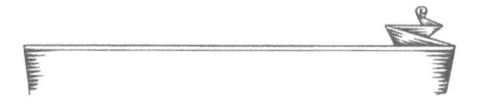

Chapter 17. The Word of Mirrion

The sunshine was as strong as ever, and dazzling after the relative dimness of the cabin. I shielded my eyes and stepped over to the gunwale, looking across at the shore and the little village of Shelter Bay.

It wasn't so far. I could easily swim it.

But what then? Soaking wet, without supplies or money, and in a village controlled by the New Dawn – how far would I get?

"If you're done below, Mr. Wraith, there's still work to do in the galley!"

The Mate was up by the wheel, watching.

"Not finished yet. I'm to collect the prisoner. The Council want to speak to him."

"Right. He's down in the hold." The main hatch was still open, a ladder had been set up, and the Mate indicated that that was to be my way below. Hidden doors were to stay hidden, it seemed.

There was even less air down in the hold than there had been in the cabin, though a similar smell prevailed. Less light as well. I peered round in the gloom, till I could make out the armourer (or The Armourer? Was he a Name?) looking at me.

"Council wants the prisoner."

"For'ard. You don't need a key, it's only bolted."

I walked forward, and as I approached the cell, I had the same unnerving feeling as I had the previous night. Ommet, even though still behind the door, was a tangible presence. I knew his pain and tiredness and desperate resolve to stay brave and strong no matter what. It was almost as if they were my own emotions – yet they were as distinctly Ommet's as the sound of his voice.

I knew the exact moment when he heard me approach. And that he immediately knew it was me.

I stopped, dizzy and confused. What was happening here?

"Arton." He wasn't asking. He was talking to me.

"Ommet." I pushed aside my confusion. I forced away the rush of emotion I felt – the sudden hope that was not my own – and unbolted the door.

There was even less furniture in the cell than there had been in my quarters at Neowbron – just a bucket. Ommet was sitting on the floor, but only because there wasn't room for him to lay down. Even in the dim light of the lower hold, I could see that he had been badly treated. His face was bruised, one eye so swollen that he could barely see out of it, his Arravine robe torn and bloodstained. The Skipper's idea of 'persuasion', no doubt.

"Come on." I reached out and grabbed his hand and helped him up, as gently as I could. "I'm sorry, but I have to take you before the New Dawn Council. The Council of the North, as they call themselves."

"You, Arton? You are taking me to the Council?"

I saw the look in his eye, and felt the hope die in him. Felt the pain of my betrayal.

"So, you're with them now? You've joined the New Dawn?"

I pulled him out of the cell. Maybe a little less gently, as I tried to hide my shame behind anger. "Well, what else could I do? Throw my lot in with you – an Imperial Agent? Serve the First Order, who have been my enemies all my life?"

"The First Order aren't your enemies, Arton. Baron Crombard, is. The Grand Duke as well, I suppose. And probably every noble who has had jewellery go missing. But they are not all of the First Order."

"So who are my friends amongst them, eh?" I pushed him towards the stairs, and his legs gave way. Too long stuffed into that cramped little hole. I pulled him up again, and put my arm round him to keep him there as we made our way to the stairs. "Your precious Empress, I suppose? Do you think she would take me as a lover when she tires of you?"

"It was never like that between us. We were never lovers in the way you think. And real love does not tire."

I made a sound intended to convey contempt for his sentimental mush, but saved most of my breath for half-supporting, half-dragging him up the stairs, with the armourer gazing suspiciously after us.

"And the New Dawn – they are your friends, Arton?"

I ignored him. We emerged back onto the deck. I paused to catch my breath.

"How much do you know about these friends, I wonder? Let me see – the Council of the North, you called them. So that's The Skipper, The Beggar, The Cook, The Matron and The Cleric, yes? And perhaps The Shopkeeper?"

"Never heard of The Shopkeeper!" I snapped at him. "Can you walk, yet?" I pushed him along the deck. He staggered, but managed to stay upright.

"So The Shopkeeper's gone, then? That wasn't unexpected. He was getting rather too powerful and independently minded. The Skipper and The Beggar would have put a stop to that. Have they replaced him, yet?"

"The Tailor." I grabbed his arm again and kept him moving. The Mate, the Bo'sun and several deckhands stood looking at us. Some were sneering, others seemed indifferent.

"Ah, yes, The Tailor. Likes to dress well, doesn't he? Wanted for murder in the south of the Empire. Killed his master when he was an apprentice. Married the widow, took over the business, then killed her as well, but this time he was found out and fled here."

"How do you know that!" I said it as sharply as I could manage in a whisper. I didn't want the crew overhearing. "And keep moving!"

Ommet kept moving, but stiffly and therefore slowly.

"Imperial Agent, remember? There are files on all the New Dawn leaders. I read them before I came up here. They are as much the enemy as Crombard or the Grand Duke."

I said nothing.

"What about the others, then? The Cook, for example. Had a position in the kitchens of a nobleman's house. He was disciplined for petty theft, and responded by poisoning the entire household. Of course, the First Order are resistant to poison as they are to disease – but a number of Second Order servants died. And some children as well."

I made no answer. He was only confirming my opinion of The Cook.

"The Matron runs a brothel. Several, actually. And she had a little side business in abortions, but she had to give that up because too many of her customers died. The Cleric actually was a cleric, you know? That is, he enrolled in a seminary, but was expelled after several incidents of drunkenness and lewd behaviour. Most unfitting for a clergyman. Always blamed his failures on First Order prejudice, and found he had more of a talent for preaching hatred than he ever had for preaching the scriptures."

"That's just what the Imperial Files would say," I muttered, though I believed every word of it.

Ommet ignored me. "The Beggar. Interesting character. Did you know he owns factories all over the North? Not nice places, from all accounts – low wages, bad conditions, harsh discipline. He employs the poor and desperate and keeps them that way. Of course, he does well out of it. One of the richest men in the province, apparently."

We'd reached the hatchway and the ladder going down to the where the Council waited.

"And then there's The Skipper. Not really a nautical man."

"I knew that!" I snapped. "Go down!"

But instead of descending the ladder, Ommet turned and looked at me. "He was an academic. Professor of History and Philosophy at a small University in the far eastern reaches of the Empire. Quite a good position for a man of the Second Order, but he seems to have harboured some resentment over the fact that he couldn't get into the more prestigious institutions. Wrote a lot of articles and tracts over the years, became increasingly outspoken. But that wasn't his downfall."

We stared at each other for a moment.

I gave in. "So what was?"

"He was found to have been abusing his students. Especially the weaker ones. For sexual favours, for money – but mostly for power, it seems. He's a small man, Arton, who wants to make himself big by dragging others down. He won't be satisfied until he's dragged everyone and everything down."

Ommet leaned forward and put a hand lightly on my shoulder.

"Be careful of these friends of yours, Arton. Please."

"How am I different?" I snapped. "I'm a jewel thief, remember?"

"You are different. You know it. And if *my* friendship ever meant anything to you – then complete my mission for me. Get those documents to the Empress."

The dirt and bruising and dried blood on his face only made the blue of his eyes shine more brightly. I stared at him, knowing the concern and desperation behind his words, struggling to find an answer.

"Hoy there! Mr Wraith!" the Mate shouted from across the deck. "Don't keep the Council waiting! Get below with him!"

I grabbed Ommet, spun him round, and pushed him down the ladder. Harder than I'd intended. He had no time to grip the rails, and fell most of the distance, landing with a dull thud on the planking below.

"Well, here he is!" The Skipper's voice came up to meet me as I descended, and a cheer followed. "Good to see that, mates! An Imperial Agent on his face before the New Dawn! We can take that as an omen, I'd say. But we can't hear him speak from down there – get him up!"

I followed him down as quickly as I could, but Silent Ghiss had already dragged Ommet to his feet and pushed him in front of the Council. He stood and stared at them one by one.

"Let me tell you a little about this sad lubber!" the Skipper continued. "He's been going by the name of Ommet, but I had a little conversation with him earlier, and it transpires that his real name is Thylan an'Darsio. As you see, he wears the habit of an Arravine, but it seems that this is no disguise for he really is of that Order. And he has confessed to me that he is also an Imperial Agent, commissioned by no less than the Bitch Empress herself!"

The Skippers voice changed to a snarl in the last sentence, Ommet's face remained impassive, but I felt his inner wince.

"So, he is twice traitor, for he has betrayed both his own kind and his religious brethren. Indeed, it seems his entire mission has been to travel to the various Libraries of the Arravines – you know how these religious love their books! – and steal their most precious volumes. For what purpose, you may ask? Why, to send all these books and dusty ancient manuscripts back to Daradura for the Empress to add to her own library – or so he tells me!"

"And what does she want with them?" asked the Beggar.

The Skipper gave Bryn an irritated look, not liking to be interrupted in full flow.

"We'll get to that in due course! My concern was what he could tell us about other Imperial spies in the North, but it seems he knows very little. The names of a few contacts, all of whom will no doubt disappear as soon as they hear that he's been compromised – just as with that family that slipped through your fingers in Muranburder!"

Bryn's turn to look irritated. He didn't like the reminder. Neither did I, remembering the servant girl's fate.

Having scored his point with The Beggar, The Skipper continued.

"The one thing that would have been of real value to us was his ring, by which his identity as an Imperial Agent is established. But that, it seems, was taken off him by the Imperials on the war-galley I destroyed, and went to the bottom with them.

That all being the case, I was set to send him off the same way, and good riddance! Still, the wretch begged that whatever happened to him, I should preserve his stolen scribblings, for they contained a great secret. He gave me some babble about these documents having the key to the future peace of the Empire, but I had no interest in that! We of the New Dawn are not in the business of preserving the Empire, but of bringing it down!"

He stopped and glared round at the room, and received the expected return of cheers and applause.

"However, since we have the rare opportunity of a Full Council meeting, I laid my course accordingly and determined to bring the man before you all. Hear what he has to say, listen to his tale and we will determine his fate together!"

The Skipper sat back and began to clean out his pipe, very obviously a man who found himself with a few empty minutes on his hands.

I had heard the Skipper's account with a certain scepticism. In particular, I found it hard to believe that Ommet had begged for anything. But if he had, it would certainly have been for the precious words of Mirrion the Prophet, and even now I felt the desperate need in him to explain matters to the Council and get them on his side.

Desperate indeed. I didn't need to feel their emotions to recognise the contempt they showed for him. His chances of persuading them were slightly less than that of a cat in a wolf pack. But there was some curiosity as well, enough to let him speak. And by my judgement, none of the counsel wanted to know the truth of it more than I did - nor had more right, considering what I'd been through over those ancient writings!

So I suppressed both my emotions and Ommet's, pushed them down and concentrated on his words.

"Members of the Council," he began. His voice sounded dry and cracked, but no one offered him a drink. "Thank you for this opportunity to speak. What I shall tell you is a secret older than the Empire itself, something suppressed and hidden for many long centuries. This secret has been kept by my Order of the Arravines, but so long has it been in the Hidden Libraries that even they have forgotten its full meaning and true value. And no one else even remembers that it exists.

Yet it does, and now it has come into your possession. And with it to power to shape the future of this land!"

The Tailor let out a loud and sceptical snort, but nonetheless, I knew that Ommet had aroused their interest.

"You and I, our goals are not so different. We all know that there must be change, that things cannot continue as they are.

There is too much injustice, too much power in the hands of those who wield it only for their own ends – it cannot be endured! The people of this land will not live like this forever. The only question is how to bring about change, and how soon it can happen."

"We've got an answer to that!" the Skipper growled, and there was a murmur of agreement.

"You have," Ommet agreed. "And now I can offer you another! I offer you a choice of ways to take. For those ancient documents that I stole and that you now have in your possession lay bare the greatest secret of our rulers – that is, how they came by their Gifts and thus became the First Order!"

Outside, waves slapped against the side of the of the ship. Wood creaked, as *Anatarna* jerked irritably at her anchor cable.

Inside the cabin, there was utter silence.

"You all know of the Gifts. The First Order live much longer than the rest of us – the First Gift, so called. And they have much greater strength, stamina and endurance also – the Second Gift. Many of those attributes sometimes termed the Lesser Gifts are simply part and parcel with the First and Second of the Great gifts – resistance to disease and to poisons, for example.

But there is also the Third Great Gift. The Gift of Understanding, it has often been called. It is the ability to know the feelings, the emotions of another. It is often overlooked or dismissed as less important than the other gifts, yet by it the First Order can know much that is otherwise hidden. For example, one of the First, in full possession of the Gifts, cannot be lied to or deceived, for they will always know the true heart of those who speak to them. Thus in ancient times it was considered the strongest and most important of all the Gifts.

But it is not so now. And for this reason: the Gifts are fading."

There was a suppressed sound in the cabin, a sort of collective sigh. To hear this, to hear the weakness of the rulers exposed, and by one of their own servants – that was something the New Dawn had not expected, and they could not help but greet it with satisfaction.

"Where once the First Order lived several hundred years, now they rarely reach a century and a half, and many do not live much past the century. They are still stronger and healthier than most people, but no longer by so great a margin. They do not let it be known, but some have suffered from maladies that would not have touched their ancestors. Some of these have even been fatal. And the Third Gift is almost unknown among them now. Only a few still have it, and that weakly."

The Skipper nodded. "This is true, and it is good to hear, but it is suspected by many, and we have had confirmation from our own sources. Tell us something we didn't know!"

"I will," Ommet replied. "I will tell you something most of the First Order do not know. I will tell you why the Gifts are fading."

He had them now. Even the Skipper leaned forward a little, his pipe forgotten.

"It is believed by almost all, First and Second Order alike, that the Gifts are innate, that the First Order are of a different race in whom these attributes are natural. The most commonly accepted theory – accepted by scholars, nobles, commoners all alike – is that the First Order came to these lands from some far distant place at a time when the native peoples were divided into tribes: primitive, fractious and often at war. It is believed that the First Order, largely by the strength of their Gifts, established peace and brought the tribes together under their rule.

That is a lie.

In actual fact, the First and Second Orders are one people, with a common ancestry. The Gifts were not inherent – rather they were, and are, literally Gifts! Gifts from God. Special blessings with which certain people were endowed by the Divine in order that they might be better equipped to serve both the Almighty and the People as leaders.

The documents I took from the Hidden Library of the Arravines are proof of this. They are the actual words of the Prophet Mirrion, written in his own hand – which can be proven, there are a few other examples to which they can be compared. In those writings, he describes how the First King of all the Tribes – himself a chieftain of the tribes, no outsider come from afar but one of the same people – this man, on the night before his coronation, prayed for wisdom and strength to lead his people. He prayed this, not from his own desire for power but out of his true love for them. And, as Mirrion attests, his prayer was answered by the bestowing of the Gifts on him and his descendants, that they might rule with wisdom and strength and – above all – with love!

For this is the secret of the Gifts: that they are based in love. And whilst that King and his descendants ruled with love for all the people, the Gifts remained strong in them, as promised by the Divine.

But in time, they became proud. They began to think of the Gifts as their natural right, and to rule not with love but with pride. Terrible things were done and the Kingdom fell into warfare and bloodshed. Kings arose who lusted for fame and glory and power, and under their rule the Kingdom became an Empire. But the truth of their past was hidden, suppressed, denied. It was wiped from the histories, it could not even be spoken of, and thus the Kingdom based on love was replaced by the Empire based on a Lie. An Empire of Silence, where the truth could not be spoken.

And as a result, now the Gifts are failing. Many in the First Order claim that it is because they have not been pure enough, that they have polluted their blood by mingling it with that of the Second Order, that they have allowed the Second Order to rise above themselves and that they must be pushed down, made into slaves and the First Order bloodline must be cleansed in order to restore the Gifts.

But the fact is that they have faded because the truth of them has been denied, and the love that was at their heart has been abandoned. And while so many of the First Order continue in this path, this arrogance and cruelty, this lust for power, this fear and hatred of the Second Order, then their gifts will continue to fade, until they are no more than common people.

The Gifts are the blessing of the Divine, the Holy sanction of the right to rule, given to enable that rule to be better, given to ensure good rule based on true love for all people. Under such rule, this was the most blessed of lands. And it can come again, for the power of the Gifts remains in the descendants of The First King. The gifts can be rekindled!

I know this for a fact. For when I met with the Empress Anatarna, I loved her – and she loved me. And you may think that an unlikely thing, that one of the First Order and moreover, the greatest in the Empire, should love such a lowly being as myself, one of the Second Order, a religious of no great value in the world – yet it happened, and I believe that this was a miracle, another Gift if you will. As all love is a gift to those who experience it, but this in particular was a Gift for the Empire, for it showed her – Anatarna, the Empress – that the gifts could be rekindled, through this love.

Let me tell what happened between us. As our love grew, and as we each acknowledged it, so the strength of the Gifts in her increased. In particular, the Third Gift. For though she was very strong in the Gifts, for one of her generation, yet only rarely had she had any sense of how another person might be feeling. And this had only occurred between her and others of the First Order, and only those to whom she had been especially close.

Yet now she began to experience my emotions. She knew her love for me was returned, for she could feel it in me. And I will tell you something even more wonderful – I could feel her love as well! This is the greatest miracle of the Third Gift, which has been hidden from the world for hundreds of years: when it is brought to life by love between First and Second Orders, then it flows both ways! When we looked on each other, our emotions rose and mingled until sometimes we could not tell whose feelings they were. There was only a great and wonderful knowledge of loving and of being loved, and there are no words in existence to tell you what an awesome thing that was."

Waves slapped against the side of the ship. On deck someone shouted an order.

I barely heard them. I was in the past, remembering.

Sitting in the sunshine, on the old bench outside our home, my elder brother with me, while father talked and showed us something he was making, some small carving. Mother came out to join us, putting round her arms round us. And love flowed from her, flowed into us – and returned from us, from Father and Brother and me. Love for her, for each other, for all of us, love flowing and mingling freely...

I could barely remember their faces – Mother and Father and my brother – but I could remember their love, the power and wonder and absolute assurance of it. I had not thought of it for a very long time, but I had never forgotten it. Nor could I, nor would I, though the memory brought tears to my eyes.

The silence was broken by a strange sort of noise from the Skipper. A sort of bark, as though he had tried to laugh but it had caught in his throat. It drew me out of my memory, back into the close and smelly cabin.

He swallowed, took a deep breath, and rapped his pipe on the table as if calling for order, though no one else was speaking.

"So this is the solution you're offering us, Friar? You want us all to fall in love?"

This time he managed a sort of laugh, and some of the others joined in.

Ommet shook his head. "No. I simply tell my story so that you know that I speak from experience. I testify that this is true, that the Gifts are what I have said and as Mirrion the Prophet wrote. All I ask of you as that you let me take those documents to Daradura. Or send them there without me, if you prefer. With those writings in hand, Anatarna will have the proof she needs to remake the Empire! She will take them before the Council of Lords, she will overrule those who wish to crush the Second Order – especially the Grand Duke, Baron Crombard and their allies! The truth will be known again, the Gifts, the true Gifts, will be re-kindled and once more we will live in a land ruled by love. True love, not simply talked about but, by the grace of God and the power of the Gifts, love which is *known!*"

"Love which is known," said the Skipper, thoughtfully. He had been re-filling his pipe whilst Ommet spoke, and now peered into the bowl. "Get me a light!" he barked.

Someone lit a taper from a lantern, and handed it too him. He puffed his pipe into life, blew out the taper, and blew a smoke ring.

"I love my pipe," he said at last. A chuckle spread round the table, and I felt Ommet's hopes die. Or was it my own I felt?

"I love my pipe," he repeated. "But it doesn't give me orders!"

More laughter.

"I love a nice glass of rum, I love a fair wind, and I love my pipe – but I love freedom above all else!"

A cheer went up, and the Cleric pounded the table in appreciation.

"You've told us a bit of history, Mr Traitor, and said some gabble about the truth. Well, let me tell you some true history!"

He pushed back his chair and stood up. He leant forward, weight on one hand and jabbed the stem of his pipe at Ommet.

"My people were once known as the Grof Varnark, the Tribe of the Sea Hawk, and we ruled these Northlands, not by love, not by gifts from some deity, but by strength and right of conquest! People call me Skipper, for I am commander of this vessel – but in those days I would have been addressed as Ahn Gravin, which means Sea Lord! In those days we were warriors who bowed to no one and our blades were feared and honoured in every trading port or fishing village along this coast and up its rivers! All of us here can trace our ancestry back to those ancient tribes, to the time when we were free people, proud people!"

He laughed, contempt in every tone of his voice and crease of his face.

"And now you come here with this prattle of 'love', and you want us to help strengthen the Gifts by which the First Order have oppressed us? Now, when – by your own admission! – they are failing at last, you want us to build them up again! You are not only a traitor but a fool. But I will tell you this, *fool,* that the future of this land will not be found in pretty little love stories or the dusty writings of dead Prophets. No, the future is blood and fire and the death of every last one of the cursed First Order! The time of the Tribes will come again, the time of our strength and our FREEDOM!"

He shouted that last word, hammering the table with his fist as he did so, and the room erupted into hammering and cheering.

In the middle of it all Ommet stood silently. I felt his sadness. And I felt his anger as well. I felt the words building in him, and I would have stopped him if I could, but with all eyes on the Friar, I had no chance to intervene.

As the applause died away, the words came out of him.

"The truth of those times was not one of pride and glorious freedom, but of constant warfare, fear and bloodshed. And you should know that, should you not, Skipper? Wasn't that your subject, the Pre-Kingdom history of the land? Back in the days when you were not Skipper, but Professor, at Imperial College in the University of Dretton? Before you were dismissed for abusing your students?"

The Skipper turned white, and for a moment was speechless. His mouth open, and he gasped, but could not form any words.

The other members of the Council might have spoken, but no one did. Perhaps they were just as shocked as the Skipper. Or perhaps not. Bryn in particular was looking at him with interest, and I wondered if this was something he had not known.

Uninterrupted, Ommet continued.

"And you also know full well that you share no blood with the Grof Varnark. For your mother was from the South of the Empire, a land that was not even part of the First Kingdom, a place the ancient tribes never ruled. And your father was from overseas, a man of Argreddon, I believe, who came to the Empire to find work as a servant in a First Order household."

Had the table not been in his way, I think that the Skipper would have assaulted Ommet himself. Instead, he found his voice.

"SILENCE HIM!" he screamed, and Ghiss stepped forward, hammering Ommet to the floor with one blow.

For a moment then, no one spoke. The Skipper continued to stand, glaring down at Ommet and panting, indeed gasping for breath, so much so that I wondered if he were about to collapse and join Ommet on the floor. But he finally managed to regain enough control to speak.

"Take this... filth, cut his throat and throw him overboard."

Ghiss, still standing over the Ommet, looked at the Beggar for confirmation. Bryn pursed his lips then gave a slight shake of his head.

"I think that, since this man has been brought before the Council, then his fate should be for the Council to decide."

The Skipper didn't look at Bryn. Instead, he clenched his fists, closed his eyes, took a deep breath and sat down.

"Very well," he said. His voice sounded strained. "We will put it to a vote. I propose that we execute this Imperial Agent forthwith. Who says 'aye' to that?"

He raised his hand, and there was a chorus of 'aye's as the rest of the Council followed suit. Including the Beggar.

I had felt a faint stirring of hope that Bryn, for whatever purpose, intended to save Ommet. But that failed on the show of hands.

"Any nays?" asked the Skipper, emphasising the point. There was no response, and of course none was expected. "Good, then that's settled. Perhaps you would have your man Ghiss deal with it?"

"Ah, no. There is one other matter to decide."

The Skipper glared down at the Beggar, the Beggar stared back with just the faintest trace of a sneer. And at that moment I realised that what was happening here was only incidentally to do with Ommet. The Beggar was launching an attack on the Skipper's authority. Ommet's revelation about the Skipper's past had given Bryn an opportunity to assert himself in front of the rest of the Council.

I wondered how long they had been playing this power game. It put Bryn's betrayal of me in a new light. The Skipper had always had plans to use me, so getting me caught by the Baron would have been a point to the Beggar. My life had just been another card for Bryn to turn over.

And how long would their game last? I had no doubt that eventually there would be a serious and fatal falling out. Both intended to be undisputed leaders of the New Dawn – and of whatever took the place of the Empire, should their plans for revolution work out.

I glanced at the other Council members, wondering if they had chosen sides yet. Perhaps it was my imagination, but I thought I saw the same calculating look on all their faces. They were obviously weighing up who best to support and who to betray.

And in that moment I saw the future of the New Dawn. If they were not destroyed by the Empire, they would destroy themselves. Any hopes I might have had of being a positive influence were futile. With these people, all roads ended in death.

"What other matter?" The Skipper ground the words out between clenched teeth. Clearly he recognised what Bryn was doing, but couldn't find a way out of it.

"Why, the proper way to dispose of him," said the Beggar lightly. "After all, it's not every day we get the chance to execute an Imperial Agent. Let's make a proper show of it! I say, keep him alive until we've taken Vorgranstern, then we'll do it in public. I have a place where we can put him, all snug and safe until then."

Ironically, that was close to what I had suggested on the voyage, but the Beggar had very different motives. It was entirely obvious to me, and probably to everyone else in the room, that Bryn wanted to chance to find out what else Ommet knew about the Skipper. And – I could almost see the thought entering their heads, one at a time – what he might know about *them*. Things that perhaps they wouldn't want anyone else in the New Dawn knowing. Especially not the Beggar.

The Skipper saw that as well, and quickly seized on the chance to recover control. "No!" he said flatly. "We've voted for his immediate death, and that's the course we'll keep to!"

There was a murmur of assent round the table, and Bryn frowned slightly, realising that he had overplayed his hand. "Very well then," he agreed reluctantly. "How is it to be done?"

There was a moments silence, as the Council considered the possibilities. It was broken by a voice from the back of the room.

"Let's shoot him."

It was my voice. I was as surprised to hear it as the rest of them. I had spoken almost without thought, but with the sudden feeling that this was the moment, the one possible moment, where I could find a little leverage, get a hold on the situation, make an opening.

"What's that?" the Skipper snapped in my direction. "Do you have something to say, Mr. Wraith?" He was frowning – with all the tension between the members of the Council, he wasn't going to be patient with challenges from another direction.

"Well, I was just thinking," I began, hesitantly. In truth, I was thinking harder and faster than I'd ever thought before, trying to keep my brain one step ahead of my mouth and making up a plan as I went along. "I don't know how many of us here have had a chance to see these new weapons of ours put to use. This would be a good opportunity to show everyone what the fire-tubes can do! And what better target than an Imperial Agent? Give me one of those things and I'll do it myself!"

I was glad that Ommet was still on the floor, still laid out cold by Ghiss's blow. But as the words left me, I felt a cold shock of betrayal coming from him. Not unconscious then. Just laying still, and listening to every word.

The Skipper was stroking his beard, and the first indications of a smile were creeping across his face. The idea worked very well for him. The chance to show off *his* weapons to the Council – and thus make it clear who held the balance of power in the New Dawn – would do a lot to restore the ground he had lost from Ommet's revelations and Bryn's undermining.

"Yes! A good idea, Mr Wraith!"

"What does the Council say?" asked the Beggar, but the Skipper wasn't going to allow any further challenges to his authority.

"The Council has had it's say! We've voted for an immediate execution, and executed he will be. But this is my ship, and I'll decide how it's to be done! The Wraith has the right of it – this is a good opportunity to show you all what fire-tubes can do."

"I'll go to the armourer, then," I said.

"Belay that! Not so fast, Mr Wraith." The Skipper waggled his pipe at me. "You've no experience with using these weapons, and this isn't the time for lessons. Besides, I think we need more than one to make a proper show. Five should do it, I think. Go and ask the Mate for five men who know how to use the arquebuses. Then take them below, and tell the armourer to issue weapons on my authority, along with powder and shot. We'll do it up on the poop deck, I think – have him stand by the rail and blast him over the side." He smiled brightly at me. "I know, you wanted to have a play with these toys yourself. There'll be time enough for that later. But since it was your idea, you can give the order!"

"Thank you," I said, forcing a smile.

"Of you go, then. Bryn, if you wouldn't mind having your man Ghiss carry this garbage up on deck? Good. The Council will reconvene on the poop deck in five minutes!"

Chapter 18. Ashore

The Wraith left nothing to chance. Weeks or months of reconnaissance, meticulous planning, all possibilities considered and allowed for. That was the cornerstone of my success, that was the way I worked.

But not now. Now I was making it up as I went along, thinking barely a step ahead of myself, with no clear idea of what that step would lead to or how to proceed further.

It was terrifying. It was exhilarating. But – for the first time in a long time – it felt utterly right. I might not know exactly where things were going, but at last I knew where I wanted to get to.

Save Ommet. That was the first order of the day, everything else could wait.

Up on deck, the Mate was by the mainmast, watching some of the hands working aloft. Repairing rigging, I supposed, or something like that. He frowned as I approached and opened his mouth to speak, but I cut him off.

"The Skipper wants five men with arquebuses on the poop deck, and he wants them now! I'm going to have the armourer make ready. Choose the five best shots and send them down."

The Mate didn't much care for my tone, and his expression turned thunderous. But before he could get out an objection I'd already turned my back and was heading for the stairs, leaving him to choose to obey or not.

As I descended, I heard him shouting names. I had been fairly sure that he wouldn't argue with an order from the Skipper, however much he resented me passing it on.

Back down at the bottom level of the hold, I paused for a moment, allowing my eyes and nose to adjust to the conditions there. A shadow moved towards, me, gaining detail as it came into the light filtering through the hatch from the deck above, and revealed itself to be the Armourer.

"What's to do?" he grunted. "You're not supposed to be down here."

"Skipper's orders," I told him. "There's five men on their way down, they're to be issued with arquebuses."

"Oh? Powder and shot as well?"

"They're executing the Imperial spy. So yes – unless they're supposed to bludgeon him to death?"

He scowled, but turned and headed back into his little kingdom, muttering that he didn't care how they killed the bastard, as long as it was done.

I followed, my eyes adapting to the dim lantern-light, and found him taking some of the heavy weapons down from a rack near the powder-room door. Behind us, footsteps announced the arrival of the selected marksmen.

"Be useful and hand these out," the Armourer grunted at me. "They're all prepared, the match is already affixed to the serpentine," He indicated the length of cord clamped into a mechanism on the side of the weapon. "But you don't light 'em till you get on deck, understand? No flame allowed down here, 'cept in my lanterns, and they's all kept behind glass panes."

I looked and saw that what light there was came from lanterns set behind small windows, so that there was no risk of direct contact with them. A wise precaution when handling fire-powder.

"How long will the match last?" I asked.

"Don't worry none about that. Takes an hour to burn a foot of slow-match. Reckon the Imperial should be well done for by then! There's fast-match as well, a foot a minute, but you'll have no need of it." He indicated some small bags on a shelf. "Shot be in there, one bag per man. I'll get the powder for them."

He was carrying the keys on his belt. I noted which one he used to open the powder room door, then turned to the men lining up behind me.

"Here, then." I started handing out arquebuses and shot-bags.

The armourer came back, carrying five small leather satchels.

"The powder's in that?" It didn't seem a very safe way of carrying such dangerous stuff.

"They's cartridges," the armourer explained, contemptuous of my ignorance. He opened one of them, showing me neat rows of paper cylinders. "Right amount of powder in each one so there's no clumsy fool can over-charge their piece and blow their face off. And then the paper's good for the wadding an' all. Thirty in each, and all counted for, so I want's all but one of them back, mind!"

He handed the cartridge bags out, with exhortations to be careful to keep enough back from each charge to allow for the priming, and not to spill the stuff over the deck or they'd answer to the Mate as well as him!

As the last man clumped his way back up the steps, I turned back to the Armourer. At the same time I loosened the marlin spike in my belt.

Six inches of Brogin Heartwood, it was. Black as night, hard as iron, densest of all woods. The point at one end, intended to open up the most tightly laid rope for splicing, flared smoothly to a rounded handle at the other. It felt heavy and solid in my hand.

"What else?" the Armourer grunted.

"That, there." I pointed with my left hand, and as he turned to look, I slipped the marlin spike smoothly into my right. Gripped it round the shaft, and swung with all my strength.

There was a solid thunk as the handle caught him neatly over the ear, followed by a dull clump as he fell to the deck.

Druthy had been right. There wasn't much that couldn't be fixed with a marlin spike.

But, despite its proven value, I discarded it and dragged the Armourer's body – dead or unconscious, it made no difference – into the shadows behind the shelving. Taking the keys from his belt I ran the few steps to the powder room door. It was open in a moment and I was inside.

I had some tricky work to do in there. And dangerous, all the more so for being done in a hurry. But I completed it, locked the door behind me and threw the keys into the shadows. I had little doubt that the Skipper would have a spare set, perhaps the Mate as well, but there was no point in making things easy for them.

Then back up the stairs, double-time, pausing only just below the deck hatch so that my emergence didn't seem suspiciously hurried.

As I emerged on deck I saw that matters had been proceeding quite briskly without me. The Council of the North had lined themselves up along the starboard side, whilst other members of the crew had assembled along the port side, or climbed into the rigging for a better view. The Mate was marshalling the five picked men into a line athwartships, just abaft the deck-house, whilst the Skipper knocked out his pipe on the starboard gunwale and smiled genially at all.

I couldn't see Ommet at first. But I felt his presence. I felt the despair, the pain, the bitterness of defeat. I felt it as if it were my own.

The Skipper saw me as I stepped over the rim of the hatch. "Come on then, Mr. Wraith," he shouted. "You're supposed to be in charge of this!"

A thought struck me, an excuse for my tardiness. "One moment," I called back, and turned for'ard, towards the galley.

Just by the galley door was kept a barrel for the waste, with a lid to keep in the worst of the smells. I picked it up by the rope handles at the side – fortunately it had been emptied recently, and was not too heavy – and carried it forward.

"I want him standing on something," I explained as I came by the Skipper. "So he goes neatly over the rail and doesn't just fall against it. I was looking below for something suitable, but then I remembered this."

The Skipper frowned for a moment, but then shrugged. "Very well, it's your show, Mr. Wraith. Get him up on it, then."

I could see Ommet now that I'd come round the deck-house. Standing at the very aft end of the deck, hard up by the rail. Standing erect, staring forward.

I felt his faith, his utter confidence in his God despite the end he was come to. I felt his fear and the intensity of the courage with which he drove it down.

And I felt his hurt, his betrayal, as he saw me coming towards him.

I tried to send back hope, and courage, and reassurance, but I wasn't sure if it was getting through. Especially as someone shouted out a joke about putting the Imperial in with the offal, prompting a wave of laughter and further ribald comments. I had to laugh along with them, to keep up the appearance for just a little longer.

I dropped the barrel down next to him. "Up you get, you bastard," I shouted, whilst all the time silently telling him 'Trust me, trust me.'

He peered at me through the sweat and dirt and caked blood. "You'll have to help me up," he said. But as he spoke I felt a shift in his feelings. A change. Something so faint that I couldn't quite identify it.

"Help me up or take the chain off," he added.

Chain?

I looked down. Half concealed by his habit, a length of rusty chain had been wrapped around his legs, with the loose ends turned over the chain itself. It was not tightly secured, but his hands were tied behind his back and it would be impossible for him to free himself. If he went in the sea, the chain would see to it that he stayed there even if the arquebuses failed to finish him.

The Skipper was taking no chances, and my tentative plan already looked like failing. But there was no changing it now.

"You two!" I called over the closest of the sailors. "Lift him up onto this."

They got round him and hoisted him up, none too gently, to stand on top of the barrel. In this position he was clear of the gunwale from the knees up. The impact of the balls would easily fling him backwards and over the rail to the sea below.

I stood back, and met his eyes.

Courage, I thought. Trust me.

Did he nod? I wasn't sure. But that unidentified feeling grew stronger, and now I was sure that I recognised it as hope.

"A moment, Mr. Wraith," called the Skipper. "Before you proceed, I have a few words." He stepped forward to occupy the centre of the little stage.

I had anticipated this. Of course he wouldn't miss the chance for a speech. Never-the-less it put another twist in my guts. How long would he talk for? How long did I have?

In the back of my mind I was counting. I had been counting since I left the armoury, but I was no longer sure if I had kept it correctly.

"This is a small thing," the Skipper announced. "Just one more life, out of how many? What does that count for? But I tell you that this is a bigger thing than you thought – for this day we make an example and we send a message! This day we show what happens to those who betray their own kind to serve the bloody First Order! This day we show that to serve the Empire is to bring down retribution!"

He paused, and those assembled responded with enthusiastic cheers.

Myself included, of course.

I glanced around, saw the seamen lined up on one side. The marksmen with their weapons at the ready, The Council of the New Dawn, all six of them, with their hangers-on,

All cheering and shouting for Ommet's blood.

But someone was missing. I looked again. There was the ship's Cook, with the seamen, there was the Bo'sun.

Where was the Mate?

"Are your weapon's charged?" the Skipper roared at the executioners.

"Aye, sir!" They responded with enthusiasm.

"Your fuses lit?"

"Aye sir!" I could see the glowing tips, the little trails of smoke.

"Then prepare to shoot straight and true – For Freedom!"

"For Freedom!" everyone shouted, and the marksmen raised the weapons to the aim.

"Mr Wraith – stand clear and give the order!" The Skipper commanded. "Death to all traitors!"

"Death to all traitors!" went up the shout, and all but drowned the cry that came from forward, It sounded to me like the Mate's voice.

I'd lost the count now. No matter, it was time to go.

I looked up at Ommet. "Take a deep breath," I said, for his ears only.

He looked puzzled, but I had no time to wait for him to understand. I could hear the Mate clearly now, as the other noise died away. And so could everyone else.

I jumped. One foot on the barrel and an arm round Ommet, up on the gunwhale with the other foot, taking him with me, then pushing off with all my strength. The two of of us, launching out into the air, and a fractional moment to think 'What have I done?' Then the sea below, the sky above, the ship behind us as Ommet and I plummeted.

The water was harder than I'd expected it to be – and colder. The double shock of impact and temperature paralysed me for a moment, and in that moment we were already several feet down and sinking fast.

My instinct was to strike out for the surface, but that was pointless with the heavy chain dragging us both into the deep. And I had no thought of letting Ommet go. Instead, I struggled to turn myself round, to reach down to his legs and uncoil the iron links.

Harder than I thought, against the water pushing past us. Even harder, as Ommet's habit was billowing up around him, tangling my arms. Vision was useless, I could see nothing but a blur of water, and already there was a desperate need for air in my lungs.

Our lungs. I could feel Ommet struggling to hold onto his breath.

We hit bottom. Sand billowed up around us, a further obstruction but it was easier to reach the chain now that we were no longer sinking. I felt its hard metal in my hands, and tugged desperately.

Pointlessly. Nothing moved.

Panic was rising in me. In me and in Ommet as well. But I forced it down – no, *he* forced it down. Helpless and on the verge of drowning he exerted control for both of us.

It's just a lock, I thought. A very simple lock. You saw how it was wrapped. You can do this.

I lifted a link, pushed it, dropped it. And took another, pulled it towards me, felt the chain's death-grip relaxing. Pulled on on side, and it fell away, loosened... then the whole thing dropped clear, and we we free.

Free, and rising, but slowly. Too slowly.

Taking a fresh grip of Ommet's clothing I kicked out for the surface with all the power I could still summon to my muscles.

My sandals hindered me, and I wished I'd thought to loosen them before jumping. Ommet's robes billowed round him and me, dragging and slowing us. Above, there was sunshine on the water, but so far above, and my lungs were ready to burst – our lungs, I could no longer tell the difference between Ommet's feeling and mine.

But we were still rising, and I was still kicking. We were both kicking, Ommet's movement's matching my own, if more clumsily, but the surface was coming to meet us, like a ceiling descending...

We burst through, gasping air back into our lungs in an instant of the most profound relief and joy I had ever experienced.

"Weren't sure if you were going to make it."

The Skippers voice. How like him to spoil the moment.

I shook water off my hair, and looked round, treading water as strongly as I could. I still had hold of Ommet, and although he was trying, I could tell that he was about to sink again if I didn't continue to help him.

"That would have been a pity," the Skipper continued. "Being as the lads are all ready for their target practice."

We were still below the stern of the *Anatarna*. The extra weight of the chain had kept me from jumping as far outboard as I'd hoped, though I doubt if I could have gone far enough to make a difference.

Above us, the Skipper was leaning on the rail and nonchalantly re-filling his pipe as he looked down. The Mate was next to him, and on the other side, the barrels of five arquebuses were pointing at us. The rest of the space along the stern rail was filled up with the Council and members of the crew.

All were smiling broadly, which did not seem too promising for us.

"Do you still want to give the order?" the Skipper asked, provoking laughter, though not from me. I was wondering if we could sink fast enough to evade the balls. Unlikely, I decided.

"What, nothing to say Mr. Wraith? Waiting for something are you?" The Skipper continued. "Waiting for this, perhaps?"

He held out his hand, and the mate passed him a short section of cord. I could see the tiny spark that glowed on one end, and the faint curl of smoke drifting up from it.

The Skipper used the slow-match to light his pipe, puffing several times to get it going.

"Surprised are we, Mr. Wraith? Disappointed that all your old friends from the New Dawn aren't blown to hell, while you and your Imperial Spy swim off to freedom?" There was a sharper edge to the Skipper's voice now. "Did you really think I trusted you enough to let you down into the magazine without having someone check what you might have done?"

I managed to get enough breath together to reply.

"No. Of course I didn't."

And there was a moment's silence, in which I fully expected the Mate to produce a second length of slow match.

But instead, he looked suddenly aghast and abruptly turned away from the rail, so I lost sight of him. The Skipper was a little slower. He first looked surprised as the Mate rushed off. But shock swiftly followed, his mouth dropped open and his pipe fell out – all unnoticed as he disappeared from my sight.

So instead I watched the pipe, as it dropped towards the sea. It struck the upper part of the rudder on the way, bouncing off with a shower of sparks.

Before it could reach the water, flames burst up from the *Anatarna*, a gigantic fireball that broke free of the ship with a roar that filled the world, and consumed the masts and furled sails in its passing.

I grabbed a breath and sank down, down into the cool water, safe from the sudden terrible heat, and kicked hard for the shore, dragging Ommet along with me.

I swam as far and as fast as I could, despite the renewed pain in my lungs, despite the even greater pain I could feel from Ommet. I swam for both our lives as objects began to splash down into the water above. Large ones, smaller ones, some floating, some sinking. Ahead of us and behind us and above us. Something bumped gently on my back, something else narrowly missed my face as it sank past me.

But I couldn't sustain it long, we both had to breath, so I angled us upwards once more and broke the surface, gasping for air.

Instead, we choked on smoke, thick billows of it, rolling across the surface of the water. Almost as thick as the seawater, and almost as deadly.

Frantically, I swam on, though I could no longer see which way I was swimming. Even though my lungs were tortured by the lack of clean air, I forced myself to keep going. I could feel Ommet's increasing distress, his failing consciousness, but I had to continue. To stop would be to accept death, and I wasn't ready to do that, so I pushed on through the water.

Coughing on every breath, still I must have managed to get something out of the tainted atmosphere, something that enabled me to keep moving, though weaker with every kick. Had there been a breeze? Which way had it been blowing? Was I swimming into deeper smoke or away from it?

My legs were screaming agony at me. So were my arms – one still hanging on to Ommet, the other pushing through the water. Only my will kept them moving, and soon that would not be enough.

But my breathing did seem to be getting easier. And the smoke was thinner. I still had no idea which direction I was going in, but it was at least away from the deadly atmosphere.

Something dark emerged in front of me. A lump of wood, deck or hull perhaps, blown far ahead of us. I made a frantic grab with my free hand as we came up to it, caught hold and pulled it closer. Got my arm over it, and hung on.

Blessed relief, to let my legs rest a moment. But that only served to emphasise the pain in my arms. Especially the one that had hold of Ommet. He was breathing, but his eyes were closed, and he was making no attempt to grasp onto the wood.

I could still feel his presence in my mind, but only just. Barely a spark of awareness remained in him, and that was fading, drifting away.

If I let go, his body would do the same. But I couldn't hold him much longer.

"Ommet," I said. I tried to shout it, but my throat felt raw, scoured by the smoke which still hung around us. "Ommet..."

There was no response.

"Thylan!" I tried his real name. "Thylan!" As loudly as I could, as close to his ear as I was able to get.

And, though his eyes remained closed, I felt a flicker of response.

I closed my own eyes, and reached out with my feelings to touch that small glow of life inside him. Touched it, and poured into it all the strength and courage and hope that I could find within me. I gave him as much of my feeling, my awareness, my life as I could force into that tiny space.

It was like fuel on a fire. I felt the life in him respond, take hold of my gift and draw it in, and grow.

His eyes flickered. Half open.

"Grab the wood," I gasped out. "Hold on, Thylan. Hold on for your life!"

He reached out. Put a hand on the rough wood, scrabbled weakly for a grip.

"Further!" I said. "You have to reach further!"

He stretched out. Found a grip, a gap in the planking, took hold. Then with a burst of effort, he pulled himself further up and got a grip with the other hand.

The piece of wreckage tipped alarmingly and dipped below the surface as his weight shifted, but then stabilised, lifted again slightly.

Freed of Ommet's weight, I rested for a few moments before getting a better grip myself.

The air was still clearing, either because the smoke was drifting away or because we were drifting out of it. I could see a wider expanse of sea now, and everywhere I looked was the shattered debris of what had once been a ship.

Distantly, there were voices. Shouts. It was hard to tell direction, but I thought it was off to our left. I supposed it to be people from the village, shouting to survivors, if there were any. Or perhaps they were out in the fishing boats, searching.

Either way, I didn't want to meet them. I started my tired legs moving again, kicking weakly to move us away from the noise and hopefully towards the shore.

I kept that going for a while, then rested. Then kicked again. The air was clearing fast now, to the great relief of my lungs, though my throat still felt as if someone had run a file over it. Ommet had made no further movement, but he still clung on, and still breathed.

The dissipating smoke might bring another problem, though. Without its cover we would be clearly visible for anyone who happened to look our way. Of course, the villagers would not know exactly what had happened, but Ommet's Arravine habit would be hard to hide – and if the Apothecary was still in the village, he would be quick to identify the Imperial Spy.

I would have redoubled my efforts, but the strength just wasn't in me. I could only go on as I had been, and hope that we were going towards the shore.

But then I could hear a sound. The sound of small waves breaking. Just ahead of me.

And now the smoke was all but gone – at least over this part of the water – and I could see it. A dull grey stretch of beach, more grit than sand, strewn with old seaweed and fresh wreckage, the most beautiful sight I'd ever beheld.

A few more kicks. I put the last of my willpower into my legs and forced them to keep moving.

Our life-saving wreckage scraped on something. An incoming wave lifted it, pushed it further up onto the beach, where it dug itself in and refused to move further.

I didn't move either. Couldn't move. My grip on the wood slackened, I slid backwards until my legs rested on the coarse sand. Then I stopped, and there I stayed.

I wanted to stay there forever. But at the back of my mind was the knowledge that this was impractical, also dangerous. The villagers would sooner or later begin exploring along the shoreline to see what or perhaps who had been washed up. It would not do for them to find us.

I'm stronger than I look. More resilient than most. I have greater stamina and recover more quickly than normal people. Not that it felt like it just now, but I knew I could still make an effort, and that I had to.

I raised my head enough to look around. The grey beach sloped quite steeply up from the waterline for about thirty feet, till it met a cliff of crumbling black rock. Not high, no more than twenty feet, but hard climbing – probably impossible in my present state, and certainly impossible for Ommet.

The good thing about the cliff was that it had shed pieces of itself all over the beach – rocks large and small littered the sand, some large enough to hide us from the village.

I pushed myself up onto my knees, and looked back out to sea.

The smoke was all gone now. So was the *Anatarna,* apart from the bits of wreckage scattered across the bay, none appearing to be larger than that which had saved us. If there was any more of the ship left, it was down on bottom.

Where we had been, I thought with a shudder. Where we nearly stayed. I decided that I'd had enough of seafaring. From now on I'd stick to dry land, the driest I could find.

Boats were moving slowly through the flotsam. Those in them were using boat-hooks to search through the debris, occasionally dragging something closer for examination or pushing it out of the way. Sometimes they hauled something inboard. The crews shouted to each other now and then: I couldn't make out the words, but the tones were not suggestive of any joyful news. They weren't finding many survivors.

I finally got to my feet, staggered along to the nearest large boulder and peered cautiously round it for a view of the village.

It at once became clear why no one had yet come to search along the beach. The cottages were simple affairs, rough laid stone and sod roofs, and none of them in the best of condition, with much of the sod appearing dead and dry. They had paid a penalty for poor maintenance, several roofs had caught fire, presumably from the *Anatarna's* blazing debris. I saw two houses with gaping, blackened holes, and a third still aflame. There was a line of people passing buckets up from the sea to be thrown over the smouldering turf.

With all this activity, and the boats still out, there had been no one to spare for searches. But that would come, I was sure.

I went back to Ommet, and shook him gently. Then harder. He looked to be in a very poor state. With all the blood and grime of his captivity washed away, his skin had an unhealthy pallor, and his breath was shallow. But I could still feel the life in him, and if anything it was growing stronger. Nothing like a little fresh air for restoring the spirit.

I slapped his face. "Come on! Wake up. We have to move." My own voice croaked and every word was painful, but that would just have to be ignored for now.

His eyes flickered open, and after a moment he focused on me. And even managed a faint smile.

"You changed your mind. About me." Barely more than a whisper.

"Decided…" I broke off to cough, which was even more painful than talking "…liked you better than the New Dawn."

"Is that what you…" he paused, tried again. "…what you do if you don't like someone?"

"Bit extreme," I admitted. "Wanted to make my feelings clear."

Ommet made a wheezing noise that might have been intended as a chuckle. "Point well made." A frown crossed his face. "Pity about…" His voice trailed off, he coughed weakly and spat out some bile.

"About the Prophet's Writings?" I asked. "Oh, yes. Glad you reminded me. We need find them."

"Find them?" Suddenly, Ommet's voice was stronger and his eyes wide open. Hope is a great revitaliser, and I could feel the hope suddenly surge through him. "They're not destroyed with the ship?"

I shook my head. "The Skipper was good enough to send them ashore first. With any luck, they're still in the village. Things look to be in some confusion just now, so we may have a chance to sneak them out. And help ourselves to dry clothes and a few supplies while we're at it."

Ommet nodded, and pushed himself upright. There was strength in him still. There was always strength in him, when it was needed. "Let's go, then."

But he staggered when he tried to walk, and I had to help him over some of the boulders. However, in spite of that inconvenience they were still more of a blessing than a curse, for under their cover we were able to make our way closer to the village.

Behind the row of cottages along the top of the beach, the cliff dropped much lower than where we had first landed, promising an exit route. Tall wooden structures were dotted here and there between the buildings – my guess was that these were for smoking fish before sending them off to market.

Up on the more solid land behind the cottages was the larger building I had seen from the *Anatarna's* deck. It looked out of place in a fishing village, and I suspected that this was an investment by the New Dawn. Likely it had acted as a barracks and perhaps a training ground for the extra crew who had manned the *Anatarna* for her assault on the *Warlord*. I pointed it out to Ommet.

"There," I said. "That's where they'll have taken the crate."

It looked deserted. The bulk of the New Dawn men had marched off towards Vorgranstern. With the fires now out, anyone left was either down by the boats or waiting along the shore. We could not hope for a better opportunity.

Even so, getting there wouldn't be without risk. The cliff at this point had dropped to about ten feet high, but even so I very much doubted if we could climb it safely. The only easy route up was near the middle of the village, where a small stream gushed out from a gap in the cliff and made its way to the sea. We would have to pass half a dozen dwellings before we could reach it, and some of them were built right back against the cliff face.

"We go behind the cottages where we can," I told Ommet. "Use whatever cover there is. While their attention is out at sea."

He nodded, but saved his breath.

We crept out from behind the last of the boulders. There was a nasty section before we reached the first cottage, where we were completely exposed to view, but no one turned in our direction. One of the boats was coming back in and all attention was on it.

We slipped behind the first building. An even sorrier place close up than it had seemed from the distance – small and shabby. No glass in the windows, just wooden shutters, scoured free of any trace of paint by windblown sand, hanging wearily open on rusty hinges.

Had anyone been inside and had chanced to look out we would have been seen at once, but there was no one.

Next to the cottage a boat had been laid upside down on trestles, presumably for maintenance or repairs. It's gear was piled up nearby. I noticed a long pole laying with the other equipment, and picked it up. There was a large iron hook in the end.

"Boat hook?" I wondered aloud.

"I think it's a gaff," said Ommet. "Used for pulling in large fish. Why?"

"It's a weapon, if we need one. Better than nothing, anyway."

We crept on. There was more cover here – big racks had been set up for drying the nets, which at least put something between us and the villagers. The boat was in now, alongside a small jetty. It was impossible to see what was happening – what must have been the entire population had gathered round – but not much imagination was required.

"They've found survivors?" Ommet suggested, but then a cry went up, Something between a shriek and a wail.

"Not survivors." I told him.

We hurried across the last open space and up the dirt track that climbed away from the beach, alongside the stream. It curved as it did so, and almost at once we were out of sight from the jetty. I allowed myself to breath a little easier. But not too much, we were still relying on the main building being empty. There was no cover to hide us should someone look out from the windows – which were all on the first floor, I could now see, and shuttered.

We approached cautiously. "It looks like a fortress," Ommet observed.

"Perhaps that was the intention? A stronghold for the New Dawn. Or a prison for their enemies. Newly built, I'd say."

And perhaps with funds gained from stolen jewellery, I thought. Had I helped pay for it?

There was no shout, no alarm raised as we approached. Nor was there any sign of an entrance on the seaward side. Reaching the near wall, we crept along it, heading for the rear of the building and hoping for a way in.

A high wall surrounded a paved courtyard, but the big gates were open and unguarded. Within, we could see an entrance to the building – a double door, and likewise left ajar.

There was also a stable block built out from the main structure, and waiting patiently in front of it a carthorse. Attached to the horse was a four-wheeled dray: and on the dray, securely lashed down and ready for travel, a large crate.

"Have you been praying?" I asked Ommet. "Because I think we have a small miracle here."

"The crate? The Prophet's Words? Truly?" Ommet could hardly believe what he saw, for the hope that arose in him.

"Truly." I confirmed. "All packed up and made ready for the road. I suppose the Skipper must have had some plan in mind for them. But his preparations will serve us just as well!"

"Come on then!" Ommet made to rush over to the cart, but I restrained him.

"Easy, there. We must trust this miracle to persist a while longer. We need clothing, supplies – and we must be sure that we're not seen making off with them. Food for the horse would be useful as well, we may have a long road to travel as yet." I pointed out the stables. "You check in there, see if you can find anything like that. I'll have a look around the main building." I passed him the gaff. "Here, take this. It's too clumsy a weapon for inside, anyway."

He took it dubiously. "I can't use this on someone, Arton. I'm still a cleric, whatever else I may have done."

I was very aware of the turmoil within him, and pushed it aside. There was no time for it. "Then just threaten them with it! But hurry. If we can get what we need and be on our way before we're discovered, then you won't have to use it all!"

He nodded, and hurried over to the stables, while I made for the entrance to the main building.

The inside looked even more like a barracks than the outside. High ceilings and wide corridors, roomy enough for armed men to pass through in large numbers. A corridor ran to the left and right along the courtyard side, dimly lit by a few unshuttered windows. Ahead were stairs to the upper floors, which appeared even dimmer.

I stood and listened for a moment, but all was quiet. At random, I turned left and walked quickly along, past revolutionary slogans painted on the whitewashed walls.

"Death to the Imperials!"

"Down with the First Order!"

"The New Dawn will Rise!"

I could hear the Skipper saying the words in my mind. Thankfully, that's was the only place I'd ever hear him again.

There was a large mess hall a few doors down, and beyond that a kitchen. I rummaged around in the cupboards, finding a rather dry loaf of bread and a few shrivelled apples. A bit of red cheese, still passable – one thing about this hard northern stuff, it did keep well. And, unsurprisingly, a good quantity of smoked fish. I stuffed as much as I could in a sack and continued my hunt.

A little further on I came across a laundry – now mostly empty, but some discarded or forgotten items remained, enough for me to change my soaking wet sailor's outfit for a torn but serviceable linen shirt and a patched pair of trousers. There were woollen socks as well, very welcome on my feet which had been feeling the cold, but no boots, so it seemed I would have to continue with my Arravine sandals. I slipped the Skipper's little poisoned blade inside the sock, thinking it more accessible there, and once more transferred Ommet's ring and my little collection of professional tools.

I'd just finished changing and was looking for something to fit Ommet, when I heard a footstep behind me.

A heavy footstep, the sort that a booted man would make. So not Ommet – though I already knew that, I would have felt his presence.

I turned round slowly.

The Apothecary was standing in the doorway, his face twisted in fury.

"You!"

I nodded. "Yes. Me." I shook my head, trying to look dazed. "Something happened on the ship. I found myself in the water. Made it to the shore, and came here, looking for help. And dry clothing."

He shook his head. "I sent men along the beach. After the boats came back... they found nothing but corpses, but I thought someone might have made it ashore. You only had to cry for help. But instead you hid, and came sneaking up here..." He raised a hand, pointed a finger. "Why do that, eh, Mr. Wraith? Why hide from your brothers of the New Dawn?"

I shrugged. "I was in a daze, I hardly knew what I was doing."

He spat on the floor. "Don't lie to me, you scum! You were hiding because you caused that explosion, didn't you? You killed them, you bastard! You killed them all!"

"Look, I told you, I don't know what..."

He ignored my protests. He had already decided I was lying. Quite correctly, of course.

"I never trusted you! The Skipper, he wasn't sure but he thought perhaps you were with us. And when you gave us that Arravine as an Imperial spy, well that proved it. Ah, but that was clever of you. Because all along it was you who was the Imperial, wasn't it?"

I shook my head. "No, it's not like that."

"Shut up, you lying Imperial bastard scumbag! I know what you are! And what you did. I know why you're the only survivor – because you did it! You blew up the ship and killed them all!"

As he said this, he was walking forward into the room. He tossed his hat aside and shrugged off his coat as he did so, revealing a rather large knife sheathed at his side. Almost a short sword, in fact – at least a foot long. He drew it and continued to advance. You can't really tell how sharp a knife is by looking at it, but this one – single edged, with a heavy blade – looked very sharp indeed.

"You think you've won, don't you? You think you'll go back to your Imperial masters and claim a big fat reward for destroying the New Dawn? What did they promise you? A free pardon from pilfering all their nice baubles? A bag of gold as well, perhaps? Well, you're not going to see any of it!"

I was backing up as he came forward, but was very aware that there was not much space left to back into. I glanced round for something to defend myself with. Back in the kitchen there had been plenty of knives, not to mention pans, ladles and other potential weapons. A pity I hadn't thought to bring any with me. Here in the laundry there was nothing more lethal than dirty socks. The poisoned blade was still concealed in my sock, but a poor match for the Apothecary's weapon. None-the-less I reached down for it. But it had slipped down to my foot, and it was hard to fumble for it whilst I was still trying to move backwards.

"I'm going to cut you, Mr. Wraith. I'm going to slice you small and slow! You killed a lot of good men today and I'll see you bleed for every one of them. You'll wish you'd drowned before I'm finished! You'll beg to be allowed the chance to drown!"

I snatched up a wicker laundry basket, and held it as a shield. The Apothecary laughed.

"Make it last a bit longer if you want. Doesn't matter. The lad's from the village will be along shortly, and I want them to see this. So as they know what you've done. And you know what, Mr. Wraith? What you've done, won't destroy the New Dawn, it'll just make us stronger!"

He leaped forward suddenly, lashing out with the knife. I jumped backwards, catching the blade on the basket. It dug deep, weight and sharpness combining so that it went through easily, cutting right down to the bottom. I twisted as it did so, trying the catch the blade and wrench it out of the Apothecary's hand, but the basket didn't have the strength for that. Instead, it fell apart

He stepped back a little, smiling. I stepped back as well, found myself up against the wall and holding two halves of a laundry basket.

"Stronger?" I said. Keep him talking, I thought. While he's talking, he's not attacking. "How are you stronger? Your leadership is dead, your fire-powder exploded, your weapons gone! What's left of the New Dawn?"

"You think that the Council were the only leaders? There's still one Name left in the North!"

"You? You think you can replace them?"

He nodded, grimly. "Who better? I've travelled all over the North for the Skipper. I know all the local groups, all the contacts. It'll take a while, but I'll have them united behind me. All the more, when they hear what's transpired this day. And we will be stronger. No more divisions between The Skipper and the Beggar. Better off without him and the others, in truth! The New Dawn only needs one leader. And as for weapons – the Skipper loved those thundering fire-tubes, but we've got other and better things."

I was feeling something. Not my feelings. Not the Apothecary's either. Worry, mostly. And coming closer.

"Oh? Like what?"

He shook his head. "You don't need to know. A pity I can't show you – I'd enjoy that – but there's no time for such indulgences. I'm going to see your blood now!"

He stepped forward again and raised his blade, but instead of striking with it, grabbed the remains of half the basket with his free hand and wrenched it away from me. I made a futile jab at him with the other half, but he smashed it down with the knife, destroying most of what was left.

"Now, where shall I start?" he wondered aloud. He held the blade up till the point almost touched my nose. "A finger, perhaps? Or shall I open up your cheek? I did want to be a surgeon once, you know. Now I'll get my chance."

I could feel Ommet approaching. He was hurrying, desperate to find me, rushing down the corridor.

I started shouting, to drown out his footsteps.

"You fool! Your cause is doomed, you are all doomed! Why do you think I left you? For love of the First Order? You know nothing! Your plans are suicide, all you will do is kill more of your own people!"

And he was shouting back. "We're stronger than you know! We will win!"

The knife in his hand pulled back, lunged forward. I jerked my head sideways and the blade struck a musical note on the wall behind me. I dropped the useless remnants of the laundry basket, grabbed at his knife arm to hold it clear. His free hand grabbed at my throat and as he did there was a swish and a dull thud.

The Apothecary stared into my eyes. He looked puzzled. Then blank. Then toppled over sideways, so that I could see Ommet standing behind him.

He had been holding the gaff, but let it go as the Apothecary fell. The hooked end was embedded in his skull, and the long wooden handle clattered on the tiles next to him. A pool of red began to form on the laundry floor.

I'd thought the gaff was too long and clumsy a weapon to be used inside, but I hadn't taken into account the high ceilings. There had been plenty of room for Ommet to swing it.

He was staring at the corpse in shock. "I – have I killed him?" he asked. Almost in a whisper. "I didn't mean to kill him. I just wanted to knock him out. I thought it would just knock him out."

"Did you forget about the pointy metal bit on the end?" I asked. With more sarcasm than I'd really intended, but it had been a very trying day. However, I regretted it immediately as I saw and felt his hurt. I shook my head. "Yes, he's dead. But he was about to kill me, so I can't say I'm sorry. And if it makes it any better, I think he killed your agent back in Vorgranstern."

"But – I took a life. I didn't mean to kill him," Ommet repeated, his eyes not leaving the dead Apothecary.

"It was an accident, then." The shock I felt in him could quickly turn to crushing guilt, I realised. I stepped over the body and gripped him by the shoulders. "Listen to me – Thylan, listen!" Using his real name helped to break through, that and the urgency I was projecting at him, and he looked at me. "You had to act quickly. There is too much at stake here – we cannot risk losing the Writings again! You did not intend to kill him, but you cannot dwell on it now. You understand me?"

After a moment he nodded.

"Good. Now look around here. There are some odd scraps of clothing. Find yourself something to change into and hurry. There'll be people up from the village soon to see what's become of him."

"They can't get in," he said. "I was in the stables, and came out to see – him – just going through the doors. I thought there might be others coming, so I shut and bolted the gate. Then..." he stopped for a moment, and looked at me. "Then I felt your fear, Arton. I felt what you were feeling."

I nodded. "So you came in with the only weapon to hand. I'm very glad you did. But even with the gate closed, we won't have long. We don't want to be trapped here, we need to be out and on our way before they come looking!"

Ommet turned away and began rummaging around, whilst I set about tidying up.

Removing the gaff was unpleasant, but fortunately not too difficult since the long handle gave plenty of leverage. It came free with a nasty cracking noise as some of the skull broke off. Ommet paused at the noise, but sensibly did not turn to look. I piled together some rags to stop the flow of blood and mop up the mess on the floor.

The Apothecary's knife had been sheathed under his left arm, with a complicated system of leather straps around his shoulder that kept it snugly concealed whilst being easy to access. I rather liked the idea. It took me a few moments to work out how to undo it, but having done so I found that it fitted me quite well, with only a minimal amount of adjustment necessary. Slipping the knife back into the sheath gave me a welcome, if perhaps unjustified, feeling of security. After being weapon-less and threatened, it felt good to have a blade to hand.

Encouraged by the good fit, I tried on the boots. These proved a size too big, but with extra socks stuffed into the toes, they would serve, and they were a big improvement on the sandals.

Ommet, who had found himself a strange assortment of clothing – ragged shirt, leather waistcoat and dirty white canvas trousers – was not impressed by my despoiling of the corpse.

"Is that really necessary?" he admonished.

"I need boots, he doesn't," I replied shortly. "And I'm also taking his hat and coat." I matched actions to words, ignoring

Ommet's discomfort. "Now, help me up with him. We need to get him out and onto the dray."

"What? We're taking him with us? Wouldn't it be better to leave him for his friends to give him a proper burial?"

I shook my head. "Think about it. If they find his body they'll come looking for his killers, and we won't be travelling fast. But if they see him – or someone wearing his coat – driving off then they'll assume he's gone about New Dawn business. I hope."

Ommet reluctantly accepted my logic, and together we hauled the Apothecary outside. We'd just heaved him up onto the dray when there was a pounding on the gate.

"Ho there!" A voice I didn't recognise. "Mr. Apothecary, Sir? Are you there?"

Ommet and I exchanged glances. "Keep quiet, they'll go away," he suggested.

There was another burst of knocking, louder. And a different voice, shouting now. "ULGROND! Open up or we'll climb over!"

So that was the Apothecary's name.

"They won't," I said to Ommet. I pulled the brim of the Apothecary's hat – now my hat – down over my eyes. "Could I pass for him?" I asked.

"You're thinner in the face, and need a shave,"

"Can't do anything about the shave." I took out the knife, cut some strips off the dead man's shirt, and stuffed them into my cheeks. "This'll have to do."

The hammering and shouting had continued whilst I did this, but suddenly and ominously ceased. I ran across to the gate and opened the watch-hole, a small wooden panel in the gate that could be slid aside to allow the gate-keeper to observe visitors. Without being well observed himself – a crucial point in my plan.

I was confronted with the toe of a boot: someone was using it as a step to help them over the top. Not easy, as it was some twelve feet high, but possible if they were nimble enough. I dealt with that possibility by putting my hand on the toe – there was just room to reach through – and pushing hard.

The boot disappeared, there was a cry of alarm and a heavy thud outside.

"What the hell do you think you're doing!" I growled through the watch-hole.

"Sir – Sorry sir, we didn't know what had happened to you!" There were several men crowded round.

"And the gates were bolted shut!" said someone else, with less respect. Most likely the one who had named the Apothecary.

"As it should have been!" I snapped back. I couldn't hope to imitate the Apothecary's voice well enough to past muster. Instead I used the roughness I already felt in my throat and exaggerated it, adding a nasty cough. "Damn that smoke, it's got to my lungs!" I commented, hoping the implied explanation would lull suspicions, before I continued. "What's in here, on the cart, could be the key to the North, perhaps to the entire Empire – and I found the gates wide open! We've had one Imperial Agent sniffing round already, who's to say there might not be others? They could have been in here and away again while we were all down at the beach!"

"What do you mean, key to the North?" said the less respectful voice. I was peering through the watch-hole, keeping my eyes as close to it as I could, as much to hide the rest of my face as to observe the men beyond. However, it had that effect as well, and I could see the owner of the dissenting voice. A truculent looking young man. "The New Dawn's finished! Our weapons are blown to hell and all the leaders with them!"

"You've found no survivors, then?"

"Not a one! They've pulled the Skipper's body from the water, but there was no life in him, and none in any others we've found. Few enough of them, either!"

"Well, that's bad news. We've taken a hard knock today, no doubt about it, but don't think we're finished yet!" I borrowed from the real Apothecary's last speech. "There's still one Name left, and I know the Skipper's plans! We'll have to move fast, but with what's on the cart we'll turn this around yet!"

"How's that then? What is on the cart?"

I snorted. "Never you mind! Less said of it the better, especially if there's Imperial Agent's around!" I saw them looking at each other. Nothing like sowing a little suspicion to keep attention away from me. "Now listen carefully. I'll be on my way with the cart very shortly. There's no time to delay. That explosion will have been heard for miles up and down the coast, and word will soon get back to the Imperials! They'll already be out looking for their missing war-galley, and it won't be long before they'll put two and two together and come sniffing round here! So as soon as you've satisfied yourselves that there are no survivors, pack up everything and leave!"

"Leave? But Mr Apothecary, Sir – these are our homes!" That was the more respectful voice. Another young fisherman, I guessed.

"And if the Imperials find you in them, they'll be your graves!" I said brutally. "So get yourselves gone! Take what you need from here, get to your boats or go by land, but be on your way tonight! In the dark, if need be – perhaps best, in case of prying eyes! Scatter, go to ground, wait for word. The New Dawn is Coming!"

There was a muttered chorus of "The New Dawn is Coming" in response. It was clear that they were no longer very sure that it was. However, the threat of Imperial vengeance seemed all too real, and it took very little more persuasion for them to head back down the road to begin evacuating their village.

"Nicely done," said Ommet. "Do you really think that the Navy will find this place?"

"If not the Navy, then the Baron!" I answered grimly. "And those lads may be misguided fools, but even so I wouldn't want them to fall into his hands. Nor us either – so let's be on our way!"

We finished loading the dray with our purloined supplies. Ommet ran back to the gate, checked through the watch-hole and then unbolted and swung them wide. I walked the horse out to the road beyond.

It was empty, for the moment. I got up in the drivers seat – Ommet had to lay in the back: if someone should happen to see two people driving off, there might be questions asked – and with a flick of the reins we were on our way again.

The road was only barely worthy of the name. Some attempt had been made to surface the area round the gate with gravel, but beyond that it was no more than a wide track, muddy and rutted. It climbed steeply up the hillside, curving to follow the little valley that the stream had cut. Progress was slow. The horse plodded along steadily, but showed no interest in picking up the pace, and I was reluctant to force the issue. We had a long way to go, and it would be foolish to exhaust the animal in the first few miles.

So I spent a lot of time looking over my shoulder, half expecting to see some of the villagers coming after us. But the road remained deserted. As we climbed higher, we could see that the boats were still out searching the water.

"Some of them on the ship probably had family in the village," said Ommet after a while.

I didn't answer.

"They'll be reluctant to leave until they know for sure," he added.

"They can be sure," I told him. "If there were any survivors, they would have found them by now."

"Yet they keep searching. Hope is a hard thing to quench."

"But sometimes a foolish thing."

I felt his disagreement. "We need hope, Arton. We all need it."

I wasn't in a mood for a philosophical debate, so I kept silent. The valley curved round the hillside, taking the road with it, and Shelter Bay was gone from our sight. To my great relief.

Once out of view from the village, Ommet joined me on the bench seat. The road continued to climb, coming at last to a wide and marshy plateau, surrounded by high, bare peaks of grey rock. The sun was well down by now, and we were about to be plunged into shadow. I pulled the horse to a halt besides a pool of dark water, fringed with reeds. Probably the source of the little river.

"Why are we stopping here?" Ommet asked.

"We have something to dispose of." I nodded back towards the Apothecary. "I'm hoping we'll reach the Imperial Highway in a few miles, and it would be best if we weren't seen transporting a corpse. People might ask questions."

"But this is no place to bury him!"

"Who spoke of burial? Give me a hand, here."

Despite Ommet's reluctance, he assisted me in pulling the body off the dray. Then, with a "One-two-three!" we swung it as far out into the water as possible.

Where it sank only a few inches before coming to rest, the face staring up at the darkening sky. The water wasn't as deep as it appeared.

"Now what do we do? The next person to come along will see that at once!"

"I know." I walked down to the water's edge, put in an experimental foot. The water was indeed shallow, but my boot continued to sink. I was down to ankle depth before I managed to pull it back out with an unpleasant sucking noise. It came up covered in black mud.

The body, however, spread out as it was, refused to sink.

"Stones," I decided. "We need to find some stones. Toss them on top and the weight will sink him."

I started looking round but, although there appeared to be plenty of stones and rocks of all sizes on the surrounding slopes, in the immediate vicinity was only water, mud and reeds. Even the cart track was hard packed earth, only kept from turning to mud by being raised several inches above the surrounding marshlands.

"I don't think you need to worry about that," said Ommet. "Look."

There were ripples in the water round the body that could not be accounted for by the light breeze that was springing up.

The loose shirt jerked a bit at one side. Then there was a distinct splash next to the head, and just for a moment something broke the surface.

There were more ripples, more little splashes, and the entire body seemed to be quivering. A tiny head popped out of the water next to an arm, and beady eyes seemed to regard us for a minute. Then it disappeared and the arm moved.

"Swamp lizards," said Ommet.

I nodded. "Smaller variety than the ones we met before. But just as voracious it seems. I don't think we need to worry about the body." I tried to sound casual about it, but of course Ommet knew my fear. As I knew his.

"Are they poisonous?" he asked.

"Do you want to find out?" I replied. There was no need for an answer. "Let's go, before they finish their feast! I want to be away from this marshland before it gets dark – or do you fancy camping the night here?"

He shook his head. "But I do feel I should say a few words. A prayer. Even he should have that much."

"Why?"

"A last mercy."

"He wasn't about to show me mercy! I don't see why he deserves any."

Ommet gave me a sad look. "Arton, mercy isn't for those who deserve it. That's the whole point. That's why its mercy."

I wasn't sure about that, but I shrugged. "Very well then. But brief ones, and do it from the dray!"

Indeed, it wasn't a long funeral service. All the same, by the time we were on the way again the water round the Apothecary's remains was boiling with little scaly bodies, while others were scampering over the top seeking flesh. No one was going to find anything of the last Name.

By the time we were out of the marshes and climbing into the higher country beyond, the sky over the mountains was glowing. Magnificent in red-gold, fading to a delicate pink at the edges, a sight to take our breath and transport us – for at least a few valuable moments – away from the mundane problems of human life.

Such as being exhausted by the events of the day. How many times had we come close to death since the days dawning, I wondered? Hardly surprising that even the stunning sunset couldn't lift our spirits for long.

All the same, I wanted to keep going. There were a few lonely lights out in the hills – innocent farms, remote shepherd's huts, or New Dawn strongholds? The men who had marched out from Shelter Bay the previous evening had to have gone somewhere. Most likely, somewhere closer to Vorgranstern, but suppose some of them were still nearby? Suppose they had heard the explosion?

All in all, best not to approach them, I thought, nor to be in their sight when dawn came again.

So we pushed on. Ommet, after nearly falling from the bench seat lay back down by the precious manuscripts and was soon asleep. I kept the horse moving, and when it became too dark to see the road, walked in front to lead it.

Until, eventually, neither the beast nor I could manage another step. I led it off the track into a wider spot where there was a little grazing, released it from the dray and tied it for the night, before laying down on the other side of the crate – borrowing the late Apothecary's position as I had his coat and boots.

It was no more comfortable than my previous night's bed had been on the deck of the *Anatarna*. The stars above were the same as the ones I had seen then, still as coldly beautiful and distant.

But something had changed. Ommet was snoring just a few feet away instead of in a cell. Between us were Mirrion's ancient writings, that we had worked so hard to take possession of. And my heart was no longer being torn in two.

Overall, I decided, it had been a good day.

Chapter 19: The Imperial Highway

I woke in the first grey light of dawn, cold, stiff, and – courtesy of a light drizzle – damp. Even so, my spirits were remarkably high. After all, both Ommet and I would have been a lot colder and stiffer had things gone differently yesterday. Being still alive in such circumstances was uplifting.

But the physical discomfort remained. There was not even the possibility of lighting a fire to warm ourselves up, there being nothing in the vicinity but wet rock and grass – unless we wanted to burn the dray, which would have been a retrograde step. I walked round for a bit, flapping my arms to generate some heat, while Ommet (who had fared somewhat better than me, having kept his Arravine robe as a blanket) searched through the supplies we had procured and prepared a basic breakfast of dry bread and damp cheese.

Then we put the horse back in its harness and set off again.

The road wound steadily upwards through the hills, the horse plodded onwards. I cast frequent glances behind, in case we were pursued from Shelter Bay, but nothing moved in the desolate landscape except a few birds, flitting here and there on business of their own.

Ommet was driving, so I took the opportunity to explore the Apothecary's green coat a little further. As soon as I'd put it on I'd been aware that it was suspiciously heavy on one side. While trying to sleep in it I'd discovered a large, hard lump on the same side, which had added to my discomfort every time I rolled over that way.

There was no obvious pocket at that point, but it didn't take me long to discover where one had been hidden in the lining. I reached in and pulled out a weighty package about eight inches long and half that in width.

"What have you found there?" asked Ommet.

"It's called a 'Pocket Safe'. Made of woven steel wire, so it can't be slit open by a cutpurse. Supposedly keeps your valuables more secure, but of course, having something like this is a good way of announcing that you have valuables – and to a pickpocket, the extra weight makes it obvious. It drags the coat down on one side, you see."

"Is it locked?"

"Of course."

"And how long will it take you open it?" he asked with a smile.

"About a second," I answered, producing a small key from a side pocket. "One of the weaknesses of the system – you need to be able to get into it yourself!"

I laid the contents out on the bench between us. There wasn't much – some papers and a leather purse, which contained ten silver crowns, some smaller silver and a few coppers. And a gold imperial – probably worth all the rest combined: the last time I had any gold, the exchange rate was twenty crowns to an imperial, and the price of gold was more likely to go up than down.

"Not a fortune, but a tidy sum to be carrying around in your coat, and explanation enough for the pocket safe." I tucked the coins away again. "Nice of him to provide for us – we'll make good use of his donation!"

I ignored the disapproval that Ommet was radiating, and turned to examine the paperwork.

The paper was thick, of good quality, and had been carefully folded to fit into the pocket safe. I unfolded the first sheet and was confronted with a bizarre collection of numbers and symbols that meant nothing to me.

"What's this? Some kind of code, do you suppose?" I showed the paper to Ommet.

Driving didn't require much attention. The horse followed the rough track a the same steady pace as Ommet held the reins loosely and glanced at the document.

"A code of sorts, indeed. Those are symbols for various chemicals, the numbers probably indicate quantities. Or perhaps time to be allowed for some process to take place. An apothecary's formula, I would think."

"That would fit with our former friend's occupation. Or at least, his Name. What is it a formula for?"

"I've no idea. There are three Apothecary's Guilds, each one has its own system for recording compounds and formulae. They do not share their secrets lightly with anyone – least of all the other guilds! I only know enough to recognise a few common symbols, and that I've gleaned from some old manuscripts that I read on the subject. My interest in chemistry was brought to an abrupt halt when I made a few polite enquiries of an Apothecary I was acquainted with: his reaction was so furious that I was forced to curtail my investigations."

He took the paper from my hand and examined it in more detail for several moments, before returning it with a shake of his head. "I would guess from the layout that this provides instructions for producing two different compounds, which must then be combined to generate some reaction. What that is I have no idea."

I shrugged. "Little help to us then. It could be anything from fire-powder to perfume."

"Not fire-powder. That would be a much simpler formula – there are only three ingredients. And I doubt if it's perfume either. Once symbol I do recognise, because it is used by all three Guilds – that skull? That is a warning. It indicates something dangerous, like a poison or a strong acid."

The skull symbol appeared at several points throughout the formula, and again, double sized, at the bottom of the page.

"Something entirely in keeping with the New Dawn, then." I laid the paper aside, and took up the next one. "Well, this one's a little easier to understand. It's a list of addresses. In fact, it's a list of Apothecaries."

"From all over the north, by the look of it." Ommet peered at the sheet. "There's one in Neowbron - 'Clake & Jormyn.'"

"And Muranburder... Scla... Jurond... Foston Hakin..." I stopped reading the names. "There isn't a northern town of any size not on this list!"

"Except Vorgranstern."

"Yes. You're right. Now why miss off the biggest city in these parts?"

"Why have the list at all?" Ommet shook his head. "Why would they need so many Apothecaries?"

I looked at the other sheet. The one with the skulls. "To make something. A lot of something."

"Something dangerous."

"But not in Vorgranstern. Where they intended to start their revolution." I thought back. "Whilst he was outlining his plans, the Skipper talked about firetubes not being his only weapon. He had some idea about trapping Crombard and his men in the tunnels."

"And what then?" Ommet asked.

"He didn't say. He just said that they'd be dealt with. Perhaps with some sort of poison?" I waved the paper in the air. "My guess is that this is what the Apothecary was about. Why he went ashore. I thought it was just to hide the Writings, but now I'm thinking that that was incidental. His real purpose was to send word, and bring together his supplies of this – whatever it is – from all the places they'd been made."

I took another look at the list. "And what's this? Every address has another name written next to it. What does that signify, I wonder?"

"Read the names." Ommet had turned his attention back to his driving. We had reached a steeper than normal stretch of the road, and unsurprisingly the horse needed extra encouragement to start up it. Ommet supplied it with a snap of the reins, and with a snort of disgust the beast began to labour up the slope.

To lighten his load – and to stretch my legs – I left the wagon and walked alongside whilst reading the names.

"Cordwald. Graylorn. Burdar. Jarken… do any of these mean anything?"

"They are all ancient heroes. Warriors and chieftains from the time of the tribes. Not well known, though, you'd have to dig into some history to come up with them."

"But the sort of names that the Skipper might have known. Given that he was a Professor of history, before he took up sea-faring." I chuckled. "He didn't like it when you mentioned that!"

Ommet shook his head sadly, and I was surprised to feel genuine regret coming from him. "I spoke in anger, which was a mistake – but yes, he would have been familiar with those names. He probably chose them for their obscurity. Unlikely that anyone would use them by accident."

"Passwords, then! Of course. Whatever this stuff was, they wouldn't hand it over to just anyone. You had to go to the right place and give the right name."

We reached the top of the slope. I climbed back aboard and we continued on our way. Ahead, the hills we had been climbing through began to fall away into a wide valley, with mountain peaks beyond.

"The Imperial Highway must run down there," I said, waving my hand to indicate the view. "We should be on it in an hour. Or two, depending how much this track bends and twists!"

Ommet nodded his agreement. "Is there any more on those papers?"

"One more sheet." I took it out. It was older than the others, worn flimsy from much handling. It had been folded so many times along the middle that it began to tear as I opened it. "This is something different though, A letter, You see the heading? The ink is faded, but I think it's from a college. Do you recognise this crest?"

Ommet glanced over. "Much faded, as you say, but it looks like the emblem for the Ancient and Noble Order of Apothecaries. One of those three that I mentioned. If so, it is likely from their College in Jurond, which is the biggest in the North. If... our late friend... did an apprenticeship with a member of the Ancient and Noble, he would most likely have attended there to complete his training."

"Except that he did not complete it, as I read this. It seems he was expelled before he graduated. Not just from the college, but from the Guild – indeed, from the profession! Apparently, the Principal wrote to all the Guild Masters naming him and requesting that he not be allowed to train in or practice the profession. On pain of criminal charges should he attempt to do so."

"That seems harsh. What offence brought on this retribution?"

"Oh, there's a list of them. Foremost seems to be 'Disrespect to Senior Members of the Profession'. But there is also 'Pursuit of experiments and activities in Forbidden Areas' - doesn't say what areas. And that good old catch-all crime: 'Actions deemed likely to bring the Profession into Disrepute'.

"'Senior Members of the Profession' would probably mean First Order," mused Ommet. "I wonder, was he already part of New Dawn? Or did this rejection direct him down that path?"

"No telling. But from the fact that he kept this letter – and read it over many times – I would say that he carried a serious grudge against the First Order."

"Not without reason." Ommet shook his head. "Such heavy handedness in dealing with what may have been a relatively small matter – and look what a bitter harvest was reaped from such seeding! Yet with a different approach, this man may have completed his studies and gone on to make a useful contribution to the world."

He caught my look – and my feeling. "Sorry, yes, I'm preaching. Well, I am a cleric, after all. And I think my point is a good one. After all, would he not have been a happier man if his life had gone in that direction?"

"Well, he probably wouldn't have ended up with a fisherman's gaff in his skull."

I regretted it as soon as I said it – I felt Ommet's pain at that reminder all too strongly. This sharing of emotions was a mixed blessing.

"My turn to apologise," I said after a moments silence between us.

He nodded. "You say the letter names him? Well, of course it must. I would like to know that name, please. I – it will help me pray for him."

Little point in praying for him now, I thought, and probably not much point before. But I buried that, quickly and deeply. I was learning that careless remarks had strong consequences between us – and besides, what did I know about prayer?

"His name..." I paused. "That part of the letter is almost illegible."

"What do you think it says?" The downward way became steeper, and the turns sharper, demanding more concentration from Ommet, which kept him from reading it himself.

"It looks like – Ommet. Ulgrond Ommet."

I had been reluctant to share that, fearing that the unfortunate coincidence would add to my friends pain. But all I felt from him was a sadness and regret.

"Yes, well, I used the name because it was common in these parts. Hardly surprising to come across it. But I wish it had been in other circumstances."

There was nothing I could add to that, so we drove on in silence, whilst I returned the papers to the pocket safe.

The descent was steeper, and the bends more frequent, than I had anticipated. Despite our early start, the morning was half gone before we reached the bottom of the hill and the Imperial Highway.

We paused as we came up to it. A proper road, of course, wide, well drained and smoothly surfaced with flat blocks of hard stone. A small river ran along the other side of it, and the whole was flanked with the first proper trees we had seen in this landscape.

"No signpost," Ommet observed. "I presume we turn left here?"

"That would be the way to Vorgranstern. But I think we should go in the other direction."

Ommet shook his head. "No. The priority now must be to get these documents back to Daradura. Only when they are safely with the Empress is my mission complete – and the quickest way is via Vorgranstern, then up the Hruchin to Muranburder and on by the Imperial Highway through the high passes."

"Yes, that's the quickest way. And the most obvious one as well – which means obvious to Crombard. And where is Crombard? Last we heard, Vorgranstern. Taking that road will be to give ourselves and the Writings straight into his hands."

Ommet reluctantly considered what I'd said. "We'll have to be cautious, certainly. Disguise ourselves. Perhaps avoid Vorgranstern itself, take the back roads north up the Hruchin valley. We don't even know if Crombard is still looking for us."

"Of course he is. You know what he's like. The Wraith and the man who freed him? He won't let that go. And as for disguises, don't forget that we're on our own now. Your network in Vorgranstern is compromised, the one in Muranburder is shut down. If we go anywhere for help, it'll get back to the Baron. Moreover, he'll be looking for the *Warlord* soon, if he hasn't already started, and that might well lead him to Shelter Bay, and what's left of the New Dawn. He'll have no trouble getting them to talk – and then he'll know that the Wraith and an Imperial Agent were on the *Anatarna*."

"Perhaps he'll think we're dead?" Ommet sounded hopeful, but I could tell that he didn't really believe that.

"He would be a fool to assume that, and whatever else he is, Crombard has never been a fool. He'll look for us to have escaped, and he'll have a starting point to look from as well." I held his gaze, poured out all the concern – indeed, the fear – that I felt. "Ommet... Thylan. We're not safe, not by a long way, and neither are the Writings. We can't take any risks. Any more than we have to, at least. We've come this far by luck or the grace of the Divine, whatever you want to call it, but our lives and your mission still hang by a thread!"

He said nothing, but I knew he was accepting my word. "What then?" he asked eventually. "Do we cross the Hruchin and then bear south-east, through the Tormrine region? That would avoid the mountains and the high passes, there are many roads we might take, but..."

"But that would bring us too close to Sonor Breck. Right in the Baron's own lands, where every pair of eyes will report back to him – from loyalty or fear, it matters not. It's not a wasteland, our passing will be marked whatever route we take. Or if we go even further east, and make use of the canals that run through those parts, then we come nearby Zyx Trethir – Grand Duke Brodon's own seat, and if there's a worse place to go than Sonor Breck, that'll be it!"

I nodded at the road. "Turn right. We go west, at the best pace we can manage."

"To Scla? But there's nothing there – unless you mean to take ship again. But that means back eastwards anyway, there's no vessels there that would take the long way round through the Northern Ocean and westwards. To find something like that would be going back, again, to Vorgranstern."

"We are not going by sea," I said firmly. "I am never again boarding anything larger than a river ferry. My mind is quite resolved on that."

"What then? There's no direct way from Scla to the south."

"We don't stop at Scla. We keep going west."

Ommet was shocked. "But that's the border! That means going outside the Empire! Across the Obsidian Mountains and into Murkarin."

"Exactly. Murkarin – where Crombard has no authority, And where there are plenty of roads going south – not Imperial Highways, to be sure, but roads non-the-less. Then we cross the Obsidian's again, back into the Empire and make our way to Daradura at our best pace. You'll be able to use your ring again there, and call for whatever help you need."

"My ring? I thought that lost on the *Warlord*."

"I rescued it. You can have it back any time you like, though I suggest you keep it hidden. Likely the Purifiers will recognise it for what it is, and perhaps the word is out to watch for it."

"Keep it then. I'm sure you're better at hiding things. But – Murkarin you say! I've heard it's a barbarous place..." Like most Imperial citizens, Ommet tended to think of anywhere outside the Empire as a realm of utter chaos.

"A lot less dangerous than Vorgranstern for us at the moment! And whilst things may not be as well ordered in Murkarin as within the Empire, they are not totally uncivilised there. I've travelled in those parts on occasion..." (most recently to sell stolen jewellery, but there was no need for Ommet to know those details) "...and I assure you, trade and travel carry on there much as they do here."

Our deliberations were interrupted by the clear, high sound of a horn from our right. From over a low rise in the road a rider had appeared while we talked, and was coming towards us at a canter. He was wearing green and gold, colours which proclaimed him to be of the Imperial Postal Service.

We held our position as he passed by. There would have been room enough if we'd pulled out – the standard width of an Imperial Highway is two carts and two horses – but the horn had clearly been a warning to keep our distance. The Post takes precedence over all except military formations on a war footing and the Empress herself.

Ommet watched him thoughtfully as he disappeared in the direction of Vorgranstern. "If I could get a message to the Grand Chancellor – my ring would give me the authority to use the Imperial Post."

"So would that gold piece that we now have possession of," I pointed out. The speed and security of the Imperial Post was available to all who could pay for it. "But Crombard has already suborned the Imperial Intelligence service and half the Northern Fleet – do you think we can trust the Post?"

Ommet sighed and snapped the reins, stirring the horse into motion and directing him westwards. "How far to Scla?" he asked.

"I have no idea. But there are stations every ten miles where the riders get fresh horses. We can enquire when we come to one."

Our lunch was the same as our breakfast, after which I took over driving for a while – an easy enough duty on this road, especially as there was little traffic. The weather had greatly improved, there were even occasional patches of sunshine. It might have been a pleasant and relaxing journey, if the horse had not been so slow and our mission so urgent. Our conversation had raised the spectre of the Baron in both our minds, and the thought of his implacable pursuit was ruining the day.

Plus which, there was something else between us, as yet unspoken but which we were both very aware of. Sooner or later it had to come out in the open, and it was Ommet who finally did that. It came as no surprise, I'd felt it building up in him for a while.

The fact that I could feel it coming was exactly the issue, of course.

"You are of the First Order." He did not exactly blurt it out, but we both felt some relief from having it spoken aloud.

"Not... exactly. My mother was First Order. Crombard would call me a half-breed."

"No. Not a half-breed or anything like that. The Gifts go with the blood in full measure, no matter if the parents are both First Order or not. You are First Order."

"The Purifiers would not accept that."

"They are wrong about a great many things."

We continued in silence for a while, both feeling some relief that the matter was in the open between us. Both sharing in the feeling.

"How long have you known?" I asked.

Ommet shrugged. "For a while. Since I first became aware that we are sharing our emotions, I suppose. Though perhaps I should have guessed earlier: you were always so much stronger than you looked. But the realisation only came on me gradually. For one thing, I did not realise it was possible. I had no suspicion that you were First Order, and even then... it is love that allows the Gift to awaken, that enables feeling to flow freely from person to person. So I experienced it with Anatarna. I did not know that it could happen... between us."

"I did not realise it could happen at all. Not until you spoke of it before the Council of the North. But when you did, I remembered. I remembered how it was. Father, Mother, my brother Satha. We loved each other. We felt each others love. Just as you described. All these years since I have not thought of it, or if I did, I believed it just a child's dream. But it was so. The Gift flowed between us."

"Is that when you decided to rescue me?" Ommet kept his tone neutral, but there was no disguising the mix of emotions he felt. Pain included, which I could not but help to share and pass back. We were both silent for a moment, while we grappled with our feelings.

"One thing I learned with Anatarna..." Ommet paused, and I got a sense of how deeply he loved and missed her, before he gently quieted that feeling. "One thing we both learned, I suppose, is that self-control must be exercised in the sharing of emotions, or they become overwhelming. We learned that we must be honest with ourselves about how we were feeling – for that cannot be hidden from the other, to attempt it only brings confusion – but also that we must be firm with ourselves. This does not come easily. I found that it sometimes helps to concentrate on something outside of ourselves."

I nodded, and stared ahead. A patch of ground between the road and the river was bright with orange flowers, a variety I did not know. I concentrated on the vivid colours until we passed them by.

"I think that I was already coming to that decision." I resumed the conversation, cautiously. "I had known for sometime that trusting the New Dawn was a terrible mistake. I thought I might be able to influence them. That was folly. Betraying you – was worse than folly. I thought I acted for all the right reasons, but everything except my reason said otherwise. So I betrayed myself as well. I..."

There was a tree near the road, who's trunk had somehow grown twisted. I looked at it very intently for a while. I did not need to ask if Ommet had forgiven me. I just needed to deal with the fact that I was forgiven.

"So your words and my memories were the final things to convince me that what you said was true," I said at last. "But how is it that the Gift is awakened between us?"

"Well..." I prepared myself for a lecture. Ommet was at his most comfortable when he was lecturing. "There was a certain scholar. Ancient even in Mirrion's day. Indeed, we only know of him because Mirrion mentions his works – but not his name. None of this scholar's own writings have survived. But according to Mirrion, this scholar quoted certain words from a language that was even more ancient than he. Incredibly old. But the wisdom of this language was that it had more than one word for love. For instance, it spoke of the enduring love that you would see, for example, between a married couple after many years together. There was another word – what the word was we do not know, only that there was a word – another word for love of ones own self. And there was, of course, a word for love as it is felt between men and women."

"Passion? Sexual love?" I asked.

"Yes, but not only that. My love – the love between myself and Anatarna – yes, there was passion, there was desire, but it was not consummated. Not physically. We still found it possible to be in love, and that love awakened Anatarna's gift. Through that gift, we shared our feelings."

"What else? Was there also a word for the love within a family – such as I once knew as a child!"

"Yes. It seems that there was. And there was also a love of friends, a love *between* friends."

"I have not had many friends," I said. I spoke slowly, carefully, the better to control my feelings as the words aroused them. "As the Wraith – and even before then – it was better to keep to myself, keep apart. Safer. I did not spend long in anyone's company, I did not get attached. Until events brought us together."

"And such events! We have been through some interesting times, have we not? Sharing such experiences will forge strong friendships."

"And if one has the Gift – it will awaken."

"So it seems."

We went on in silence for a while. It was better that way, so as not to stir up more emotion, while we coped with what was already there. But that was not so difficult a thing to do now that it was understood..

"There was another sort of love as well," Ommet said. Back to lecture mode. "That was a word used for the special sort of love which God has. And, since the Gifts are all from the Divine, it follows that..."

"You're preaching again," I interrupted.

"Ah. Well, thank you for pointing that out. As a friend!"

"Sometimes, you really need that sort of friend!"

Laughter bubbled up from both of us. Sometimes, you really need to laugh.

Late that afternoon we came, not to a post station but to an Inn. Well, it was a post station as well, but this offered food and lodging to all travellers, not just the Imperial Post riders, and stabling for horses.

We debated our choices as we approached. "It's too early to stop," said Ommet. "We should keep going whilst we can."

"True. We have no time to waste."

"Though the horse is tired. It might be wise to rest it here. We could stay an hour or so, have a hot meal, and carry on a few more miles before it gets dark."

"A good plan," I agreed. "Though, I don't know how far apart Inns are on this road, but I doubt if we'll reach the next one before then."

"No, probably not. Perhaps we can buy some blankets, get some firewood as well."

"Yes, that would be wise. If we're going to spend another night out in the open, we should certainly do that."

We didn't have to say anything to know that the thought of another night in the open was less than appealing to either of us.

"Poor old horse has worked hard today. It deserves a longer rest," I mentioned casually.

"A good night in a warm stable would benefit it, I'm sure." Ommet agreed.

There was no further need for discussion. We both knew what the decision was, and both agreed with it.

We didn't actually ask the horse, but it certainly made no objection when we unhitched it from the cart and put it in the care of the stable-boy.

An hour later we were eating hot mutton pie, washed down with good ale, and an hour after that we were in the common dormitory – the Inn not running to the luxury of individual rooms, not at least for the likes of us, or who we appeared to be in our rough clothing and with our old horse and cart. Our gold piece, or even some of the silver, would have gained us better accomodation, but not without attracting more attention than we wanted. And in any case, after the last few nights, a real bed under a roof was luxury enough.

Ommet was concerned about leaving the Writings out in the cart, in their box, but I pointed out that to insist on bringing them in with us was to shout from the rooftop that we had something of unusual value with us. Staying unremarkable and unnoticed was our best security. He accepted the argument reluctantly, but once he'd laid down with a warm blanket and a full stomach weariness soon overcame lingering doubts and his snores filled the room.

I lay awake a little longer. Partially because of the snores, but also because I was still grappling with this new thing that had happened to me. I had been alone so long that I had forgotten any other condition was possible. But now I had a friend. A friend who I could trust to the death.

It was a wonderful and frightening thing, but too much to really grasp all at once. Especially not when I was so tired. I let the thought drift away, and slept.

※

I WAS UP WELL BEFORE Ommet, waking shortly after dawn. I was feeling surprisingly strong and refreshed. The Gifts, I supposed, were all stronger in me than ever before.

Leaving my friend still snoring, I went down for an early breakfast and to exchange gossip with whoever might be around. I was wondering if word had yet got out concerning events at Shelter Bay. Surely that massive explosion must have caught some attention, even in so remote a place.

Not so, it seemed. No one mentioned any such incident, and I was careful not to show my hand by too obvious questioning. However, I did learn a thing or two which set me thinking.

Ommet made a bleary eyed appearance while I was finishing my second bowl of porridge. He got his own and sat with me. I could tell that he didn't have much conversation in him as yet, so I allowed him time to emerge into wakefulness whilst I sipped on a mulled wine – a very good start to a day, I've found.

While he was still eating, a horn blast sounded outside, still some distance away but high and clear even inside the inn. A young man jumped up from his seat, pulled on a green and gold tabard, and rushed outside.

I went to the window and looked out, in time to see him ride out from the Inn yard. Another Post rider appeared, his horse panting: he handed over the mail pouch and the fresh rider was off at once. Not at a gallop, of course. It was ten miles to the next post station, where the rider would change horses, and that would be covered with a mixture of trotting and cantering.

I went back and sat down again with Ommet. "That's the morning mail. He'll be in Vorgranstern by this evening. There'll be three more pass here in that direction today, and three going the other way."

Ommet raised an eyebrow at me.

"I was chatting with that lad earlier. He tells me that this is a lonely stretch of road: most traffic between Scla and Vorgranstern goes by sea. It's only because it's an Imperial Highway that it's maintained at all, I suppose. But that's been a policy for centuries – to have good roads everywhere."

"For the post," Ommet grunted.

"For the post, and local traffic, certainly. But of course the real reason, that no one talks about, is that Imperial troops can march anywhere in the country with all speed – to confront invaders, or to put down rebellion."

Ommet grunted again. He'd turned down the mulled wine in favour of some local ale. "Very interesting. Why are we talking about it?"

"Well, I got to thinking. A cart with two men and a large box, on an empty road – it's noticeable."

"Yes." Ommet rubbed his face and yawned. "But who's to notice, when there's no one else there?"

"The Post riders. They'll notice. That one that passed us yesterday – he noticed. He blew his horn to keep us from impeding him. And he'll have been in Vorgranstern before we stopped here last night."

Ommet was waking slowly. "You're thinking that he might mention us?"

I shrugged. "Crombard only has to set a man to talk to incoming riders. And who will refuse to talk to the Baron's men? Why would they? Think of it - 'Did you see anyone on the road?' 'Not many. Two people in a cart, that's all.' 'And what did these two look like?'"

"Right. I see your point." He sipped on his ale and took a few more spoonfuls of porridge. I waited until he *had* seen the point. When he suddenly paused with the spoon half-way to his mouth, I knew that he'd got there – and I felt the shock of realisation run through him. "If he hears that from the Post rider, then he'll send men out looking for us!"

"Yes. Hopefully, he might expect us to head for Vorgranstern. But he's no fool, to sit and wait to see if we turn up. He'll have people out on the road. And not just from Vorgranstern. I've no doubt that he commands others in Scla, and anyone of these Post riders could have been carrying his instructions to be on the lookout for us."

"Or to send men to seek us! They'll be coming from both directions." Ommet looked at his porridge like a man who has suddenly lost his appetite. "We're trapped!"

"Not quite. There's a few turnings off the Highway. Some going only to small places like Shelter Bay, down on the coast. Or up in the hills. Dead ends. But a mile beyond this inn is the road to Casterlayne."

"Casterlayne." Ommet furrowed his brow. "Now, I know that place. Heard of it, at any rate. Slate mines, right?"

"Slate quarries. Scla slate is reckoned to be the best in the Empire, and half of it comes from Casterlayne, or around there. And how does the slate get down to Scla?"

A light dawned in Ommet's eyes. "Lord Tunward's Railway!"

"Right. Thirty miles from Casterlayne to Scla, and difficult terrain – but its all downhill, and they say the railway never takes more than three hours to descend. Rumour has it that its been done in less – two hours has been claimed!"

"Yes, I heard that, but two hours would be an average speed of fifteen miles per hour, which seems unlikely."

"Yes, but in any case, three hours is much faster than a man on horseback could manage."

"Indeed but…" Ommet resumed eating his porridge, but slowly. There was a faraway look in his eyes. "How long would it take us to get to Casterlayne?"

I shook my head. "I'm not sure. I didn't want to ask – in case word gets back to Crombard. But, from what I can recall, it's only a few miles off the Highway. If we left now, we might be there by midday, or early afternoon at least. I don't know how often the slate trucks run down to Scla, but with good fortune we might even get there by tonight. That's least as soon as if we carried on along the Imperial Highway. And if the Baron has got men out looking for us, this route would avoid them."

Ommet finished his porridge. "You know, I've always wanted to see Lord Tunward's Railway. Longest in the world, they say!"

I grinned at him. "Well then, it would be a pity to miss it since we're so close anyway!"

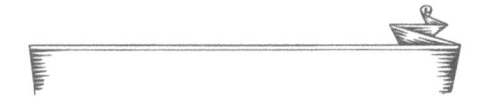

Chapter 20: Casterlayne

Once again, we were climbing, going even higher than before. But these hills were different from those near the coast. Drier. A small stream gurgled its way along the valley below us, but there were no great expanses of bog-land, not even when the road climbed out of the valley and onto a plateau. This was all dry stone, with thin patches of vegetation nestled into cracks and hiding behind boulders. They sought shelter from the harsh wind that swept over the landscape, but up on the cart we found none and it poked icy fingers through every small gap in our garments.

There was at least some sun to give a little warmth, and no cloud to shade it. In the distance, round-shouldered hills rose even higher, and beyond them were sharper peaks.

Ommet pointed to them as I drove. "The Hayata Mountains. Highest peaks in the Empire. The tribes which once inhabited these parts believed that God lived there."

"A good place to watch the world from, I suppose."

"A mistaken view of God. He does not watch the world from a distance, but walks amongst us."

I could think of several different answers to that, many of them sarcastic. But I was too well aware of Ommet's sincere belief. When he said that God walks amongst us, he was thrilled by the thought. I valued that in him, and so said nothing that would hurt it.

But of course, he knew. "You don't agree?" he asked.

"I don't disagree. But I have no reason to believe in God walking with us. If he's anywhere at all, he seems very distant. Perhaps on top of those mountains?"

I could feel Ommet wanting to argue the point. But he was as sensitive to my feelings as I was to his. "Then perhaps you need to climb higher!" He said it as a joke, but I could feel the seriousness behind it.

"For now, I'll just be glad to get to Casterlayne!" I replied in the same tone.

"Ah, yes. Casterlayne. How far did you say it was?"

"My estimate may have been a little wayward." I agreed.

It was about noon, and the road across the plateau continued on ahead of us, without any indication of human habitation. Not so much as a shepherd's hut, far less a town.

We had at least managed to replenish our supplies at the Inn. We stopped to rest the horse and made a good lunch from cold meat, fresh bread, red cheese and fruit, with a flask of wine to wash it all down.

"One thing," said Ommet looking back the way we'd come, "If anyone comes after us we'll see them in good time."

"In good time for what?" I asked. "There's nowhere to hide a horse and cart. We'd just have plenty of time to watch them catching up."

"Hmmm. Best to keep moving then."

Another hour passed, and one of the distant high hills suddenly shifted its perspective and became a lower and much closer mound. Not a natural hill at all, in fact, but a vast pile of broken rock.

"Did you know that for every ton of good slate that's dug out of the ground, there can be up to thirty tons of worthless rock?" Ommet nodded at the fake hill. "That's what that is, I'm sure of it. There'll be a quarry or a mine shaft somewhere nearby."

"I didn't know that, but it's a hopeful sign. We must be getting near Casterlayne. Nearer, at any rate."

The rock pile had been there for some time: moss was slowly covering the stones, and small clumps of grass were taking root in cracks and niches. The road took us round its base, then along the rim of a vast hole in the landscape just the other side. The quarry Ommet had predicted. Now silent, empty and abandoned, a huge scar in the ground surrounded by heaps of rubble,

"They might at least have tidied up after them," Ommet grumbled. "Why couldn't they put the worthless rock back in the hole instead of leaving all their rubbish?"

"Where's the money in that?" I asked him. "Whoever owns these hills and the slate in them – Lord Tunward, I suppose – isn't going to concern himself over how it looks afterwards. He's not here to see it!"

A little further on and we saw more rock piles some way off to the left of the road, but this time accompanied by distant noises. The ringing of many hammers, an occasional louder crash as of falling rocks – the sounds of a working quarry. Another road joined from that direction, with some traffic on it. Stout carts, laden with blocks of grey slate and pulled by teams of four horses each. Their drivers gave us curious looks as we drew near.

One of them was forced to a halt as we passed in front of it. "How far to Casterlayne?" I shouted.

"An hour's drive or so. Move along! We've got slate to move and we'll not get paid while you block the road!"

"Friendly folk round here," I commented to Ommet.

"They're paid by the trip," he explained. "The more slate they deliver, the more they earn – but it's not a lot. A man with a family will need to make four or five trips a day to keep them fed and clothed and the rent paid. Plus he must feed his horses and maintain his cart. They've got little time for pleasantries!" He saw my look – or felt my incredulity. "I read a lot. And this slate trade is fascinating, not least because of the railway built to service it. Lord Tunward is one of the wealthiest of the Northern Lords because of slate – after Lord Endranard and Grand Duke Brodon - but he pays his workers as little as possible."

"That's common enough. Especially amongst these Northern Lords. It's no surprise that the New Dawn grew so strong in these parts."

"Yes, indeed." Ommet nodded an emphatic agreement. "I saw documents back in Daradura where it was estimated that almost a third of the population hereabouts oppose the rule of the First Order. Not necessarily members of the New Dawn, they're too extreme for most people, but there's a lot of resentment against the Lords especially. And perhaps another third would be in favour of change, if not the complete overthrow of the First Order."

"And this Lord Tunward - would I be wrong in presuming him a staunch supporter of the Grand Duke and Baron Crombard?"

"You would not. Tunward actually spends much of his time down in the capital, where he leads the Duke's Party in the Lord's Council when the Duke himself isn't there. Which he isn't very much of late, since he and the Empress had a falling out!"

I felt a shift in his mood as he mentioned the Empress, and he fell silent. I knew the ache in him, the longing.

"You still miss her?"

"Of course. I love her. I always will."

"And yet here we are."

"Yes." He looked round at the barren landscape, the heavy-laden wagons, the distant hills. "Here I am," he continued quietly, "for the sake of love and the salvation of the Empire." He sighed. "Change must come, my friend. I only hope that what we do will help to bring it peacefully."

"The New Dawn's finished, and their mad dreams of blood and fire finished with them!"

"I know, and I suppose I'm glad of it – though I wish there had been a better way, even with them! Yes, yes I know!" He added that as he felt my reaction. "You had no choice in what you did. I don't blame you, you know I don't. But it was still a lot of lives ended, a lot of grief remaining. And the sad thing is that it could happen again. All the pain and anger that simmers here," (he gestured around him) "will find an outlet in one way or another. People like Tunward – and Crombard, and Brodon – think they are maintaining order and keeping control, not seeing that they merely stoke the fires that will consume them."

The road was descending now, and widening. It needed to, for empty carts were toiling back up to the quarry to collect another load. Yet another side road joined, adding further to the traffic, so we were now trundling along with our horse's nose very nearly in the cart ahead, and another as close behind us. The air was full of the clatter of wheels, the creak of harness, and the occasional shouts of the drivers – along with the mingled smell of horse sweat and rock dust.

"It was more peaceful up on the high plateau," I said wistfully. "Still, at least no pursuers will be able to catch up with us now!"

We soon had our first view of Casterlayne. The valley, about a mile wide at this point, opened up ahead of us, then the road turned to the left, following the valley wall and descending. The town was directly below us.

"Grey, isn't it?" said Ommet.

Everything below the blue sky was grey. Casterlayne was a jumble of grey buildings – dark grey, light grey, purple and blue-grey, but all grey. Around it the landscape was littered with heaps of grey stone. More waste from mines and quarries. Above the town, the hillsides were gouged and torn, as if some immense giant had gnawed at them, leaving bare grey rock exposed to the sun.

"And that'll be the railway, I suppose?"

I pointed to where wagons were arrayed in several long lines, parallel to each other. Sunlight reflected of lines of bright metal that led away from the wagons and off towards Scla – the metal rails from which the 'rail way' derived its name.

Some kind of framework had been erected over some of the wagons, supporting an assembly of ropes which were being used to hoist loads of cut slate into them. A team of horses were harnessed at one end, and as each wagon was filled they strained themselves to pull the entire line forward until the next one was beneath the framework.

"That's it. Looks like there's a rail-train being loaded – and another one about to leave."

Faintly we heard the sharp ringing of a bell. Men gathered round one line of wagons, and set themselves to push. The bell rang again and as the pushers exerted themselves, the wagons began to move forward.

The bell rang once more, and the men drew back. The rail-train continued to move forward, its speed increasing as the ground sloped down away from the rail-yard. The lines of rails drew together until just two remained, down which the rail-train travelled. I watched until it disappeared round a bend.

Our progress was frustratingly slower than the rail-train. Caught in the long queue of wagons, it took us another hour to reach the valley floor. After that, things became easier, as they turned off to leave their slate at the factories where the great blocks would be split and cut and prepared for transport down to Scla. We found our way through the grey streets until we came at last, late in the afternoon, to the railway.

Men were bustling around the long lines of wagons. I called out to one of them.

"We travel to Scla – who do we talk to?"

"Rail Master's Office," he shouted back. "Over there!"

A small building at the far end of the rails. Grey, of course, but with a red-painted sign that confirmed that it was the Casterlayne Rail Master's office. A busy place, with men running in and out all the time.

We left the cart and went inside, finding ourselves in a queue. I picked up snatches of conversation.

"I've got a hundred tons that must get to the docks by tomorrow night..."

"There's an order in directly from Lord Abberdy of Garanford..."

"Findal's Shaft isn't producing more than five tons of good slate a day, there's no money in it..."

"I can't get enough splitters, not at those wages..."

Eventually we reached the front of the line, and were confronted by a harassed looking man in a (grey) suit, seated behind a desk awash with paperwork.

"We need urgent passage down to Scla..." I began.

"Next passenger train is nine tomorrow," he snapped. "Schedule's by the door!"

"But this is..."

"Tomorrow, I said! Next!"

We were pushed out of the way by an angry foreman whose shipment of new tools hadn't yet come up from Scla and who wanted to know why. With little choice in the matter, we went back outside, stopping to check the schedule on the way.

"Only two passenger trains a day? It's a disgrace!" I fumed.

"Well, it is a slate railway, after all," Ommet pointed out. "Lucky we're not going the other way. There's only one passenger train up from Scla, and that doesn't leave until midnight. Look, we'll find an inn, get a good meal and a nights rest. Tomorrow we'll be on our way first thing! How does that sound?"

"It sounds... too late."

"What?"

Ommet followed my gaze.

From the rail-yard, we could clearly see the road down which we'd recently come. Traffic was still heavy, but a line of black-clad horseman were nevertheless forcing their way through.

"Purifiers!" Ommet gasped. I felt his shock and fear. It matched my own. "How did they find our trail so quickly?"

"Perhaps they didn't. It might be that Crombard simply sent men to every possible place we might have gone. It doesn't matter. They'll be down here in much less time than it took us."

"There are roads up into the hills – or even down to Scla..."

"They'll soon track us down. We can't outrun them, and we can't hide in a little place like this. Not for long."

"Certainly not until the next passenger train. So what...? Ah!" Ommet raised a finger. "My Imperial ring, of course. We just need to write an order to commandeer a rail-train and put the Imperial seal on it."

I shook my head. "We don't have paper or pen to hand, and I doubt if there's time to find it before Crombard's men catch up with us. And besides, if you use the Imperial seal it's as good as shouting 'Here we are!' in Crombard's ear. At the moment, they may not be sure if we've even been in Casterlayne. Better to try and slip away quietly, and leave them guessing."

Ommet managed a smile, though I knew he was feeling desperate. "Spoken like a true Wraith! So how will we accomplish this feat."

I climbed back up into our dray. "Come on."

"But where are we going?"

"We will take the next train down to Scla. By one means or another."

I drove us round the Rail Master's office, and down between the rows of rail-wagons. Close up they were bigger than I'd realised, half again as big as a normal wagon, made of varnished wood framed in black iron. They were joined by heavy chains into lines of twenty.

Coming to the head of the line, I saw that one of the trains had been pulled forward on its track, and the last of its wagons was under the loading frame.

"That'll be the next one to go," said Ommet.

A smaller wagon had been connected to the front of the train. This one was painted blue, with a large white number '10' on the sides. A man in dark blue uniform was walking round it with an oil can.

I pulled up next to him. "Good day to you. Are you in charge of this rail-train?"

He looked up. A strongly built man, grey eyes and curly black hair. He gave us a wary look.

"Aye, I'm the Brakesman." Strongest Northern accent I'd heard since Neowbron. "Do something for you, ah?"

"We need passage down to Scla. Us and a box, that's all."

He was shaking his head before I'd finished. "Nay. Can't help you. No passenger's on this trip, ah? Tomorrow morning's the next one you can get – ask the Rail Master."

I got down from the dray. "We can pay," I said. "Pay *you*, that is."

He raised an eyebrow – not surprisingly, considering the fact that we were mostly dressed in laundry discards. We didn't look like we could pay for a drink, let alone a ride.

"Are you fafwangling me?" he asked suspiciously. Northern idiom in a northern accent: I could feel Ommet's confusion.

Fortunately, I'd heard the phrase before, and knew that it referred to silly or foolish speech.

"Not at all," I promised him. "We can make it well worth your trouble."

"Well, that's as maybe, but like I said, I can't help you," he said firmly, and with a touch of irritation. "Payment or not, it's more than my job's worth to risk..."

He broke off as I held up our one gold piece.

And in that moment I felt something change in him. It was the first time I'd felt anything from anyone other than Ommet, but I recognised it at once. The sight of gold took him from a definite no to a very possible yes in a heartbeat.

Suddenly I understood how powerful this Gift could be.

"An Imperial Crown." I held it out to him. "The two of us and that box on the dray, down to Scla. You can drop us off before you get there if you wish, we're not going to tell anyone we rode with you."

He looked at me, at Ommet, at the box on the dray, and at the gold. He was hesitating, but I knew the decision was already made.

"That's true gold?" he asked.

"See for yourself." I tossed it into his hand. He felt it, felt the weight of it, and then bit it in the traditional fashion.

"Gold, eh?" He gave me a shrewd look. "That's more'n I make in a year. You must have pressing business down in Scla, ah?"

"Very pressing," I agreed.

"Right then." He swung open a door in the side of 'Number 10'. "Get in the brake wagon. Keep well down, if the Rail Master's Assistant sees you he'll stop me and haul you off. There's room for your cargo as well. Don't touch anything! I have to check the brake linkages and the coupling chains before we can leave, but I won't be long, ah?"

"What about the horse and the dray?"

He shrugged. "Can't take them with you, can you, ah? Leave them be. Someone'll claim them soon enough. Always needing another horse and another cart round here."

We unloaded the box and put it into the brake wagon before climbing aboard ourselves. The metal sides came to just above my waist, and when we sat on the floor with the box between us our heads were well below the top. The Brakesman nodded and shut the door, rendering us invisible from any casual outside observer.

How casual would those Purifiers be, though? Would they insist on searching all the Scla-bound wagons? If so, our only chance would be to leave before they arrived. But, gold or not, the Brakesman didn't seem inclined to rush things.

I wondered if perhaps we should attempt to take matters into our own hands, and leave at once. With or without the Brakesman. The thought had been in the back of my mind before – after all, how hard could it be? The rail-trains ran downhill under their own weight, and didn't even have to be steered. However, looking at the bewildering array of wheels and levers that clustered around the front end of the brake wagon, I reconsidered. It might actually be more difficult than I'd realised.

Besides which, I recalled seeing the previous departure as we were coming down the hillside. It had taken a lot of pushing by a lot of men to start the train off. Not something we could do by ourselves.

Ommet was also studying the brake car's controls, but not with any thought of theft. He was just fascinated by the technicalities of the system.

"See those big levers there, on each side?" He pointed them out to me. "If I'm not mistaken they operate brakes on all the wagons in the train. Simultaneously! That will be the brake linkages he was talking about... and those wheel things, they must be the brakes for this wagon. More graduated than the levers, finer control I expect. I wonder what the smaller levers are?"

"Hardly important now," I said. "Do you think I could risk a glance over the top? I'd like to know if those riders are in sight."

"Best not to," Ommet cautioned. "If anyone were to see you peeking out, we could get ourselves thrown off the train!" He indicated the brake levers again. "Did you know that this was all designed by an Arravine? Brother Rartienne. I met him once, we had a fascinating discussion,"

"I'm sure you did."

"It's an interesting story," Ommet insisted, despite being well aware of my disinterest. Trying to distract me from worrying about the Purifiers, I thought. Or trying to distract himself. "There was another rail-way before this. Only about five miles long, and not very successful. When Rartienne heard that Lord Tunward was considering building one of his own, he wrote to him with some ideas for improvements. Ended up being in charge of the whole project."

"Must have been lucrative for him," I commented drily. "I thought the Arravines weren't supposed to work for money."

"He didn't," Ommet said sadly. "Tunward had agreed to give a generous donation to the Arravines in return for Rartienne's help. But in the end he gave nothing at all! Rartienne's work wasn't even acknowledged. But we know the truth of it."

The door opened again, and the Brakesman climbed in. He shut and bolted it behind him, gestured at us to stay low and quiet, and leaned over the side to exchange words with someone invisible to us. I tensed, imagining a Purifier making enquiries. The Apothecary's long knife was still inside my coat, the Skipper's poisoned dagger was in my sock. I put one hand on each. To be ready, in case the door was flung open and Crombard's man peered in.

The last thing he would see would be the bright shine of steel!

Ommet saw, and knew what I was thinking. He rested a hand on my shoulder, caught my eye, and shook his head. Then nodded at the door. I forced myself to relax and listened to the conversation – which was all on technical matters of loading weights and brake wear. It came to an end and the Brakesman turned back to us.

"Won't be long now," he said. "Just waiting on the Rail Master's Assistant to sign off on the load and we'll be rolling, ah?" He took of his cap, scratched his head. "Name's Curril, by the way. Jedster Curril, at your service, ah?"

"Arton Dowder," I identified myself. "And Mr. Ommet."

"Mr Dowder – Mr Ommet." If Curril was at all sceptical about the names, he didn't show it.

Instead, his attention was taken by something happening outside of the brake car.

"Now what's that a-goin' on back there, ah?" he wondered aloud.

"What is it?" I asked urgently. "What do you see."

"Horsemen. A dozen or so, all dressed in black. They look to be gathering outside the Rail Master's Office." He gave us a shrewd look. "And would they be anything to do with you, ah?"

We shrugged, and he nodded thoughtfully. "Well, here comes the Assistant. So we'll be on our way directly, and they'll be no concern of ours."

He leaned over the side again, engaged in another technical conversation with someone out of our sight. A paper was signed, and Curril at once turned to the array of levers and wheels, slamming some into different positions, unwinding others.

A metal pole was fastened at each front corner of the car. From one hung a lantern, unlit and unneeded in the daylight. From the other was suspended a brass bell, not unlike one of those on a ship.

Curril took hold of this and rang it sharply, three groups of two chimes each.

Before the last chime had died away, he leaned over the side and bellowed out.

"NUMBER TEN, READY TO ROLL! PUSHER'S UP!"

"And here come those horsemen," he added to us.

"What?" I had to see for myself. Twisting round, I raised my head a fraction above the rim. But of course, there was little to see from that position. Most of the view back down the line was obscured by the big slate wagon behind us. All I glimpsed – before Ommet dragged me back down – was one of the pushers, a brawny young man, inserting a short wooden pole into a slot on the side of the wagon.

"Stay down!" Curril hissed. "They're just trotting along the line at present, and they've no authority to intervene – at least, none that I'm going to recognise!"

He rang the bell again, three times. A pause, then once more.

A shout went up – from the pushers, I realised, as they leant into their poles and exerted themselves.

Slowly, slowly, the rail-train began to move.

There was another shout from behind. Not from the pushers, this was one voice.

"What's this?" asked Curril "Another one, galloping up from the Rail Master's Office by the look of it!"

The rail-train was picking up speed. Walking pace now, as far as I could judge from inside the brake car. A slow walking pace.

More shouts. Indistinct, with the increasingly loud rumble of wagon wheels to compete with.

"They might be calling on us to stop," Curril said thoughtfully. "But I couldn't say for sure. And who are they anyway? Only the Rail Master has authority to stop a train. In any case, we're on the slope now!"

He rang the bell once more, and shouted. "PUSHER'S AWAY!"

Our pace was still increasing, but slowly. And I could hear hoof beats, growing louder.

"Stop!" someone shouted. "Stop, damn you! By order of Baron Crombard!"

"Crombard?" Curril rested one hand on a brake wheel, but the other he cupped to his ear. "What? Can't hear you!"

"STOP! STOP NOW or I'll have your head!"

We were at a run now. A man's run, that is, and the horseman had no trouble keeping up.

Horsemen. I could see from the way Curril's eyes flickered from side to side that we were flanked. More than that, I could feel the growing fear in him.

And I could feel something else as well. An anger, a hatred. It had been growing slowly for the past few minutes, and at first I hadn't distinguished it from the tension that had simultaneously increased in myself – and in Ommet. But now it was clear and distinct, and coming at us from both sides of the brake car.

I pulled the long knife free, and braced myself.

"Can't stop!" Curril was shaking his head. "We're rolling. Stay clear! STAY CLEAR, I SAY!"

Then his fear spiked. It matched a spike in the fury alongside us. And in the next moment, a sword blade crashed against the bell, setting it ringing on a strange note.

"STOP! NOW!"

Faster, faster... the huge weight of the slate wagons was pushing at us, but the horses were still keeping pace, and Curril's hand was tightening on the brake wheel. I could feel the uncertainty in him, fear and anger at odds within.

There was a crash, the brake wagon shook, and there were hands gripping the side of the brake car. Ommet's side. Then an arm was flung over, and a face appeared.

A young looking man, thin, blond hair and a ruddy flush in his cheeks. His eyes were pale blue, and something in them, or in him, told me that he was older than he appeared. That he was First Order.

Our eyes met. "I'll..." he began to snarl, but I didn't give him chance to continue. Leaning over Ommet, I smashed the hilt of my knife into the man's face, using all the strength I could muster.

With a shriek, he fell back, his hands disappearing from the edge of the brake wagon.

No hope now of keeping our presence secret. I jumped to my feet, turning to face the other side – and fell back again as the sword slashed through the air in front of me.

The horse was at a full gallop now, clearly struggling to keep up, but the rider was forcing it on. Long brown hair and beard, dark eyes glaring, black cloak billowing behind him. On his chest, a splash of colour against the black leather. A badge, waving lines of orange and red. A burning heart.

And in his hand a cavalry sabre, with which he now struck again.

But I was ready this this time, caught the blade on my knife and riposted with a slash at his arm. He screamed and dropped the sword, then pulled his horse away, shouting curses.

There were other horseman behind, but our speed was still increasing and they were beginning to fall back. Moreover the rails were dropping down into a cutting, whilst the road the horsemen were on remained level.

I checked the other side of the brake wagon. No sign of the one who'd tried to get on board, and no more room for any horsemen. Just beyond the rails the ground dropped away, down about ten feet to a small river. Which explained the man's desperate jump – he'd run out of road.

Curril was still standing by his brake levers. He'd gone a little pale, which was understandable.

"I think we've outrun them," I said.

His eyes, looking past me, suddenly widened. "Get down!" he shouted and dropped into the bottom of the car.

Something whipped past my head, struck one of the brake wheels and was deflected away to the side. I turned and leaned out to look behind us.

Just in time to see one of the horsemen levelling a crossbow. I ducked back, the bolt slammed against the outside of the brake wagon.

Curril grabbed at my arm. "We've got to brake!"

I shook my head. "We can't! They'll catch up again, and we'll be dead meat." I pointed to the road above us. "From up there they'll be able to shoot straight down into the wagon. But we're outrunning them! Their horses are tired, they won't be able to keep up. We have to keep going!"

He shook his head. "You don't understand! There's a bend coming up... if we don't brake soon, we'll be going too fast to take it. We'll be off the rails and down into the river, with all the slate wagons coming down on top of us!"

"But if they catch up with us..."

Another bolt flew over our heads to emphasise the point. It struck one of the smaller levers and was deflected into the front panel, where it impacted with sufficient force to penetrate the thin metal. It's not easy aiming a crossbow from a galloping horse, but these fellows seemed to have had some practice.

Curril looked at the wicked little thing, flights still quivering a bare foot from his arm. "What have I got myself into?" he asked.

Chapter 21: Lord Tunward's Railway

I took his question to be rhetorical, and ignored it. "How far does the road follow us?"

The brake wagon was shuddering as it hurtled down the track, still picking up speed. More bolts came our way, but went awry as the range increased.

"Not far, it turns off to the right... but then it comes out above the track, after we take the bend. If we do take it!"

I swore, loudly and it didn't even get a reaction from Ommet. "And beyond that? Does it run all the way down to Scla?"

"No, after that it goes up to a mine... but we have to take that section slowly! We've got a right hand bend coming up, and then there's a left-hander onto a bridge. That takes us over a ravine and away from the road, but there's no way we can do it at this speed!"

"We have to get to that point before they reach it! Their horses are tired, they'll be forced to slow down. We just have to take the turn as fast as we can."

Curril ran his hands through his hair, and looked again at the bolt next to him. It seemed to be a source of fascination. "Yes. Yes, I understand. But we need to slow down, all the same, and we have to start soon!"

Ommet had got up and taken a swift glance behind. "I can't see them behind us any more. I think you can start braking."

"Right!" Curril jumped into action, heaving back on levers and winding wheels. A horrendous screeching broke out as the brakes engaged, but our headlong pace began to slow.

None too early. The track had already begun to curve to the right, pushed that way by a bend in the river. Gently at first.

"Too late, too late!" Curril shouted.

As the bend sharpened, the tortured scream of metal wheels on metal rails increased, and we felt the brake wagon beginning to sway outwards.

"The wheels are lifting! Lean! Lean!"

Curril threw himself to one side, grabbing the rail and leaning as far out over the inside of the curve as he could. We followed his example. Below me I could see the wheels coming clear of the track... spinning uselessly in the air.

"If we go, the rest will follow! Lean out!"

Curril flung a leg over the side, so far out of the wagon that his shoulder was brushing against the shrubbery that grew alongside the line. I followed his example, whilst next to me Ommet was doing the same.

With a crash and a jolt, the brake wagon righted itself. Ommet shouted as the shock loosened his grip and one hand came free. I clutched at him, gained a handful of clothing and pulled him back against the wagon.

Curril was still staring wildly back along the line. "If one of the slate wagons goes over..." he began, but even as he said it it became clear that they were round the bend, and still upright.

I scrambled back over the side and into the relative safety of the brake wagon, then gave Ommet a hand to follow me. "Take the brakes off!" I told Curril as he clambered in.

He shook his head. "No! We can't pick up speed again. The next bend, the left hander, is even sharper, we'll never make it if we go any faster"

"We're slowing down too much!" I retorted. "Do you want a crossbow bolt in your skull? How far until the road meets us again?"

"Half a mile, perhaps? But I don't know the distance along the road, I've never been on it."

"Well, take some brakes off until we get there, then. We must outrun them."

He bit his lip. "Madness!" he muttered, but attended to the levers. Some of the squealing died away, and I felt us pick up speed again.

To our right rose a steep slope. Wooded, but not thickly enough for my liking. To our left the ground fell away even more steeply. I saw glimpses, between the vegetation, of two rivers meeting in a tumult of white water.

"The Slatebrook comes down through Casterlayne," said Curril. "Meets Perrican Brook just here, ah? That comes from up near the Perrican Mine. We're following it now, but then the ground starts to rise, so the rails go left, over the Perrican Bridge. The road is directly above at that point."

"There's no slope on the tracks at all here," said Ommet. "We'll come to a stop!"

"No, there's a small incline. Just enough to keep us moving up to the bend. We're still going faster than I like!" So saying Curril made further adjustments and I felt us slowing once more.

Above us, the slope was steepening to near vertical, but there were no more trees or bushes to screen us.

"There's the bridge." Curril pointed. "Ahead and to the left. See the wooden towers? They support the weight of the rail-trains crossing."

"Another Arravine design!" Ommet put in, with a certain amount of pride. "But where's the road?"

"Up there." Curril nodded at the slope above us. "About two hundred feet."

"Long range for a crossbow," Ommet said hopefully.

"But they'll be shooting directly down at us," I said. "And they're good." We'd slowed right down now, to little more than a fast walking pace. "Damn it Curril, speed us up a bit."

He shook his head. "There's the bend, see?"

Constrained by the contours of the land, the builders had had to fit the turn into the only space there was between the ravine on one side and the upward slope on the other. It was a tight fit. Even to my untrained eye, I could see how sharp it was – and after our recent experience, I well understood Curril's reluctance to take it at speed.

Ommet and I looked up the slope. No sign of any riders. We looked ahead. A hundred yards to the bend. Perhaps less.

I needed no Gift to feel the tension in the wagon.

"Did you see their badges?" I asked, conversationally. "Orange and red, looked like flames. A burning heart."

"That's the sign of the Purifiers. The Knights of the Pure Heart. First Order fanatics. They serve Grand Duke Brodon now, with Crombard as their Commander, but they were created by the First Emperor, Eckharden to enforce the purity of the First Order – and to suppress the true nature of the Gifts. Thus began the long decline of the First Order... the flames are supposed to symbolise the purifying power of fire, I suppose."

I thought of flame badges, and flames, and thrust the thought aside before it brought back memories I'd rather not visit.

Sixty yards? Or seventy?

"These Purifiers?" Curril asked. "They're these ones in black that are after you?"

"That's right," I confirmed.

He didn't reply, just looked up at the slope. I followed his gaze.

A horseman had appeared there. Looking down at us. Two more arrived. Then others. They dismounted, and began winding crossbows.

I looked at Ommet, sharing his dismay. "If we get right against this side," he said, "And as low as possible, we'll be out of their line of sight."

"There isn't room for three of us!" I pointed out.

"The slate wagon!" Curril snapped. "Quickly! The slates aren't packed right to the side, they don't want the edges chipped. Depending on the size of the slates there might be a foot of space – you should just have room to squeeze in."

Ommet turned, and looked at the gap between the brake wagon and the first of the slate wagons. "What about you?" he asked Curril.

"I have to take the brakes off as soon as we get round the bend. There's no incline on the bridge, if we don't start picking up speed again we could come to a dead stop! Go!"

A bolt thumped into the wooden floor between us. Above there was a cheer, I looked up and saw a Purifier kneeling to take aim.

"GO!" I shouted.

Ommet went, scrambling up the rear of the brake wagon and leaping across the gap without hesitation. A bolt hummed through the space he'd been in and I ducked low. When I looked up again he was dragging himself over the side of the slate wagon.

I followed – but faster. One jump up, then a jump across, grabbing at the rim of the slate wagon as Ommet disappeared over the side.

Something slammed into me, a massive blow on my ribs that knocked most of the breath out of me. My left hand lost its grip and I hung desperately by my right hand, gasping, grasping, feet flailing uselessly against the wagon and the rail directly below me, the big steel wheels rumbling under the wagon ready to crush and slice and mangle...

Then Ommet was leaning over, grasping my arm with both hands and heaving me up, heedless of the bolt that chipped the slate just above his head and flew on down to the river.

I tumbled in after him. The cut and finished slates were packed into wooden frames, lashed tightly to stop them shifting, and as Curril had promised there was just enough room for us to squeeze into the gap. Our heads were far enough below the top of the slates to put us out of sight of the Purifiers.

"We've done some mad things the last few weeks," Ommet observed. He was trying to sound casual, but there was a shake in his voice. "That may have been the worst!"

I shook my head, feeling equally shaky but striving to keep my voice steady. "No, I think diving off the *Anatarna* just before she blew up was worse. We only had to make a little jump this time."

"With Crombard's Purifiers shooting bolts at us while we did it."

"Yes, but moving targets at this range? Nobody's that good."

"Then Nobody must have shot that one." Ommet indicated my coat. The green coat I'd taken from the Apothecary.

It was quite ruined now, with a massive rip down the left side from the chest almost to the bottom, where a crossbow bolt hung, its black vanes caught in the seam. The sharp edged head was blackened steel, the wooden shaft was black as well. Nasty looking thing.

"Oh. I thought I'd hit something on the wagon. That should have gone to my heart!"

I explored the place the bolt must have struck. Underneath the point where the rip began was the big knife that the Apothecary had tried to gut me with. The tough leather of the sheath was torn, but the knife blade had turned the point away and directed the bolt downwards. With sad results for the coat, but better ones for me.

I took a moment to contemplate the irony.

"They've stopped shooting," Ommet observed.

"No targets." I peered forwards, being careful to keep my head behind the slates. I could see the front of the brake wagon, but of the Brakesman himself there was no sign. Probably because he was laying down and making himself as small as possible.

Or because he was dead. I decided not to pursue that thought. Instead I looked ahead towards the bend and the bridge.

"Not far now. Twenty, maybe twenty five yards until we turn into the bridge," I told Ommet.

"Good... Arton! We forgot the Writings! They're still in the box – it could be full of bolts by now!"

In sudden panic he grasped the top of the slates and started to pull himself up, perhaps to get a better view of the box and its precious contents. I pulled him back down just before two bolts flew past, one of them impacting on the slates where his hand had just been.

"They're very good at that." I commented. "Probably too good to be wasting bolts on a wooden box that they are unlikely to understand the significance of. If anything hits it, it'll be by mistake, and it's a strong box."

"But..."

"But if we try and rescue the box they will kill us."

He met my gaze, and I felt his mixture of frustration and despair. "Arton – if I am killed, you will see that the Writings are protected, won't you? Protected and delivered to Daradura?"

"You're not going to get killed – not unless you do something foolish like stick your head out for target practice. You'll deliver those dammed Writings into the hands of the Grand Chancellor personally!"

He opened his mouth to answer – from his up-swelling emotions, he was probably going to rebuke me for my language in respect to the sacred words of the Prophet Mirrion – but he was interrupted by a shout from above.

"Ho, down there! Hear me well! I command you, in the name of Baron Crombard, Lieutenant of the North – stop that train and surrender yourselves! Do it now, and I will spare your lives. Disobey and your death is certain!"

In the silence that followed, the creak of the wagons, the rumble of wheels and the squealing of the brakes was clearly heard. I could even hear the splashing of Perrican Brook below us.

Nobody spoke, but looking ahead I could see that the bend was certainly less than twenty yards away by now.

I also saw Curril's hands come into view, reaching up to a brake lever, and for a terrible moment I thought that he was about to put it fully on and bring us to a halt.

Instead, he pushed it the other way. With some difficulty, given the awkward angle he was working at – but it was released. Some of the sound of metal on metal died away, and the rail-train began to pick up speed once more.

There was an angry shout from above, and another bolt struck into the floor of the brake wagon, joining several others that were already there. Curril, who had been leaning across the wagon towards the brake on the other side, pulled back hastily.

Ommet was peering over my shoulder. "The right-hand lever operates half the brakes, but the rest are controlled from the other side. If Curril cannot release them, we might still come to a halt on the bridge!"

How long would it take for the Purifiers to get to us then, I wondered? Not long. They'd have ropes to help the scramble down the hillside, or else they'd send for them, while keeping us pinned down. Even if we escaped the marksmen's aim, we wouldn't get far on foot and carrying the Writings. Leaving them behind wasn't even to be considered.

"Curril!" I called, trying to pitch my voice for his ears only, not wishing the Purifiers to hear our plans. "Curril!"

"What?" I heard him call back.

"Stand ready to release that brake! I'll distract them!"

""Make it quick!"

I raised my voice to a shout. "UP TOP THERE. Do you hear me? Stop shooting at us for a moment so we can talk."

The answer came straight back. "Show yourself, then! Stop your train and show yourselves!"

"Yes, I'm showing myself! Don't shoot!"

I took a deep breath, gripped the top of the slates and pulled myself up until my head was clear of them. Half expecting to get a bolt between the eyes.

"I'm here! Why are you shooting at us? We are just travellers going down to Scla on business of our own – what's your issue with us that you must seek our lives?"

Directly above me, a line of black-clad men were kneeling with crossbows aimed. The spokesman stood behind them. "Stop and surrender! We know who you are – no innocent travellers, for certain. A renegade priest, a jewel thief, and a disloyal employee of Lord Tunward's Railway! Give yourselves up and I see you get a fair trial before Baron Crombard himself! Defy me and be shot down like dogs!"

"He's got that all wrong," Ommet muttered. "I was never ordained as a priest!"

"His negotiating skills certainly leave much to be desired. But I think I have his attention... best to make sure. Push me up!"

"What? Expose yourself more?"

"Do it!"

Ommet pushed on my feet, and I scrambled up to stand on the top of the slates.

"As soon as you like, Curril," I said. "They're all looking at me now." I raised my voice again, and my hands. Nothing attracts attention like waving hands. "Sir, you are mistaken..." I began.

And as I did I felt the sudden burst of activity from Curril. Out of the corner of my eye I saw him leap across the brake wagon, grasp the lever and slam it across.

There was a shout of fury from above. I dropped flat onto the slates, and rolled myself off, falling on top of Ommet. Just ahead of a sleet of bolts that hammered into the slates where I had been just a moment before.

The only thing that saved me was the distraction that Curril had provided – as I had provided a distraction for him. For a crucial fraction of a second their attention had been divided between two possible targets.

"Curril – did he make it?" I gasped.

"How could I know?" Ommet grunted from underneath me. "What about you?"

"They missed me." I managed to get myself off him and looked forward.

There was no sign of Curril, which was good. The bend began just ten yards ahead now, and with the brakes fully off the rail-train was building up speed once more.

More bolts from above. They were concentrating their fire into the brake wagon, perhaps hoping for a lucky rebound that might kill or injure our Brakesman. But most of the bolts seemed to be digging into the wooden floor, punching into the thin metal sides, or flying off down to the brook.

"Curril – are you hit?" I called out.

"Not yet!" he answered. "The bastards are still trying, though! Hold on, we're almost at the turn!"

Five yards. Fast walking pace.

Ommet plucked at my sleeve. "Arton – when we go round the turn, we'll come into their line of fire!"

I looked round, assessing the angles, and swore. Even now, Ommet managed a wince at my language, though only I would have noticed it.

"Right – you get down there, right at the back of the wagon, as low as you can get. Squeeze yourself into the smallest space you can manage."

"What about you? You'll still be exposed!"

"I'll go over the front of the wagon. There's footing on the framework, I can hang on there for a few minutes. Long enough to be out of range."

He didn't like it. But there was no time to argue, and no other choices.

"Turn!" Curril shouted, voice almost drowned out by the screeching of metal wheels on rails as the brake car reached the bend.

I jumped, grabbed at the front of the wagon, pulled myself up. I hadn't had time to plan the manoeuvre, but I'd hoped to vault smoothly over. Instead, it was at that precise moment that the wagon reached the bend and lurched into it. I lost my grip, flopped over the top on my belly and fell head first towards the rails.

A desperate grab gave me a precarious hold on the chain joining the wagons – a chain that was itself swinging around, hanging slack then coming tight in unpredictable response to the movement of the rail-train. Each time it went loose it encouraged my fingers to slip in between the links to gain purchase. Each time it pulled taught it threatened to crush or nip off any fingers caught between the links.

And my legs were following me down, sliding off towards the side of the wagon as I scrabbled for a purchase... which I found, just before my feet disappeared underneath and the rest of me followed them onto the rails and the steel wheels.

There was an extra piece of wood fitted to the front of the wagon, clearly to absorb the impact if two wagons came together. It ran below the coupling chains and extended several inches out – a very chipped and battered piece of timber, but it caught my flailing limbs.

There was a similar beam on the rear of the brake wagon. I got an elbow on it, managed to twist myself round and pull myself up.

The rumbling of the wheels changed to a loud clattering that steadily increased in volume as each wagon in turn came safely round the bend and out onto the bridge.

Bolts were still coming down from above, but were hitting nothing but slates or metal. And the bridge was not a long one. I risked a quick glance out at the side, and saw that the brake wagon was nearly clear, and beyond it a gentle turn would take us into woodland and out of sight of the Purifiers.

Then I felt a bust of intense pain shoot through me, and I screamed.

Or Ommet did. Or we both did. I heard him at the same moment that I felt the pain.

It was radiating out from my shoulder, but when I looked there was nothing there. I touched it, but there was no blood. And already it was fading. No, not fading – withdrawing. I could still feel it, it was agonising – but it was not my pain. It was Ommets.

I pulled myself up and looked back into the slate wagon.

Ommet was huddled up in the rear of the wagon, stuffed down next to the slates where I'd told him to be. He was looking up at me with an expression of pain and chagrin, and there was a bolt in him. In his left shoulder. Just where I'd felt the pain.

I ducked down again, but there were no more bolts now. We'd gone too far, the Purifiers could no longer see us behind the bridge and the wagons, and even now the sound of the wheels was changing again as we came back onto solid ground, and our speed was picking up.

I braced myself, and once more pulled myself up and over the side.

"What happened?" I asked as I reached him. "Did you stand up? That bolt's in your front – were you facing them? Why? What a damn stupid thing to do, what were you thinking…"

Ommet was shaking his head, and finally managed to get a word in. "Of course I… didn't stand up. Or face them." His voice was shaky, his breathing laboured, his emotions clouded with pain, but I could still detect a trace of humour in him. "Did you think… I was waving them… waving goodbye?"

"No. Of course not. So how did it happen."

"Not sure. It was so fast. I think… it hit something and bounced back at me."

There was a metal rim round the edge, and other places where a hard-driven bolt might strike and go tumbling back at random. Just bad fortune that such a thing should happen. Cruellest of bad fortune that it should strike, point first, into Ommet's flesh, unprotected by anything more than the grubby rags that he'd picked out of a laundry basket a few days before.

But looking at it I could see now that it could not have been a direct strike. Those bolts could penetrate light armour if they struck true from a fully wound weapon. Ommet would have been spitted through and through from such a shot. But this bolt had lost most of its energy before it reached him. All the same, it had had enough power left for the head to go deep into the flesh. And its unstable trajectory had caused it to leave a long, jagged entry wound that was bleeding profusely.

I pulled off my coat, took out the Apothecary's big knife and began slicing strips from my shirt.

"I can't take the bolt out," I explained as I did so. "The head is barbed, it would do more damage if I tried. It will have to be cut out, but not here. One sway of the wagon and I'd cut too deep. We'll get you to a doctor as soon as we reach Scla. For now, the best I can do is to try and stop the bleeding. And – I'm sorry, but I can do nothing for the pain."

Ommet nodded. "I understand. Don't trouble yourself about me, Arton. The Writings. Protect them at all costs! They are much more important."

"To you, perhaps," I muttered. Under my breath since I didn't want to add to Ommet's distress – as it surely would if he thought I would abandon them. As carefully as possible I put a padding of shirt strips round the wound and used longer lengths to bind them in place. But I couldn't avoid nudging the bolt several times, and each time Ommet's pain spiked. Feeling it made my hands even more unsteady.

"You must cut yourself off from me," Ommet whispered.

"What do you mean?"

"Disconnect yourself from feeling what I feel. Otherwise my pain will impede you."

"I don't know how to do that. I don't know if I can."

"You can. Anatarna and I... we learned how. It was necessary. Not to deny the feelings, but to... keep them at a distance. Or else they can become overwhelming."

I met his gaze. "I don't want to abandon you. To leave you alone with your pain."

He forced a smile. "I know. I can feel that. It is a comfort, to feel your... steadfastness. You are a rock, Arton. You strengthen me. But... I am weakening you. And that cannot happen. Cut yourself off. I will survive all the same. But not... not if my pain... stops you from helping..."

He sank back, eyes closing. Still conscious, but exhausted.

Just as I was myself, I realised. I was carrying my own burden of relatively minor bumps and bruises, but Ommet's much greater hurt was draining me.

I sat back, closed my eyes. Focused my mind on the agony that flooded into me from him. And very deliberately – shut it out. Pushed it back away from me, back into Ommet. Closed myself off from it.

It was still there. But distant. An awareness of a pain that was happening – somewhere else. In him, not me.

I opened my eyes but his remained closed. Taking a deep breath, I resumed my task of dressing his wound. It went more quickly now that my mind was no longer fogged by what he was feeling. Once or twice he groaned as I had to apply pressure, but as I finished he slipped into unconsciousness.

The bleeding had stopped, or at least slowed, but the makeshift bandage was already soaked in red.

I threw off the tattered remnants of my shirt, and rolled it into a makeshift pillow to put behind Ommet's head. In the cramped space there was nothing more I could do to make him comfortable.

I stood up and put the green coat back on. With Ommet's pain distanced, I was all too aware of a great many aches of my own. Some of them acute. I put those away from me as well. If there was no time for his pain, there was certainly no time for my own.

Instead, I went back to the front and looked over into the brake wagon, where Curril was standing with hands resting on the brakes, but making only a few adjustments. This section curved gently round the hillside, with no more than a slight incline that kept the rail-train rolling steadily. And quite slowly, it seemed, at least after the wild ride we'd had earlier

I climbed back into the brake wagon and joined him. "Not to tell you your job, of course, but couldn't we be going faster than this? The bends don't seem to be as sharp as those we came round earlier."

"You mean that place where we nearly came of the rails and rolled down the hill with a few hundred tons of slate on top of us? Yes, we're going slower than that!"

"I see. And I do understand your point of view. But what concerns me is that those lads with the crossbows will right now be heading back to the rail yard as fast as their tired horses can take them. And once there, they'll commandeer the next rail-train and be after us with all the speed they can force out of the Brakesman. At sword-point if necessary! How long do you suppose that will take?"

Curril was unworried. "At a guess, about twelve hours. Perhaps more."

"Twelve hours! But..." I felt his amusement before I saw the smile. "What aren't you telling me?"

"They can't come after us until tomorrow morning. Sword point or Baron Combard's name, it doesn't matter what they use, it's physically impossible."

"And why is that?"

"See, there's ten rail-trains down to Scla everyday. This is the last. There are plenty of wagons up there still, of course. Getting loaded for tomorrow. But there's no brake wagons. Not until the horses bring them up in the night, along with the empty slate wagons. No Brakesmen either – tomorrows shift will come up with the brake wagons. It's a slow business, hauling all those wagons thirty miles back up hill. Takes all night. And they can't start until I reach Scla – no place to pass, ah?"

I thought about it. "And they can't just take a normal wagon down?"

He snorted. "Only as far as the first bend! You saw what that was like, even when we were braked. Without the brake wagon, there's no way to slow down at all. No, they'll not be after us till morning."

"Then they'll get fresh horses and come down by road!"

"Let them. It's a lot longer by road than it is by rail-train, and a lot slower. Especially at night. I promise you, they can't be in Scla before mid-morning at the earliest."

"That's good. However – we still need to make the best possible time down. My friend – Mr. Ommet – he was hit. Nasty wound in the shoulder. He needs to get to a Doctor as soon as possible. How soon can we make it to Scla?"

"I'm sorry to hear about that, ah?" Curril declined to answer my question, though. Instead, as we approached another bend he wound a handle, applying a gentle braking that slowed us just a little. "But I was wondering - who were those lads, ah? Right handy with crossbows, so well trained. Not ruffians or common bandits, then, but not Imperial troops either. First Order, they looked, and they used Baron Crombard's name. But I've seen Crombard livery, and that wasn't it."

"No, it wasn't," I agreed. What was this about, I wondered? I could not feel his emotions with any clarity, or understand what his intentions were.

"They had a badge though. Knights of the Pure Heart, did I hear your friend say? First Order killers in the service of Grand Duke Brodon himself?"

He glanced at me and I nodded.

"Yes. Purifiers. Nasty buggers."

"Oh, aye!" He laughed, though without much humour. "That's clear enough, ah? But my question is, why are they after you? What do they want with a ragamuffin pair like yourselves – no offence, but you're not really dressed for mingling with First Order Lordlings. Or is that box they're after? What might be in there, I wonder."

He glanced back at it as he spoke, and I followed his gaze. As Ommet had feared, it had taken a hit or two. One bolt had hit the lid full on and gone deep. By my estimation, deep enough to have reached the crystal sheets that surrounded the Writings themselves. Could it have been powerful enough to break the crystal and expose the fragile ancient documents themselves? I had no idea, and now was not the time to investigate. I hoped Ommet wouldn't find out.

Looking forward again, I saw that we were round the bend and onto a straight section. But Curril didn't ease the brakes. Instead he wound them down, and we slowed further.

His face was expressionless as he gazed at me. His emotions were confusing. There was tension there, and fear, and determination, but I could not deduce anything from that. Was he planning to betray us after all?

"Now, I do recall what that loud-mouth shouted back there." Curril looked directly at me as he continued. "He talked of a disloyal employee of the railway. Which I presume to be me, ah? Though I reject the charge of disloyalty! Then there's the renegade priest he mentioned. Which of you two is that, then?"

"That'll be Ommet. Though he'd tell you that he's no priest. Never ordained, that I know of. He'd say he's just a humble Friar of the Arravine Order."

"An Arravine? Indeed. Well, I've known Arravines. Good people. I attended one of their schools for a while. Quiet, scholarly men, the Friars. This..." he swept his hand round the brake wagon, still littered with spent bolts, "... does not seem like an Arravine sort of thing."

"It's not a normal situation," I agreed. "Believe me, Mr. Ommet would not be part of this had he better choices to take."

"Now that I do understand and concur with." Curril nodded. "But that makes you the Jewel Thief, if we are to believe what those Purifiers were saying."

The tension in him was very clear now. It was reflected in my own. I eased away from him, giving me space to snatch out my long knife should I need it. Curril had no obvious weapons, but there was a tool box secured to the floor. What might he have taken out of that, I wondered? Perhaps he had a spanner hidden up his sleeve, a knife in his pocket?

"You'll have to make your own judgement on that," I answered.

"Hmm. I suppose I must." Curril put out a hand, and rested it on another lever. Unlike the rest, this had been painted bright red, which made it stand out. "Do you know what this is?"

"Of course not. I'm not a Brakesman, am I?"

He snorted. "Indeed not. Whatever you might be, you're not that! Well, Mr Dowder – this is the emergency brake. I pull this, and it releases an anchor. Not one such as you'd find on board ship, of course, But it has a similar function. A metal claw, driven downward by a powerful spring. It will dig into the earth, catch on to the timbers that support the rails and halt a rail-train dead, no matter how fast it's going. And once it's down, there's no quick way of raising it again. Powerful springs, like I said. Men have to come all the way up from Scla with winches to get the emergence brake off and the wagons moving again." He looked directly at me. "Not to be used lightly, of course. There's a pin in there normally, so the lever cannot be pulled by accident. But I have removed that pin, ah? I pull this lever now, and we travel not one foot further."

So that was his weapon. More subtle, and more powerful than any spanner.

"I understand. And what can I say to persuade you not to pull it?"

"Right, well here it is then. You're perhaps a Jewel Thief, and I'm a law abiding man. You're in trouble with Baron Crombard, and I've got a family to think of: by rights I should turn you in as soon as maybe, ah?"

I said nothing.

"Still... it occurs to me that there are a lot of thieves around and about. And most of them will gladly help themselves to a bit of jewellery if they have the opportunity. But why would the likes of Crombard be concerned with such as they? What would cause him to send out his elite, his private army of First Order killers to track down a common thief?"

He paused, but I remained silent. I could still discern nothing in Curril beyond the mounting tension.

"So I thought to myself – but suppose this isn't just some common thief, ah? Because there *is* one man who might warrant Crombard's personal attention. One person well known all across the North for having despoiled First Order Lords and Ladies of their finest jewels. One who, rumour has it, has even been to Crombard's own seat of Sonor Breck and robbed the Baron himself!"

Curril put out a finger and poked me firmly in the chest – though keeping his other hand on the emergency brake.

"And is that man you, Mr. Dowder? Are you that particular jewel thief? Are you The Wraith?"

So there it was. Curril's concern, out in the open. And I had no way of knowing what the best answer was. The Gift couldn't help me here, it only showed me the tension in him. And I'd known the man too short a time to guess which way he might incline. If I admitted to being the Wraith might he then pull that brake lever? To avoid punishment or perhaps gain reward. Or if he was more subtle, he might carry on down to Scla and then turn us in at his earliest convenience.

But if I denied it, then I was just a common thief, not worth taking risks for. Whereas the Wraith was a hero to some. A champion against the First Order.

And the First Order were not well thought of in these parts. Lord Tunward owned the slate, the mines, the railway, the towns and villages, the wealth – and the people. He had not proved to be an easy master.

I'd long been in the habit of concealing my identity. That was what came naturally to me. But perhaps it was time for a new tactic, the old one was played out.

And besides, and above all this, I knew what Ommet would say. He valued honesty. So it was for him as much as for myself that I decided.

"Curril, do you remember about three years ago, Lord Tunward's strong room was despoiled, he lost over ten thousand gold Imperial's worth of jewellery? Well, that was me. I was the thief. I am the Wraith."

It felt surprisingly good to say it out loud. Even better to see – and feel! - Curril's reaction.

"It's true!" He threw back his head and laughed. "Damn me, I thought it must be – but it's true! Heaven's above, I've only got the real, the actual, the Wraith himself riding with me!"

He turned back to me, grinning broadly, and his emotions on fire with excitement. "Every time we heard news of another noble house robbed, people drank to the Wraith in every pub in Scla and all along the valley! When word came out that he'd visited that bastard Tunward, the publicans and landlords were giving free drinks to anyone who'd raise it to his health! Ah, and more of the same when there was just a rumour that you'd been to Sonor Breck and tweaked the nose of Baron Crombard himself! There's been more pints sunk in your honour than to any man in history!"

"Really? I..."

"Yes, really! Minstrels sing songs about the Wraith – sing them quietly, if the First Order are around, but everyone knows the words! Children play at being him! Young women sigh over him! There's not a man of the Second Order in any mine, factory, shop or dockside between Casterlayne and the Murkarin border who wouldn't be proud to stand alongside the Wraith – and here you are, in my brake wagon!"

"Yes, here I am," I agreed. Curril's enthusiasm was overwhelming, but I could still feel Ommet's pain, and the urgency of our mission. "And in a hurry to get to Scla, so..."

I motioned towards the brakes. Curril had taken his hand off the red emergency lever, and now began releasing the others.

"In a hurry, ah? Well, I'll tell you Mr Wraith – there's not a Brakesman working this line that doesn't dream of setting the record for the fastest run! And now I'm going to do it. Hold on tight, this is going to be a hell of a ride!"

The rumbling of the slate wagon wheels grew steadily louder as our speed increased.

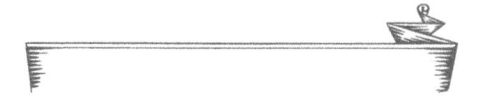

Chapter 22: Talinge

What Curril promised, he delivered. While the track followed the Slatebrook valley, it was smooth travelling – gentle inclines, easy curves. Curril barely touched the brakes as we hurtled down the track. The wind of our passage left trees shaking behind us, and made my eyes water as it blasted into our faces. Curril took his hat off, tucked it into a pocket and instead donned a set of goggles.

"How fast are we going?" I asked him. I had to shout over the noise of wind and wheels.

In reply, he reached into one of his boxes and took out a small clock – chained to the box, I noticed.

"See the white posts we keep passing?" he pointed one out. "They're a mile apart. Take the clock, and next one we pass, press the lever on the side. Then again, the post after that. Watch that red hand!"

I followed his instructions, he read the result off the dial, and made a mental calculation.

"About twenty miles an hour!" he announced with a broad grin. "Probably more than that, especially on the straights! That's ten miles an hour more than regulations allow!" He laughed out loud.

"Why do they restrict it so much?" I asked. "We seem to be running well at this speed."

"Running well until a deer gets onto the line!" he saw the look on my face, and shook his head. "Not to worry. The track is fenced off, I've never seen a deer. A few rabbits, sometimes a fox or badger... but the real problem from going so fast is damage to the track. Especially on the turns. These heavy wagons can push the rails out of alignment at this speed. Means the up train might be delayed while the engineers make repairs – but that's all to the good, slows down any pursuit by those Purifiers!"

I nodded. "Right. But – won't this get you into trouble?"

"Oh, it probably means my job. But don't you fret on that, ah? That gold piece, it's enough for me to move my family out of Scla. Likely we'll go up the coast. Wife's got family up there, always complaining she never sees them! I'll buy a boat, take up fishing... I'll be ready for a slower pace of life, ah?" He laughed again.

"That sounds like a good plan," I agreed. "But if I were you, I'd do it in a hurry. Be on your way before the Purifiers reach Scla and start asking questions."

"Right enough. But those Purifiers may have a hard job getting answers, especially not if people hear that the Wraith is involved!"

"I don't know about that. They have a forceful way of pursuing their aims, and I don't want people getting hurt by them on my account."

"But it won't be on your account! This will be a way we can all push back against the First Order. You're just giving people the opportunity to do something they've always wanted to. I can tell you, those Purifiers get too forceful then they'll find the whole town against them!"

"No, that mustn't happen!" I had a fearful vision of Scla rising in rebellion, and of the terrible retribution Crombard would visit on them in return. And all due to my mere presence. What had I stirred up? It could be as bad as any of the Skipper's mad schemes. "We have to keep all this as quiet as possible. Trust me, what

Ommet and I are about will mean better times for all in the future, but for now it has to be softly softly! So please, no mention of the Wraith."

I could feel his disappointment. "Some people will have to know," he protested. "You're going to need more help than I can give. Your friend Mr. Ommet is going to need proper treatment, for a start. The name of the Wraith will procure that better even than gold!"

He had a point, especially since I had no more gold – and little enough of silver or even copper. "Well then, tell who you must. But only them, and make sure they know to keep it to themselves. If it once gets out that the Wraith is in Scla, Tunward and Crombard together will turn the place upside down to find me – and they won't care how much Second Order blood they shed in the process."

"As you say, then," he agreed. With glum reluctance. "But you don't realise what a sacrifice that will be. I reckoned to get free drinks for a year by telling about how I rode down from Casterlayne with the Wraith!"

"We get through this, I'll buy you free drinks for a year!" I promised. "You'll have earned them."

The thought raised his spirits. "As long as you have a few with me, then!" He started pulling on brake levers, adding a horrendous screeching to the noise. "Need to slow it down some now. Coming out to the Scla Valley soon, gets a bit more interesting from here on!"

I didn't much like the idea of 'more interesting' but there wasn't a lot of choice.

As the Slatebrook Valley dropped and opened out into the main Scla Valley, the rail track followed a long curve to the right. At this point, the Scla Valley was wide and flat at the bottom, but very steep at the sides. As we came out of the curve, we found ourselves on a narrow ledge, just a few feet wider than the slate wagons, with vertical walls of rock on our right and a precipitous drop to our left. Curril kept our speed in check as the track followed the contours of the cliff, with occasional little bridges or short tunnels to take us over deep cracks or through jagged outcrops. Not as desperate as the beginning of our journey, but still quite enough to raise my heartbeat.

"Wonderful view!" Curril commented – perhaps noticing my white knuckles as I gripped the front of the wagon and stared ahead. "Look, you can see practically the whole valley from here!"

The distraction was welcome – and it was indeed a magnificent view.

Although it was getting on towards early evening, the sun was still high in the west. But the far side of the valley was already in deep shadow from the Obsidian Mountains, their jagged peaks clawing at the sky and marking the boundaries of the Empire.

The rest of the valley was bathed in golden light, a patchwork of fields dotted with villages and farms. The town of Scla itself was a grey sprawl with the wide sea beyond – dockyards, dwellings, places of business and commerce, places of worship and recreation, all built of the slate that brought it wealth.

"See there?" Curril was pointing in the other direction, up towards the head of the valley. On top of a high hill was a magnificent castle – not grey, but of some stone that glowed where the sunlight shone on it.

"Nordbras Castle," Curril informed me. "Lord Tunward's seat."

"I know. I've been there."

"Oh yes - of course you have!"

We were descending the cliffs quite rapidly now, and soon lost the view as lower hills intervened.

"I've had a thought," Curril said. "Bearing in mind that you want to keep your name out of it. If I bring this Number Ten in early, littered with crossbow bolts and with two illegal passengers – one of them wounded – it's going to create a stir, even without mentioning the Wraith, ah? Word will get out."

"It will," I agreed. "And it wouldn't surprise me if Crombard already has men watching the railway. Just in case we do arrive by that means. So what can be done about that?"

"Well now, that's my thought. In a few miles we turn away from these cliffs and follow a ridge down into the valley. At the end of that ridge, we're only a mile or two from the terminus, but before then we run past a village. Talinge. The tracks cross over a road there, so there's gates, and a gate-keeper to mind them and stop traffic when we pass through. He's a friend of mine. I'll slow us right down and have a quick word with him as we pass. Get him to meet us beyond the village, with a wagon for your friend and your – ah – cargo. Have him get the healer to look at your friend as well."

"That sounds like a good thought. Except – a healer?" To my mind, that suggested an elderly lady who delivered babies and sold nice smelling packets of herbs. Probably told fortunes as well. "Is there no Doctor?"

"There's Doctor's in Scla, right enough. But they're all First Order. And expensive as well. Common folk go to the healer, and I know this one. She's good."

The choices were limited. "Then we'll go with your plan, and thank you."

The mountain shadows had lengthened by the time we reached Talinge, but had not yet reached our side of the valley. Curril slowed us down to a walking pace and began ringing the bell vigorously. As we came up to the road, a man rushed out of a nearby cottage, struggling into his jacket and swearing loud enough for us to hear as he hastily swung gates across to open up the rail-way and close off the road.

"What's this, Curril," he shouted red-faced as we trundled by. "Did you have brake failure or something? You're not due yet, not by an hour or else I've gone crazy! And who's that in the wagon with you, ah? By thunder, if you're carrying passengers it's trouble for all of us – you know I have to report it!"

Curril laughed. "Sorry, Mure, did I wake you?" He waved him closer "Listen – for your ears only…"

He leaned over the side and spoke quietly. But not so quietly that I couldn't hear the word 'Wraith' mentioned a few times. So Mure must count as one of those who needed to know. I just hoped that he could keep it to himself.

At least the name worked. I could feel the moment when his anger turned to amazement, and I saw his jaw drop as he glanced at me.

"You've got that, then?" Curril asked, and Mure nodded.

"I'll see it done, ah?" he said. "Freskan Woods, with a cart and the Healer, and as soon as maybe. And I'll write up the books to show you came past at the proper time! Which is a pity, because you must have set some sort of record on this run!"

"That I did," Curril agreed. "But there's more important things at hand than that just now. Away with you, ah?"

He released brakes and we were soon out of sight of the gates and the little village scattered around them. But before long he was putting them on again, and brought us to a full halt in a leafy wood.

"Will you be able to get the wagons moving again, without the pushers?" I wondered.

"No problem on this slope," Curril assured me. "We can wait here as long as need be, ah? Mure should be along soon enough, the healer lives in the village. Do you need to check on Mr. Ommet?"

I didn't, in fact, since I knew exactly how he was – deep in a pain-wracked sleep, only a little way above unconscious. Never-the-less I went and looked over the end of the wagon at him

– which confirmed what I knew already. He was in a very poor way. My makeshift bandage had perhaps slowed the loss of blood, but with the bolt still in him it was impossible to stop it altogether, and his clothing was soaked scarlet.

I forced down my own emotions. This was not the time for them. Instead I turned to the task of helping Curril pull spent bolts out of the floor and sides of the brake wagon. There was a worrying number of them.

"A dozen!" He tossed them out into the forest. "And that doesn't count all the ones that missed or were deflected away. The last of them he weighed in his hand, looking at it. "I might keep this. For when I can tell the story to my lads, ah?"

"Better not be caught with it, then – or you'll be telling the story to the Purifiers!" I pointed out, and he reluctantly threw it after the rest of them.

A rough track met the railway at this point, and shortly after we had disposed of the bolts a horse and cart emerged from it. Mure the Gate-Keeper was driving, and the woman riding beside him I took to be the healer. Younger than I'd expected, sharp features and sandy-blonde hair, but what struck me first was the unusually strong emotion that radiated from her. There was curiosity, and some apprehension, but mostly there was concern. Whatever her skills were, it was clear that she had a healer's heart. It was so powerful in her that I barely registered the awe that Mure was directing at me.

"Where is he?" she asked as the cart drew up alongside.

"In the slate wagon. Sleeping. I did my best with a bandage, but he's lost a lot of blood."

She hoisted herself over the side, and took a long look before dropping down again.

"I can't do anything while he's like that. Have him out and in the cart. We'll take him back to my house, and with all speed."

Little trace of an accent. An educated woman, I guessed – not who I'd expected to find filling the role of healer in a little Northern village.

"We need to get to Scla," I told her. "In haste. We are pursued."

"So I hear." She gave me a brief but searching look. "So you're the Wraith? Not surprising that you are pursued, then, given your reputation! Well, you carry on to Scla if you must. But your friend here stays with me, or he'll be dead by morning." She didn't wait for me to make a decision on it. "Mure – Curril – lift him out of there, if you please. Gentle as you can."

Gentle was difficult in the cramped space. I felt Ommet's pain spike as they lifted him out and lowered him down to where myself and the healer waited to take him. He moaned, and his eyes flickered open.

"Arton..." he whispered.

"I'm here," I told him. "There's a healer. She'll help you."

He gasped as we laid him in the back of the wagon, then slipped back into unconsciousness.

"Well, Mr. Wraith – what's it to be?" the healer asked.

"I can't leave him now," I said. "Scla will have to wait. Curril – could you and Mure pass that box down?"

The Healer clicked her tongue with impatience as the Holy Writings were unceremoniously dumped out of the brake wagon and into the cart with much less care than had been given to Ommet. But then, they couldn't feel anything.

"Curril," I asked, "those slate wagons – are they ever washed out?"

He looked puzzled. "No. Why should they be?"

"Well that one because it'll have a big pool of blood in it. And if the Purifiers find it, then they'll know that one of us is wounded."

"And then they'll come round looking for a healer who might have treated a man with a crossbow bolt in him." Curril finished the thought for me, looking grim. "I'll do what I can, but if I start washing out slate wagons that's going to attract attention in itself. There's a lot of wagons down there, though, it might take them a while to find that particular one."

"Don't do anything to get yourself in more trouble. You've done more than enough already. Take your family and go somewhere safer."

"We will. Be safe yourself, Mr. Wraith, and God Speed you on whatever this venture of yours is." He held out a hand. "It's been an honour to ride with you!"

I shook his hand warmly. "An honour for me, Brakesman Curril – and a ride I'm never going to forget!"

"Me neither!" he laughed.

"That's touching, but I've got a very sick man here!" Impatience radiated off the healer. "Mure, get this cart moving. Mr Wraith can come, stay or catch up as he wishes!"

"I'm coming!" I jumped up in the back of the cart as it started back up the lane, leaving Curril leaning over the side of Number Ten and waving us off.

It was getting darker under the trees. The Healer was wiping Ommet's face with a cloth, and my nostrils were filled with a strong scent. The cloth smelled, somehow, of warmth and rest.

"What is that?" I asked.

"It's a blend of herbs and oils that I make myself," she said, without taking her attention away from Ommet. "The skin absorbs it and it eases pain, among other things. The scent is beneficial as well."

She was right. I felt myself calmed by it, and I could feel Ommet's pain easing.

"That's all I can do for now," she continued. "But we'll be back at my house shortly."

"May I ask your name?"

"Viennive. Viennive Alacade. And what should I call you – or do you only go by 'Wraith'?"

"Arton Dowder. 'Wraith' is not a name I would have chosen, but it seems to have attached itself to me!"

"Well, it's not such a bad name at that." She glanced up at me. "When Mure told me that Curril had brought the Wraith down from Casterlayne, I thought he must be drunk. Even now, I'm having trouble with the idea. You're not what I would have expected. But this –" she indicated the bolt in Ommet's shoulder "– supports your story, I suppose. And if you truly are the Wraith, then you'll find only friends here."

I felt her sincerity. "Thank you. That's good to know. But, as a friend, I should warn you that those who did this to my friend will be in pursuit – and any who help us will incur their wrath!"

"Time enough to worry about that later, Mr. Dowder. For now, my priority is this wound. We'll discuss the rest later."

The cart emerged from the forest and turned onto a narrow country lane with fields to one side and houses ahead. The closest of these was a substantial dwelling of red brick, with a wide yard to the side that Mure turned the cart into.

Viennive was out of the cart before it had come to a halt, calling out names and giving instructions to those who responded. "Jennine – is the Master back yet? Then you will have to assist me. Go and prepare the surgery. Galton, lend a hand here – Mr Dowder, if you could help him with your friend? - take him directly to the surgery, Galton. I'll be along as soon as I've prepared. Mure – my thanks for this days work. You'd best get yourself back to your cottage – and if you happen down to The Woodsman for some ale later, be sure you don't mention this matter! Joskin, see to the horse, please, and get the cart scrubbed out. They'll be blood in it, and I don't want any trace left. Well, come on, let's be to it!"

She rushed inside, while I helped Galton. Not that he needed much help, he was a big lad, and had Ommet cradled in his arms like a baby once we'd eased him off the cart. My role was to go ahead and open doors at his instruction, and within a few minutes we were laying Ommet gently down onto a table.

It was an unusual table, the surface being all shiny white tiles. So was the rest of the room, the surgery as she had called it. It was all unrelentingly white and fastidiously clean.

The young woman, Jennine, came in with two lamps that burned with such a clear and brilliant light that the Illuminators of Vorgranstern might have provided them. There were no dark places in the room for the light to escape to, and my eyes ached with the whiteness of it. I wondered if this was a normal thing to find in a healer's house. I had little experience of such places, thanks to my First Order heritage.

Viennive followed, having changed into a smock of clean linen – white, of course. "Thank you, Galton. Please show Mr. Dowder into the lounge, and get him some refreshment. I'm afraid this may take a while, Mr. Dowder, and you are in no great shape yourself, I think. Go and rest, while I see to your friend."

There was no space for argument in her voice, and indeed I saw no reason for any. Ommet was in as good a care as he could be: the compassion and confidence I felt from the Healer was assurance of that. She was concerned for him, she knew what to do about it. I went without argument.

Galton showed me into a room at the back of the house, and left to get food.

Through the windows I could see a pleasant garden, bright flower beds edging a well tended lawn. It was now approaching sunset, and a warm golden light shone through trees and bushes. It was still bright enough to show the lounge to be a comfortable place, with well used but quite serviceable furniture, several rugs in warm colours, and an interesting collection of watercolours on the walls. I took a closer look at them. Landscapes, local scenery I thought. Probably done by a local, or at least by someone having some talent but little training. They were interspersed with formal portraits of people from past generations. Ladies and gentlemen in stiff clothing with expressions to match.

I sat in one of the armchairs, and felt myself begin to relax for the first time in... how long? Days, certainly.

Perhaps years. I couldn't remember a time when I'd ever been completely at ease. But there was that about this house that encouraged it. A faint scent in the air – sweet, but not cloying. More than that, a feeling of peace.

Perhaps it was the compassion I'd sensed from Viennive, permeating the building. I couldn't feel it directly any more, but the memory of it lingered. Perhaps it was simply the fact that I could no longer feel Ommet's pain – which had been ever-present since the bolt had struck him. But it had faded now. Perhaps he had been given something more to ease him.

Galton returned, with a tray, which he set on a low table before leaving me alone once more. I found myself suddenly ravenous – perhaps not surprisingly. It had been an eventful day, and I hadn't eaten since our sparse meal up on the high plateau above Casterlayne.

There was a thick vegetable broth, warm and tasty, with some soft bread, recently baked. A tankard of ale, a platter of assorted fruits and some covered dishes.

I set to with a will, and having quickly finished the broth, I turned my attention to the rest of the fare. To my delight, when I removed a lid I found an actual selection of cheeses – not just the usual hard red Northern variety, but several others as well. A white and salty goat's cheese. A crumbly yellow cheese which I thought must be from Murkarin. This close to the border there was a good deal of local traffic in delicacies that would not travel much further.

And there was a soft cheese. Pale yellow, with a rough white rind.

I cut a small piece off, sniffed it, A very delicate scent, hard to define but familiar.

I tasted it. Slightly nutty flavour, smooth texture. Stronger than the scent suggested, and probably a little past the best, but still good.

"Ferabard," I whispered to myself. "Or from one of the farms nearby. Local milk, from the red-brown local cows, eating the local grass mixed in with the hedgerow weeds that the cows love."

Ferabard was ten miles from my home. From where I'd grown up. My father had made a cheese very similar to this. He had blended some herbs with it, that gave it a distinct flavour. He'd promised that one day he would show me how to do that, what herbs he used and how he did it.

But he'd died before he could do that. The secret was lost with him. No one would ever make that cheese again.

They'd hung him from the tree that grew in the yard between the barn and our house. They hung him and my brother and my friend from the next farm who had come to play. We played hide and seek, and I was hiding when the men rode in. My mother ran out of the house, screaming, shouting to my father to get the boys and run, but they had already surrounded the farm. They charged from all directions, men on big horses, men in black leather with bare steel in hand, men with flame-badges on their chests.

Their leader, broad-faced, black bearded... he hit her, knocking her down. Then dragged her up and forced her to watch whilst they threw ropes over the branches and hauled the three bodies into the air, twisting and jerking. He made her watch until they were still. Then he threw her over a horse and they rode off. All but the ones who went into the house and the barn and the other buildings. They carried torches, and smoke and flames were soon pouring out from every window. Blazing buildings, blazing badges, flames everywhere. Flames and black smoke billowing into the sky, black cloaks billowing behind the last of the riders as they galloped away.

I'd longed for this cheese, missed its delicate taste. But now I couldn't eat it. It dropped onto the plate as I sank back into the chair, sobbing and exhausted by the years and years of grief.

Chapter 23: The House of Healing

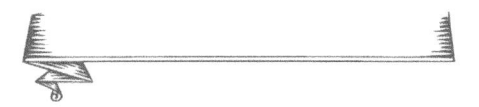

I woke slowly, consciousness rising painfully from some deep, dark place within me. Before I was even properly awake, I was aware of three things.

Firstly, that I was not alone. Secondly, that the person with me was First Order. And thirdly, that he was not a threat.

I opened my eyes. They felt painful, and my face was stiff with dried tears. The room was changed now – curtains drawn across the windows, lamps lit. Not the brilliant white light of the surgery, but a more normal lamplight, golden and gentle. The food tray had been removed as well, and someone had put a blanket over me.

The man who sat opposite looked to be in his twenties, but I knew he was older. Though not as old as I was. Dark blonde hair, darker beard close cropped to his face. A warm smile.

"Welcome," he said. "I'm Padran. Viennive's husband."

Suddenly, a great deal became clear. Padran was a First Order man in whom the Gifts were fully expressed. A man who shared a love with one of the Second Order. The empathy which that released had extended to every member of the household and had permeated the entire place. I'd felt it as soon as I'd entered, or would have done if I had not been so focussed on Ommet's pain.

I sat up, rubbing my face. "Sorry, I fell asleep... my friend. Ommet. Is he – how is he?"

Padran smiled. "Sleep is good, and you're welcome to rest here. As for your friend, Viennive has got the bolt out, but there are complications. It carried threads from his clothing deep into his flesh, and they must all be removed or infection will follow. A delicate matter, to find and extract all of them without making the wound worse! But not to worry, she is very good at this. She'll come and talk to you later. I'm sorry I wasn't here when you arrived – I'd gone out to tend to someone at a farm some distance from here."

"So you are both Healers?"

He chuckled. "Indeed we are. But she's better at it! I tend to the easier matters – today it was a young man with a broken leg – but for the more challenging cases Viennive is much the better choice, I promise you."

I believed him. It was impossible not to, since his sincerity, his truthfulness, resonated within me. There could be no deceit between two people of the First Order with their Gifts fully awakened. The implications of such transparency were both profound and frightening.

As that knowledge struck me, I saw and felt Padran's own recognition of that, and realised that for him as well, this was the first time he had met with another of the First Order with the same strength in the Gifts. There was an instant of connection, of knowledge, and I knew Padran. Not his thoughts, not the facts of his life, but his nature, his character, his being. I knew his courage, honesty, compassion, love and strength. And his fears and doubts and rage against injustices.

In that same moment, he knew me as well.

We both pulled back, instinctively shielding ourselves.

"That... that was unexpected," said Padran after a moment.

I nodded. "For me as well. I have never met with another of the First Order who was so strong in the Gifts. At least, not since my own became more alive."

"Nor have I. In fact I thought that I might be the only one who had developed in this way. They say that the Gifts are fading. I thought that I was an anomaly." He smiled. "The last thing I would have expected was to find a kindred soul in my lounge. Especially not one whom I'm told is an infamous jewel thief! The Wraith himself, no less."

There was no point in denying it. He could see the truth of it in me.

"If you are an anomaly, then so am I! But the fact is, Padran, this flowering of our Gifts is what is supposed to happen. Their fading in so many of the First Order is because the truth has been suppressed."

"What truth is that?"

I sat back, scratched my head, and considered how best to answer that question. How to tell Padran something that would upend his whole understanding of the world and his place in it. Something that, in truth, I was barely coming to terms with myself.

"Tell me, when did you first begin to realise that your Gifts were increasing in strength?"

"I suppose it was when I was at Medical School. While I was training to be a doctor."

"And was that when you met Viennive?"

"Yes." He smiled. "She was one of the very few Second Order students there."

"She trained to be a doctor? Not... a healer?" I only just managed to keep from saying 'Not just a healer'.

"That's right. There was a time when most doctors were of the Second Order. Not surprisingly, for the First Order rarely needed medical aid in those days, accept for accidents or injuries. The Gifts kept illness at bay, and quickly healed minor wounds. So Viennive has a family history of medicine. Both her parents were doctors, and she had grandfather who was a surgeon of some renown." He nodded at one of the portraits. "But that has changed. As the Gifts have faded, the First Order have come to need doctors more and more. Especially as they grew older – and they grow older more quickly now than in the past."

"And they didn't trust Second Order doctors?" I suggested.

"Indeed not. But it goes beyond matters of trust – at least, up here in the North. I hear that things are more relaxed in other parts of the Empire. But at the Northern Medical College, near Vorgranstern, it was made very clear that the Second Order were not welcome. Not even Viennive."

"In spite of her family history?"

"And in spite of the fact that she was very clearly the best of us all." Padran shrugged. "Perhaps because of that. There was a lot of jealousy. She, and the few other Second Order students faced opposition and discrimination from the start. But as our studies progressed, and she continued to excel, it became apparent that there was more to it than some petty rivalry, or even prejudice. There was an active campaign to force all the Second Order out of the College – and it did not originate amongst the other students, but with the faculty. And even beyond them, I believe."

"So this was a matter of policy?"

"That's right. I didn't realise it at first. But I saw how the Second Order students were constantly belittled, their confidence undermined. No matter how well they did in exams, they were marked down. They were given gratuitous punishments, made to work extra hours on demeaning tasks. And one by one, they gave up and went home. Until only Viennive was left. But she..."

He broke off, shaking his head at the memory. I felt from him how much he'd wondered at her, how he had come to love her strength.

"She was indomitable. And no matter how much they tried to undermine her, her ability stood out. She not only had a deeper knowledge of the academic side of medicine, but she had the heart and soul for it as well. She simply cared more, I think."

"I'm not surprised that you fell in love with her!"

He smiled. "I think I might always have been in love with her, from the moment I saw her. Does that sound silly? I know it's a staple idea in some novels. But in truth, I was always very attracted by her. And the worse the persecution became, the more passionate I became in her defence. The injustice of it infuriated me, the grace and courage with which she faced it inspired me. And I started to challenge her treatment."

"That must have gone down well," I said dryly.

"As you'd expect! I became more and more isolated from the other First Order students. But I didn't care, because Viennive and I became closer and closer. But then one day I was called into the Chancellor's office."

Emotions were gusting out from Padran as he spoke. Old feelings, but strong ones. Memories that still stirred anger in him. An unnatural feeling in a gentle soul, but all the more powerful for that.

"The Chancellor was there, and another. Someone who I had not met before, but I knew their name. And their reputation. Baron Crombard, Lieutenant of the North, nephew and right-hand man to Grand Duke Brodon himself."

I winced, considering such a meeting. "That must have been unpleasant."

"You could say that... To be honest, it started well enough, as the Chancellor complimented me on my on my progress and assured me that I should have no trouble in qualifying. Providing, that was, that I focused on my work, and did not allow myself distractions.

By which, of course, he meant Viennive. He then pontificated about the need to preserve our superiority as members of the First

Order – our 'natural heritage' as he called it. He talked around the fact that the Gifts were fading, but made it clear that this was why the Second Order could no longer be allowed into the Medical Professions."

"Ah! If Second Order doctors are called on to treat First Order patients – then the fading of the Gifts will soon be common knowledge!"

"Exactly so. And he went on to tell me that I needed to use any influence I had with Viennive to persuade her to leave the College. She should use her gifts to work amongst the Second Order, he suggested. But she needed no qualification for that.

Of course, I rejected his proposal outright.

Then Crombard took over, and gave me a furious tongue-lashing, cursing me as a traitor to my Order, a fool who would sully my pure bloodline with a debased Second Order slut – yes, he called her that! - a weakling and a disgrace to my family. And so on. He went on to tell me that Viennive would be cast out of the college one way or another, and if I didn't help get rid of her then I'd be gone as well."

"A fearful experience." I knew it was. I could feel the echoes of it in him.

"The really frightening bit was yet to come. I had been standing in front of the Chancellor's desk up till then, but Crombard come close and pushed me back into a chair. Loomed over me, and spoke directly into my ear. I can still remember every word. 'If you think to leave with her, that will be an insult to your entire Order and I will take it personally! I have men trained to deal with such as you. My Purifiers will cleanse the Empire of all traitors!' Then he simply walked out, without another word."

"Purifiers?" A shock ran through me. Images sprang to mind: a badge of fire, burning buildings. "He threatened you with the Purifiers?"

"That's right. You know of them." It wasn't a question, Padran felt my reaction.

"They are the ones who chased us out of Casterlayne. And – I have a history with them."

"I hadn't heard of them before then. Except as a rumour, a legend even. Knights of ancient times who upheld the rule of the First Order. But when Crombard spoke of them, I knew that they were no legend, but real and terrible. And I understood why they were called Purifiers."

"What did you do?"

"I went at once to Viennive. We realised that things had gone beyond academic persecution. Our lives were in danger. We fled that same night, looking for somewhere where we could practice our healing in safety, I hid the fact that I was First Order. We married, we made a new life for ourselves. And we kept watch for the Purifiers. Eventually, we came here."

"And now I have brought them upon you," I said softly. "I am so sorry."

Padran raised his hands. A calming gesture, echoed by the emotion he sent my way. "I don't deny, I regret that. But in truth, it was always a possibility. And in any case, they are not yet at the door. From what I hear, they cannot get to Scla for some hours yet. We have time to make preparations. But you were telling me of the Gifts. What do they have to do with Viennive?"

"It's love, Padran. Love between the First and the Second Order, in particular. That's why they were given in the first place, that is what kindles their power. And it is the denial, the suppression of that truth that has caused the decline in the Gifts."

I proceeded to tell him what I'd learned from Ommet, the things he had revealed to the New Dawn. I went on to explain to him about the Writings we carried with us, and how Mirrion's words offered hope for the future of the Empire. And as I talked,

I felt wonder and excitement grow in him, which burst out as I finished.

"Then there is hope! Hope for us and for the whole Empire! We will not need to hide ourselves forever!"

"There is hope," I agreed. "But only if those Writings get to the Empress in time. Without that proof, she cannot act to reverse the lies. Even with it, it will be hard, and especially hard up here in the north. I don't think that the likes of Brodon and Crombard will accept such a truth. Not willingly."

Padran nodded soberly. "There are hard times ahead, perhaps. But at least there is a chance for something better to come. What can we do to help? What's your plan for getting to Daradura?"

I couldn't doubt his sincerity, but neither could I accept his offer. "I can't tell you. The less anyone knows of my plans the better. I know you would not willingly betray me – but if the Purifiers take you and Viennive..." I let my voice trail off.

He closed his eyes, fear surging through him at the thought. "I see. I understand that – but there must be something we can do?"

"You're already doing it. Or your wife is. Healing Ommet is the most important thing you could do. But apart from that, just get us to Scla, and as soon as possible."

Viennive came in at that point, still wearing her white gown, though it was now stained with blood. Ommet's blood. Focused on Padran, I hadn't notice her approach, but now she was here I was aware of her tiredness – and her concern.

"Get you to Scla?" she said. "Yourself, Mr. Wraith, certainly. But not your friend. He won't be fit to travel for a while."

"How is he?"

"The bolt is out, and he is sleeping. But it had cut deep and was well embedded. I've repaired what I can, and cleaned the wound, but there was a great deal of damage. Not just from the bolt, either. He's been through some hard times of late, I think. He looks to have been badly beaten, and was probably weak already. With all the blood he has now lost, he can only recover with rest and care. A lot of rest and care! He'll not be fit to travel, to Scla or anywhere else, for a long time to come."

"And yet he cannot stay here," I said gently, and raised a hand against her objections. "Not because the care is lacking, of course not! But as I have told your husband, we are pursued by Baron Crombard and his men. Including the Purifiers!"

I felt the fear in her as I said it. "Truly? But why?"

"I'll explain it all later," Padran told her. "But I fear our guest is correct. Once it is known that Mr. Ommet was wounded – or even of the mere possibility – they will be scouring the entire countryside up and down the railway. And there are no healers living any closer than us."

"There are few enough healers anywhere in these parts," Viennive admitted. "None that I'd trust with anything more than a bruise! But people round here have no love for the likes of Crombard. No one will give his men information."

I shook my head. "Somebody will. If not for gold, then for fear. Who will keep silent when their family is threatened? And the Purifiers have no restraints. No, Ommet is not safe here – nor anywhere else you might move him to. I have to get him away, by one means or another." I paused then added another thought. "Nor are you safe. Crombard knows you from the past, and he does not forget such things. If his men bring word of a husband and wife, healers of unusual skill, he will most likely come and see for himself – and even if they cannot connect you to us, he will still have his revenge on you, just for being together. To him, the joining together of First and Second Order is a crime in itself, and he will destroy you for that alone. It's not just myself and Ommet that need to leave. You and all your household must be gone before the Purifiers come looking."

Viennive shook her head. "No, we can't – our work here, the people..."

Padran took her in his arms. "We must, for a while. Our mere presence could bring Crombard's fury down on the entire village. Especially if they tried to protect us, and you know that they would." He looked over at me. "Feelings in these parts run high against the First Order. Lord Tunward has not been a kind overlord, and there's been talk of a rising. Indeed, there are rumours that one is already planned – perhaps you've heard of the New Dawn?"

I smiled grimly. "Oh, I know all about the New Dawn. Be assured, they will not be causing any more problems. But in times like these it only takes a few hotheads to start something that soon runs out of control. Reprisals will follow, and they will be harsh. Yet, if things remain calm for just a short while – if I and Ommet can complete our mission – then there is hope for a better future, without the bloodshed."

Viennive gave Padran a searching look.

"It's true, my love. I'll tell you the details later. But all that he says is right." She relaxed as she felt the reassurance come from him. Total trust, that was the blessing that the Gift could bring to a relationship.

Padran looked at me. "We have made plans. It was always possible that this day would come. There are places we can go for a while. But perhaps Mr. Ommet should come with us. We might get him safely to Scla, but I doubt that he'd survive a longer journey."

"I know. It seems that he and I must part company for a while." I said it calmly, but Padran knew the depth of feeling behind the statement, and nodded his sympathy. "But if he were to stay with you it would increase your risk. I will make – other arrangements for him. But we have to be in Scla."

"Very well. Viennive, can you prepare him? Galton can take them into Scla with the cart. He has family there, I'll tell him to stay with them for a while. Joskin can get the wagon out and help us pack up, then go to his parents in the village. I'll ask him to spread the word that we've gone away for a while – and tell them that if anyone comes asking, they're to tell everything they know. Jennine will come with us. Let's be at it! We must be on our way by dawn."

Viennive may have been the better healer, but Padran was a leader. The decision was made and acted upon at once, and the entire household was thrown into a bustle of sorting and packing.

Anxious not to get in the way, I wandered outside, where Galton was hitching the horse back up to the cart, whilst Padran and Joskin eased a huge wagon out into the yard. 'Wagon' was a poor description – it was more like a cottage riding on six great wheels, all polished wood with painted panels, proper windows, a high driver's bench at the front and a chimney projecting from the roof. I lent a hand, heaving and straining to roll it forward.

Padran looked at it with some pride. "Our first home," he told me. "After we left the college and married. We couldn't go back to our families – mine wouldn't have me back with her, and she couldn't put hers at risk – but we found refuge with the travelling communities. In time, we got our own wagon. After a year or so, we decided it would be safe to settle down. But we keep the wagon stocked and sometimes use it to visit the more remote parts. So we can be on our way quite quickly."

He gave me a knowing look. "You have your doubts." It wasn't a question.

"Only that this seems very conspicuous for someone trying to hide from the Purifiers."

"It would seem so. But there are travelling communities here and there all over the north. They keep to themselves, and have little to do with outsiders – but our healing gifts won us friendships, and amongst them, such things are not forgotten. We will join them – and vanish! Hidden in plain sight, as it were."

"But if Joskin or Galton talk about the wagon?"

"They won't. And if they did, the Purifiers would have a long hard search to find the right one! Not to mention a dangerous one. Travellers protect their own and whilst they are loyal friends, they are also implacable enemies."

He clapped me on the shoulder. "The Empire itself will be changed before the Purifiers find us – especially if you finish your mission!"

Joskin was bringing out horses for the wagon – big, powerful beasts, snorting with annoyance at having their rest disturbed. Or perhaps with eagerness to be off? Padran turned to go and help, but I remembered something.

"One thing I must ask you about…"

He turned back, raising an enquiring eyebrow.

"How did you come by the Ferabard?"

He frowned. "The what?"

"The Ferabard. That soft cheese? I know it seems a strange thing to ask about but…" I stopped and shook my head. "It has some significance for me."

Padran gave me an intent look. "Yes. There are strong emotions there for you. Not pleasant ones. I'm sorry, if I'd known – but it was in the kitchen, so Galton put it out for you."

"Don't concern yourself, I was surprised, that's all. I haven't seen any of it for years. They don't have it in these parts. I wondered how it came here, that's all."

"Ah, yes. Well, we have had something of a problem in obtaining proper medical supplies. We do what we can with local herbs, but some medicines, some equipment, are less easy to come by. Especially as we cannot use the normal sources, not without giving ourselves away. So, every so often I must travel further afield.

Sometimes I go into Murkarin, but for some things I go south, into other parts of the Empire."

"And you buy cheese?"

"In these times, in these parts, you have to be able to give a reason for what you do and where you go. So I say that I am a lover of exotic foods, including fine cheeses. And I show samples I have bought to support my story. In truth, I am developing a taste for them. But that is how I came to have this – what did you call it? Ferabard?"

"I see. Well, perhaps someday I will bring you some samples of southern cheeses at their best. If you have a taste for over-ripe Ferabard, then you would love them!"

"I shall look forward to it!" he said. "God speed you, Mr. Wraith – you carry our best hopes for the future."

Chapter 24: Scla

The journey from Talinge to Scla was a lot slower than the one down from Casterlayne. And a lot less exciting, though that was no disadvantage. I dozed through most of it, laid out in the back of the cart with Ommet and Mirrion's Writings, but the rough road and the unsprung cart prevented any deep sleep. Ommet did better, still under the influence of the healer's potions. I roused myself to check on him several times, worried that a particularly deep pothole might have started his wound bleeding again. But for all Viennive's concern about letting Ommet travel, her work held up.

In the first grey light of dawn, we rattled across cobblestones and down the streets of Scla. More colourful than you would expect from a town built mostly of slate, because here they had the pick of the best, and it wasn't all grey. Many buildings were faced and tiled in shades of green, pink and blue, whilst the grander dwellings and public edifices had imported red or yellow brick.

At my request, Galton took us directly down to the harbour, which was already busy even at this time. Over on the far side, fishing boats were discharging their catch from the night, and the air was filled with sea birds, screeching loudly as they swooped and dived to fight over the scraps. The same sounds that I had heard around the great rock of Vorgranstern. But here in Scla their cries were interspersed with a surprisingly loud hissing from small flying lizards – distant kin to the swamp lizards we had had previous acquaintance with. I was happy for them to stay over with the fish.

Nearer at hand, the quays were full of two masted trading vessels of the same ilk as the *Anatarna*. More unpleasant memories! These, however, were fully engaged in legitimate business, unloading various cargoes and loading slate.

Set back from the busy dockside was a row of taverns, inns and hotels, of various degrees ranging from the rough and bawdy to the quiet and respectable. I chose one of the latter, the sort of place where passengers might await their ship or a sea-captain might take a rest from his. We aroused the landlady and obtained a room, after first assuring her that Ommet's condition was due to an accident from which he needed time to recover. Not (as she feared) extreme inebriation or some dreadful infection acquired in foreign parts. My remaining silver – well, technically the Apothecaries silver – served to sooth her fears and compensate her for the early start.

Galton carried Ommet up to his room, laid him gently on the bed, and went back for the box. He hadn't said a word in the entire journey, so I was somewhat surprised when, on taking his leave, he shook me warmly by the hand, and refused the coppers I offered him for his trouble.

"No, sir, I need no payment," he assured me. "It's been my honour and privilege to assist you."

"Well, my thanks anyway. Best be on your way – there's trouble following us, and I don't want you caught up in it."

He gave me a knowing look. "Trouble, ah? But you'll slip away from it, I think – like a wraith!"

I wished I had his confidence. Looking out at the brightening sky, I was aware that the first rail-train down from Casterlayne would have departed by now. There were probably already Purifiers here in Scla, alert for us if not actually aware of our presence, and once those from Casterlayne got here with the news, the search would begin in earnest. And what of the Baron himself, I wondered? Where was he? Not far away, I could feel it in my bones – not the result of any Gift, but simple apprehension.

Ommet continued to sleep peacefully. Following Viennive's written instructions, I carefully administered some more of the medicine she had provided. Then set about my business. I had a great deal to do, and I couldn't be sure how long I would have to do it in.

Breakfast arrived, along with writing materials that I had requested. Whilst eating, I wrote out three documents, two of which I then stamped with the Imperial Seal contained in Ommet's ring. Now my ring, I supposed, as I slipped it onto my finger. I briefly amused myself with the thought that the great jewel thief was now reduced to stealing a ring with a fake stone from his friend. I do enjoy irony.

But there was no time to dwell on it. The sun was well up, the day promised to be dry and bright, Scla was awake and the Purifiers were coming.

I left the hotel and made my way to an especially imposing building near the town centre – not slate, nor even brick, but a polished stone which must have been imported from the south at considerable expense. By such means do banks demonstrate how much of other people's money they have.

Another privilege of wealth is that you don't have to get up early. The bank had not yet opened when I arrived and it took a lot of hammering on the very grand doors before a junior member of the staff peered out and ordered me away with some annoyance. Clearly, he was unimpressed by my ragged appearance, but I handed him one of my documents and his jaw dropped in a satisfying manner when he saw the Imperial Seal.

"What is this?" he asked, incredulous. "How did you come by this?"

"I suggest you take it directly to your manager," I told him. "And be quick about it – you do recognise that seal, I hope?"

He slammed the door in my face and left me on the doorstep, which gave me cause for concern. There was little doubt that should the Purifiers already be here, and perhaps in control of the bank, they would have scant respect for the seal or the bearer. But otherwise? No doubt the bank manager was Tunward's man – it was Tunward's bank, after all – but would he take it upon himself to delay or deny an Imperial agent?

To my relief, after a few minutes the door opened again and I was ushered inside with considerably more respect. We went directly to the Manager's office, where a flustered man of the First Order persisted in saying 'Most irregular, most irregular," to every request I made of him. Never-the-less, I left the premises shortly afterwards with a good sized bag of gold and another of silver.

I had no doubt that my note with its all-powerful seal would be shown to Lord Tunward before it was dispatched to Daradura, and likely to Baron Crombard as well. Hopefully I'd be across the border before that happened.

Fund's secured, I next visited a tailor, one which specialised in clothing for those embarking on long journeys. They may have raised eyebrows at my dishevelled appearance, but the sight of my gold reassured them, and I quickly and gladly exchanged my New Dawn rags – and the Apothecaries green coat – for fresh linen shirt and undergarments, topped with trousers and jacket of red leather, and a thick fur-lined cloak to complete. Very suitable for a merchant travelling across the mountains in the closing weeks of summer.

I debated treating myself to a new pair of boots. But my current pair, though a little too big, were comfortable, and I had no desire to risk the blisters that breaking in stiff new leather could entail. These would do well enough for now.

THE HIDDEN LIBRARIES

The most common route into Murkarin is along the coast road. It is busy, well travelled and has a large customs post, well manned and supported by a garrison of Imperial troops. I fully expected that the Baron would have his own men there as a matter of course. Much safer from my point of view to use one of the more remote mountain passes. They were still guarded, of course, but less rigorously, and for anyone travelling to the southern regions of Murkarin the route is more direct.

However, those are not roads suitable for wheels, so my next stop was to buy myself a good riding horse and three pack-horses. Along with all the necessary tack, of course, and horse fodder for three days – the mountains are short of grazing, and I had no intention of stopping at any Inn this side of them. Considering which, I also needed my own supplies – something that the stables were happy to provide, for a price of course.

I left the horses to be prepared, with further instructions to load up other items that I'd be sending over. Yet another extra expense, but one that the Imperial treasury could well afford.

Then to a booksellers. Murkarin was not entirely the cultural wilderness that most citizens of the Empire assumed. Most of the educated classes there could read, not only in their own language but also the script of the Empire. However, there was a shortage of reading material for them to use, and consequently a flourishing trade in books. Excellent cover for someone wishing to smuggle some ancient documents across the borders. To further support that cover, I added to the assortment of popular titles some religious tomes and a few rather ragged scrolls of scriptural passages. Which would be unlikely to find a market in Murkarin or anywhere else, but of course the bookseller made no comment, probably being only too glad to be rid of them himself.

Next, an armourers, to buy a sword. A serviceable weapon, without any decoration but of fine steel. Travellers in Murkarin need to be cautious, law and order there are not as well enforced as in the Empire, particularly in the borderlands. Carrying a sword gave notice that I was prepared and able to defend myself and my goods. If that proved insufficient, then I still had the Apothecaries big knife in its damaged sheath under my new jacket.

I also had the Skipper's little poisoned dagger in my boot, but it wasn't much of a deterrent, and I hoped never to use it. Still, a blade is a blade, and you never knew when another might come in useful.

Preparations nearly done, one more visit to make. Out on the street, it was looking like a normal day, with all the usual bustle of people going about their business. There were a few guards around, but they were just the Scla Watchmen in brown uniforms, carrying staves but only looking to discourage petty thefts and public brawls.

The Purifiers must have reached here by now, surely? Were they still searching the train yard? Had they gone to the Baron for further orders, or up to Lord Tunward's castle to request reinforcements?

Probably all three. They were here, I was sure of it, but not moving openly. I hoped Curril and his family had got away.

The Scla river curves round the west of the town before reaching the sea just beyond the dockyards. The land inside that curve was originally low salt marsh, dank and liable to flooding. Mostly built over now, and with flood banks set up to protect against all but the highest tides, yet it is still unhealthy. Mud often seeps hrough poorly laid cobblestones, and mould creeps up the walls.

This is where the poorest inhabitants of Scla are forced to live, and this is where I found the Arravines.

They had, in fact, a fairly substantial establishment on a slight rise which would protect it from the worst of the damp or flooding.

Three buildings stood round a well paved courtyard, the central one standing higher than the others by a full storey. The courtyard gate stood open, and a line of ragged people were receiving soup and bread from the kitchens along one side. Peering through windows I saw that classes were already taking place within as the Friars followed their calling to teach.

An elderly man in Arravine robes stood watching the activities in the courtyard. He greeted me with a bright smile as I approached.

"Good morning!" he said. "If you're in need of food, do get in line – there's plenty for all. But you don't seem like one of our normal clientèle – is there some other need we can help you with?" His gentle smile matched the warm concern I felt from him.

An educated voice with a faint western accent. That, and the clothing, brought Ommet vividly to mind. But amongst the Arravines he was Thylan an'Darsio, Friar and scholar. Not my friend and companion through all these recent adventures, but a stranger. I held onto that thought, hoping it might make what I had to do easier.

I shook my head. "No, but I have something for you. The Arravines have been good to me in the past, and I now find myself in a position to repay you somewhat. Here – a donation to your work."

I dropped a small purse into his hand, and saw his eyes widen as he felt the weight of gold. "Why, this is most generous! I assure you, it will be put to good use."

A better use than it would have had in Lord Tunward's bank, I thought. "I'm sure it will," I agreed. "And there is something more. Some information that may be of interest to you. Here."

I handed over the second of the three documents, the one lacking the Imperial Seal. I felt the Arravine's curiosity as he began to open it up.

Without further conversation, I turned and strode quickly away. The gold had not been given merely to support a good cause, but to insure that my message got quick attention. However, I did not wish to remain whilst the document was read. That might lead to questions which I had neither time nor inclination to be answering.

Back to the stables, then.

But on the way I happened to pass an Apothecaries shop. A town the size of Scla would be expected to have several such establishments, and indeed I had seen one earlier. But this caught my eye.

Nordrum & Son, Apothecaries, read the sign that hung above the door, along with the usual symbol of a pestle and mortar. I recognised that name. I had read it on the list I had found in the green coat I had recently been wearing, that belonging to one Ulgrond Ommet, named the Apothecary in the New Dawn though not actually qualified as such.

I had kept the list, as well as the formula it had been with. Taking it out of an inside pocket, I checked it again. There was no doubt. Next to 'Scla' was 'Nordrum & Son'. And a single word, which we had deduced to be a password - 'Burdar'.

I had had no intention of investigating that matter. And I really didn't have the time just now, I told myself.

And yet, here was the very place mentioned on the list, right before me. And I had the password.

It wasn't just idle curiosity, I told myself as I crossed the street. It would be useful to know what the New Dawn had been planning. Certainly, the Empress or her Grand Chancellor would be interested. And it should only take a few minutes. After all, there was no sign that the Purifiers were yet here in strength.

I entered the shop.

I have not had a lot of experience of Apothecaries, but this seemed a fairly typical example of its type, if somewhat small and shabby. Long shelves lined with bottles containing various potions, racks of small drawers with neat labels no doubt filled with powders or pills. Larger containers lined one wall, bearing the names of various herbs, and a strong smell filled the room. Or rather, a mingling of many smells to give a strange olfactory result: a kind of sharp-edged mustiness which seemed likely to make my eyes water given long enough exposure.

The narrow faced young man behind the counter seemed unaffected, as you would expect. He looked at me expectantly. "Good morning sir, what might I do for you, ah?"

Strong local accent. "Good morning. I'm here regarding Burdar."

The effect was immediate. His eyes widened and I felt his emotion switch from mild boredom to sudden intense fear.

"B..Burdar?" he stuttered. "You are here for..."

Without finishing the sentence, he turned and ran to the back of the shop and through a doorway. I wondered for a moment if I should follow him but he returned almost at once with another man – older, but so much like him that I deduced that this must be Mr. Nordrum, and the younger man the '& Son'.

Nordrum elder was just as frightened. "I'm told you asked for – Burdar?" Apprehension radiated from him.

"That's right. Burdar. Is there some difficulty?"

"No, no, not at all, not at all!" He licked his lips. "Only you are not the gentleman who gave us the commission."

"Of course not. Why do you think you were given a password? That gentleman is detained on other business. Is this going to be a problem?" I kept my voice calm, but put an edge on the last sentence.

"Oh no, no indeed, certainly not, no problem, no problem at all sir!" Nordrum was desperate to reassure me. "If you would come through to the back, sir, the commission is completed and awaiting you... Vister, close the shop! We want no interruptions, ah?"

Nordrum Junior ran quickly to lock the front door, whilst Nordrum Senior ushered me through into a small workroom. More shelves, more assorted bottles and boxes. The centre of the room was occupied by a large, rather battered table, strewn with various tools of the trade. There was a large safe in the far corner, which he opened, and removed a small metal case.

"There you are, sir. Six items contained within, all exactly as specified." He put the case on the table, took a small key out of the safe, and offered it to me.

There were three key-holes. Which seemed like excessive security, especially if there was only one key. Though there were some arrangements I had heard of in which locks must be opened in a specific order.

"Open it," I said, and felt his fear spike again.

"Yes sir," he said with obvious reluctance. He picked up the key, inserted in the central hole and turned it. Then turned it back the other way, a full turn. He repeated that procedure in the left hand hole and finally – with great reluctance – the right hand. There was a click after each one, but the final hole produced a much louder noise. Not just a click but a clunk, as of some mechanism operating, and Nordrum jumped.

Biting his lip, he opened the lid with extreme care. I stepped closer and he stood aside so that I could see the contents.

The inside was padded with thick leather, shaped to hold six round glass jars, each about six inches tall and three across. I reached out to pick one up, and Nordrum let out a squeak of anguish.

"Oh, be careful, please sir, I beg of you!" He had gone beyond fear now, and was approaching terror. A malicious part of me was tempted to toss the jar into the air just to see his reaction, but I restrained myself. Not only would Nordrum probably make a bolt for the door (or suffer heart failure) but it would be foolish to ignore his reaction. He knew exactly what was in the jar.

So I removed the jar with extreme caution, and held it in both hands while I examined it carefully.

It was filled with some translucent yellowish liquid, but in the middle of the jar I could see there was a cylinder of something darker. The top was covered with a glass cap, held firmly in place with a wax seal.

"And this is as specified?" I asked, hoping to elicit information without revealing my ignorance.

Fortunately, Nordrum rose to the occasion. "Yes, sir," he confirmed. "The outer jar contains Substance A, as the instructions labelled it. The thinner glass container within contains Substance B, just as was required."

Thinner glass. So if the outer jar was broken, the inner one probably would be as well, allowing the substances to mix – with what result? "Have you tested it?" I asked.

Nordrum gulped. "Well, yes, I – we – thought that it would be best, to be sure that we had produced the substances correctly."

"And the result?"

"We, only used a few drops of Substance A, and one drop of B – so that the proportions were correct. We put them in a sealed tank containing some rats and a few lizards. The result was very effective. The gas was produced immediately and everything within the tank was dead within a few minutes. The animals, that is. The vegetation we had placed inside took a little longer."

Gas.

I now understood the Skipper's plan for Vorgranstern. Have the Baron and his men packed into the tunnels, seal them, and throw in the jars. The tunnels would fill with the deadly fumes... of course, that would probably wipe out half the civilian population of the city along with Crombard. But that would have have been an acceptable sacrifice in the Skipper's thinking.

"How high did it rise?" I had a chilling vision of pure death boiling out from the tunnels and enclosing the whole city in its embrace. "And how long did it remain?" I asked, wondering if the tunnels of Vorgranstern would have become permanently uninhabitable.

"It filled the tank, but that was a confined space. I could not experiment further, but the gas is heavier than air, so should not rise further than, perhaps, one storey of a house? More if some current of air should draw it up. It loses it's virulence after an hour or so. It would be less, of course, in the open air or a ventilated space. But we put in another rat after that hour was up and it survived."

Throughout this conversation, Nordrum's eyes had not left the jar in my hands, and I now fully appreciated his concern. If I dropped the jar, we were both dead. Very carefully, I moved to put it back in the case.

As I did so, I noticed a small hole in the leather padding. Looking more closely, I could see a gleam of metal, a sharp point just within the hole.

Three locks, which had to be operated in a specific order. A distinctive noise when the last one was turned – as of a mechanism being activated. Or deactivated. Glass jars. That all made sense now.

"And the case itself? Did you test its performance?"

"No sir. I just followed the instructions that came with it. Always unlock in the sequence 'Middle – Left – Right'. A full turn back for each one. Re-lock in the same order."

"Good." I laid the jar gently in its place, to Nordrum's evident relief, and closed the lid. "Lock it up, if you would, Mr. Nordrum."

He complied, and handed me the key. "May I ask, sir – do you intend to use this... locally?"

I gave him a cold look. "That is not your concern."

"No, no, of course not," he assured me with some desperation. "It is only that – should it be in Scla – that is, I have family here..." He stared at me in anguish as his voice faded away.

I could feel the turmoil within him. He had probably been nursing this fear ever since he had finished producing the evil stuff. Desperate to be rid of it, frightened of what it might be used for. The New Dawn would have cared nothing for that, but I was not the New Dawn.

"To the best of my knowledge, there are no plans for its use here in Scla."

His relief would have been evident without the Gift. "Thank you sir, thank you. Please be assured of my loyalty to the cause, of course, it's only that..."

"It's only that you prefer that this be used somewhere where you don't have to confront the results of your handiwork?" I said bluntly, and he looked at his feet. "I shall be leaving now. But one more thing – the formula from which you produced these substances?"

"Destroyed, as I was instructed."

"Then we have no further business. I advise that you now forget this whole matter!"

I had no doubt that Nordrum and his son – who was waiting, white faced, by the door – would be glad to do just that.

The case was provided with a leather handle. I picked it up and left. I did a little mental arithmetic as I did so. There were twenty Apothecaries on the list. One hundred and twenty jars of poison. At least that, some of them might have been supplied with more jars and cases. But more than enough to turn Vorgranstern into a charnel house. And perhaps some left over for other projects.

If ever I'd had any inkling of regret for what I had done to the Anatarna, it was fully gone now.

Back at the stables, my horses were fully prepared and loaded with the books I'd brought. I added the case to one of the packs, taking great care to see it secure.

Then back to the docks.

It still felt like a normal day, which was becoming more worrying by the minute since I knew very well it was nothing of the sort. The Purifiers were about, I was certain of it. I reassured myself that they must be thinly spread. They'd be watching exits from the town. The docks, the river bridge. They'd be looking for two men, one with bright red hair, the other in a green coat. I was a merchant, travelling alone, leading a string of pack-horses. They would have no interest in me.

I reached the hotel without incident, took my horses into the yard at the rear, and slipped the stable boy a copper to keep an eye on them until I got back. Then up to the room. Ommet was still sleeping. His breathing seemed easy and his colour was good. I opened up the box and began taking out the sacred Writings of the Prophet Mirrion, with more haste than reverence. They were still packed in their canvas bags, which made it easier.

The crossbow bolt which had pierced the box lid had penetrated far enough to crack the crystal sheet that protected one of them. The parchment beneath had been pricked, and the rest of the document exposed to the air for the first time in centuries.

Ommet would have been appalled, if he'd been awake to see it.

But, considering that Mirrion himself had sat and penned these very words some three thousand years past, it was incredible that they had survived so long at all. All things considered, they were doing quite well.

Better than they would if the Purifiers got to them! I shouldered the first two packs and took them down the stairs.

It took several trips and longer than I wanted to get all the Writings safely packed away on my horses, and then I had one more trip to make, to clear out all trace that I had ever been there. Not that there was much. On my way out, I paused by the bed and looked down at my friend for one last time. Relaxed in sleep, he seemed very young. It was far too early in his life for all that he had done, all he had endured.

The scabs and bruises stood out clearly on his pale skin, legacy of recent adventures but particularly of the Skipper's hospitality. Neither of us had had sight of a razor since we left Layfarban, but whereas my beard was growing out smooth and dark, Ommet's was patchy, bushy, and a shade redder than his hair.

I watched him for a while. Trying to find words for a goodbye, even though I couldn't speak it. I spent too long doing so: he stirred and his eyes flickered open. "Arton?"

"I'm here." I gripped his hand.

"I'm very dry," he whispered.

I poured a glass of water from the jug by the bed, and helped him sip it. I had added some of the healer's potion to it earlier. It would be better for him to sleep, whatever happened next.

"What's happening? Where are we now?" he asked with a stronger voice.

"We're in Scla. We found a healer. Your wound should heal well, but you need to rest."

He smiled faintly. "Rest. Rest is good..." Then a frown crossed his face. "Purifiers! We can't rest! They're after us. The Writings..."

He made to push the covers away, but I restrained him gently. "No. The Writings are on their way to Daradura. You must rest."

He looked at me long and hard, and I knew that he felt the untruth, or at least the half-truth.

"The Writings are loaded on pack-horses, Ommet. I'll take them to the Empress myself. I promise you. But you must stay here, and rest."

He understood. I felt his acceptance. And his trust.

I released his hand and stood up. "I have to go. I've made arrangements – the Purifiers will not take you."

"They might. But that's not important. The Writings are. And all that they will mean." For a moment, his eyes seemed to burn with the same intensity that I had first seen in that dark cell in Neowbron. Then he closed them and sank back. "Go, my friend. And thank you."

I sought for something more to say. Nothing came to mind. I turned to go, and then he spoke again. "Arton – perhaps you can satisfy me on one point – I've wondered about it – what's your real name?"

His eyes opened again, just a fraction.

"It really is Arton," I told him. "But not Dowder, of course. I was born Arton di Ferabard."

"Arton di Ferabard." He said it thoughtfully. "Arton of Ferabard. Arton from Ferabard. The south-east. Teilisin Peninsula."

"That's right. And that's more than anyone has known of me for... for a very long time."

He smiled, although his eyes had shut again as the potion began to take hold. "But there should be another name. A family name. In those parts, it goes through the mothers line, does it not?"

I had not told anyone my family name. Ever. But Ommet – Thylan – I wanted him to know. To know who I really was.

"My full name... is Arton di Ferabard r'ha Sahal Crombard. Arton from Ferabard, son of Sahal Crombard."

I wondered what his reaction would be. Shock? Horror? Fear? But what I felt from him was surprise. And sadness.

"Your mother was a Crombard? Related to the Baron?"

"His sister."

"And your father… was Second Order? That explains a lot."

"It does, doesn't it."

Ommet understood. He knew me, and all I felt from him was his sympathy, his care, his love. Which slowly faded into sleep.

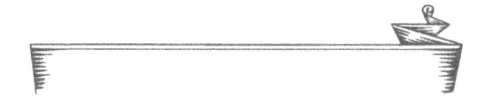

Chapter 25: To the Border

I had lingered for too long. It was nearly noon, and my stomach rumbled at good smells wafting from the kitchen, but there was no time to stop for lunch. Instead it was out to the horses, a final quick check that the precious Writings were securely stowed, then up in the saddle and away.

I took quiet side streets as much as possible, but had eventually to come back to the main road that ran down to the docks. As I came near, there was a sudden disturbance. Carts were being pulled to the side, people scurrying out of the way. City Watchmen with staves were encouraging them, and not gently From my Gift, I felt the prevailing mood of the crowd, normally as mixed and variable as their physical presence, become suddenly one of shared alarm.

Though my way ahead was now blocked, from my mounted position I had a good view over pedestrian heads. I heard the clatter of hooves, and then mounted men came by at a good canter.

Men-at-arms in mail, with silver and green surcoats. Lord Tunward's colours. A full troop of them, heading down to the docks. But what alarmed me more was the black clad figure at their head. In the glimpse I had there was no sign of a flame-badge, but I didn't need that to know a Purifier when I saw one.

Once the troops had past, the crowd began to clear again, as people went back to their business – though now the prevailing mood had swung to a surly anger. My own feeling was more of apprehension. I had convinced myself that the Purifiers would be content to watch secretly, and in small numbers. Clearly, their strategy had changed – perhaps because Lord Tunward had sent his men to support them. With greater numbers at their disposal, they were coming out into the open and would be more active in their search.

My first thought was to turn back to the docks and get Ommet to safety. But to do so would be to put my plans in danger, and risk losing the Writings. If they fell into Crombard's hands, all that we had worked for would be lost.

Cursing under my breath, I rode on, but no longer bothering with the side streets. There was no more advantage to be gained there. Speed was of the essence now, and the main road was a better route than the narrow and winding side ways.

Never-the-less, I had barely got my horses moving again when there was further delay. Once again, people moved to the side of the road, though this time I felt more respect than alarm or anger. A group of Arravine Friars came by, on foot, panting and sweating, but still making good time. One of them was the man I had spoken to earlier: I dropped my head and looked away as he passed, but he had no interest in the crowd and went by without a glance in my direction.

I was relieved to see them. I had hoped for a more urgent response from the letter I had sent, if not because a fellow Arravine was wounded and in trouble, then because this Arravine was the notorious Thylan an'Darsio, who had plundered their Hidden Libraries of the most valuable documents. Surely word of him must have been spread to all their houses by now? Though they would not yet have heard of the latest outrage at Kalanhad.

Still, if they had taken time to make the decision, they were trying to make up for it now, and if they'd run all the way from the Arravine House then their hot and sweaty faces were excused. It might be, I speculated, that they had got wind of Lord Tunward's men moving into the town in force, and whatever their feelings in regard to their errant Brother, the thought of leaving him to First Order justice had energised them.

Of course, the troops would be at the docks before them, but the Purifiers first concern would be to stop us leaving by sea. So they would stop all vessels sailing and search every ship in the harbour before turning their attention to the hotels and inns. Even with the extra numbers, that would take time – time enough for the Arravines (having the advantage of knowing where to go) to get Ommet and whisk him off to safety. Of course, I wouldn't put it past the Purifiers to invade the Arravine house once they discovered who had him, but if the Friar's book learning translated into any degree of common sense they would put him somewhere better hidden.

It was out of my hands. The traffic was flowing again, and I went with it, heading out of Scla.

There were three main routes by which I could leave the town. One road went up the valley, going south to Nordbras Castle – but that would put me on the wrong side of the river, with few places to cross. And those easily guarded. The Imperial Highway ran to the east and Vorgranstern in one direction – the wrong direction, for my purposes. In the other it crossed the river by a large and well constructed bridge and went west to the Murkarin border. That was the road I had to take.

Of course, it's named the 'Lord Tunward Bridge', built by him and decorated with several statues showing the Lord himself in various authoritative poses. It wasn't hard to understand why he was unpopular.

As I approached it, (passing under a large archway topped by, as you would expect, a statue of Lord Tunward) the traffic thickened and slowed. There was a long queue of laden carts – most of them carrying slate – interspersed with carriages, pack-horses, lone riders and pedestrians. Watchmen were bustling around, trying to keep things moving and people calm.

"What's up, ah?" shouted the driver of a cart in front of me.

The Watchmen he'd addressed shouted back. "'s the Lord's men. Checking for someone. They do say it's the Wraith himself they're after!"

"The Wraith, is it? Well good luck to him, is my word on't!"

The news was passed around, and the sentiment seemed generally agreed on. Indeed, I felt it, as the mood of the crowd flickered between irritation at the delay and warm support for the iconic jewel-thief. It was as I'd been told – the Wraith was something of a hero to these people. Which was encouraging, but wasn't going to help much if I was arrested.

The traffic started to move again. More slowly, but steadily, until I was actually on the bridge. It rose slightly in the middle, and by standing up in my stirrups I could see ahead, to where men-at-arms in green and silver were stopping everyone who passed by and checking them against papers they held.

I remembered something the Skipper had told me, back in Vorgranstern.

"The Beggar Man's sent word from Muranburder. There's posters up all over town, leaflets being given out in the market places, with a fine drawing of your good self, and a reward offered for knowledge of you!"

That's what they were checking. They had those drawings, and they were comparing them with all who passed by.

A cold chill passed over me. There were at least twenty men at the checkpoint, and well armed. Crossbowmen stood to one side, weapons loaded. Fighting my way through was not an option.

Neither was turning back. The bridge was divided down the middle by a low wall, with traffic flowing smoothly in the opposite direction. I could probably get my riding horse over it, and the pack-horses as well, though perhaps with more difficulty. But such an action would be obvious and suspicious. The Watchmen were patrolling the bridge, and Lord Tunward's soldiers would come to investigate, I was sure of it.

The line moved forward a bit more. Then stopped. A carriage was opened and a young man was made to step down. Dark hair. I couldn't tell from where I was, but he might look a bit like me. They commenced searching the carriage. Looking for a red-haired Arravine Friar, perhaps? Or a box of suspicious documents sealed in crystal?

How much did they know? Perhaps they only had the drawing to go by, and that had been made some time back. The artist would most probably have seen me in the jail at Neowbron, and would have worked from his memory of that – or perhaps even from descriptions given by the jailers. It couldn't be that close a likeness.

Plus which, I'd been clean shaven then. I scratched my beard, now getting to be a respectable length. Would someone have thought to add a beard to the drawing?

The young man was bundled back into his carriage, and the traffic moved on. Only to stop again when a cart driver got into a shouting match with on of the men-at-arms. His cart had a large canvas sheet covering its cargo, and they were insisting on removing it to look underneath.

I took the opportunity to climb down from the saddle and go back to my pack-horses. Under the pretext of checking the harness, I tore some pages from one of my books and stuffed them into my cheeks. Hopefully, a fat cheeked, bearded man would look nothing like the thin faced, clean shaven man who had been in the cell at Neowbron.

Ahead, the canvas sheet had been ripped away from the cart by the impatient men-at-arms, revealing only a heap of straw, which now began to blow away in the breeze that was coming upriver from the sea. Swords were thrust into it, disturbing the pile even more. Finally satisfied that there were no fugitives hiding there, they allowed it past, with the sheet tossed aside and the cargo diminishing steadily. The driver's furious complaints were dealt with by a blow from a cudgel. He was lucky not to have been arrested, but they were after bigger fish.

The line moved forward. Those who had seen what happened to the cart driver were much more co-operative.

I focused my attention on the men-at-arms, trying to separate their emotions from the rest of the crowd. Bored, impatient – apprehensive? I couldn't sure. The sergeant in charge glanced often at a man standing off to the side. Inconspicuous dress, he looked like a casual bystander. Purifier, was my guess, and tried to gauge his feelings. But it was like trying to distinguish one voice in a shouting crowd.

There was only one cart ahead of me now. Driven by a grey bearded man and clearly loaded with slate. He was waved past with barely a glance, and I trotted my horses forward to draw level with the sergeant. Looked down at him, and nodded a greeting.

His feelings were clear now. And yes, he was mostly apprehensive. Worried that he might miss something? He looked up at me, looked at the drawing in his hand, and frowned. Looked at my little train of horses.

"This all you've got?"

"Yes, just what you see. Books for Murkarin."

"You've got papers for crossing the border?"

I had a warrant with an Imperial stamp, but I wasn't about to show him that. "Oh, I'm not crossing the border. I'm meeting a dealer on this side. He comes regularly, buys anything I can get him." It was hard saying a long sentence with all that paper in my cheeks. I stopped talking in case I inadvertently spat a wad in his face.

He glanced again at my packs, obviously wondering if he should check them. Then looked across at the bystander.

There was a jerk of the head. So slight, I wouldn't have noticed if I hadn't been looking for it. I felt boredom and impatience coming from him.

"Right, on your way." The Sergeant stepped back, attention already on the next person in line. I rode past.

Once out of sight of the bridge, I leaned from the saddle and spat out the soggy pages. They tasted awful. I felt some sympathy for whoever might end up with the book. They would never know the ending unless they found another copy. I hate when that happens to me.

ABOUT TWO MILES OUTSIDE the town, I turned south, following a dusty lane up into the foothills. There were better roads going in that direction, on both sides of the river, but those would be the ones most likely to be patrolled. I didn't know how many Purifiers the Baron had at his disposal, but he had sent at least a dozen to Casterlayne against the mere possibility that we might go that way. And now he had Tunward's full strength supporting him.

Against that, it was a considerable task to guard all ways in and out of Scla, whilst also searching the docks, the shipping, and the rest of the town. I was certain that they would also be looking up and down the rail-way for any sign that we might have disembarked somewhere along the line, and they would be particularly looking for any and all healers who might have assisted us.

This all added up to a lot of resources that the Baron had to commit in his search for myself and Ommet. I was gambling that he would have a watch on all main roads, but would not be able to watch the multitude of side roads, lanes, farm tracks and bridle-paths that laced the countryside. With pack-horses I had greater freedom in my choice of routes than I had had with horse and cart, and that was my greatest advantage. If the Baron spread his net wide, then he must spread it thin, and I could weave my way through the gaps.

I hoped.

So I followed quiet little ways that wound through villages and past farms, steadily working my way up into the foothills of the Obsidian Mountains and further south all the time.

It was a pleasant enough afternoon, and I focused my attention on that. On the sweet smells of the hedgerows, the warmth of the sun (before it dropped below the mountain peaks – evening came earlier on this side of the valley), the rolling patchwork of fields and woodland, with the sea falling steadily further behind. It helped to keep me from worrying about Ommet. I hoped the Arravines had got to him before the Purifiers did. I hoped they'd be able to keep him safe when the Purifiers came to search the Arravine House, as they inevitably would. I hoped that they would not treat Ommet too harshly themselves.

I hoped he would not think too harshly of me, when he realised I had betrayed him. Again.

By the time the mountain shadow reached the river, I was well up into the foothills. As I crested a ridge I paused to look across to where the Casterlayne side valley opened up. I couldn't see where the rail-train ran, but I could trace its probably path down the valley wall and out along a wooded ridge. That group of buildings at its far end was probably Talinge. I hoped that Padran and Viennive had managed to lose themselves amongst the travelling families.

Too many people to worry about, when I'd only worried about myself for so many years. Too many changes in my life since Neowbron. Hard to cope with it all. Oh, how I longed for the simple life of a jewel thief! The Wraith had never had to think about anything more than his next job.

I continued south, whilst watching the shadow-line creeping up the far side of the valley. When the last of the sunlight was glowing on the eastern peaks, I decided to make camp for the night. There had been villages, some big enough to boast an inn where I might have stayed. But people would see, would remember, would talk. A casual word that got back to the Baron's men might mean disaster: better to remain unseen and unnoticed.

A small, well wooded valley seemed secluded enough to risk a modest fire, and after seeing to the horses – a long job on my own – I made a passable meal from my supplies. Then, by the flickering firelight, I took some time for a little project I had been thinking about for a while.

The Skipper's little assassination blade was not ideally situated in my boot. It kept slipping down out of easy reach, and was somewhat uncomfortable when it did. So I undid the wide leather belt that had come with my new outfit, and did a little work on the stitching where the buckle was secured.

It was a trickier job than I'd anticipated, especially as my only tool was the big knife bequeathed by the Apothecary. I had no intention of actually unsheathing the small blade itself unless I intended to use it for its lethal purpose. I had too much respect for the poison on it to employ it for mundane purposes.

But the job was completed with some success. Sheath and blade were concealed within the belt, just enough of the hilt showing to allow it to be drawn, and that well hidden behind the ornate buckle. Which I had chosen with this purpose in mind.

I still hoped never to use the nasty little thing, but if I needed to, it was ready. The first lesson of being a Wraith: plan ahead. Even plan for eventualities that might never occur.

I WAS UP WITH THE DAWN, cold and stiff, my blankets damp with dew. I soon warmed up with the business of reloading the horses, and broke my fast in the saddle.

It was a grey sort of day, though I was glad to see no sign of rain – especially as up in the mountains, rain could easily become snow, even at this time of year. A little sunlight leaked through the clouds here and there, illuminating my side of the valley. Far below I saw the turrets of Nordbras. Perhaps Crombard was staying there, enjoying Lord Tunward's hospitality while the search continued. I wished him a good breakfast and a quiet morning, undisturbed by any news of the Wraith. Though if he were to choke on something – say, a piece of hard red northern cheese – that would be even better.

I was no longer following even the faintest of paths, but had struck out on my own across empty hillsides and was navigating by instinct. My biggest fear had been that the approaches to the mountain pass would be watched and the closer I came to that destination, the greater the danger. But they couldn't watch a path that I made for myself, I reasoned. Of course, following my own route brought with it the risk of getting completely lost, especially as I found myself in a region of broken country – sharp rocky ridges that my horses couldn't cross, narrow winding valleys that led nowhere, thick patches of woodland with no way through. Several times I was forced to turn back from a promising route and try a different way.

But, as I reminded myself, safety was more important than speed, and patience was my best ally. Fortunately, I had a good sense of direction and at least a general knowledge of the area, having left Nordbras Castle via the same mountain pass on my previous visit. On that occasion, I was carrying some of Lord

Tunward's best jewellery. I had no intention of ever coming back then, and could never have imagined following this route with such strange treasure, but the experience served me well. Occasional glimpses of Nordbras down in the valley gave me a good idea of my general position, and I was starting to recognise the alignment of mountain peaks.

Around midday I made a brief pause for lunch and to rest the horses, and shortly afterwards I rode past a shepherds hut and found myself on a gravelled road wide enough for two laden horses to pass. A highway, after the last few hours, and one I recognised as the main route up into the Obsidians and through the pass. Kenrall Pass, it was named on the maps, though no local folk called it that. It was just 'The Pass', the only sure route through the mountains until you reached the coast.

I had struck on it quite high up, well above the other roads that joined it, which was all according to plan – if there had been watchers, I would have expected them down there. All the same, there was some tension in me as I turned to follow it upwards. From this point the valley walls draw in, and there was no way off the path. Only forward or back.

I continued forward, though checking my weapons as I went. The sword slid smoothly from its scabbard. My jacket was unlaced, despite a sharp wind coming down from the pass, so I could easily reach the big knife. And the Skipper's poisoned blade was in my belt, for what good that might do. If it came to it, I was prepared to fight my way through, though that would be a desperate move and probably my last one.

It was with a some relief that I came in sight of the Kenrall Pass Customs House. Not an impressive building, a squat two-storey blockhouse nestled into the side of the valley, but it marked the final boundary of the Empire and the last obstacle to my mission.

Of the Border Guards themselves I had no fear. The Imperial Borders and Customs Service was renowned for being perhaps the least corruptible of all Imperial agencies and offices.

This hadn't always been the case. Several hundred years past, borders were administered by local Lords, using local people, which led to smuggling and corruption on a large scale. So large that it threatened to choke off trade entirely in some places, and the Imperial revenues were suffering considerable loss. So the Emperor of the time – I forget which one – instituted a new force. The Borderers are trained to a very high standard in the capital, and it is an unbreakable rule that they are never sent to a border near their homes. Nor are they allowed to form any but the most superficial relationships with local people. They take an oath of personal loyalty to the Empire and to their service, and in all the time since its formation, there has never been any suggestion that this has been broken.

So, although the Purifiers had infiltrated members into the Imperial Navy and most probably the Army as well, I had no fear that they would have done the same with the Border Guards. Once at the Custom's House, I was beyond the Baron's reach. They would certainly respect my warrant with its Imperial stamp, and send me on my way into Murkarin without hindrance.

I glanced nervously over my shoulder once or twice as I neared the Customs House, but there was no sign of Purifiers galloping up the road behind me. A tension I had scarcely been aware of began to ease itself: I rolled my head and twisted my shoulders to work the last vestiges of it out of my body.

The Border Guards were alert. I saw two of them in their green uniforms come out of the Customs House as I approached and stand waiting for me.

Strangely, I felt tension increasing again as I approached. A disconcerting feeling, since there seemed no reason for it. Another glance over my shoulder showed the road behind remained clear, yet the close I came to the Guards, the stronger the feeling became.

It was only as one of them stepped out in front of me with raised hand that I realised it was their tension I was receiving. But why? What cause had they to be so much on edge?

I looked at them more closely as I brought my horses to a halt. The one who had stopped me bore the insignia of a Sergeant-Commander, a sergeant given charge of a border post. Equivalent to a junior officer in the army. Why was such a person of this rank dealing with the routine of inspecting a passing merchant?

For a Sergeant-Commander he was sloppily dressed, not at all up to the usual standard of the Border Guards. In fact, his uniform appeared a size or two too small. The tunic was stretched very tightly across his broad shoulders, and his wrists projected well beyond the cuffs. His short sword and cudgel were in his belt, though, and he had a hand on each.

His companion moved forward to grasp my horse's reins. His uniform fitted better, but he seemed to have put it on in a hurry and had missed several buttons. Moreover, he was wearing black riding boots, instead of the short brown boots that were normal.

"Off the horse!" The Sergeant-Commander was curt, even hostile. Both in his voice and in the glare he was giving me.

Something was wrong. I couldn't understand what. Unless – perhaps Crombard had warned them against me? I could imagine a message to the effect that a wanted man, the infamous Wraith, might be attempting to cross the border. But if that was the case, it was soon dealt with. The Imperial stamp would trump any message from a Baron.

I had it ready, rolled up inside my jacket. I held it out to the Sergeant-Commander. "Please look at this first."

He took it, opened it up, and nodded as he read it. "Well, that confirms it. Imperial Agent, eh?" He tossed it aside and drew his sword. "Off the horse! Now!"

I was stunned. "But – but the stamp..."

He laughed in my face. "Oh, yes, that stamp. That carries no authority here! Not over the Knights of the Pure Heart!"

Purifiers? My stomach knotted in fear and shock. "How..." I began.

"Never mind how!" he interrupted. "Off your horse, Mr Wraith, or I'll cut you from it!" He raised the blade and levelled it at me.

There was a moment when I thought about drawing my own sword, of knocking his aside and cutting down the man holding the reins. If I got the horses to a gallop I could be away ahead of them, and in Murkarin before they could pursue and catch me.

But even as I thought it a movement caught my eye. The flat roof of the Customs House was battlemented like a small castle, and from behind the battlements three crossbows were pointing down at me. The men behind them wore black, not green.

The Sergeant-Commander – or rather, the Purifier wearing his uniform – saw my glance and smiled. "Go on, try and run for it. The Baron would prefer you alive, but he won't mind a few holes in you, either!"

The sense of triumph from him as I got off the horse was all but overwhelming.

Chapter 26: The Baron at Kenrall Pass

In the cell of the Customs House at Kenrall Pass, there are no stone blocks to count.

All in all, it was a much more pleasant place than the Neowbron town jail. There was a window – small, and of course barred, but it let in a good amount of light. There was an actual bed, with a straw mattress and a blanket, as well as a bench. I was not manacled, and they even let me have my clothing back, after having searched everything thoroughly, even down to my small clothes. They removed all the lock picks, of course. Not that they would have made much difference to my situation. There was nothing as sophisticated as a lock on the door – just a good strong bolt on the outside, quite impervious to any lock picks smaller than a sledgehammer.

I didn't know if they'd found the Skipper's little knife, since they didn't return my belt, perhaps fearing that I would hang myself and so deprive the Baron of his pleasure.

The walls were plastered and whitewashed, which gave the whole room a light and airy feel, though it does of course cover over any bricks or stone blocks. It was the best cell I had ever occupied, but I missed not having stone blocks to count.

In their absence, I spent a lot of time looking out of the window. Since the cell was at the back of the Customs House, there wasn't much of a view. A small yard, stables, a steep hillside and the high peaks of the Obsidian Mountains looming over all. They aren't really made of obsidian, of course, but of some other dark rock. Not as shiny, but the peaks do look very sharp. On the other side was Murkarin, almost in sight but entirely out of reach.

Once again, I had underestimated the Baron. I knew he couldn't suborn the Border Guards, I had not expected him to simply replace them. I didn't need to ask what had happened to them, their bodies were still stacked up in the courtyard. There was nowhere to bury a corpse, I presumed. But later that day the bodies were dragged away and a big fire set outside the wall.

The Purifiers didn't want the smell of rotting flesh hanging round when Crombard arrived.

It was not simply his ruthlessness that had confounded me. In so casually eliminating the entire garrison he had committed a crime against the Empire – an act of rebellion, in fact. It might be that he intended to put the blame on bandits, perhaps border reavers out of Murkarin. Such things had happened before, though not for a long time. But he was taking a huge risk, for such an incident would be investigated thoroughly, on both sides of the border, and who knew where that might lead? War with Murkarin was a distinct possibility

The chilling implication was that if he was willing to take such a risk, then he was very likely planning for a war. A civil war. Or his Master, Grand Duke Brodon, was, which came to the same thing. This trifling incident on the border would be of no consequence at all if the Empire was consumed by blood and fire.

I'd thought the Skipper's plans for revolution bad enough, but the prospect of a full scale conflict between Grand Duke and Empress was appalling. Inevitably, it would also become North against South, First Order against Second Order... nowhere and no one would be untouched.

My mission may have been the last hope of avoiding this future. My failure may have insured it.

I stared out of the window again, trying to find some distraction. I counted flagstones in the courtyard, bricks in the stable wall, but it was hard to concentrate.

My horses at least had been taken care of. The packs had been taken off them, and were presumably in the Custom's House. The Purifier's hadn't yet begun to search through them – or at least, they hadn't searched the metal box from Nordrum and Son, or we'd all be dead. Most likely they were waiting on the Baron before they began that task, which meant that there was a good chance that Crombard would be amongst those killed when the case was opened and the gas released. It was a hope that I clung to. Of course, it would probably mean my own death, and my mission would still have failed, but to take the Baron with me would be some compensation.

They had taken the key, of course. It was possible that one amongst them might realise the significance of three locks, but surely they would not anticipate the danger? As far as I knew, even amongst the New Dawn only the Skipper and the Apothecary knew about the deadly substance he had concocted.

But for now, all was on hold, awaiting the Baron.

My guess that he was at Nordbras was confirmed. The Purifiers had told as much when they'd thrown me – literally – into the cell.

"Don't worry, you won't be there long," they said. "We've sent word to Nordbras Castle, and the Baron will be on his way up here. Wants to see you in person, he does! I think we can expect him tomorrow, midday at the latest."

That was one advantage Neowbron had had – Crombard was further away and I had longer before he arrived. Long enough for Ommet to come and rescue me.

That wouldn't happen this time.

It was a long night, with little sleep for me. In the morning, a cheerful Purifier – the same who had impersonated the

Sergeant-Commander, though now wearing his own clothing – brought me a breakfast of cold porridge.

"The Baron's on his way!" he told me. His bright smile was genuine, I could feel his pleasure. "Eat well, you might not be around for luncheon!"

"How about letting me have my belt back?" I asked. "These trousers are a bit loose on me. Bad enough I have to stand before the Baron, without having my trousers fall down when I do!"

He laughed. "Think the Baron'll care about that, do you?" Just mentioning the Baron added to his happiness. It was apparent that he expected some commendation for his part in this. After all, he was the one who had finally caught the elusive Wraith! He was looking forward to his master's approval.

In that, I saw a small opportunity.

I shrugged. "He might. You'll know him better than I do, but I doubt if he's in the mood for comedy. I'm afraid he would probably be annoyed by such a thing. It would seem like a silly joke, a child's trick. Though I don't suppose it'll make much difference to me."

"You're right, it won't!" he said, and left, but I could sense a change in his mood. A sliver of worry, a hint of uncertainty. After an hour or so the door was opened again and my belt was tossed in.

I put it on, surreptitiously checking for the knife as I did so. It was still there, concealed inside the belt and behind the buckle! My spirits lifted for a moment, before I considered just how much of a chance it gave me. There were five Purifiers guarding me, more probably on their way with Crombard, all well armed. One little knife was not going to tip the balance significantly, however strong the poison.

Still, at least it was a weapon they didn't know about, and that was a positive thing. I'd take all the positive I could get just now.

AS FAR AS I COULD JUDGE from the light outside, it was still a little short of noon when I heard the sound of hooves coming up the road towards us. And at about the same time, I felt their approach.

I was discovering that it was difficult to distinguish the emotions of one individual in a group, especially at a distance. They tended to blur together and cancel each other out. But here, one person seemed prominent.

I closed my eyes, trying to focus my empathic sense, and in that darkness saw them as colours. An orange-red of anticipation, but at its heart a tight knot of red and black. Anger and hate.

That was the Baron. I didn't have to see him to know him. Who else could it be?

They halted outside, my captors rushing out in eager anticipation – laced with concern. The Baron's wrath was something to be feared even by his most loyal followers. But as he strode into the building, I sensed that his deep fury was now overlaid with a golden glow of triumph.

I'd expected to be dragged out at once, but instead he seemed to spend some time questioning his men. I couldn't hear the words, but I felt the tone of them, and guessed that he was going over the details of my capture. I wondered if he would choose to examine my baggage at this point, in which case we'd all die before I had chance to meet him. That would be a pity, I thought.

Instead, two of the Purifiers came down the corridor. The bolt was pulled back, the door slammed open. I was given no chance to walk out with any dignity. Instead they grabbed me, hustled me out and along the corridor.

The front ground floor of the Custom's House was taken up by one large room, which seemed to perform various functions. A common space for the garrison, a ready-room for those on duty, an office for dealing with official paperwork, an armoury and storage space for equipment. Also a place to search for contrabrand, with a long table against one wall, on which all my packs and baggage had been placed.

Large though the room was, it now seemed quite full. In addition to the five Purifiers who had captured me, there were six others who had presumably arrived with the Baron. These were all arrayed around the edges of the room, leaving the centre open for the main performers. Myself, and Baron Crombard.

I was thrown down onto the floor as we came in, and then dragged up again, and pushed into a chair.

The Baron stood before me, hands behind his back. Like his men, he dressed all in black, leather and linen, cloak lined in black fur. On his chest, the bright image of heart and flames stood out clearly against that background.

"So, this is the infamous Wraith." His voice was a low growl, his tone was contempt, his feelings were – as always – anger and hate, suppressed at the moment but always ready to burst out.

I looked up at him, and was shocked by what I saw.

The image I had of him from all those years ago was of a huge, broad-shouldered man, black haired and black bearded. Looking down from my hiding place in the barn, I had had only glimpses of his face, but in my mind it was square jawed, with full cheeks and a prominent nose.

He must have been about sixty years old then, young by the measure of the First Order, and appearing no more than thirty by Second Order standards. And that was forty years past, so if he had not now reached his century he would be close to it. His appearance should not have changed to any great degree. It is not uncommon for the First Order to live past one hundred and fifty years, and to show no significant sign of ageing until near their end. In my time at Sonor Breck I had only seen the Baron at a distance, and so was not prepared for how he looked now.

The beard was thin and straggly, streaked with grey. His hair was cropped short, perhaps to disguise the fact that it, too, had grown thin. His cheeks were sunken, the skin looking thin and tight and yellowing, whilst his eyes seemed to have retreated deeper into their sockets, from where they glowered at me.

There was still strength in him. I could feel it. But it was a strength of will not of body. And even as he stood and glared at me, the broad shoulders were sagging, and it was only by conscious effort that he kept from stooping.

The Gifts were weak in him.

"You are something of a disappointment, Mr. Wraith." His tone was all amused contempt. "From your reputation, I would have expected someone more imposing. Instead – what do we have here? Some scrawny little gutter rat? A sly, dirty-fingered Second Order piece of offal who forgot his place in the order of things – that's what I see!"

"I didn't need imposing looks to..." I began, but before I could finish my retort, a fist smashed into the side of my face, knocking me half off the chair. Only a firm grip from behind stopped me falling all the way. I was hauled back into position without any attempt at gentleness.

"You don't speak until you are given permission, scum." The Baron sounded just as he had before, but despite the pain in my face and dizziness in my head, I could feel the glow of triumph brightening in him. There was no doubt but that he was enjoying this. "And then you don't stop speaking until you're given permission!" He leaned forward a little. "Let me explain how things are going to be. I am going to ask you about a great many things. I want to know all about your recent adventures. I want to hear about your companion, the Imperial Agent, and what his business is with the Arravines. I want to know what you took from them, and why. I want to know about your involvement with those pitiful fools who call themselves the New Dawn, and what happened at Shelter Bay, and where the Imperial Navy's ship went. I want to know how many Lords you have stolen from, and what you did with their property, and in particular I want to know who helped you steal from *me*!"

His voice rose to a shout at that point, and I felt his anger rise with it. The thefts from other Lords were annoying, but the fact that I had taken his property was infuriating. I smiled at the thought, but only to myself.

He drew breath. "Yes, I will have the names of every wretch who aided you, everyone who handled my jewellery. And you will account for every single piece of it, and tell me exactly where it went and where it is now, or I will cut the knowledge out of you with hot knives! Is that clear to you, scum?"

"Yes," I said, and received a blow on the other side of my face.

"You will address my as 'sir', or 'My Lord'. There will be nothing but respect from you, do you understand?"

"Yes, sir. My Lord." I answered quickly.

"Good. Perhaps we can proceed then. If you answer quickly and truthfully and to my satisfaction, you may save yourself some agony before you die. If you lie or prevaricate – well, what you don't tell me here you will spill out soon enough once I've got you back at Sonor Breck."

He waited expectantly, but I said nothing.

"Very well," he continued. "Let's start with your true name. No more of this Wraith nonsense, and don't think to use that 'Arton Dowder' alias again. Who are you?"

The last was shouted as he leaned forward.

I lifted my head and met his gaze. "Sir, my full name is Arton di Ferabard r'ha Sahal Crombard." And thought to myself that, after forty years without saying that name, I had used it twice in the last few days.

There was dead silence in the room.

From most of the Purifiers, it was a silence of incomprehension. Or of anticipation as they waited to see how the Baron would respond to this effrontery. But in the Baron himself there was a different reaction. Shock, yes – I had the satisfaction of seeing his jaw drop. But I felt something else in him as well.

Beneath the red anger and black hatred that drove him, something else boiled up from a place deep inside. Something that my mind could give no colour to, or even name at first. Until I recognised it as fear.

"Where..." he stopped, licked his lips, and made a huge effort to reassert control of himself. "Where did you hear that name?" he finally asked.

"From my mother, sir. Your sister, that is – Uncle."

"LIAR!" He leapt across the room and slapped me across the face with a gloved hand. "Liar!" he repeated, backhanding me. Then he grabbed my hair, pulled my face close to his and shouted. "That child is dead! I killed him, I killed the whole vile little nest of them. Liar!"

The slaps hadn't hurt as much as the fists from the Purifiers. I looked back at him, face just inches from mine, and spoke calmly. "You killed my father, my brother, and my friend who had come to visit. We were playing hide-and-seek. I was hiding up in the barn. I saw it all, My Lord."

"We burned the barn!"

"And the house and all the outbuildings. I know. I didn't stay there when the fire started. I went out from the back, and ran to the neighbouring farm, whilst you rode off with my mother. You missed me, Uncle."

He stepped back, breathing heavily, hand going to his sword. "Liar!" he said again, but without conviction. He glanced around, suddenly aware that his men were staring at him, and I felt the fear swirling and rising in his soul.

"They don't know, do they?" I asked softly. So softly that only the Baron and the two holding me heard. I felt the truth of it reflected back from him. "You've kept it secret, all these years, how you..."

"SILENCE!" The Baron had his sword out, pointing at me. For a moment, I thought he would run me through. Instead he rested the point lightly on my chest. "Be. Silent." he hissed at me.

The Gifts were not strong in him but his mind worked well enough, in spite of the blow I had dealt him. "This filth has impugned my family honour," he announced. "That makes this a personal matter, and I will therefore continue this interrogation alone. On your feet!" he concluded, flicking the flat of his blade against my chin in emphasis, and I stood up.

"My Lord, are you sure this is wise..." one of the Purifiers behind me began, but stopped when the Baron glared at him.

"Are you suggesting that I cannot deal with this unarmed little runt?" he snarled.

"No, no, not at all, My Lord, not at all!" The man nearly spluttered the words out in his haste to reassure his master, and I felt a surge of fear from him.

"Good. I'm glad to know that my men still have confidence in me!" Crombard said with biting sarcasm. "And I have another task for you all. I want a full search made through all his possessions, all the baggage from his horses. Check and list every item. Be alert for hidden compartments or secret places. By the time I've finished with him I want to know exactly what he was trying to smuggle across the border. Am I clear?"

He glanced round the room and received a chorus of 'Yes, My Lord.' It was quick thinking on his part, to divert his men's attention away from what I had said, and from speculation on what it might signify.

It was also their death, if they carried out his full instructions. But even if I had wished to warn them, his sword point was still at my throat. I said nothing.

Chapter 27: Matters of Revenge and Honour

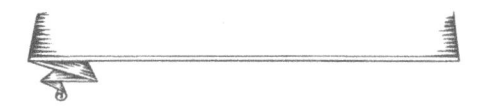

Baron Crombard lowered the sword, gripped my shoulder, and pushed me through the door. Halfway down the corridor a set of stairs led upwards, and with the point of his blade the Baron indicated I should go that way, and quickly.

The upper floor contained just two rooms. The staircase led into a large dormitory, clearly the living quarters for the men of the garrison. But Crombard herded me along to the front of the building, where a separate room appeared to be reserved for the Sergeant-Commander. At least, there were uniforms with that insignia hung on a rack near the door, A neatly made up bed was on one side of the room, a table and chairs on the other, and there was a desk in the middle of the room, facing the door.

The Baron followed me in, and slammed the door shut behind him. The latch clicked into place, holding it firm.

"There, that should give us some privacy."

"I understand why you would need privacy." I turned to face him, and met his eyes. "Not something you want to talk about in front of your men, is it? How you murdered an entire family – your sisters family!" It felt good to say that to his face, to hurl the accusations that I had carried with me for forty years.

"Hah!" he said, and then without warning kicked me in the stomach. I dropped to the floor, doubled over, gasping for breath. "Now we can discuss family matters," he continued in a matter of fact tone. "And let me first say that disposing of a few Second Order scum is not a matter of concern for me or my men. But in regard to my sister: the shame she brought to my house, the dishonour to my name and blood, that is not something that should be talked about. I thought that matter long sorted, but it seems you know more than you should. So, I will find out just what you know, and how you came by that knowledge."

I managed to get some air into my lungs and strength in my limbs. Crawling to the desk, I pulled myself upright.

"You claim to be Sahel's youngest, do you? In that case, you can tell me this: what was your father's name?"

"Drahane." I had to force the words out, my lungs were still struggling. "Drahane di Ferabard r'ha Temasti."

"And where did you live?"

"A farm. About ten miles from Ferabard, and counted in that District. Under the Governorship of Lord Harrani."

"Where did they meet? Your parents?"

"In the Imperial Park, by Lake Sh'thran. In sight of Daradura, at the centre of the capital."

He raised an eyebrow. "Indeed. I knew it was in the capital. But the Imperial Park – that was a detail I have not heard before. Unless of course, you're making it up."

"Then let me tell you this! That day you came to our farm, you had about half-a-dozen men with you. They surrounded the farm from a distance, then all rode in at once, so we had no chance to escape. Father was out in the fields, with my elder brother. They dragged them in from there, with ropes. My friend was in the yard, searching for me. He stood looking up at you, not understanding, until one of your men jumped down from his horse and smashed him to the ground with one blow.

Mother was in the house. You had her dragged out. She pleaded with you. 'Brother' she called you. And a name she used. Urquan. Who else knows that name?"

"Some." He watched me impassively whilst dark emotions coiled and strained within him like great serpents.

"You made her watch whilst your men hung my father and brother and friend from the tree outside the house. Then you had her bound over a horse and you rode off with her. You left two men behind to put our house and all the buildings to the torch. I ran from the back of the barn. They didn't see me."

"Well perhaps it's true then." The Baron dropped his sword point a little and stepped back. "Damnation. I thought that I'd cleaned that little rat hole out completely. Now look at you – come back causing trouble and stealing my jewels!" He stared at me as if I'd crawled out from a rock. "This is what happens when abominations are allowed to live."

Not a trace of regret or remorse. Not even for my murdered friend, who had been innocent of even the tenuous offence of being half First and half Second.

I was listening hard, trying to hear what might be happening below us. I thought there might be some noise from my baggage being torn apart, but the floorboards were thick and double-layered. No sound came to my ears.

A sight came to my eyes, though. Looking past the Baron I saw, hanging on the back of the door, a sword. Not one of the regular issue short swords of the Border Guards. This was a longer, slightly curved cavalry sabre. The Sergeant-Commander's personal weapon, no doubt. Crombard had shut the door behind him without looking. He hadn't seen it.

But to get to it, I would have to get past him, and although he had lowered his blade, he was still alert.

"Abomination?" I said. "That's a poor greeting for your long lost nephew!"

His face twisted with hate, and his blade flicked out, too quickly for me to dodge or duck. I felt a sharp pain in my cheek.

"Abomination is what you are! Your existence is a stain on the world and an affront to me! That my dirty slut of a sister should mingle our blood with some wretched piece of Second Order flotsam – that is an insult to my family and our entire order. Not surprising that you became a thief with your tainted blood!"

Better a thief than a murderer, I thought, but decided it would be best not to say it. Just a little more provocation and he would take my head off. Instead I lowered my gaze, pulled a shirt tail out of my trousers and tried to stem the flow of blood with it.

"So, how did it happen that you became the Wraith?" Combard asked. "Was that your plan, to get revenge by stealing my jewellery?"

"There was more to it than that. Revenge was only part of it. My first thought was to rescue my mother, and when I reached the neighbours farm, I was calling on them to send men out to find you and bring her back. Of course, they did not do that. They were farmers, not warriors, and fearful of the First Order. They did take me in, but they were in dread that if word of my survival went out, you would return. They had already lost one son, they could not afford to lose more. So they took me to Ferabard and apprenticed me to a cheese merchant. Under a different name, of course."

"A cheese merchant? Hah! A long way from jewel thief."

"Indeed. But I was obsessed with tracking you down and finding my mother. No one knew of you down there, we had few dealings with any of the First Order."

I shifted my weight to slide a few inches along the desk. If I could get a clear passage to the sword on the door, I might be able to dive past Crombard and snatch it from its scabbard.

At any moment, one of the Purifiers might try and open the case. They might, by chance, turn the keys in the right order, but it was beyond any likelihood that they would do the double turn in each. That, of course, was the purpose of the system.

And when they did, there would be a brief moment when they would be filled with terror, before the gas overcame them. I would feel it, I was sure. And perhaps Crombard would as well. The Gifts were very weak in him, that was clear. I had no sense that he was feeling any emotion from me at all. But surely the death-throes of his men would be strong enough to reach him? In which case, I could expect a strong reaction, and I must be ready to move.

I slid a little further along as I continued my story.

"There was a Jeweller's shop nearby the cheese merchants. Not a grand place, but occasionally some minor noble of the First Order might come by to order a piece made. That, I thought, was the way to gain knowledge. Jewellery could give me access to the First Order that cheese never would. So, after a few years, I left the cheese merchants and took a job with the Jewellers."

"And began stealing!"

"Not at first. I learned the trade. I left Ferabard, and began my travels, taking work here and there, learning what I could along the way, and listening always for that name. Your name!"

"I trust that did not take long." Pride flared. His position, his importance – that meant everything to him.

"I learned eventually. Baron Crombard. Nephew to Grand Duke Brodon. Lord Lieutenant of the North. Brodon's strong right arm. The enforcer of his will, with more real power than many Dukes. More wealth, also. The most feared man across half the Empire."

Maybe I exaggerated slightly, but I was looking for a reaction. And got it. Not in his face, but I felt the glow in him as I fed his self-image. And the sword point dropped a little further. The flattery relaxed him – and his arm was growing weary.

"After many years wandering and seeking, I found my way to Sonor Breck. But there was no way in. I could not gain access even to the estate, let alone the house. So I travelled further, exploring these Northern parts, seeking news of my mother, seeking ways to get into your house."

"And stealing jewellery."

I shrugged. "I needed to finance my travelling. Pay for bribes. Buy information. I had no compunction about stealing from the First Order. They were wealthy enough to sustain it, even the lesser nobility who I began with, and seeing how most of them treated their Second Order servants, I judged them to deserve it. But after a while my activities became noticed by those with a wider agenda than my own."

"The New Dawn, you mean?"

"Not at first. There are others, less radical. But the New Dawn proved to be behind many of those as well."

"So you became a revolutionary, as well as a thief."

Below us – was that a noise? A crash as of a metal box roughly handled? Perhaps picked up off the floor and dropped onto a table for examination? I couldn't be sure.

"I wouldn't have labelled myself thus. Oh, I agreed with their aims, by and large. Overthrow the First Order – yes, certainly. I had no problem with that! Apart from the injustice done to me, I had seen more than enough cruelty and arrogance from the Lords and nobles to justify that. But my own concern was still the same – to find out what had happened to my mother, to rescue her if possible – and to deliver a little justice as well, if I could!"

Crombard spat, contemptuously. "I see that Second Order blood is strong in you. Whining about injustices, complaining against your betters. You people think you can overthrow us and rule yourselves? Pah! You have not the strength of body, mind or character!"

While he was speaking, I felt it. Coming from below us. A sudden burst of shock, fear, pain. Bright colours of agony and terror flared in my inner vision. And in my ears – was that a noise like bodies falling? The sound of limbs thrashing in torment? Men coughing, choking, gasping for one last breath of air.

"You people sicken me, with your weakness and stupidity!" Crombard ranted on, showing no awareness of what I felt so clearly. Could the Gift be so weak in him that he did not even feel the death that had overtaken his men? "Your ingratitude and spite! You lack the intelligence even to know your proper place. You must be crushed and broken for your own good!"

Below us, there was no more feeling. It was as if someone had snuffed out all the little candles that had been burning there. We were alone in the building. But Crombard did not know it.

"That's why your family had to die," he continued. "Tainted blood like yours is a threat and an affront to the proper order of things. Mixing the purity of the First Order with the debased nature of the Second is the most vile thing that can be done – and my own sister..."

He almost choked with the intensity of his emotions. I was waiting to see if the gas would rise to this floor, in which case we would both choke, and die of it. No more than one storey – that was Nordrum's estimation. But it was only an estimate.

The Baron recovered his breath. "Continue your story. I want to hear how you came back to Sonor Breck, and how you gained entry."

"So it was that I made common cause with the New Dawn. I made use of their organisation, for intelligence and assistance. In return, my thefts aided their funds." (Not an inconsiderable amount, either, despite what the Skipper had said). "But I think it was more valuable to them that they could spread the story around. They invented the name – the Wraith. It helped to stir opposition to the First Order, to show them as weak and vulnerable."

"Ignorant fools!" The Baron snorted contempt. "To think that losing a few jewels would make a real difference to the natural order of things?"

"It was the symbolism of it that the New Dawn valued. They had other plans for making it a reality."

"Oh, indeed?" That got his interest. "Tell me of these."

"They intended to instigate an uprising in Vorgranstern. This would, of course, be crushed, brutally: which would be both the signal and the cause for a wider rebellion. Their intention was that you yourself would be lured into the tunnels and die there."

Crombard glared at me for a moment, and I prepared to duck another slash from his blade. But instead he let out a noise that I knew from his emotions signified amusement, though it sounded more like a dog clearing its throat. "Fools! We knew all of these plans, of course. Nothing would have come of them. My Knights of the Pure Heart were already in Vorgranstern, in strength. The New Dawn would have been eliminated as soon as they showed themselves."

I nodded, as if in agreement. "So you had plans for dealing with their fire-tubes?"

He frowned, but beneath that I felt a shock. He hadn't known. And therefore most certainly hadn't known of the Apothecaries deadly concoction.

"Fire-tubes? Is that what they told you? Perhaps they obtained one or two, and showed them off to convince weak minded fools like you of their plans. They would have made no difference."

"I saw hundreds. And some large ones as well. How do you think they took the '*Warlord*'? Your Purifiers who had command of her were cut down in a moment! And if you think you knew their plans – that was because they arranged it that way. They wanted you and your men in Vorgranstern, in strength, to meet your doom."

I took some pleasure in telling him this, despite the horror I'd felt on hearing the Skipper's plans. It was nice to feel his consternation. But the anger that followed was less amusing.

He had his sword up again, the point an inch from my eyes, even though I was leaning backwards as far as I could over the desk.

"Fire-tubes or not, the Second Order are no match for any man of the First!" He spat it out, and for a moment I felt his readiness to emphasise the point by skewering me. But he reasserted control, and brought the sword back a little way. "Later, you will tell me about these things in full detail. But never think for a moment that you lesser beings could ever defeat us, your Lords and Masters! Only fools and madmen could think otherwise!"

I shrugged, whilst thinking that it would have been amusing to see Crombard and the Skipper engage in a debate. At the same time I moved a little further along the desk. A natural if futile attempt to keep clear of the Baron's blade – or so I hoped he would think: but it gave me clear path past him. Not, however, one that would take me beyond the reach of his sword. My hands, resting on the desktop, moved slowly along it, questing for something I could use as a distraction.

"And yet they had a great deal of support in the North, especially in those places where the Lords ruled with a heavy hand. They heard most of what went on in the great houses – information that helped me greatly in my work."

"Your thieving!" He jabbed the sword at me in emphasis.

"Yes. Thieving. It was from them that I heard of an opportunity to enter Sonor Breck." I was finding nothing on the desk. I moved a little further, stretched my hands out more.

"The building work." He nodded to himself. "I never wanted to bring in labourers, but the architect assured me it was necessary. So you sneaked your way in to dip your dirty fingers in my treasure chest!"

"No. Not my main intention. As I told you, my first concern was to find out about my mother. Naive of me, but in some depth of my heart I still held a hope that she might be alive." My questing fingers touched against something.

Crombard barked his laughter again. "Her fate was, and remains, known only to myself and a very few of my most faithful men. You will never know what happened to her!" He finished with a sneer.

"So you hid her away? Where?" I leaned forward, as if searching for an answer. If he had had anything at all of the gift, he would have known that my desperate eagerness was faked. I already knew the answer. But I wanted to know what he would say about it. And I wanted to keep him distracted from my fingers, surreptitiously curling round the object on the desk.

"Oh, yes. Very well hidden away." He found that idea amusing. "I was searching for her for fifteen years, so I had plenty of time to plan and prepare for her to disappear. I will tell you this though: she has had every opportunity to regret her actions. She has bitterly repented that she ever gave birth to you!"

I felt the malicious pleasure he had in saying this, his desire to inflict the maximum pain. And indeed it hurt. But not as much as he intended, because I knew the lie.

I leaned back again, and shook my head. "I shall tell you what happened. What you did to her. You brought her in at night, when you thought that the house was all asleep. But your house never sleeps. There are always servants up and about. Cleaning those places that are busy in the day. Preparing food. And just being awake should there be a call in the night. You take these things so much for granted, you do not even notice them. But all that happens is seen by someone!"

His attention was all on my face, my words. He did not notice my fingers curling round the object on the desk. Something small enough to grip. Hard. Heavy for its size.

"What if they did? No one would dare talk of it!" he snapped.

"Oh, they talked. In whispers, perhaps, but they talk to each other. Your sister, she was well remembered. People had affection for her. They knew when you brought her back. They knew about the cell you had had made, two floors underground, with its concealed entrance in a disused storeroom. Disused by your order – did you think that such a thing would go unnoticed? The Lord of Sonor Breck, suddenly concerning himself with such mundane matters?"

He opened his mouth, but shock kept him silent. So I continued.

"Yes, people knew, and they talked! Quietly, indeed. And fearfully. But the cruelty you showed to your own sister, that still angered them. You are hated in Sonor Breck, Baron – did you know that? Feared, yes, but hated more, and not least for what you did to my mother!"

"I care nothing for their hate!" he snarled.

"You should! Hate will overcome fear and loosen tongues better than gold, I've found. I heard how you kept her down there, alone in the dark. Fed by those who you trusted, but never spoken to, except sometimes by you. Left to wither and eventually die."

I had to stop. When I'd first learned of it, the thought of my mother's fate had all but unhinged me with grief and rage. The Baron had been away from Sonor Breck at the time, or I might have taken the first opportunity to attack him, which would have meant my own demise. By the time he returned I'd planned a more effective vengeance.

"So, you learned that much, eh? Well, know this as well – your Mother was quite mad, by the end! Sitting in her own filth, daubing herself with it, crying and wailing and cackling..."

"Uncle, I know when you're lying," I said, and the shock of that silenced him. "My mother's Gift was strong, and it is strong in me. Far stronger than it is in you! So I know untruth when I hear it. And in any case, I heard a different story from the servants at Sonor Breck. They talked with her, did you know? When you were away, some would visit her, bring her extra food... She suffered terribly, Baron. But you never broke her. And in the end, you could not bear that, the fact that she was, after all, stronger than you. She only died because you stopped feeding her."

"ENOUGH!" Crombard's bellow would have been heard below, if there had been anyone alive to hear. "ENOUGH I SAY! I will hear no more of this! You're mother was a slut, a whore, a traitor – and you are an obscenity that should never have existed! The Gifts are for the Pure of Blood and Heart, and them alone, your tainted blood cannot bear any trace of them and when I've learned all I need to know I will throw you into that same dungeon where you can be reunited with your mother's *bones!*"

By the time he had finished his rant, he was screaming and waving his sword around wildly. It was an opportunity.

I snatched up the object I'd found on the desk, and in the same motion flung it at his face.

But the Baron's reactions were good. Or lucky. He flicked his sword up and across, catching the object with the flat while it was still a foot from his face.

It was a glass inkpot, with a stopper in the top. The impact sent it off course, tumbling through the air. The stopper came out as it did so, and black ink sprayed out.

I was leaping forward and diving down, trying to drop below his back-swing whilst still keeping momentum towards the sword on the door.

The inkpot flew away over the Baron's right shoulder. The fan of ink splashed across his face and into his eyes, blinding him as he cut at me. The blow landed, but not cleanly, the flat sliding over the leather on my back and the tip catching in my hair... and I was past, scrambling across the floor whilst the Baron staggered, off-balance from the missed swing and pawing at his eyes with his free hand.

At the door, on my feet, I snatched at the sword hilt, getting an awkward grip and pulling at it. But with it hanging high up on the door, the angle was wrong, it caught in the scabbard, half-way out.

Crombard was wiping his eyes on his sleeve, smearing ink across his face and pouring out a stream of obscenities whilst waving his sword blindly in front of him.

I heaved on the scabbard, trying to get it free. But the belt by which it hung tangled as I pulled desperately on the hilt, My wild attempts to free it were hampered by the fact that I was looking over my shoulder at the Baron.

Crombard was blinking the last of the ink out of his eyes, fixing a bleary glare on me. With wordless roar he leapt forwards, swinging his blade in a vicious down-stroke aimed at my head.

With a burst of desperate strength I ripped the hook out of the door and brought the sabre up and round in a clumsy parry with the scabbard still half on. Unconventional, but it worked well enough, deflecting the blow away from my head. Momentum carried the Baron forward, crashing into me and crushing me up against the door, snarling, ink-smeared face just inches from mine until I brought my forehead down hard into his nose and he stumbled backwards, cursing. As the space opened up again, I thrust at his chest, but the scabbard was still on and the blow only served to push him back faster. He parried as he did so, which would have been too late for him if my blade had been clear, but it caught on the leather, and dragged the scabbard free.

We stood facing each other. I adjusted my grip on the sabre, feeling its balance. Crombard wiped his face on his sleeve again, this time mingling blood from his nose with the ink. The streaks of black and red made him look bizarre, like a masked demon from some theatrical production.

He looked at me and laughed, white teeth adding another colour to the display. "Little man's got a sword, eh? Going to make a fight of it, then? Good. This should be fun!"

"I'm glad you're enjoying it," I answered. "I hope you'll still be laughing when you feel sharp steel in your guts!"

"Big words, but empty ones!" he retorted. "Do you really think you can best me? My father put my first sword in my hand when I was just four years old, and I have held one every single day since then. Every day! I have fought duels and battles without number and I have killed or maimed every man who ever opposed me with sharp steel! You – you I will slice up slowly, and will leave enough to take back to Sonor Breck and your mother's dungeon! After a spell in the questioning chamber, of course! Take your guard, filth!"

He adopted a formal fencing posture, and advanced. I could feel his total confidence. With a sword in his hand he was in his element.

I moved to meet him, which he hadn't expected, but it didn't put him off at all. He feinted a thrust at my face, then flicked the point down towards my groin.

I beat his blade down and away to my right, riposted with a cut at his leg but I had underestimated his strength and control: he had his blade back up far faster than I had anticipated, took the blow neatly on the forte, and with a twist was thrusting at my face again, but this time for real, and I couldn't get the heavy sabre up in time to block.

Instead I dropped, down on one knee, so he missed, but cut back again, back and down before I could get back to my feet, too fast for me to dodge, and I just barely got my guard up in a clumsy, badly positioned block that would have cost my my fingers if the sword had not had a knucklebow that deflected his edge onto my blade and away.

I threw myself back and to the side, rolling and back on my feet as he came on again, just in time to engage him with another parry, better executed this time. This time, I didn't attempt a riposte. He was too fast, too skilful, and I was unused to this sword, to the balance of the heavy sabre blade, which put me at a disadvantage compared with his longer and lighter rapier.

He pulled back. "So, you at least know how to hold a sword!"

I shrugged. "I was a long time planning my revenge, Uncle." It annoyed him when I called him that. "I learned many skills along the way. Fencing, for example. And lock picking. The lock on my mother's cell, I had that open in five minutes. It would have been quicker, but it had rusted up and needed time for the oil to penetrate."

"You were in the cell!"

"Oh yes. I found her at last. As you'd left her. Still chained to the wall." I thought I'd dealt with all the grief, but found it was still there, welling up. I pushed it away, it was not the time. But I allowed the anger to leak through.

"Then you know your own fate!" he snarled at me. "The rats gnawed on her, and they will be ready for you when I put you by her side!"

"She's not there any more, Uncle. I took her away and buried her properly. With tears, and the right words said to send her to her peace. She's beyond you now and forever out of your reach!"

"You think so?" he snapped. "You'll tell me where you put her remains and I'll dig them up and bring them back for you to share the cell with!"

"That will never happen!"

"I say it will!" he shouted and launched another furious attack.

I'd learned from our first round, and made no attempt to riposte. Instead I stayed on the defensive, gave ground, backing away and using the space to negate his advantage of reach. I could feel the subtle play of his emotions – the sharp anticipation of a strike, the wariness as he watched my own blade move, the cunning of a deceptive move. The fine nuances of his feelings led the lightening- flicker of his blade by the merest fraction of a second, but that was enough for me to block and parry and dodge his every attempt to pass my guard.

That and my own sharpness of mind and speed of reflex. They wouldn't have been enough on their own, and probably nothing would have been enough if I'd come against him in his heyday. But he was older, and slower, and all his experience could not make up for that.

I felt the tiredness growing in him, the weight of the sword on his arm, the tightness in his lungs as he struggled to get air. I felt him slowing, and his increasing frustration as every attack failed, every trick was anticipated.

He was trying to back me into a corner, pushing me back to the space between the bed and the wall, where I would be trapped. Growing desperate to wound me before his strength failed.

Desperation and weariness led to carelessness. That and the fact that it had been a long time since he fought anyone who seriously wanted, or dared, to injure him.

I fell back, allowed him to think I was going where he wanted. I felt the triumph in him, and then as he thrust towards my right shoulder, I changed tactics. It would have been a simply parry, especially if I'd stepped back. But instead I dropped my guard, twisted to let his blade pass me by a clear inch, and stepped in close, left arm coming up and my elbow coming back into his face.

He was too slow now, and too committed to moving forward to avoid it. There was a crunch of bone, a shock I felt all through my own arm, and as he staggered back, I brought my arm down again to trap his sword hand against my body.

I was still turning, pivoting on my left foot and forcing him round. He was dizzy from the blow and off balance, already stumbling as my right foot tripped him.

I released him as he fell. Struck his sword aside and pinned his sword arm with my foot, whilst my own point went against his throat.

And there I stood, staring down at him, our eyes meeting.

I don't know what he saw in mine, but I knew what was behind his. The rage had been stripped away, the hate pushed aside to make way for what dominated him. What had always dominated him, but was now fully revealed.

Fear.

"Don't..." he said finally. Working the words out with an effort.

"Why not?" I asked.

"Safe passage!" he gasped out. "I will let you go. Across the border. No pursuit!"

"I already have safe passage," I said. "As soon as I kill you."

"Kill me and my men will have no mercy!"

"Your men are dead, Uncle. Did you not feel them die? No, of course not. You don't have that Gift at all."

"They can't be..."

"They are. A little parting gift from the New Dawn. You should not have told them to search my baggage."

He stared up at me. "I will give you whatever you want!"

"Oh? Can you give me back my family? My friend?"

"I have gold!"

I laughed. "Do you think I want your gold? I already took your jewellery, remember? And let me tell you something – I didn't really want that, either."

I knelt down next to him, keeping the blade across his throat. "You wanted to know where it had gone, didn't you? Your treasure? I knew it was important to you. You loved to show off your wealth. That's why I took it in the first place. But I didn't keep it. Oh, there were a few bits that got smuggled out. One of your own guards had them in his saddlebags when he rode out to search for the thief. I thought that was amusing!"

I could see from his glare that he didn't agree.

"But in any case, that was just a fraction of what I got out of your chest. Just some small pieces for expenses. Most of it... oh, you're going to love this... most of it, Uncle, never left Sonor Breck!"

"What?"

"That's right. It's still there. In the same house!"

"No. I had them search. Everywhere, and more than once. You're lying!"

"Not everywhere, Uncle. There was one place that they couldn't go. A place you would never look. Can't you guess?"

I felt it growing in him. I could picture the colours. A slowly brightening gold of understanding, tinged by green of horror.

"That's right. I put it all in the cell. After I had taken my mother's bones out to bury them, I put your treasure in there. Not even hidden. Just on the floor, in plain sight, where only the rats ever go."

I leaned closer, and whispered. "And that, Uncle, is my revenge. Where you hid the person I valued most in the world, I hid the things that you valued most. Fitting, don't you think."

I got up again, and stood regarding him. "So what to do now, Uncle. What do you think? Shall I take your life? After all, quite apart from matters of revenge or even justice, if I let you live you'll just keep trying to kill me. I'll spend the rest of my life looking over my shoulder for some Purifier or hired assassin."

"No – promise, I promise, I will not seek your life. I will not seek you, not now, not ever. My word on it, my word of honour!"

"Well, that's nice to hear. But all the same, perhaps better to finish it now." I raised the sabre. "I'll make it quick, which is more than you were planning for me. Heart or throat?"

"NO! No – I beg of you!" He was all fear now. Nothing else left in him.

"My mother begged you," I reminded him. "Why should I give you mercy?"

But even as I said it, I remembered Ommet. The horror in him when he killed the Apothecary. His words when we disposed of the body.

'Mercy isn't for the deserving', he'd said. *'That's why its mercy.'*

I looked at the broken shell of a man on the floor, and understood. Or at least, began to see what understanding might be like.

"There's no point in killing you," I decided. "You're dying anyway. All the Gifts are failing in you, not just the Empathic Gift. The Life Gift is failing as well. And the Strength. How long do you have? Once one of the First Order starts to show age like you do, it can't be long. A year, perhaps, at the most." I shook my head. "You had it all wrong about the Gifts, Uncle. It was never about purity of blood. My mother knew, and I have learned. It's about love. That's the real gift, and all the others depend on it.

I turned away, picked up the Baron's sword, and went over to the desk to drop both weapons on it. Behind me I could hear Crombard slowly getting to his feet.

"We'll need to wait about an hour before its safe to go down," I told him without looking round. "An hour at a minimum, that is. I'd be inclined to wait longer. But you can feel free to go any time you like. There might be an exit from this floor down to the stables, I don't know. If so, that should be safe enough. I just hope that the horses were not effected. I.."

He had been coming towards me. Stepping very softly, but I didn't need to hear him. I could feel him coming closer, and I knew that the fear had been drowned by a rising tide of pure black hate.

My hand was still on my sword. When he leapt forward, I snatched it up and swung round.

But once again, I had underestimated the Baron. He was closer and faster than I'd allowed for, and he had a dagger in his hand, drawn from some concealed place, and striking down at me. I caught his wrist in my left hand, but the impact pushed me back onto the desk and at the same time his free hand had grabbed my sword arm,, smashing it down on the edge of the desk so hard that my fingers jerked open and the sabre fell to the floor.

He loomed over me, superior in weight, pushing down on the dagger, forcing its point toward my eyes. His other hand clutched at my throat, squeezing.

My right hand was free, scrabbling uselessly over the desk, unable this time to find anything to use as a weapon. The knife point was coming nearer, and I couldn't breath.

"It was never the treasure I valued," he hissed at me. "It was honour! Can you understand that, you scum? Honour is the important thing, the only thing. For honour I killed your family, for honour I destroyed my sister, for honour!"

I had one weapon.

I reached for my belt, for the buckle, for the little knife concealed there. Trying to find the strength to hold off the dagger, trying to draw the tiniest little bit of air into my lungs.

THE HIDDEN LIBRARIES

The knife came free. Little thing. Blade barely two inches long. Was it sharp? It had looked sharp. I hadn't tested it. Was the poison strong, or had it faded with time? Would it act quickly?

With the last of my strength I drove it into Crombard's body. Into his ribs. Through the leather and black linen just below his fire-bright badge, into his flesh.

His eyes opened with shock.

"What?" he asked, and I felt his grip on my throat loosen. "What?" he said again. He was feeling puzzled. He didn't understand the sudden sharp pain or the numbness that spread through him so quickly.

I managed to draw breath, a strained gasp of delicious life giving air. I twisted, pushing him off to the side, and his dagger fell to the desk with a thud.

"You never had any honour," I whispered. I couldn't manage to speak louder, even as his hand fell away from my throat. "You only had pride. It's not the same."

"No," he said, but I couldn't tell if he was arguing or just denying what was happening to him.

Then his eyes were blank, and his body slid off the desk to the floor.

I nearly joined him there, but instead half sat, half leaned on the Sergeant-Commander's desk and enjoyed breathing.

✕

MY THROAT WAS STILL sore when I finally left the room. I had found a little wine, which helped, but the Baron's grip on my windpipe had been very firm. I would have to wear a scarf to hide the bruises.

I gave it two hours, or thereabouts, before making my way cautiously down the stairs and out to the stables. The horses, fortunately, were unharmed, the gas having apparently been confined to the ground floor of the building. If any had escaped, it had dissipated harmlessly into the air.

All the same, I left it a little longer, then opened the doors from the outside and allowed plenty of fresh air to blow through before I dared to enter the main room to recover my baggage.

It was not a pretty sight, with corpses everywhere, and they had not died easily. I made haste to recover and repack my belongings.

It was too late to get across the border that night, but I had no intention of remaining in that charnel house. I loaded my horses and set off up the road. A few miles beyond the Customs House I found a suitable place by the roadside, and made camp there.

At first light, I was up again, and on my way. By midday I was through the steepest part of the pass, and making my way down into Murkarin.

Chapter 28: The Imperial Park, in view of Daradura

It was ten years almost to the month since the demise of Baron Crombard that I found myself in the capital, and took a stroll through the Imperial Park. As I often did when visiting those parts.

It was a fine summers day, with many people out to take the air, enjoy the sun and admire the view. Lake Sh'thran, with its many islands, glittered in the light, and the great bulk of Daradura, fortress and imperial palace, dominated the scene. There would be a concert later, in Damarl's Theatre, but for now music was supplied by street musicians and buskers who performed along the lakeside paths. Walk far enough along the shore, it was said, and you could hear every kind of music that the Empire had to offer, and some from beyond.

The mingled emotions of the people flowed over and around me, as much part of the background as the various pipes and drums and strings and singing voices. Years of practice had made me proficient at disregarding feelings that I didn't want to experience, but today it was all the pleasant emotions of people enjoying sunshine and good company. Children playing added excitement, and there was contentment from those eating and drinking, sharing picnics or sitting at one of the many little stalls and bars set up by the lake.

If I cared to, I could still see those emotions as colours in my mind, and today the entire park glowed in gentle pastels.

Until, a little way ahead of me, someone flared in bright orange-red. Someone familiar.

I quickened my pace, searching with my eyes to confirm what I felt, and soon saw him. He had become aware of me as well, and was standing up, peering in my direction. He waved when he saw me, but I already knew, for I felt the surge of joy from him, matched and mirrored back from me.

He was sitting at a table outside one of the larger restaurants. I almost ran the last few yards, but preserved some dignity until we stood in front of each other, then he grabbed me and pulled me into the strongest and warmest hug I could ever remember.

Finally we stepped back, and looked at each other.

"Arton," he said.

"Ommet." I answered.

He laughed, a full throated and immensely happy sound. "I haven't been called that in a long time!" he said.

"I still go by Arton Dowder," I told him. "My true name carried too many associations, I found."

We sat down. He had been eating sausages and drinking some herbal tea, but without us needing to discuss it, he waved a waiter over and ordered wine. "A bottle of something suitable for a celebration," he said "and the best you have!"

And after that, we could find nothing to say. "How are you?" seemed too trite for the occasion, so we sipped on a surprisingly good wine and simply enjoyed the fact of each others presence.

"You no longer wear the Arravine robes," I said at last, stating the obvious. "Do I take it that you left the Order? Or did they cast you out?"

"It was something of a mutual decision, in the end. I'm afraid that what I did has still not been forgiven by many of my former brothers."

"That was painful." I stated it as a fact, I could feel it in him. "But at least they didn't give you up to the Purifiers!"

"No, I don't think they even considered that as an option. Indeed, they went to great lengths to keep me safe. Here's the irony – when Crombard's men came searching, they concealed me in the Hidden Library!"

We both laughed over that. "I didn't even know that Scla had a Hidden Library!"

"Well, that's the point of it being hidden! It was just a small one, with no volumes that had any bearing on my mission. Big enough to hold me for a while, though. When the search ended and I had sufficiently recovered they smuggled me out and back to Kalanhad."

"To the cells again?"

"Once I'd fully recovered from my wound, they put me in there for a while. Mostly because they had no idea what else to do with me. I was not the only Arravine ever guilty of theft, but the only one who ever stole from the Hidden Libraries! There was talk of convening an Extraordinary Judicial Prior's Council. However such a thing takes time to set up, as it requires a number of Priors to gather. So the case was deferred to the next General Priors Council. But by the time that came round, everything had changed. The Empress had announced the Breaking of The Silence: the truth about the Gifts, proven by the Writings of Mirrion and other items I had obtained from various Hidden Libraries, was proclaimed throughout the Empire."

"Which proved you had been right to do what you did."

"Certainly, I thought so!" Ommet agreed with a smile. "TheArravines as a whole found it rather difficult to adjust, though."

"Not as difficult as some of the First Order," I observed. "Grand Duke Brodon, for example."

"Ah, yes. Well, after his rebellion, things were rather difficult in the north, and there was no question of convening any Councils. When things had finally calmed down, they decided to deal with me locally. So I was invited to resign from the Order, with the understanding that if I went quietly it would be better for everyone."

"And did you?"

"Oh yes. I agreed, really. It was sad, to put aside my robes and my calling, but I had long accepted that this would be the most likely outcome. It was a small sacrifice to make, all things considered." He paused to pour more wine. "But what of you, Arton? What happened after you left me in Scla?"

I shrugged. "Not much, really. Had a little trouble getting over the border, but after that it was a mostly uneventful journey down through Murkarin and back over the border."

Ommet gave me a long and amused look. "You can't lie with the Gift. Even shading the truth becomes obvious between those who are close enough. And besides, there was the matter of Baron Crombard and some of his most trusted men, found dead at the Kenrall Pass Custom's House. Which doesn't sound like 'a little trouble' to me."

"Oh, all right then," I sighed. And gave him a more detailed account of my border crossing and the final meeting with Crombard. Which led to further explanations about my family history and my issues with the Baron.

He was silent for a while afterwards. "I always knew you were carrying a burden," he said at last. "Even before the Gift grew strong between us. But I had no idea how terrible it was."

"It is in the past now. And I have found a peace about it. I have you to thank for that, in large measure."

"What? How so?" His eyebrows raised.

"At the end, I was able to show some mercy towards Crombard. Perhaps even forgiveness. I'm not sure how far that went. But when I saw the man's soul... there was really nothing left in him to punish. He was dead inside, destroyed by his own hate and fear."

"Just the opposite of the love by which the Gifts are released," Ommet observed.

"Yes, exactly. But here's my point: for all those years I was driven by exactly the same hate that drove Crombard. True, I had justice on my side. And also true, I did kill him in the end. He gave me no choice. But if you had not come my way, to teach me otherwise, I fear I would have ended up just like him. So thank you." I raised my glass to him. He acknowledged with his own glass, but I could feel how deeply moved he was.

We were silent for a while, before our conversation resumed.

"What have you been doing these last ten years?" Ommet wanted to know

"Oh, travelling around, back and forth. On Imperial Service at first. The Grand Chancellor decided that, since I already had the ring, I might as well carry on being an Imperial Agent. I saw his point, and was sent back up to the north. Firstly, to track down the rest of those evil potions that the Apothecary had had made, and see them destroyed. Along with all copies of the formula. After that – well, he had other work for me."

"Did you come across any of our old friends while you were up there?"

"Some. In fact, I'm still in touch with a few of them. You remember Mebbers?"

"Of the boat's crew? He with the impressive shoulders?"

"The same. Well, I found him running a little dockside inn just along the coast from Vorgranstern. He'd been invalided out of the Navy and now stumps around on a wooden leg – the story of which he will tell to anyone who asks! It involves us, actually – indirectly."

"Really?" Ommet raised an eyebrow. "How so?"

"Well, you'll recall that the *Wave Dancer* had already left when the *Anatarna* began her attack on *Warlord*?"

Ommet shuddered. "Yes indeed. Terrible business."

I nodded my agreement. "Of course, they heard the noise and Druthy at once put about to see what was going on. But, canny man that he is, he went round to the far side of the Seals, and so was out of sight of the New Dawn. Mebbers and Druthy crept ashore on the Seals and observed all that took place, but when *Warlord* was destroyed the debris rained down on them. Mebbers took a burning timber right on his leg."

"How awful!"

"Well yes, though exactly how awful is hard to say, since the size of the timber varies in Mebbers telling of the story! But yes, it was certainly bad enough to end his sailing days. The *Wave Dancer* was badly damaged as well. But Druthy, fine seaman as he is, effected repairs and got back to Layfarban with the news – if somewhat too late to make any difference, of course. And too late for Mebbers' leg, which had to be taken off. But he has settled very comfortably into the Innkeepers life and keeps his clientèle well entertained with rousing sea stories!"

I paused for a sip of wine. "But what about you? I'm surprised you didn't stay in the Imperial Agent business yourself. After all, you did do rather well at it!"

"Thank you, but I'd had quite enough of that! No, I went back to doing what I was always best at – teaching. I opened a little school in a place called Tynam. It's done rather well over the years, I'm happy to say."

"But the Empress – surely you must have gone back to see her?"

He looked over the water at Daradura. "I couldn't. There are still those who hate this new sort of Empire she has brought. If it was known who I was, and what love there was between us, then she would be made vulnerable by reason of that. I can't risk all that we did, all that she has achieved as a result – all the reforms, or the hope of this new Empire – not just for my happiness, or hers."

"That's hard, though. To sacrifice love, when it is love that has been at the heart of all this." I felt the sadness in him, and reached out to grip his hand.

He accepted the grip with a smile. "Thank you. But truly, I am content. Love does require sacrifice, and the price is a small one for an Empire at peace with itself and rediscovering the truth of the Gifts it was blessed with. Besides – I come here as often as I can, and look over at Daradura, and think of her there. And when I do, I can feel her love. The Gifts are stronger in her than in anyone, I think, and so I believe she can feel my love for her."

"I'm sure that you're right," I said gently, and we looked at each other and smiled.

"And – correct me if I'm wrong," I continued "But I see a ring on your finger that I don't recall from before. Can I assume that you have found other love as well?"

"Yes, yes I have." Ommet looked down at his hand as if surprised by what he saw there, and his feelings were a strange mixture of gentle warmth and mild embarrassment. "There was a lady who came to work for me when I opened the school. A widow, who had two sons. They were my first pupils and she..." he shook his head. "I am still baffled by how many different sorts of love there can be. That which I felt for Anatarna, and still feel – is like, yet different from what I know with Halise. Not greater or lesser but different. And whilst I did not ever think that I could love as much as I loved my Ana', I've found that there is always room for more love. The Gifts show us that." He looked up at me. "You showed me that, Arton. Who could love more than someone who risks his life for you?"

"That worked both ways," I said.

"Of course. Love always does." Ommet shifted his glance to my hand. "No rings there! Not even an Imperial one. You didn't go back to being the Wraith, did you?"

"Oh no! Like you, after Brodon was finished with I had had quite enough of Imperial Service, and in any case, I was no longer required. The Grand Chancellor gave me a handsome parting gift and sent my on my way with his blessing – and the proviso that I should not return to theft as a career. I hadn't planned to in any case, and I'm an honest businessman now."

"Oh, really? In what line? Still jewels, or perhaps you're a locksmith? You were very talented, as I recall."

"No, none of those things. Like you, I went back to my roots, and now I deal in cheese!"

"Cheese?" Oh, wonderful! I remember how bored you were with all that hard red cheese up in the north!"

"That's in the past. There are lots of other and better cheeses available in those parts now. I decided that there was a distinct gap in the market, and I have spent much of the last few years educating the north in the wide variety of cheese that there are in the world. My business buys, transports and sells all manner of cheeses up to Vorgranstern, Scla and all the way over to Neowbron!"

"I would love to try some of those cheeses. Do you think that you could perhaps arrange for some to be delivered to Tynam?"

"I shall bring them myself." I paused, took a breath. "There is something I need to give you, Ommet. And then something I must ask you. I – think I am sure of your answer, but I would very much like to hear it."

"Of course! What is it?"

"First – take this." I took a small, rather worn, leather pouch from an inside pocket. "I took this from you. For good reason, and I put it to good use – and by rights it should have gone back to the Grand Chancellor – but I kept it. A sort of talisman, perhaps. Or a memory. I didn't know if I would ever see you again, but I always told myself that I would give it back if I could."

I emptied the pouch onto the table. A big green stone in a gold setting. Cheaper than it first looked. More powerful than any ring should be.

"You can't use it, of course! Not without causing a huge upset across the water there..." I nodded at Daradura "...and probably getting yourself arrested!"

Ommet picked it up, and looked at it, with a slow smile dawning. "I knew you had it. Suspected, at any rate. Goodness, what memories this holds for us both!"

He tried it on a finger, then slipped it into a pocket. "I'll keep it safe. Perhaps I can use it to prove the story someday! But what did you want to ask me?"

I met his eyes, still the same brilliant blue I had first seen in the cell at Neowbron.

"Do you forgive me?"

"Forgive you? Why? Whatever for?"

"For betraying you. Twice. First to the New Dawn, then to the Arravines."

He met my gaze and gripped my hand again. "Arton. My friend, my dear, dear friend... the first time, you were seeking to do the right thing, with no clear understanding of what that was. It was a difficult situation. Confusing. I'll not deny, I was greatly hurt when I thought you'd abandoned me. But you made it right, you rescued me, and to tell the truth, I wasn't surprised that you did. Deep down, I'd always known you would make the right decision in the end. As for the second time – well, that saved my life! So I have nothing to complain about on that score."

"I – I would still like to hear you say it. It has been something that has troubled me, over the years."

His gaze hadn't shifted, but the firmness of his grip increased.

"I forgive you," he said. "And I love you."

And the world had never been more right, nor my soul more at peace.

Afterword: The School House, Tynam

My name is Anatarna an'Darsio. I am the daughter of Thylan and Halise an'Darsio.

My father told me something of his adventures in the past, and of his part in the great events that changed the Empire. He always played down his role in them, but I learned more from his friend, Arton Dowder.

Uncle Arton was a frequent visitor to Tynam. As a child, I only knew him as Papa's friend who always brought lots of cheese. But he told me many things about my father that I would not have known otherwise.

After I had put these things together in a written history (which you may have read, it is published under the title of 'The Empress's Lover') he brought this manuscript to me. It was mostly a collection of notes, jottings and various recollections in no particular order. At his request, I spent some time going through them, and put them into the order that you now see.

Even as I write this, though, I am still amazed by the story. It is hard for me to believe that my dear and now very aged father, and his much loved friend my Uncle Arton, had such great adventures and did such incredible things. Yet this is the truth of it, and in proof my father showed me a ring with an Imperial seal.

It is on the desk beside me now. It is too large for my finger, but I often hold it in my hands and wonder at the great events of which it was part.

Also by Paul H. Trembling

The Empire of Silence
The Hidden Libraries

The Reality Escape Commitee
Minutes of the Reality Escape Commitee (Volume 1).

Watch for more at https://yearningblue.weebly.com/.

About the Author

Paul Trembling began making up stories in his head before he could even read - let alone write! Since then he has been many things - a seaman, a missionary, a janitor, a CSI, etc. - but he has always been a story maker. It's a habit he has never been able to break, and has no intention of trying. Paul currently lives in Bath, England with his wife Annie and a fluctuating household.

Read more at https://yearningblue.weebly.com/.